Sergeant Lamb's

AMERICA

402

ROBERT GRAVES

Sergeant Lamb's
AMERICA

Published in 2000 by
Academy Chicago Publishers
363 West Erie Street
Chicago, Illinois 60610

Copyright © 1937 Robert Graves. Renewed 1965.

First printing 2000

No part of this book may be reproduced in any form whatsoever
without the permission of the publisher.

Library of Congress Cataloging-in-Publication Data

Graves, Robert, 1895—
    Sergeant Lamb's America.
    Lamb, Roger, b. 1756. 2. Graves, Robert, 1895—
    Series. Locations. 3. Great Britain, Army—Biography.
    United States—History—Revolution, 1775-1783—Fiction.
    I. Title.
    PR6013.R35S47 1998   823'.912—dc21

Academy Chicago Publishers

Published in 1995 by
Academy Chicago Publishers
363 West Erie
Chicago, IL 60610

First printing 1986

Library of Congress Cataloging-in-Publication Data
Graves, Robert, 1895-
      Sergeant Lamb's America.
      1. Lamb, Roger, 1756-1830—Fiction. 2. United States—
      History—Revolution, 1775-1783—Fiction. 3. Great
      Britain—History, Military—18th century—Fiction.
         I. Title.
      PR6013.R35S45   1986   823'.912   86-22154
      ISBN 0-89733-213-X (pbk.)

Foreword

I FIRST came across the name of Sergeant Roger Lamb in 1914, when I was a young officer instructing my platoon in regimental history. His experiences conveyed little to me at the time, because of my truly British ignorance of America and the Americans. However, I visited the United States twenty-five years later and stayed for some weeks with American friends at Princeton, New Jersey, where Washington's defeat of the Hessian Division of the British Army was a proud tradition of the town. It happened to be the time when King George and Queen Elizabeth were being magnificently welcomed by the President and people of the United States; and as an Englishman I came in for my share of the popular warmth. I naturally remembered Sergeant Lamb as a representative British soldier of the period and looked up his story. This novel then suggested itself as a means of learning, as I wrote, why and how the Americans had separated themselves from the British Crown. These were for me very serious questions—for I now regarded the American Revolution as the most important single event of modern times—and I had found them as equivocally treated in American as in English text-books of history.

Since *Sergeant Lamb's America* is not presented as straight history, I have avoided footnotes or other documentation. All that readers of an historical novel can fairly ask from the author is an assurance that he has nowhere wilfully falsified geography, chronology, or character, and that the information contained in it is accurate enough to add without discount to their general stock of history. I am prepared to give that assurance. I have invented no main characters, not even Chaplain John Martin, Sergeant Buchanan, Dipper Brooks, or the child born at the Quaker's house in the forest by Lake George. All the opinions on the war which are here put into the mouth of Lamb or quoted from his friends and enemies —however shockingly they may read now—are actual opinions recorded during the American War of Independence.

The date of Lamb's death is not known, the record having apparently perished when the Four Courts were blown up in 1922 by the Irish revolutionaries: but from information that Mr. Dermot Coffey of the Irish Public Record Office has been good enough to supply, he appears to have lived until at least 1824. After his discharge from the Army in 1784 he became schoolmaster of the Free School at White Friars Lane, Dublin. He married Jane Crumer by banns in St. Anne's Parish Church, Dublin, in January 1786.

R. G.

Galmpton-Brixham, Devon
1940

Roger Lamb's
Note of Explanation

I CANNOT readily convey to paper the vexations and disappointments which attended the publication of the autobiographical book on which I had for so many years laboured, after school hours, and during the whole of my holidays, while master of the crowded Free School of White Friars Lane in this city of Dublin. I had written it as a faithful memoir of interesting events, not shrinking from any confession of error or boast of success, so long as I should keep to the truth.

In the year 1808, when it was concluded, I showed the manuscript to one or two of my old military comrades who resided in Dublin. They considered it pretty well as story, and had little fault to find with its exactness as historical writing. But with the booksellers it was an altogether different matter. Few of these would deign so much as to look into the work, which they said was clearly of tedious and inordinate length as the life-story of so obscure an individual as I was; others read a page or two and then asked me, affecting to like it fairly, whether I would pay them a hundred guineas for the risk of publication. But I was a poor man, with a parcel of debts, indifferent health, and a numerous family to support; and had expected the tide of money rather to flow in the opposite direction.

The chief subject treated of was my campaigning experiences in the American War of 1775-83, which these booksellers professed to regard as 'a Lazarus'—their trade term for a subject that was not only dead but stinking.

They refused to listen to me when I argued that the present hostilities with France would greatly favour the book, as calling attention to the thankless heroism once displayed in America by the same regiments then triumphantly engaged under Lord Wellington in the Spanish Peninsula.

This American war had, admittedly, been a war lost, and so was in general not a pleasant subject for the British people to dwell upon; and a shameful war, too, as fought against men of our own blood, the American colonists; and still more shameful in that these had been leagued after a time with our natural enemies the French, against whose aggressions we had so recently defended them. Yet in spite of all this, we (if I may speak for the survivors of the British expeditionary forces in America) had nothing with which to reproach ourselves, nor could we hold ourselves the inferiors in either skill or courage to Lord Wellington's troops. Our common conviction was that it was not we who had lost the war—indeed there was hardly a skirmish or battle in which we had not been left in victorious possession of the field—but that it was lost by a supine and ignorant Ministry seconded by an unpatriotic and malignant Opposition. Nor could our view be readily disputed.

I put all this, perhaps almost too hotly, to Messrs. Wilkinson and Courtney, two enterprising booksellers of Wood Street to whom finally I brought the manuscript of my book. And I asked this question of old Mr. Courtney: 'When is it, sir, that old campaigners speak most earnestly and warmly about the hazards, fatigues, triumphs, and frolics that they have lived through together?' 'It is' (I informed him in the same breath) 'when a new war is in progress and when the regiments whose badges and facings they once wore with pride are again hotly engaged, as now. Can such a subject as the American War be therefore called "a Lazarus," except in the sense that Lazarus was by a miracle raised from the dead and acclaimed by the crowds?'

Mr. Courtney admitted the justice of my observations, and agreed that a great many retired officers could perhaps be found in Ireland and elsewhere to subscribe to a book which gave an account of campaigns in which they had themselves sometime fought.

Young Mr. Wilkinson then undertook to read the book through, which he did; and a few days later proposed to come to an agreement with me, as follows. Mr. Wilkinson should have authority to solicit subscriptions in my name for a work entitled *A True and Authentic Journal of Occurrences in the Late American War,* in which he would include the more general and striking parts of my story and fat it up with extracts drawn from dependable works of travel and biography. He would excite the compassionate interest of the nobility, clergy, and gentry in me as a worn-out old soldier now surprisingly turned writer, and he would expunge from my work all judgments and incidents not consonant with that humble character. He fully expected an edition of fifteen hundred copies to be taken up; and undertook to pay me five pounds down and sixpence for each copy subscribed, which he represented to be very handsome payment indeed. If matters turned out as he hoped, he would publish the remainder of my writings, a more particular *Memoir of His Own Life: by R. Lamb,* as a separate work of a highly moral tone; he would not handle this himself but turn it over to a hackney writer, some hedge-parson or other, who could strike the note of contrition that the middling public would heed. For this work I should receive nothing but the glory of being the author of a second book, until after one thousand copies had been sold, when my reward should be at threepence a copy.

This was a wretched offer and at first I refused it with indignation. But presently I swallowed my pride and signified my acceptance, because of my great want of money and the wretched importunities of the tradesmen who were my creditors, small men almost as impoverished as myself.

Mr. Wilkinson allowed me to assist him in the editing of my book. It was excessively painful for me to sit and watch him run his lead-pencil through its choicest passages with a reiterated groan of 'No, no, Mr. Lamb, this will never do.' *This* was trifling, *that* was vulgar, *the other* would not only cause pain and offence but dry up subscriptions like a styptic. However, I now had somewhat less urgent

need of money than before, since my recent application
for an out-pension from the Chelsea Hospital had been
immediately and unexpectedly granted—through the good
offices of General H. Calvert (by whose side I had once
fought) with His Royal Highness the Duke of York. I
therefore wished to tear up the signed agreement made in
an evil hour with these *cognoscenti* of literature, repay
them the five pounds and have my book back. But they
held me to my signature and I had no legal remedy against
them.

Not once did Mr. Wilkinson respect my plea to allow
some particular or other to stand in his version. I therefore
soon left him to finish his butcherly work alone; and I
confess that I was sick at heart when the *True and Authentic Journal* was finally presented to me bound in calf,
handsomely printed and with hardly a sentence left as I
had penned it. That I received my twenty guineas was
poor consolation, or that the list of subscribers to the
work included such great names as Major-General W. H.
Clinton, M.P., the Quartermaster-General of Ireland; Lieutenant-General Sir Charles Asgill, Bt., then commanding
the Eastern District; and the Earl of Harrington himself,
Commander-in-Chief of His Majesty's Forces in Ireland—
it was no longer my book, no longer the truth as I had
wished to tell it. The second volume was yet worse, a
sad hotch-potch of religious sentiment and irrelevant anecdote; but it was at least gratifying for me to know that
if I got nothing from it, the publishers got less than
nothing (though they had shared their risks with a Welsh
printer named J. Jones of South Great George's Street),
for hardly a copy sold.

Much mortified, I prevailed upon an underling of Mr.
Wilkinson's (paying him a guinea) to find and restore to
me the pencil-scarred manuscript; which Mr. Wilkinson
continually pretended, when I applied directly to him, that
he could not lay his hand upon. Then I set myself, as a
sort of penitential task, to rewrite the original story again,
and in a manner that displayed even less regard than before
for the susceptibilities of the nobility, clergy, and gentry;
at the same time correcting numerous errors of detail that
I had committed, or that had been fathered on me by the

ingenious but unhistorical Mr. Wilkinson. I trust that I have now done my duty by the jealous nymph Clio, whom the ancients figured in their legends as the Muse of authentic history.

R. LAMB
(December 1814)

The Free School,
White Friars Lane,
Dublin.

The British Regiments of the Line which are here mentioned as serving in America now bear the following names:

4TH FOOT: The King's Own Royal Lancaster Regiment

7TH FOOT: The Royal Fusiliers, City of London Regiment

8TH FOOT: The King's Liverpool Regiment

9TH FOOT: The Royal Norfolk Regiment

10TH FOOT: The Lincolnshire Regiment

14TH FOOT: The Prince of Wales' Own West Yorkshire Regiment

20TH FOOT: The Lancashire Fusiliers

21ST FOOT: The Royal Scots Fusiliers

23RD FOOT: The Royal Welch Fusiliers

24TH FOOT: The South Wales Borderers

26TH FOOT: The Cameronians, Scottish Rifles

29TH FOOT: The Worcestershire Regiment

31ST FOOT: The East Surrey Regiment

33RD FOOT: The Duke of Wellington's West Riding Regiment

34TH FOOT: The Border Regiment

43RD FOOT: The Oxfordshire and Buckinghamshire Light Infantry, First Battalion

47TH FOOT: The Loyal North Lancashire Regiment

52ND FOOT: The Oxfordshire and Buckinghamshire Light Infantry, Second Battalion

53RD FOOT: The King's Shropshire Light Infantry

57TH FOOT: The Duke of Cambridge's Own Middlesex Regiment, the Diehards

60TH FOOT: The King's Royal Rifle Corps

62ND FOOT: The Duke of Edinburgh's Wiltshire Regiment

64TH FOOT: The Prince of Wales' North Staffordshire Regiment

65TH FOOT: The York and Lancaster Regiment

Sergeant Lamb's

AMERICA

❀ ❀ ❀ ❀ ❀ ❀ ❀ ❀ ❀ ❀ ❀ ❀

CHAPTER

I

THERE are more ways than one of telling a story. I could perhaps plunge as Homer does—whom I have read in translation—*in medias res* with my arrival at the city of Quebec in May 1776, when the American War had been already in progress for a year; and tell the story backward from that point until overtaking it again. But I consider it both more workman-like and more soldier-like a method to do as follows: first, to relate some particulars of my early life and peace-time service with the British Army in Ireland; next, before coming to my own experiences in the war, to venture upon a general account of its origins and commencement. Here I beg leave to point out a grave historical lack: namely, an impartial Detail of the more minute but no less important occurrences of the war which, as secret springs of a clock, actuated the visible pendulum and turned round publicly the hands of time. The only attempt at such a Detail of which I have knowledge is a work published in America, and written by a Member of Congress, but which I find to be exceedingly partial.

I first heard the name of America from my father, an industrious Dublin tradesman who dealt chiefly in seamen's necessaries, on the occasion of the news reaching our city of the British capture of Quebec in Canada from the French under M. de Montcalm. This was in November 1759, the year of victories, when I was not quite four

years old. Great cheering and shouting were heard in our
humble street, which lay contiguous to the Arran Bridge
on the River Liffey, because it was a Protestant street and
here was another victory to be celebrated over the
Papists of our vicinity. My big brother Tom came bounc-
ing in with the news, blackthorn in fist, huzza-ing and
twirling in the air his frieze cap. But my father, upon
learning that the gallant and affable General Sir James
Wolfe, who had been Quartermaster-General of the
Forces in Ireland but a year previously, had fallen in the
hour of victory, sternly rebuked Tom's enthusiasm. He
made him sit down quietly upon a stool and hearken to a
geographical lesson upon the subject of North America
which (my father said) was wholly ours now, for ever.
This was, as I say, the first time that ever I heard tell of
America, and the name was thereby endued for me with
solemn associations of glory and grief. My father, I must
observe, was a man of much reading which strong native
powers of intellect had led him to digest and methodize;
but he was by no means pious and gave me no regular
religious education, though he taught me at an early age
to read, cipher, and write a fair hand.

For many weeks after, a favourite play in our back
garden was the 'Capture of Quebec,' in which my brothers
played the part of the British forlorn-hope that swarmed
up the Heights of Abraham (a withered apple-tree) to
the Upper City of Quebec (the roof of a wood-shed),
where two of my younger sisters and myself did duty for
the French Army. Tom was the eldest, and I the youngest
of our family of eleven, of whom four were boys. In the
following year Tom sacrificed his life in defence of his
country, dying of a wound received on board a British
frigate during a fight in the English Channel. My father
was gravely afflicted by the news, which took the sweet
taste of perpetual victory from his mouth and left only
bitterness. Hitherto he had used to take me every Sunday
afternoon along the North Wall and describe to me, in
the most interesting and familiar manner, the latest naval
engagement of which news had reached him; pausing now
and then to illustrate the manœuvres of the ships with
marks scratched in the mud. He used the point of his

stick, a curious twisted piece of ivory, the spear of a sword-fish. But there was now no more of that, for when one day I asked him: 'Father: tell me a battle!' he shook his head and tears came into his eyes.

He replied: 'Ah, Gerry, dear child, I see your little breast has been fired with the accounts I have given you. But I only related these things to form your judgment: I would not have you become a fighting man, no, not on any account. I have lost one fine boy already in fighting for his country. Let us have no more talk of battles for a while.'

A year or two later, my two remaining brothers (as well as my favourite sister) died of the confluent smallpox, so that I was left the only son of my parents. I was nearly carried off myself, and being thus preserved unexpectedly was for some time so cosseted and indulged by my mother that I became very wilful; and when my father began again to discipline me for my faults I resented it greatly. I openly defied him, and allowed him no alternative but a sterner discipline yet. My mother took my part, but secretly, because she stood somewhat in dread of my father, who was of powerful body and of temper difficult to govern.

I constantly visited the quays on the banks of the Liffey and soon acquired the art of swarming up the masts of the vessels moored thereabouts. One day at the age of six I came near to destruction by imitating the acts of some grown lads whom I had seen that same morning strip off their clothes and jump from the steps of the old dock, in the place where the new customhouse now stands. But whereas the boys had leaped into the river at low tide, when the stream did not rise above their middles, I inadvertently chose a time when the water was ten feet deep. I plunged to the bottom like a stone and, my legs sinking in thick mud up to my knees, I was caught there fast. I would infallibly have drowned had not one of my father's customers, who was passing with a messmate, happened to see my plunge and happened also to be an expert swimmer. Observing, after a time, that I did not rise again to the surface, he immediately leaped in and took me up, almost dead. I was quite unconscious; but this excellent fellow laid me on the ground in the sun and stretched himself beside me. He blew with his mouth into mine, closing my nostrils with one hand, as with the other he expelled the air by pressing my chest closely. Then calling to his mate to continue the treatment, he also gave me a tobacco clyster, puffing up smoke of tobacco into my bowels with the broken stem of his pipe; and next rubbed my belly with his neckerchief. The last remedy of this series was a pinch of snuff in my nostrils. I sneezed, vomited, and so painfully recovered my senses.

This adventure, far from deterring me from the water, only made me eager to learn how to swim; and after some time I became such a proficient that, from off the bowsprits and round-tops of ships, I frequently leaped head-foremost into the river. I also delighted in the summer-time to float about in the sea at the river's mouth, lying quite stiff and straight, and suffering myself to sink till the water entered my ears; thus committing myself to the discretion of the tides. I could remain for several hours in the water in this manner, and would continue often until I grew drowsy and took little naps as I floated. I recommend swimming to the rising generation as a most healthy accomplishment, and immeasurably more useful than many which are at present taught at a very great expense.

My mind still ran upon naval battles and the seafaring life in general, and since my father no longer indulged me in my fancy I would prevail on seamen who came to the shop to tell me of their own experiences in the wars. My father was vexed at this curiosity of mine. He therefore took me by the hand one holiday morning and said: 'Come, Roger, my froward son, let us to-day walk farther than our usual custom. Let us visit the Four Jolly Rogers.'

I could not conceive what he meant by this play on my name, and hoped to meet with—I hardly know what, perhaps four big playmates. He took me along the South Wall and near the pigeon-house, in the direction of the light-house, talking to me of the hardships and dangers of the seafaring life, and enlarging on my own intractable disposition. At last he pointed to some large objects hanging above my head and said solemnly: 'There swing the Four

Jolly Rogers, Roger, my froward son, and be careful
that you don't one day make a fifth. For it is directly to
those rusty chains that your present inclinations are leading you.'

The four hanged men, whose mouldering and tattered
bodies were swaying in the breeze above me, on gibbets
(as terrible examples to the people of Dublin in general
and myself in particular) were Peter M'Kinley, boatswain;
George Gidley, cook; Richard St. Quintan and Andrew
Zikerman, mariners.

'These ruffians,' my father told me, 'conspired together
and murdered the master, mate, and cabin-boy of a
merchant ship, the *Earl of Sandwich* (out of Oratova,
laden with wine, Spanish dollars, gold dust, and jewels),
and also a Captain Giles, his wife, his young daughter,
and a serving-boy. They then altered the course of the
ship, which was bound for London, and landed some
leagues from Waterford, where they loaded the ship's boat
with treasure and left the *Earl of Sandwich* with her
ballast-port open to sink, as she soon did, together with
two cabin-boys whom they barbarously left on board. The
four men subsequently came to Dublin and lived for a time
in great luxury and excess.

'However, the ship was in some way buoyed up from the
ocean-bed and a few days later came ashore near Waterford. That there was found no damage to her hull or
masts caused much speculation; and upon M'Kinley dispos-
ing of about £300 worth of dollars to a Dublin gold-
smith, the plot was suspected. Presently all four criminals
were laid by the heels: who severally confessed to the
commission of this horrid crime.'

He added many vivid circumstances to the narrative,
with which I will not trouble my readers, though they still
remain indelibly impressed upon my mind.

This was the first sight that I had ever had of corpses,
and it caused such alarm and disgust in me, their flesh
being rotted from the bones so that their anatomies
showed plainly under their ragged clothing, that I said
not a word but began to whimper and begged to be taken
home at once. I could not sleep that night, and the day
following I was found tossing in a violent fever of the

brain. When this left me, I had no desire left for a sea-faring life, since in the height of my delirium I imagined myself to be a cabin-boy sucked down with the ship; and this was a recurrent dream with me for many years following.

At the age of eleven I was taken under the charge of a youth of fifteen named Howard to stay for six weeks in a village of West Meath: at the house of his uncle Mr. William Howard, a merchant of Jervis Street, and a close friend of my father's. I had never before left my father's roof or lived in the country and the experience delighted me, though I was astounded at the pitiable condition in which these country people lived. Their only fare was potatoes and buttermilk, and their small, smoky cabins seemed to be pigsties in which humans were housed, rather than human habitations with occasional accommodation for pigs and poultry. On the first day that I was in this village I presented a little piece of sugar-candy to a ragged peasant boy of my own age: an act for which old Mr. Howard reproved me, saying that the child had never tasted such a delicacy in his life. To give him a touch of it was cruel, as creating a new appetite and so making him dissatisfied with his lot. Mr. Howard was a very religious gentleman, but, I remember, stoutly opposed a project sponsored by the rector of the nearest parish, to set up Sunday school for the poor children: advancing the same reason, that it would lead to trouble as educating them above their station, and unsettling their minds. Perhaps he was right, for they seemed a happy, singing people in spite of all; and notwithstanding the drab hue of their faces, which could be ascribed to continual curing by peat-smoke, robust enough in frame. 'I envy them,' sighed Mr. Howard, 'with all my heart I envy them. Not an old man among them has the gout, an affection that is slowly killing me.'

I was here accepted as the hanger-on and errand-boy of Mr. Howard's son, who was a year older than his cousin, and had just obtained a commission in the Fourteenth Regiment, then stationed at Boston in America. They appeared very grand gentlemen to me, and I soon learned the newest oaths—'Od's triggers,' 'As God shall judge me,'

'Prick my vitals,' and the like—together with the fashionable London manner of speaking: to their great amusement. Mr. Howard's son fancied himself as a swordsman,
and so did the nephew, and together they taught me the
rudiments of small-sword fencing. I became proud of this
elegant accomplishment, which I took up seriously on
my return to Dublin, though it was not altogether consonant with my station in society. I even entertained the
idea of becoming a professional duellist—of the sort employed at that period by some great persons to fight their
battles for them. The two Howard cousins amused themselves at the same time by putting me on a spirited horse,
in order to see me tossed off; but somehow I managed to
keep my seat, and before long, by perseverance, became
a tolerable horseman and could even leap low walls and
ditches.

Mr. Howard's son was pleased with my usefulness to
him and flattered by my devotion, which came very near
to downright worship. At my instance, he wrote to my
father, asking whether he might take me with him to
America. My father was ready to comply with this unusual
request, for I had been a great trouble to him at home;
but it proved in the event that no situation in The
Fourteenth could be procured for so young a boy as I
then was. I was obliged to remain at home and the disappointment distressed me. I resolved at all events to depart
for America as speedily as possible, and there attach myself to my hero. What ensued is a familiar sort of story,
and I will therefore spare particulars of it: how an adventurous child goes to the captain of a vessel sailing
for the Indies or America and asks to be engaged. The
captain either laughs and tells the boy to run home, or
else (which is more common) he engages him and then
betrays him to his father, asking a sum of money for his
release. Mine was the commoner case. My father paid the
money, and took tribute from me with a stout stick.

At that period the administration of justice was greatly
relaxed in the city of Dublin. It was almost impossible for
persons to walk through some parts of the city (particularly on Sunday evenings) without encountering the
most violent and sometimes dangerous assaults. Lower

Abbey and Marlborough Streets on the north side of the city, and the Long Lane near Kevin Street on the south, were the places of general rendezvous for 'Club Law,' as it was vulgarly called. Here numbers of daring, desperate fellows used to assemble and form themselves in battle array according to their religious persuasions: then to batter one another with well-managed blackthorn sticks, showing neither mercy nor remorse.

In the case of death, which was frequent, the murderer was seldom discovered. On only one occasion that I remember was such a man apprehended by the watch and tried for his life by the civil power. He did not deny that he had struck the fatal blow or profess any regret, pleading ancient usage and that it was done in sport. Evidence was then advanced that the victim's skull was particularly thin, and the jury, upon retiring, instantly brought in a verdict of 'innocent,' the foreman announcing very grandly on their behalf that 'a man with so un-Hibernian a cranial formation had no right to stroll down Lower Abbey Street at five o'clock of a Sunday evening.'

I took no part in these encounters. As a small-swordsman I considered the blackthorn club beneath me, but would often condescendingly watch the battle from a distance, sword in hand lest I should become involved in a charge of the Papists. My only regret was that in my walk of life I did not encounter sufficient adversaries armed with my own weapon to keep my hand in practice; affairs of honour which called for recourse to the sword being a prerogative of the higher orders of society.

After the age of seventeen, when I had been for two years employed as clerk in the counting-house of a respectable tallow-chandler and soap-boiler, I grew weary of my lot. It was a continual regret to me that my father's means and interest were insufficient to secure me a commission in the Army, for which I considered myself by nature fitted. I read several treatises on strategy and military engineering, but this practice seemed to no purpose and I desisted. I thought then of persuading my father to let me change my employment and learn surgery in the hospitals, so that I might become an Army surgeon. But he would not grant me even this request. My disgust with tallow-chandling increased and I grasped at whatever distractions of a novel sort were offered to me by the city. The cockpit outside the barracks was my favourite place of call and I would wager there as much as half a guinea on a main, though my wages did not warrant my staking so much as a sixpence.

One memorable day, the 10th of August 1773, I was challenged to lay against that oddity, a hen-cock—that is to say, a cock with plumage resembling a hen's—which was to meet a famous shift-wing red, owned by a drummer of the garrison, that had won six good fights in a row. I offered to lay a shilling, which was all that I had of my own money in my pocket, but this was considered un-handsome by my challenger, an evil, black-browed, sallow fellow with a little grey cock tucked under his arm. So I dared to clap down on the board a whole guinea with which my father had that afternoon entrusted me—I was to take it to a tailor in discharge of a debt. The shift-wing, after a long quailing, was prevailed upon to set to the hen-cock, but with such evident alarm and dismay at what seemed to him a fowl of the opposite sex masquerading in spurs, that the hen-cock made short work of him: first tearing his throat and then, volleying over, striking him through the brain with the first heel-blow.

I had lately been forced to pledge my sword and a laced hat owing to similar mischances of play, and had no other resources left for concealing my peculation. I am sure that had I played the prodigal son and, going to my father, fallen on my knees with: 'Father, I have sinned against Heaven and before thee and am no more worthy to be called thy son,' he would have rebuked but forgiven me once again. But pride would not permit this Christian course, nor a recollection of his good-humoured scorn at my parade of cock-fighting lore. Instead of re-turning home I thought to myself: 'I am a man now and have no more fear of a father's curse than I have use for a father's blessing. To the devil with my father, the guinea, the tailor, the block-browed rogue, and that theif of a hen-cock! I still have a shilling to stake on the last fight.'

This fight was between the little grey cock and another

of the same breed, but rather dark-winged. It ended in confusion, the company clamouring that the 'black fellow with the jaw on him' had played his cock foul. They fell on him in a body, but somehow he extricated himself unharmed from the hurly-burly and darted down the street, the little grey cock under his arm. I kept my shilling and the sport ended. Then I said to myself, 'Damn the whole lot of 'em! I still have a shilling for rye whisky: a man can get drunk as a tinker's wife for less than half that sum.'

I soon found myself in the public-house opposite the lower barrack gate, calling for rye whisky and puffing out my chest. Sergeant Jenkins, who kept the house, was a recruiting sergeant. He noticed that the top of my head overpassed the chalk line on the lintel that marked five foot six and a half inches, which was the height below which, at that time, no soldier could be accepted for enlistment. He therefore flattered me and gave me another drink, this time at the expense of the house. Then followed a close inquiry after my state of health: had I ever been troubled with fits, was I ruptured, had I the sight of both eyes? I satisfied him with these particulars without even considering his reasons for asking them, and he began to stroke my shoulders and croon over me: 'Aye, a fine, tall, brave dandy young fellow: the proper cut, the exact proper fit!' It so closely recalled an old farmer exulting over a pig to be carted off to market, that I laughed in his face. However, he joined heartily in the laugh, and soon he had me nobly drunk. Within half an hour he had trotted me before a Justice of the Peace and sworn me in; and lo, I was a recruit of His Majesty King George's Ninth Regiment of Foot, and committed to a martial career after all.

But Sergeant Jenkins was himself a trifle drunk and did not consider that I was enlisted in good form until, after the event, he had made me his customary recruiting speech in the following well-worn phrases:

'To all aspiring heroes bold—in which I include you, Mr. Lamb—who have spirits above flattery and trade, and inclinations to become gentlemen by bearing arms in His Majesty's Ninth Regiment of Foot, commanded by the magnanimous General Lord Ligonier, let him repair to the drum's head (Towrow-dow!) where each gentleman volunteer shall be kindly used and honourably entertained and enter into present pay and good quarters. Besides which, gentlemen—meaning yourself, Mr. Lamb—for your further and better encouragement you shall receive one golden guinea advance, and a crown besides to drink His Majesty King George's health. And when you come to join your regiment you shall all have new hats, caps, arms, clothes, and accoutrements and everything that is necessary and fitting to complete a gentleman soldier. God Save their Majesties, and success to their Arms!'

'Huzza, huzza,' I replied fervently, gripping his hand.

When I came to my senses the next morning I was sick and sorry for what I had done; but another drink or two of whisky soon restored me, and I was able to go home to my father, accompanied by Sergeant Jenkins, and civilly informed him that I had joined the Service. I repaid him therewith the guinea out of my enlistment money and promised to settle another small debt from the sale of my present wardrobe so soon as a set of regimental clothes should be issued to me. He took the news pretty well, grasped my hand, and wished me good luck in my new life since I had failed so signally in the old. It is curious that his chief regret was that I had joined the Army in preference to the Navy: forgetting, I suppose, his former objections to my entering on a seafaring life. The Navy, for which my father had a predilection, having once served in a King's ship as boatswain, despised soldiers heartily. It was a preferential saying of seamen: 'A messmate before a shipmate, a shipmate before a stranger, a stranger before a dog, a dog before a soldier.'

The Army, it may be remarked, returned the odious compliment. 'Sailor' was a term of peculiar affront in the barrack-room; and in an officious hand-book issued about this time it was ordered that: 'You must enlist no strollers, vagabonds, tinkers, chimney-sweepers—or sailors.' And in another similar work it was remarked: 'Sailors and colliers seldom make good soldiers, being accustomed to a more debauched and drunken way of life than what a private soldier's pay can possibly admit of.' The severest and most disgraceful punishment that could be inflicted upon a soldier, beyond any quantity of lashes, or the Wooden Horse, or even the Scavenger's Daughter was *Removal to the Navy*. I think it a great pity that such reciprocal abuses were and still are exchanged between the two Services: they breed jealousies and ill feeling that has often been fatal to our arms in a combined expedition on land and water. My father, I believe, regarded my choosing the Army in preference to the Navy as a slight both upon himself and upon my dead brother's memory; though, as I say, he took the news pretty well.

My mother was disconsolate and could not say a word of good-bye, but only wept.

❋ ❋ ❋ ❋ ❋ ❋ ❋ ❋ ❋ ❋ ❋ ❋

CHAPTER

2

I WAS lodged at the barracks for four days and employed there in a number of menial and disagreeable tasks for which I had not bargained. without even the satisfaction of being given a red coat to wear. I was also refused a pass through the gate lest I should be tempted to desert. On the 18th of August three other recruits and myself, under a Corporal Buchanan, were marched a distance of seventy-six miles by road to Waterford, where my regiment was then stationed. Of these three men, one was a 'dipper' or pickpocket recruited in Dublin Jail, and one a gin-shop keeper whose only means of escape from his creditors had been to join the Army. The third was a delicate young fellow named Richard Harlowe who was a man of some education and evidently owed his presence among us to some personal misfortune; though in all our long acquaintance he never let fall a single word as to his antecedents, and I was always too delicate to inquire into them. Harlowe and I struck up a sort of friendship on our march together, and I protected him from the insults of our two fellow recruits who sneered at him for a fine gentleman who found their company too low for him. I knew something of the art of boxing and made it clear that any malice that they showed towards him I would resent equally as if it had been directed against myself.

Our way lay through Timolin, Carlow, Kilkenny, and Royal Oak. It was for Harlowe and myself a matter of melancholy interest to contrast the magnificence of the country seats of the nobility and gentry, and the decency of the dwellings allotted to their retainers, with the sordid cots of the unprotected peasantry. Castle Belan, two miles beyond Timolin, was a case in point, the residence of the Earl of Aldborough. The house, which we turned aside to visit, stood near the junction of two streams, the Greece and the Arrow, with before it a wide lawn gradually sloping from a grove of high fir-trees to the gently flowing Greece, between two rows of elm and ash. The Earl was very busy at this time on the modernization of the house, which was built in the plain style in use under King George I; and this process when complete was to include a fruitery, hot-house, green-house, ice-house, a chapel, a theatre, a pheasantry, and two porters' lodges to each of the six approaches—twelve in all—and stone piers and sweep walls. Each approach was an English mile in length from the house. There were artificial waters in the pleasure grounds besides the two streams aforesaid, namely, ponds, canals, and a small lake replete with carp, tench, trout, pike, cray-fish, etc., and with all sorts of domestic and foreign waterfowl. His Lordship had, moreover, erected a spacious inn and planned to construct forty slate farm-houses for the Protestant tenantry of his out-domain. But a mile or two away from this island of opulence we came upon a cluster of Papist cabins in the pitiful old style, of mud and turf. We should have thought it impossible for human beings to exist in such abject poverty, sloth, dirt, and misery: which was worse even than anything that I had seen in County Meath as a boy —indeed seldom in all my subsequent travels did I see such 'looped and windowed raggedness' or such pinched, greenish animal faces as there.

A toothless old man to whom we spoke, told us among

other particulars that there were not more than a half dozen ploughs in the whole parish; that these were let out by their owners at a high rate, but that for the most part the spade ruled hereabouts. The labourers were paid by their titular employer, an absentee rector, not in money but in small potato-plots of an acre apiece, for which they were charged six pounds a year; which they worked out at the rate of fivepence a day. They ate no bread, but only potatoes, even on feast-days. Some of them were also, as a charity, allowed the grazing of a cow. This serfdom was aggravated by their compulsion to pay tithes (though illegally) on potatoes, turf, and furze, for the support of a religion which oppressed and detested their own. At the time that we passed through, there was almost famine in the village: as was customary in the months of July and August when the old potatoes were exhausted and the new not yet come to maturity. The cottiers were obliged to fall back upon boiled cabbages and nettles with a little milk, so that many, as usual, were dead of the flux. But once every week when their tyrants, the tithe-proctor and the tithe-farmer, and the other Protestant gentry were safely away at church together down the road—where a wretched out-at-heels curate officiated— they would bleed the cattle fattening on the summer grass to make themselves a holiday meal of black pudding. The tithe-farmer bought the tithes from the tithe-proctor (who managed for the rector) and each turned a profit by the transaction. The peasants were the slaves of the tithe-farmer and were made to draw home his corn, hay, and turf for nothing, and to give him their labour and that of their children whenever called upon.

I presented the old man with a sixpence, which he gazed at with wild joy and wonder. It was, he assured us with tears, the grandest coin that any man in the village had seen since Chrismas; and he would be careful about taking it to some friends a great distance off to change it into half-pence, lest the tithe-farmer should get wind of his riches. He wished me abundant prosperity, health, glory, etc. etc., which grateful oratory I cut short by remarking that a stout gentleman was coming towards us who had the very air and complexion of a tithe-farmer.

CHAPTER 2

The old man took to the hedge like a hare and I saw him no more.

In our journey we passed many places hardly less wretched than this.

Corporal Buchanan was of the blustering sort. He soon had cause for gratitude to Harlowe and myself, though he did not mitigate his severity towards us on that account; for just after dawn, in the barn where we were lodged, near the ruined Abbey of Craigenamanagh, I awoke to see Brooks the pickpocket rise secretly and rifle the pockets of the Corporal's coat. I raised the hue and cry and out he ran across the fields. I pursued him; but he had his shoes on, whereas I was unshod. He would have escaped, had not Harlowe pulled a stake from the hedge, caught and mounted a horse that was pasturing in a field, and ridden the fugitive down in the Abbey grounds. Brooks was conveyed for the rest of the journey with his hands firmly secured behind his back. There was, by the bye, a prophecy current in these parts that the fine ancient octagonal tower of the Abbey would fall down at last on the day when the Devil passed through Craigenamanagh. But it had a solid enough look.

On our arrival at Waterford, on August the 24th, we were put into the hands of an old drill-sergeant of the name of Fitzpatrick, who was a remarkably devout man— for a person of his profession. There were sixteen of us in his awkward squad, and on the first morning Sergeant Fitzpatrick addressed us as follows: 'My dear lads, now that you are set under my charge I will teach you to become good soldiers, if you will closely heed me. The Ninth Foot in which you have the honour of serving is the best regiment in the Army—barring always The Twenty-third, the Royal Welch Fusiliers, with whom I served throughout the Seven Years' War. For you know, my lads, that it is with a regiment as with a wife: you espouse her for life and are one flesh with her, you must never permit the least reproach to be spoken against her, as you love your own honour. I am, as it happens, a twice married man; The Ninth is my second wife and I honour her accordingly, but I cannot be untrue to the memory of my first. The Royal Welch Fusiliers were ever the boldest corps in the King's Army, and the truest on parade: and, what is more, we fought at Fontenoy, Dettingen, and Minden under the guiding eye of the Most High God and the inspiration of His saint, the Reverend Charles Wesley. But The Ninth is a very good regiment likewise.

'Understand, then (it is an order): The Ninth Foot is to be for you the *ne plus ultra* of martial perfection and you shall strive with all your might to keep it so.

'Next, my gallant lads, pay strict attention to what I say. These are my instructions with regard to you, viz.:—

'The Recruit is to be taught the several duties of the soldier, by gradation and regular stages, as follows:

'First—his body is to be formed, the air of the clown to be banished, and a manly, soldier-like deportment to be acquired.

'Secondly—he is to learn to march with ease and gracefulness, and to be taught the Step.

'Thirdly—the handling of his arms and the Manual Exercise.

'Fourthly—firing, and the Platoon Exercise.

'Fifthly—firing with ball.

'Now, in the first stage, you must learn from me the true position of the soldier: fixing your eyes upon me and making me your fugleman. You must keep your body erect, without constraint. Observe, my heels are close and in a line, my toes a little turned out, my belly rather drawn in than otherwise, my breast projected, my shoulders square to the front and braced well back, my hands hanging down my sides with the palms close to the thighs. Observe especially my head: how it is turned somewhat to the right, so as to bring the left eye in a direct line with the centre of the body, with my looks directed to an object to the right—the soldier's wife's chemise yonder hanging on the line.

'Come now, my brave boys, and we'll make a lucky start. Fall back against the wall of the privy in a line, the tallest soldier on the right, the shortest on the left.'

He had us back against the privy wall (our heels, calves, shoulders, the backs of our heads and palms of our hands all touching it) and kept us standing there, after correcting our position with stern judgments upon our boorishness, for fifteen or twenty minutes. The term 'Friday's children' was his most solemn abuse, by which he intended us to understand that we still formed part of the great animal kingdom, which included bears, asses, mules, puppies, and the round-shouldered ourang-outang. These the Almighty Lord created on the fifth day, Friday, before perfecting Man on the Saturday afternoon, and resting on the Sunday morning. Having then an immobile audience fixed before him, he would preach to us on the excellence of military discipline as moulding the man for duty and propriety in general, how it forms not merely good soldiers but good citizens and subjects to benefit the commonwealth. Sometimes in these addresses his eloquence carried him away, and we were like to faint in our upright posture; waiting for the sermon to finish, which, by the bye, it seldom did without the name of the Rev. Charles Wesley being somehow introduced into it.

It may be observed that the Rev. Charles Wesley and the Rev. George Whitefield, both Methodists, had been much persecuted in their early missionary journeys through Ireland and particularly by beneficed clergymen who happened also to be Justices of the Peace—the Cork Grand Jury made in 1749 a memorable presentment to the effect that 'We find and present Charles Wesley to be a person of ill fame, a vagabond, and a common disturber of His Majesty's peace; and we pray he may be transported.' However, the effect of their severe teaching upon the troops stationed in Ireland was approved by the commanding officers, as conducing to good behaviour and improved discipline; and the persecution died down. It has been said that the true victor of Minden was not Ferdinand of Brunswick but the same Charles Wesley whose inspiration made perfect Ironsides of our marching regiments.

Instead of beating us over the shoulders with a cane, as most drill-sergeants do, to correct the faults of recruits, Sergeant Fitzpatrick would chasten us in Biblical language. But, even this failing, would give the order, 'On your knees, down!' 'Now,' said he, 'you shall in unison humbly pray God to give you both the will and strength to become good soldiers of Christ and King George'—which order we were bound to obey, mumbling the words after him. When Smutchy Steel, the gin-shop keeper, stealing a sidelong glance to his left laughed aloud at the sight of his comrade, Brooks the Dipper, thus praying to order, Sergeant Fitzpatrick grew enraged. He seized Steel by the collar, swung him up in the air, though a heavy slouch, and hustled him off the parade-ground so powerfully that his heels seemed hardly to scrape the gravel; and threw, rather than gave, him in charge of the Main Guard. Smutchy Steel was instantly confined and spent the remainder of the day in the dark cell, with bread and water as his only subsistence. 'Well, then, my brave soldiers,' cried the Sergeant, returning very red in the face, 'you see the rapid fate that overtakes the man who dares interrupt your devotions. On the feet up! Now that you are refreshed by prayer, it is an opportune time for you to attempt the Right Face, the Left Face, and the Right About Face. Therefore watch me, pray, with close attention. To the Right Face. First, place the hollow of the right foot briskly behind the left heel' (etc.).

This dark cell, or Black Hole, was a place approved of by general military regulations: it was ordered, however, by the Adjutant-General that though as dark and dismal as possible, the Black Hole should be free from damp and supplied with clean straw once a week.

It was our misfortune that we did not continue long under the instruction of good Sergeant Fitzpatrick: he was poisoned by a meal of shell-fish, of which, in the excessive hot weather then prevailing, he should have had the sense to beware, and narrowly escaped with his life, his face and extremities swelling to an alarming degree. His charge was handed to a sergeant, nicknamed 'Mortal Harry' from his extravagant use of swearing, who completed with us the twenty-one days set aside for our first stage of training. 'O you truant offspring of a Drogheda pig and a Belfast chambermaid' he would shout at young Harlowe, for whom he reserved his choicest objurgations. 'Another false step and I'll pluck out your smoking liver with my own fingers, by the Holy Syssop and Vinegar, so I will! I'll eat it raw with salt on—and relish it too, God damn me all hues and colours!' He taught us the Slow or Parade step, of seventy paces to a minute, timing us with a battered silver watch, and the Quick step of one hundred paces to a minute. The length of the pace was to be exactly two feet four inches, from heel to heel, and he hobbled our legs with straps so that we should not exceed this allowance. He would buckle on the straps himself and took delight in so tightening them that they constricted the flesh painfully. This cruelty roused our indignation but we were too wise to protest to an officer. At the end of that period, having at last, in the opinion of the Captain who came to inspect us, rectified the most prominent appearance of our awkwardness, we were each given his regimentals—coat, waistcoat, breeches, hat—a set of accoutrements and a Tower musket with its bayonet and ramrod. This musket, which weighed fifteen pounds, was a fine and trusty weapon, though most inaccurate at a longer range than fifty paces; and the yellow flint supplied with it was only good for fifteen rounds—the black flint used in gentlemen's fowling-pieces, with which the American armies were afterwards supplied from a rich vein at Ticonderoga, was good for sixty. For the loss of a musket we were fined one pound, ten shillings; for a bayonet, five shillings; and for a ramrod, two. Our complement of necessaries, valued at three pounds sterling, may be interesting to the reader to compare with that of the present trousered, booted, and short-haired days. They comprised: three shirts, two white stocks, one black hair stock with its brass clasps, three pair of white yarn stockings, three pair of oiled linen stockings to be worn on the march under half-spatterdashes, one pair of these same half-spatterdashes, two pair of black linen gaiters, one pair of long black woollen gaiters, one pair of linen drawers, one red cap, one cockade, one knapsack, one haversack, one pair of shoe-buckles and one of garter-buckles, one of black leather garters, two pair of shoes, and a machine to cut and cock hats. In addition we carried a cartouche case to contain four-and-twenty rounds of ball and powder, which were not to be used but in cases of necessity; for ordinary service we were expected to make our own cartridges and run our own bullets. We also carried two spare flints, a powder bag, a ream of whited-brown paper, a spool of pack-thread, three spare musket locks, a dozen of screw pins, three spare priming-pans, six iron ramrods, a bullet-mould, a cartridge-mould, an iron ladle to melt lead in, a worm for extracting cartridges that were fast in the breech, a turnkey, a hammercap, and a stopper. One pound of lead, half a pint of powder and a yard of paper made about fifteen cartridges.

We were next taught how to salute an officer of the Army or Navy, standing fast, giving him a full front, at the same time pulling off our hats with the left hand, and letting them fall in a graceful manner to the side. These hats were wide awkward affairs, not looped three-corner-wise, as in the time of the German wars, but only before and behind, so that they afforded neither shade to the eyes nor protection against sunstroke. The tall caps worn by the Grenadier companies were lighter and at the same time more noble in appearance.

Thus prepared we marched every morning from the barracks to the bowling-green near the water-front, to be instructed in the Manual Exercise. We learned how to stand with a firelock, how to shoulder, order, and present arms, how to fix and charge bayonets, and, finally, how to load and fire with ball. We were drilled for four hours every day.

The words of command and instructions which accompanied this exercise may be of interest, and I shall therefore as a specimen detail the loading instructions then in use. (The firelock at the start, is dropped to the primary position, and at half-cock.)

Handle Cartridge! Draw the cartridge smartly from the pouch with the right hand. Bring it to the mouth, holding it between the forefinger and thumb. Bite off the top of it.

Prime! Shake a little powder into the priming-pan. Shut the pan with the three last fingers. Seize the small of the butt with the same three fingers.

Load! Face to the left on both heels, so that the right toe may point directly to the front, and the body be a very little faced to the left, bringing at the same time the firelock round to the left side without sinking it. It should in this momentary position be almost perpendicular (having the muzzle only a small degree brought forward) and, as soon as it is steady there, must instantly be forced down within two inches of the ground, the butt nearly opposite the left heel, and the firelock itself somewhat sloped, and directly to the front; the right hand at the same instant catches the muzzle, in order to steady it. Shake the remaining powder into the barrel from the cartridge, putting in after it the wadding and ball. Seize the top of the ramrod with forefinger and thumb.

Draw Ramrods! Force the ramrod half out, and seize it backhanded exactly in the middle. Draw it entirely out, and turning it with the whole hand and arm extended from you, put it one inch into the barrel.

Ram down Cartridge! Push the ramrod down, holding it, as before, exactly in the middle, until the hand touches the muzzle. Slip the forefinger and thumb to the upper end, without letting the ramrod fall farther into the barrel. Push the cartridge well down to the bottom. Strike it two very quick strokes with the ramrod.

Return Ramrods! Return the ramrod to its loops, strike the top of the muzzle smartly so as to fix the ramrod and bayonet in position.

The primary position varied between the ranks. For the front rank of the platoon, who dropped upon the right knee when it came to firing their volley, this position was fixed at the height of the breeches' waistband; for the centre rank, who stood fast, it was at the middle of the stomach; for the rear rank, who moved one pace to their right, it was close to the breast. The firelock was in each case kept horizontal. For discharging the firelock, the orders were *Make ready, present, give fire!* A trained platoon could fire two aimed volleys in the space of one minute, following these orders, and the motions became so mechanical that I have seen a man who had been knocked senseless in battle with a blow on his skull, yet continue loading and firing in exact perfection of discipline—though what mark his bullets were striking I could not well determine.

These instructions were simple by comparison with the old words of command, with their relevant explanation, that hung in a frame in our Sergeants' Mess, showing a date of ninety years before: when a musket was fired with a slow match, not flint and trigger, and supported on a rest.

The orders for firing, unloading, and reloading a musket were a sermon in themselves, viz.

March with your rest in your hand	Present
March, and with your musket carry your rest	Give fire
	Dismount your musket
Unshoulder your musket	Uncock your match
Poise your musket	Return your match
Join your rest to your musket	Clear your pan
	Prime your pan
Take forth your match	Shut your pan
Blow off your coal	Cast off your loose powder
Cock your match	Blow off your loose powder
Try your match	Cast about your musket
Guard, blow, and open your priming-pan	Trail your rest
	Open your charge
Charge your musket	Withdraw your scouring stick
Draw forth your scouring stick	
	Shorten your scouring stick
Shorten your scouring stick	Return your scouring stick
Put in your bullet and ram home	Recover your musket

But at the present day a great improvement has been made even upon our expeditious orders; so that only ten words of command are given from start to finish in the same exercise.

❀ ❀ ❀ ❀ ❀ ❀ ❀ ❀ ❀ ❀ ❀ ❀

CHAPTER

3

MORTAL HARRY's language outraged my sensibilities but broke no bones. Some of us recruits, namely Harlowe, Brooks, and myself, suffered far worse at the hands of

Corporal Buchanan who had marched us down from Dublin and who was now in charge of the mess to which we were assigned. He drew our pay for us every Saturday, and on the specious pretence of guarding it safely for us, so that we should not run into temptations of women and drink, squandered the greater part of it himself. It paid the expenses of his weekly score at the public-house. According as it was thirsty weather or not so thirsty, we received a greater or lesser proportion of our due; but, though provisions were very cheap in Waterford at the time, the allowance he made us was always below our needs. We complained continually in private among ourselves, but such was our inexperience that we did not dare state our grievance to the Captain commanding our company. Had the complaint been properly made, with the interference of a sergeant, we should most certainly have been redressed: but none of us came forward to bell the cat. Our apprehensions were increased by the fact of the Corporal's being a favourite with Lieutenant Sweetenham, our platoon officer. This Lieutenant was a well-intentioned but negligent gentleman, having been over-long in the service and without interest to secure his promotion: he suffered many abuses in his command to pass with impunity.

The first of us to contemplate desertion was Brooks the Dipper, but he did not confide in us, knowing of our objections to him. He was a dirty soldier and a liar, and would not relinquish his old trade when embracing that of arms; we were therefore not sorry one Sunday, when we were awakened by the morning gun, to find him gone. It added to our satisfaction to hear that, before absconding, he had stolen the whole of our pay from the pockets of our cruel Corporal: for we hoped now to reclaim it for ourselves. But the Corporal boldly told Lieutenant Sweetenham that the money was his own, all but a few shillings, since he had advanced us money earlier in the week for the purchase of pipe-clay, hair-powder, soap, and missing necessaries to lay out for the general inspection of our belongings that had been held. We were a pack of spendthrifts, so he had the impudence to tell the Lieutenant, in our presence too—and he eyed us malignantly as who would say: 'Dare to tell on me, my beauties, and you'll be confined in darky for ten days, every man Pat of you,' which was his common expression. Such was Corporal Buchanan's ascendancy over us that none of us durst nail his lie to the bench.

That evening Harlowe said to me: 'Lamb, a bargain is a bargain. I swore to serve the King as a soldier, for a certain payment. That payment is withheld from me and I am half-starved for want of it. The exercises are severe and I am punished for every trifling fault which my bodily weakness makes me fall into. I am resolved to desert the Service. If the Dipper can get off free, why not I? What I have suffered is enough to turn a man rank Jacobite. Aye, Waterford is a harbour of good omen: it was from here that King James II escaped from his enemies and sailed to freedom in France.'

I remonstrated with Harlowe, pointing out the manifest dangers of such a course; but he persisted in it. He said that the vessels in the Newfoundland trade that sailed from Waterford with cargoes of pork, butter, and potatoes were frequently shorthanded, and he could no doubt stow himself aboard one of them and work his passage to America, which was his object. The harbour of Waterford extended about eight miles in length in nearly a straight line, all the way deep and clear, and having no rocks or sands that could obstruct the navigation; and that many small vessels were tied up in lonely parts would facilitate his escape. The name of America struck sympathetically in my ears, and, near desperate as I was myself, I began to think that his project was not so rash as I had judged. That evening, after a particularly warm day under Mortal Harry, I became fully determined to ally myself with Harlowe.

There was a manner of breaking out of barracks, known to two or three of us, which presented no difficulties to a pair of active men. The route began with the necessary-house. One man would there mount on the other's shoulders in order to climb a ten-foot wall, and pull up his comrade after him; a short stretch of this wall brought the venturers to a holly-tree, into the prickly branches of which they must leap, and so descend. A sentry had his walk along the outer wall of the barracks; but he could be eluded even on moonlit nights by making the passage in three stages. The first stage was to choose, for the leap into the tree, the moment when the sentry had turned the corner of the barrack wall, and to wait concealed in the foliage until he had reappeared and passed on again. The second stage was then to shin down the tree and lie concealed behind an elder bush. The third was to wait for his second reappearance and subsequent disappearance, and thereupon to dash across a paddock and out of sight behind a hedge.

Corporal Buchanan was dead-drunk as usual on the night for which we planned our evasion, which was pay-day night of the ensuing week; and we therefore had no fear that our long absence at the necessary-house would be noticed by him. We stole out, about an hour after the evening gun, Harlowe carrying two wretched suits of slops which he had bartered at a marine-store against the fine silk handkerchief and decent hat in which he had enlisted. We undressed in the necessary-house and put on these patched and ragged duds, rolling up our regimental clothes and burying them in a sand-heap outside. It was a cloudy night and a little rain was falling.

We mounted the wall cautiously and silently and observed that the sentry was at that moment disappearing round the corner. We crawled along the top of the wall, which was irregular and difficult, and each in turn catching hold of a projecting bough of the holly swung ourselves into a crotch of the tree: where we crouched panting. Soon we heard the sentry's steps approaching and presently saw him ground his firelock in a very unsoldier-like fashion and begin to whistle and dance a jig to the tune of 'The Top of Cork Road.' We recognized him as 'Mad Johnny Maguire,' a very humane and merry Northerner who had been among our comforters in these troubles. He had urged us repeatedly to bring our complaint to the company officer and brave the consequences, and undertook that all would be well if we did so. My heart pricked me that, should we succeed in deserting, poor Maguire must bear the blame and be confined for our fault: for our regimental clothes would be discovered and it would be known that we had passed through his walk. He might well be suspected as a confederate. However, it was too late now to turn back.

Hardly had Maguire shouldered his arm again and resumed his march, when we heard whispered curses and a rattle of stones, and two men came along the wall after us. For a moment we thought we were lost, and that this was a party sent to apprehend us. We lay perfectly still, not daring to move, and suddenly some one took a great leap off the wall into the tree, kicking Harlowe on the head as he went, and landing on my thighs. My assailant gave a muttered cry and seized me by the throat, but Harlowe instantly interposed, recognizing him. 'Hist, Moon-Curser,' he said. 'Leave off now, for God's sake. We are all friends. This is Gerry Lamb and I am Gentleman Harlowe. We are deserting too.'

Terry Reeves (nicknamed 'Moon-Curser' from his having been a link-boy before he enlisted) and his comrade Smutchy Steel were recruits of the same company as ourselves but of another mess; they had by a coincidence chosen the same moment for desertion. Terry was drunk and Smutchy a very oafish fellow; both were in their regimental clothes. It was a great embarrassment to both parties that we were simultaneously engaged on the same venture, for the risk of capture was thus more than doubled. But neither would 'give the wall' to the other, and Mad Johnny Maguire had come whistling back before the whispered argument in the crotch had finished. We were piled one upon the other, like fish in a creel, or like corpses along the covered way during a hot assault.

Then came a diversion: from the next sentry post on the right, a sudden hoarse challenge of 'Halt, who goes there?'

'Rounds,' was the reply. This surprised us, for the visiting sergeant of the watch was not due until midnight.

'What rounds?' the sentry called again.

'Surprise Grand Rounds.'

'Advance four paces, Grand Rounds, your Honours!' So quiet was the night that we could hear the smart slap of the sentry's hand at the swell of the stock, and the click of his heels as he presented his arm. For it was Major Bolton, the Commanding Officer of the Regiment, who, accompanied by his adjutant officer, a drummer with a lantern, a sergeant, and a file of men, was making an unexpected inspection of the posts. Maguire's strolling step briskened up into a parade-ground stride, he ceased whistling, and retired around the corner again to await the officers' approach. While the Major was questioning the sentry in his duties and finding fault with him for being short of two buttons on his coat, we decided on a bold move. I slid to the ground and helped down Harlowe, who ran across to the elderbush. Then I stayed to assist the two others, for I reckoned that, since we must all sink or swim together, it was to my interest to do so. How we managed to push the heavy-footed Smutchy Steel under cover of the bush without Maguire hearing and challenging us, I do not know; but I imagine that his attention was so fixed upon the approach of the Grand Rounds that he discounted the nearer noises as unworthy of his attention. There were, as it happened, an ass and her foal pasturing near by, for the steps of which perhaps he mistook ours.

From behind the bush we heard Maguire challenge, in his turn, very fiercely, and after the same exchange as before, Major Bolton, the adjutant, and the drummer with his lantern came into view. Major Bolton warned Maguire to be on his guard that night, for there was a report that two soldiers contemplated desertion. 'And if you fail in your duty, my man, it will not be for lack of warning.' They passed on, and soon we were able to make the next stage to the hedge.

On the previous day we had marked out the vessel in which we proposed to stow ourselves away, moored at about a mile's distance from the barracks. She was a large, half-decked, cutter-rigged vessel, of the sort named 'droghers,' and was evidently sailing soon, and for some distance, to judge from the water and live stock being carried aboard her as we watched. The cargo was birch-brooms and potatoes. Our two comrades had broken out in a blind despair rather than with any preconcerted plan, and they therefore attached themselves to us as guides to salvation; nor could anything that we might object make them quit our company. We passed along the road down which we were marched every morning to our drill, but took to the ditch every time that footsteps approached. After a few hundred paces we heard a regular tramp of feet in the distance and the sharp cry of a non-commissioned officer giving his men the step. We leaped into the ditch in no time, and soon a party of six men went by with fixed bayonets. Mortal Harry was in command and in their midst we descried the stumbling and miserable figure of Brooks the Dipper, his hands gyved behind him.

'Yes, my heathen jewel,' Mortal Harry was exulting, 'the drummers of The Ninth are Goliaths and Behemoths; they lay on like the red fiends of Hell itself. Won't they lift the skin off your eel's body, hey? Old Pontius Pilate's crew of Romans couldn't do better, by the Almighty God, no, they couldn't! By the time they have entirely done with you, you'll be howling for the raw hide of a cow to lap yourself within, my poor damned monkey, lest you bleed to death.'

An indescribable horror seized me at these words, spoken in such cold malevolent tones that they felt like the hand of death on my heart. To go forward, or return —either course now seemed equally perilous. Harlowe was for going forward at all events; therefore I went with him. We arrived without further hazard at the water-front, but I remember that it was rather with relief than anguish that I observed our potato-ship in the act of casting off and slipping down the tide.

'Now,' says I to Harlowe, 'you can do as you please. But I, for one, am returning. Be sure that it was the man at the shop from whom you bought these rags who betrayed us to Major Bolton; for we communicated our design to no one, and these two drunkards here acted on a sudden motion. We have no chance of escape; but we have a chance at least of making good our return, if we start at once.'

They all felt too miserable for disputation, and without a word turned homeward with me. After the passage of half an hour we were back again at the hedge and then ran across in pairs to the elder-bush. But Smutchy Steel, the awkward creature, put his foot in a rabbit-hole and turned his ankle, letting out a great screech. Mad Johnny Maguire was still on his watch, for it wanted a few minutes of midnight. He was standing at ease under the holly-tree. I had the presence of mind to anticipate his challenge, by crying out: 'Hist, Maguire, for the love of God raise no alarm! It's I, Gerry Lamb! Let me come forward and explain our case to you.'

He proved a good comrade to me once more; for, though risking a severe punishment for such a breach of discipline, he consented to let me approach unchallenged. I detailed what had occurred in a few words and pleaded earnestly with him to let us return to our duty, explaining that we had felt at the waterfront the reviving energy of loyal motives, which had induced us to turn back in time. He revolved the matter for awhile in his head and then remarked quizzically, 'So it's deserting backwards you are, my fine cocks? By Heaven, it's a big thing you're asking me, Gerry boy. For if I were now to arrest the whole four of you, wouldn't it mean great glory to me, and perhaps a guinea from the company officer in recompense, beside?'

'Yes, John Maguire, we are indeed at your mercy. But pray hasten your decision, or the Visiting Rounds will be upon us.'

He winked at me, shouldered his piece, and retired beyond the corner, as much as to say: 'Well, then, my name is Billy Hare, I know nothing.' So we returned safely, though it was a great business, hoisting Steel into the crotch and hauling him across to the wall; we could not prevail on him to stifle his groans. We were safely back at the sand-heap, and hurriedly changing back into our soldiers' clothes, before midnight tolled from the chapel bell, and the distant cries marked the progress of the Visiting Sergeant.

As Harlowe and I re-entered the barrack-room, Corporal Buchanan awakened suddenly at the noise and turned up the lantern burning small beside him.

'From whence, in the Devil's name, do you soldiers come?' he inquired in the hoarse whisper of sleep.

'From the necessary-house,' we replied. 'We have, both of us, a touch of the colic.'

'How came that sand on your coats?'

'We tripped over a mound of sand in the darkness.'

'You drunken strollers, get you to bed at once,' he roared at us, and an instant later fell asleep.

Harlowe turned down the lantern wick, lest finding it still burning high in the morning he should be reminded of the incident; and then we crept back into bed. Never before in my life had I been so glad to be between blankets, as then. We had taken the precaution to thrust our ragged clothes, with a stick, deep into the night soil at the necessary-house, and there was now nothing more to fear.

A court martial sat upon Brooks the Dipper the next morning and he was found guilty of desertion, aggravated by the theft of his comrades' pay, and the additional crime of resisting arrest by the party sent to take him at the peasants' hut where he was found hiding. The sentence was three hundred lashes at the halberts. Major Bolton had accelerated these proceedings instead of letting Brooks lie a prisoner for a week or so, which would have been the more usual course. For he desired to make him an example to the two unknown men who, from the evidence of the slop-shop man, seemed also to be contemplating desertion. The sentence was promulgated at noon, and at three o'clock the regiment was formed up in a hollow square to witness its execution under the superintendence of the Drum-Major, who was answerable that the cat did not have more than nine tails, and with the surgeon standing by to decide at each stroke whether the continuance of the punishment endangered the man's life or his further usefulness as a soldier. I will say this for Major Bolton, and so will any man who ever had the honour of serving under his command, that he was an officer who combined strictness with magnanimity to a most remarkable degree. He avoided flogging as much as possible, and only resorted to it for such great crimes as required extraordinary coercion. For the common breaches of military laws and duties, he used to send the offenders to the drill field for a few hours, sometimes (to show his keener displeasure) making them wear their regimental coats inside out as examples of ill behaviour and disgrace. They were moreover prevented from going on any command or mounting the principal guards.

On this occasion, he did not shirk the horrid spectacle

of Private Brooks' castigation, though it was well known that he had told the surgeon that his stomach churned within him on such occasions, and that he had great difficulty in restraining his vomit. I shall spare the reader the details of the proceedings, informing him merely that during the infliction of the punishment on my comrade's bare back, by the regimental drummers, the warm, youthful emotions operated in me to such an extent that I cried like a child. Harlowe, who stood next to me, fainted clean away, his firelock falling with a clatter at my feet.

The third drummer had just completed his tale of twenty-five lashes—each one of which was like a stroke against my own heart—and the victims' shrill screams had already turned to great sobs when Major Bolton, evidently much affected, strode forward to the halberts where he was bound, and in very moving, compassionate tones expostulated with Brooks on the greatness of his offenses, and asked him, had he suffered enough?

When Brooks signified his repentance in grimacings, being unable to find a voice, Major Bolton ordered him to be taken down and remitted the remainder of the punishment, on Brooks's promise of future good conduct. The parade was then dismissed.

As we came off parade, my feelings still very warm, I remarked to Terry Reeves, in the hearing of Corporal Buchanan: 'Twenty-five was for resisting arrest, Moon-Curser, twenty-five for desertion, but the remaining twenty-five, as the Major said, was for *that meanest of all crimes, stealing his comrades' pay*.'

The Corporal turned round sharply, but I was too wild to mind his glaring eye, and I believe that had he spoken a word of reproof, I should have called him a thief to his face. However, he made no remark; and, fearing, I suppose, that his peculation might be made known to the Captain, he gave us that very night nearly two shillings apiece of our pay, holding back only the odd shilling of our due. However, the next week and the week following he still kept us on very unfair allowance, and I should yet have gone hungry had not Sergeant Fitzpatrick and his wife employed me to teach their young son writing and arithmetic. These people were very kind to me, frequently inviting me to their table, where they both plied me with the Rev. Charles Wesley's opinions and merits as well as with excellent porter. They paid me, besides, at the rate of one shilling and sixpence a week. I also managed to pick up an odd sixpence or so by making out reports for other sergeants and corporals; and was thus able to relieve my unfortunate messmates who still, however incredible this may seem, preferred starvation to complaint.

Harlowe, though a man of better education than myself, was unable to undertake such writing tasks as these, because he had never learned a clerkly hand, and had such a crabbed gentleman's fist that his writing was quite illegible.

❊ ❊ ❊ ❊ ❊ ❊ ❊ ❊ ❊ ❊ ❊ ❊

CHAPTER

4

DURING our stay at Waterford I fell into many irregularities. The common girls of the town were lavish of their favours to the military, whose handsome facings and well-set-up appearance exercised a sort of fascination upon them; and since the Roman Church regarded such errors as venial, so long as the men they chose were not known to them to be married, I had much gratification at little expense. I also acquired a taste for the raw spirit distilled by the peasants from potatoes, which was as potent as it was easy to come by. However, my strongest prepossession was for gambling, and 'the Devil's picture book,' as the Methodists term a pack of cards, was now my favourite study. Being inexperienced in barrack-room life, I was a regular loser in whatever games of chance I attempted. In Dublin I had acquired a sharp eye for those forms of cheating in which cards are secretly removed from the pack to the dealer's advantage, or the pack is arranged beforehand and only a pretence of cutting and shuffling made. But I had yet to learn the maxim, which it cost me a large sum of money to frame for myself: never to use an opponent's pack more often than my own. For though in The Ninth no one, I dare affirm, marked his cards with the faint thumb-nail scratches and notches used in the fashionable clubs of London, there was not a pack in use among us of which each card had not acquired a distinct character of its own by constant handling. A shepherd knows every ewe in his flock by some slight difference of appearance, which would certainly escape the eye of the stranger unless one happened to be blind, lame, or tailless: in this same way every owner of a pack knew his own cards at a glance, soon as dealt, even though there might be no broken corner or torn edge among them. This knowledge put him in the ascendancy over players who knew only a half dozen of them at most, even after playing several times with the pack.

Sergeant Fitzpatrick and his good wife used to counsel me strongly against my passion for gambling. He used to say: 'Private Lamb, the practice will involve you in severe difficulties. Even where money is not risked, the playing of cards administers to idleness and dissipation; and where money is risked, the winner proceeds with ideas of avarice, and the loser to recover his losses; until the precipice yawns equally for both.' And she would quote from a poem of which I do not recollect the title:

> *Cards are superfluous, with all the tricks*
> *That idleness has ever yet contrived,*
> *To fill the void of an unfurnished brain,*
> *To palliate dullness and give time a shove.*

To supply the expenses of gaming, the privates sold their necessaries, besides squandering their pay: on such occasions they dreaded an officer's inspection of the barrack-room when they had to lay out their belongings for his scrutiny. But they almost invariably managed to elude punishment, by borrowing shirts, gaiters, stockings, and other articles of regimental appointment from comrades who happened to be sick or absent on guard duty. It was, among us, held a matter of honour to pay gambling debts within twenty-four hours of incurring them, and a man would rather commit crimes which even common and statute law punishes as capital offences than fail to meet such obligations.

In July, 1774, our regiment received the route for the North of Ireland, and on our arrival there, by way of Dublin—where, to my satisfaction, I found my father more friendly disposed towards me—the companies were distributed among the various towns of Ulster. I happened to be ordered on command, in a detachment of twelve men under Lieutenant Sweetenham, to Saintfield, ten miles distant from Belfast. It was a small but neat town once extensively engaged in the linen manufacture; but then in decay. The neighbourhood of Belfast was very ill disposed to the British Government, because of the way in which its ministers had played fast and loose with Irish trade and industry. The greater cheapness of living and labour in Ireland had always rendered her a dangerous commercial rival to England. First of all we were forbidden to export cattle, so our land-owners turned their land into sheep-walks, and a flourishing woollen industry was presently begun. This industry, which employed thirty thousand families in Dublin alone, was crushed in my grandfather's day by laws prohibiting the export of Irish wool or cloth, not only to England and the colonies, but to any country whatsoever. In compensation, a promise was made that our linen and hemp manufacture should be encouraged; but no sooner was the linen trade well established than innumerable restrictions were put upon it so that Irish should not compete with English and Scottish linen (which were subsidized by the Government) in any country in the world—nor even with Dutch linen, for fear the Dutch, in retaliation, ceased to buy English woollens.

As a result of this jealousy of the English manufacturers ten thousand or more weavers had since five years been obliged to emigrate to America, whence they wrote home letters full of rancour. The spirit of these weavers, who were all Presbyterians, was the Dissidence of Dissent, and was more obnoxious to our Protestant ruling classes even than Popery. Many thousands of Presbyterians had previously emigrated to America, being driven from their homes at the beginning of the eighteenth century by the inquisitorial Test Act, though they had been among King

William's staunchest supporters at the Protestant revolution. These had become backwoodsmen of the Western Border, and were to be among the fiercest and most redoubtable foes with whom we had to contend in the American War. From a great many inhabitants of Saintfield we therefore received black and sullen looks; none the less, the women here, as in the South, appeared very ready to court with our men, especially where there seemed a prospect of matrimony.

There was a very beautiful girl living at Newton Breda, two and a half miles distant from the inn where we were quartered, the daughter of a retired English merchant captain and a former lady's maid in the household of Lord Dungannon, whose seat of Belvoir lay adjacent. Father and daughter resided together in humble circumstances, the mother being lately deceased. I conceived a great passion for Miss Kate and would have made her my wife had she consented, since she was a Protestant like myself, and there was no obstacle to our union but my poverty. But she put me off with a tender firmness, and would not so much as allow me the smallest familiarity with her. I did not suspect that I had a rival, at least among the soldiery. The Saintfield horse-barrack lay empty at this time and I flattered myself that of all my comrades there was none to whom she could give the preference over me.

She continued to treat me with friendship and did not discourage my visits. Nor was her father at all averse to my visits at the house, though he made it clear enough that I must not deceive myself with any hopes in regard to his daughter until I held at least a corporal's rank. With my education, he said, and my natural talents, I might within a few years rise high in the Service.

To be brief: this Kate Weldone, who was dark-haired, well-featured, and of a gracefully rounded figure, and had, besides, remarkable wit and spirit, told me one day during her father's absence from the house that she was in great grief. She said that she would do almost anything in the world to recompense me if I would risk a crime for her sake.

I resented this question, and asked her whether she mistook me for a rapparee or bully.

But her misery was so remarkable that I softened towards her. Indeed, I presently assured her that I would commit almost any crime in the world, just for the satisfaction of pleasing her, so long as it were no vulgar crime, of theft or murder, and did not injure any of my comrades.

At this, she ran into my embrace and kissed me wildly. She swore that what she asked was in the interests of her own greatest happiness and would not hurt any one at all, least of all any comrade of mine.

'A strange sort of crime that hurts nobody, yet benefits you, my dearest Kate,' said I. 'Very well. On condition that it is indeed exactly as you say, I hereby swear by my honour to do for you whatever lies in my power: and I shall leave the assessment of my reward to your generosity.'

Her father happened to approach the room at the moment, but we broke our embrace in time, warned by his difficult breathing. On his entry he did not observe the emotion under which both of us were labouring, and called for a dish of tea.

'I hear from the innkeeper, Private Lamb,' he said, after we had exchanged our usual civilities and his daughter had busied herself in blowing up the fire, 'that even were I willing to give you my daughter, which I am not, the marriage could not now be solemnized. Your Commanding Officer has to-day issued a general order to prevent private soldiers from marrying without written licence signed by the officer of their company or detachment. He has desired the ministers of the places concerned not to solemnize the marriages of soldiers without calling for such a paper from them.'

Miss Kate affected indifference to the news, and Captain Weldone then went to repeat a rumour that orders were soon expected for us to be sent to Boston in New England, where the colonists were at this time in almost open rebellion. Major Bolton's action was read as a precaution against more soldiers' wives being taken than could be received aboard the transports when we embarked for America. 'It's an ill wind, etc.,' he said. 'If you are sent, and a campaign develops, your promotion is likely to

be accelerated, and on your return I shall, I trust, find
no reason for refusing you my Kate, if she be still willing.'

This made me suppose that there was an understanding
between the Captain and his daughter on the subject, that
she had confessed to her liking for me, and that only my
lowness of station and my poverty prevented the consum-
mation of my hopes. I returned to our quarters in an elated
frame of mind, and after buying drinks for the whole company called on my comrades for a game of cards. We
played a while for very trifling stakes, since they were so
far reduced in wealth that most of them had been forced
to keg themselves: that is to say, they had taken a common
form of oath not to borrow, lend, touch spirituous liquors
or lose more than a penny a game at cards or dice, until
they had saved enough of their pay to repurchase the
necessaries which they had sold. The restriction seemed to
irk my friend Harlowe, for he asked in a tone of challenge
whether there was not a soul present who would dare to
bet with him in visible coin. 'I have just bought a new pack
of cards,' he said, 'and I'll break the seal for any one
who will match me through the pack, card against card,
the ace to take precedence over the king.'

He fetched the cards, broke the seal and shuffled them
while I fetched drink for the two of us. He was my messmate and much obliged to me for a variety of services, and
I therefore did not do him the discourtesy of watching him
at the shuffle. He dealt out the cards alternately, so that
we had half the pack each. They were smuggled Spanish
cards, a sort which we favoured because they were both
stout and cheap. They ran forty-eight to the pack, and
Primero was our favourite game with them.

We matched card against card at threepence a sight,
and when at the eighth card he was a shilling and threepence ahead of me, I called on him to double the stake:
which he did.

At the twenty-fourth card I owed him eight shillings
and ninepence and, desperate at the greatness of this sum,
called on him to double the stakes again. He refused, saying that he would not run me into such a thicket as would
tear the clothes off my back, thread and thrum; but I

insisted, and my comrades called him a coward and told him in the language of the cock-pit to 'beak up and fight it out to the throttle.' So he consented, though with an appearance of comradely reluctance and concern: and when only eight cards were left to play I owed him sixteen shillings. I doubled the stakes again, and he consented 'to give me a chance to win the whole sum back.' But I continued to lose, at two shillings a card, twice out of every three times; and when the last card had been turned up, and I lost even that, my debt to Harlowe stood at the prodigious sum—for us—of twenty-nine shillings and nine-pence.

There was dead silence for a while, and I sat stupidly fingering the cards with my left hand and drumming the Devil's tattoo on the table with the fingers of my right.

Nobody laughed, for it was well understood that I could not afford to quit my debt within the statutory time. I was well enough liked by the men, many of whom would have been willing to accommodate me with a loan, had they been able; but they were kegging themselves and could do nothing. For Harlowe they had no liking and avoided his company as much as they decently could, he being a bird of another feather than their own. Mad Johnny Maguire offered me one shilling and sixpence, which was all he had, and Terry Reeves two, which was more than he had in coin; but this sum, added to what I had in my pockets, still fell short of the debt by a guinea. All those present behaved like mourners at a decent funeral.

I burst out laughing and shouted: 'Oh, by the Holy, it's come to this, has it? Well, down goes the whisky, and that's the last drink I'll swallow for a long while, for now I'll be kegging myself to Harlowe.' As an alternative to paying a debt, if the sum exceeded one month's pay, a soldier might keg himself to the victor: that is, abstain from all drink and gaming and make over all his pay, except one shilling a week, to his creditor. Nevertheless, the creditor had the right to refuse to compound in this manner if he distrusted the debtor; and the debtor was then bound to obtain the money by some other means.

Harlowe looked narrowly into my eyes. 'And what if I refuse to let you keg yourself to me?' he inquired. 'Have you always treated me in so comradely a way that you should expect generosity or mercy now?'

I could not in the least understand what he meant by this, nor could any one else present. There were murmurs of astonishment and indignation. However, Maguire said: 'This is none of our business, lads. There's a she in the case, I'll be bound. Let us leave these bucks to settle it between them in private.'

'Comrades, I have nothing whatever on my conscience,' I declared, 'in regard to Private Harlowe. Indeed, since the time when we were recruits together, I have treated him with far greater delicacy, I think, than many persons of my acquaintance.'

There was a laugh at this, for only the night before I had dissuaded Smutchy Steel, whom enforced abstinence had made quarrelsome, from daubing the tap-room wall, as he threatened, with Harlowe's entrails.

'You must come outside,' pronounced Harlowe, 'if you wish to talk compound with me.'

We went out for a jaunt down the Newton Breda road.

'How have I offended you, Harlowe?' I inquired. 'For I know that you would not refuse me to keg myself to you, unless you considered yourself in some way injured.'

He did not answer me outright, but paced along by my side in a silence which greatly annoyed me.

I stopped in my stride, faced about, pulled him backwards by the shoulders and told him: 'Gentleman Harlowe, if you will have your pound of flesh, then by God, say so plainly like an honest Shylock. For then I'll go on the pad, cut the purse and throat of some innocent traveller and the money will be yours by morning, though I swing high for it.'

'No, Gerry,' he replied softly, 'it need not come to that. But I'll remit the whole debt and present you with my painted snuff-box, which you have so long coveted, into the bargain, if you will but give me the help, not of your side-arm but of your pen.'

I thought for the moment that he had gone out of his wits. I inquired, 'Am I to write out the whole of Pope's *Essay on Man* in a flowing hand, like a schoolboy punished for orchard-robbing?'

'No,' he said, 'two words would serve, almost.'

'Don't tantalize me further,' I cried. 'What joke are you driving?'

Thereupon he explained: 'I am bent on contracting marriage with a girl of this town. Not only is our scheme unknown to her father, who would object to it, but there is a general order posted this morning which prevents such marriages from being solemnized without the written permission of an officer. You know that Lieutenant Sweetenham has a strong antipathy to me, at any rate, and that he would reject my request, did I dare make it, with contempt. You write a good hand and are used by the Lieutenant as his amanuensis. You are therefore familiar both with his composition and his signature. Now, my proposal to you is that you shall counterfeit the Lieutenant's signature to the licence and accompany me with it to the minister's house, to arrange for the solemnization of my marriage. If you will do all this, you are quit of your debt; and the snuff-box, too, is yours.'

I stared dumbly at him and many strange emotions stirred within my breast. How thankful I now am that I did not do what came uppermost to my mind, which was to take him by the throat and choke him in rage, scorn, and envy. For, like a flash, the explanation of the evening's events came upon me. The woman with whom he contemplated marriage could be none other than Kate Weldone. Her careful amity with me had been a mere pretence to conceal her infatuation for my comrade Gentleman Harlowe—against whom her father had conceived a strong prejudice on our first arrival at the town and whom he had told bluntly, he was an unwelcome visitor at the cottage. The petition that Kate had been on the point of disclosing to me and that I had undertaken in advance to grant, for love of her, was the very same that Harlowe had now converted into an obligation, by a downright cheat. For I was suddenly convinced that the cards had been rigged by him with this very object. I was sensible enough to reflect, however, that this fraud must have been unknown to Miss Kate, for otherwise she would not have troubled to plead with me in so melting a way; and that I could therefore not justly be incensed with her.

I therefore contented myself by saying shortly to my companion: 'I must think this over a spell.' I turned on my heel and left him standing there.

It was a starry but moonless night and I had the luck to recognize old Captain Weldone as he passed me on the road, he not recognizing me. I could now count upon gaining admittance at the cottage and speaking to Kate, without recourse to any stratagem. She had already retired to rest, as I knew by the candle-light at her window; but I threw up a pebble and she presently put her head out and called, 'Is that you, my sweet Dick?'

Dick was Harlowe's name, so I knew that I had read the story aright. But nevertheless I carried on with my game.

'No,' said I, 'it is no sweet Dick, nor no common Tom or Harry, but it's myself, Private Roger Lamb. I have come to hear the service that I am to do for you, since it weighs so heavy on your mind.'

She descended after a while, with her hair loose upon her shoulders, and, upon my urging her, disclosed to me the very same plan of forgery that I had just heard from Gentleman Harlowe's lips, though she was more frank than he in naming him as her intended spouse. I simulated grief, surprise, and a great unwillingness, but she urged that I had given my word. I agreed at last, making one condition only, which she swore on her honour to keep: that she was not on any account to reveal to Harlowe her request of me, and that the very next words she spoke to him would be begging him to propose the plan to me himself as an act of friendship. 'If he does so, I will agree readily,' I assured her, 'and thus persuade him, against truth but in the interests of your own honour, that the object of my visits to this house has always been rather your father than yourself.'

She considered this more than handsome on my part, and with expressions of unmistakable affection, which I need not rehearse, promised never to forget the heavy debt that she was incurring. Presently I said good night and we parted.

On my way home to our quarters, I smiled sourly to myself at the comedy which would ensue: Harlowe would agree, at Miss Kate's instance, to urge me for friendship's sake to forge the document; and yet be greatly troubled in his mind lest I reveal to her, at my next visit to the cottage, in what manner that crime had already been forced upon me.

My spirits were totally restored by an incident upon the road. I passed by a poor thatched cabin from which issued the agreeable sound of a fiddle very masterly played; and the melody so plucked at me that I turned aside, pushed upon the door and entered. It was a scene of the most distressful poverty. That the inhabitants were Papists was shown by the wooden crucifix hanging on the rough earthen wall. I found them to consist of a sick man groaning on a straw pallet; an ailing young woman crouched before a low fire, over which potatoes were boiling unskinned in an old iron pot on legs; three half-naked dirty children tumbling in a corner; four starved fowls roosting on a beam; and an old grandfather with ragged white hair seated on a stool at the opposite side of the fire from the woman. It was he was playing upon the fiddle, and his face was away from me as I entered.

He put down his instrument and spoke something to me in the Gaelic tongue without turning round. The woman translated for him. 'He says you are welcome, your Honour, and to be seated on this stool. He has not the English and he is blind; but he has the Sight. He told us this morning that a tall young soldier visits us this evening.'

I asked: 'What was that tune he was playing? It seemed to invite me to enter.'

She replied that the Gaelic words concerned a woman for whose sake a wise man would not trouble himself. She repeated them to me, and they may be Englished thus:

> *O woman shapely as the swan*
> *Should I turn wan*
> *   For love of thee?*
> *O turn those blue and rolling eyes*
> *On men unwise—*
> *   They wound not me.*

The old man spoke again. The woman informed me: 'My man's father says that he played the tune for your comfort.'

'Thank him kindly,' I said, 'and pray give him this shilling if he will consent to take a fee. But how in the world could he have known my need of it?'

'I tell you, he has the Sight,' she returned.

The old man pocketed the shilling with satisfaction and, seizing up his fiddle again, resumed his playing to such an effect that my breast swelled with the strangest alternations of enraged despair and amused equanimity; and, having thus amused himself with me for awhile, let the music drop into a lullaby so compelling that I felt myself falling off into a deep sleep where I sat on the stool.

I awoke with a startle, to find that the music had stopped and that the old man was laughing at me.

'He has all the ancient gifts of music,' said the woman.

'It was a shilling well spent,' I rejoined, rubbing my eyes, and thereupon went over to shake my host by the hand. He retained my fingers in a surprisingly powerful grasp, and I had the conviction that he was able to read my inmost thoughts while so engaged.

He spoke at last and (as the woman gave me to understand) ran through many exact particulars of my past life, including the story of my early escape from drowning and my attempted desertion, promised me happy issue to my present troubles, but a long and hazardous life to follow. He also assured me of a future event so fantastical that I laughed outright to hear of it: that when next I attempted desertion I should succeed in the attempt and that I should be thanked for my pains by a general with a shining star on his breast.

I returned to the tap-room in a sort of dream, but the familiar close smell of the room restored me to my usual senses. I recollected the plan of conduct that I had drawn up for myself before the distraction of that fiddling lured me from the road.

As I pushed open the door, all eyes turned on me.

I said to Mad Johnny Maguire: 'Maguire, my good friend, I'll not require your loan, nor yours neither, Terry Reeves, though I thank you from the bottom of my heart.'

Terry Reeves asked: 'Have you compounded then with the Gentleman?'

My staunch resolve was that in no possible respect would I be beholden to my successful rival. I replied shortly: 'I am permitted to keg myself to him after all.'

Harlowe started, but said nothing, for I continued: 'He has asked me also, in return for this permission, to perform a certain small service for him, and I have consented to that.'

Harlowe raised his eyebrows in an inquiring manner; I nodded good-humouredly in his direction.

He fumbled in his pouch and drew out the snuff-box, which was a pretty enough piece, with a painting on it of the Limerick coach with its four matched horses at full gallop.

'I accept the token, Gentleman Harlowe,' I said softly. But, after helping myself to a pinch of snuff, I threw it to the back of the grate where the fire was crackling hotly under a kettle hung from a chain.

This seemed so droll and unaccountable an action that nobody had the wit to snatch the box from the fire for his own use: the company watched it slowly scorch and char, scrutinizing our countenances between-whiles as if to read the riddle. Both Harlowe and I sat impassive, and they remained nonplussed.

Harlowe was the first to speak: 'Well, it was yours, Gerry Lamb. You have a right to burn or squander whatever is yours, I suppose.'

'I have kegged myself to you, Gentleman Harlowe,' I said, 'and I shall have arranged the other matter to your satisfaction before the coming pay-night.'

I was as good as my word, and Fortune assisted me smilingly. The next day was the 28th of July, which was kept in The Ninth as an anniversary of the Relief of Londonderry in the year 1689; at this exploit The Ninth had assisted, when the *Mountjoy*, with some of our musketeers aboard her, broke the boom across the river, and King James consequently raised the siege. Lieutenant Sweetenham called me in, an hour or two before his celebratory dinner, to copy for him in a fair hand some official papers to which he would then attach his signature. I considered whether to smuggle the marriage licence in among these papers, bringing them to him just before he sat down to

dine with an ensign and another lieutenant, invited by him
from neighbouring commands. But I rejected this project
as too daring, though he was a man who, for negligence,
seldom read through even the most important paper before he signed it.

Throughout the next day he was incapacitated from
duty by a surfeit of roasted goose and of Madeira wine,
four cases of which had been ordered up for this celebration; and on that afternoon, at four o'clock, Private
Richard Harlowe was clandestinely married to Kate Weldone by a curate of Saintfield whom I had imposed upon.
In Northern Ireland in those days it was not difficult, I
confess, to find a minister to solemnize a marriage in a
hurry and without proper ceremony: if he were visited in
his front parlour at any time after noon, when it was ten
chances in twelve that he would be perfectly inebriated.

I afterwards brazened it out with the Lieutenant. Upon
his recovery, I reported to him, in a casual manner, that
the marriage had passed without incident and that Private
Harlowe had drunk his officer's health with grateful devotion.

'What marriage in the Devil's name is that?' the Lieutenant asked petulantly. 'I sanctioned none, so far as I am
aware.'

'Oh, doesn't your Honour remember signing the permission after dinner last night, which I brought to you at your
own urgent request?'

'I remember nothing at all of last night's events,' he complained. 'If you now told me that I stripped myself naked
and waved my small-clothes in the air like a flag, shouting
"Death to the Papist pigs," I would believe you, Private
Lamb; not being able to swear to the contrary and knowing you for an honest man.'

'It is exactly what your Honour did,' I said, very truly,
'for we all witnessed it.'

Lieutenant Sweetenham did not push his inquiry into
the marriage-matter further, but buried his head remorse-
fully in his feather pillow; and that was the first and last
that I heard of it from him. But I faithfully kept my keg-
ging-contract with Harlowe, intending that every penny I
paid him on a Saturday night would scorch his palm.

Old Captain Weldone took his daughter's marriage ill, and would not permit his son-in-law to lodge in the cottage during all the time that we were stationed there. However, he did not suspect my hand in it and I continued with my visits to the cottage, in order both to gratify the old man, who enjoyed my society, and to displease Harlowe. To Mrs. Harlowe I was very civil and said nothing to wound her feelings. She would entrust messages to me for her husband, which it tickled my crooked humour to deliver to him with every outward show of good comradeship.

It was in this year that the octagonal tower of Craigenamanagh Cathedral fell down; and when we heard the news, we shook our heads. That the Devil was loose again in Ireland was ill news. It was said that he had not been sighted for certain in our country since his apparition to Saint Moling, near a thousand years before.

✺ ✺ ✺ ✺ ✺ ✺ ✺ ✺ ✺ ✺ ✺ ✺

CHAPTER

5

IN THE beginning of the year 1775 The Ninth was ordered to Dublin and Major-General Viscount Ligonier, the Colonel of the Regiment, arrived from England to inspect and take the command of it. His Lordship, who had fought at the battle of Minden, was generous, affable, and greatly beloved by the men. A regiment commanded by a peer can in general congratulate itself on this score, because as his coronet has elevated him above the society of his officers he can afford to unbend towards the rank and file to a degree that commoners would not dare—for fear of abating something of their dignity. Moreover, a peer can often win for his regiment privileges and advantages from the civil government that would be refused to a person of less consequence. It was said that, but for His Lordship's interest at the Castle, another regiment would have been given the Dublin duty, which was the most popular in Ireland.

Lord Ligonier's eye soon fastened upon Private Harlowe and myself as persons of superior education, fit for promotion as corporals; and the Sergeant-Major of the Regiment, under whose immediate command the non-commissioned officers came, and who was a complete sergeant, a good scholar, and a sensible, agreeable man, spoke up for us to His Lordship. There was increasing talk of our being sent across the Atlantic, and His Lordship held that a scattered sort of fighting would be likely to prevail in the woody and intricate districts in which America abounds. It was therefore to the common advantage that non-commissioned officers should be able to send intelligible messages in writing to their company officers. Harlowe and I were among the non-commissioned officers chosen to be instructed in the novel light infantry manœuvres, lately introduced into the Army by General Sir William Howe and strongly approved by His Majesty the King. These manœuvres were intended for use in broken country, the set hitherto employed having been designed rather for the open battlefields of Germany and the Low Countries. They were six in number and well designed to their purpose, and we of The Ninth were sent to the Thirty-third Regiment, then also quartered in Dublin, to learn them.

I am bound to record here that I felt a certain shamefacedness, on visiting the barracks of The Thirty-third, who were commanded by the young Earl of Cornwallis, to compare their high state of appointment and the steadiness of their discipline with the slovenly and relaxed bearing of most of our own companies. One can always correctly judge a regiment's capacities by the behaviour of its sentries. I have already described how Maguire performed his sentry duty at Waterford, and might well have remarked then that his behaviour was not exceptional. I have seen men go on duty in The Ninth dead drunk and scarcely able to stand. But with The Thirty-third the sentry was always alert and alive in attention; when on duty he was all eye, all ear. Even in the sentry-box, which he never entered unless in a downpour of rain, he was forbidden to keep the palm of his hand carelessly on the muzzle of his loaded firelock; for this was considered as dangerous an attitude as it was awkward. During the two hours that he remained on his post the sentry continued in constant motion, and could not walk less than seven miles in that time. The Thirty-third thus set a standard of soldier-like duty which made me secretly dissatisfied with The Ninth, and which I have never seen equalled since but *by a single other regiment* which was brigaded with The Thirty-third under the same Lord Cornwallis, in the later campaigns of the American War. I resolved at least to bring the men who were under my immediate command into a state of discipline for which I should have no cause to blush.

On my return to the Regiment I was appointed to take charge of a squad of light infantry, thirty-three in number, for passing on to them the knowledge that I had acquired. I soon learned the accent of authority without which it is impossible to make men jump to their tasks, and Major Bolton was pleased to congratulate me upon the neat agility and grace with which my pupils performed the new manœuvres. My employment did not preclude me from other duties such as guard-duties, and on more than one occasion I was appointed for the important Newgate Guard.

It was our ill luck, however, to be under the nominal charge of a captain, an Irish nobleman, who was noted more for punctilio and the flippancy of his tongue than for the acquisitions becoming his rank. He had not taken the pains to acquaint himself with the new exercises and when he appeared upon parade, usually far gone in liquor, to take over the direction of the squad from me, his orders were always confused and contradictory. I was then placed on the horns of a dilemma—whether to allow the men to be misled and mismanaged, or whether to interpret the Captain's wishes by supplying the correct words of command. In the first case I should be wanting in duty to the Regiment and the King, in the second I should be wanting in respect to my immediately superior officer, and in face of the men too. I chose the second evil and, when twice I had capped an impossible order with the correct one, he turned on me in a rage, threatening me with his cane if

I would not pay him the proper respect. He added, with shocking imprecations, coupling the name of the Deity with expressions drawn from the common bawdy-house, that if I did not mind myself he would make a devil of me. I had the sense to reply with the becoming and respectful tone of a non-commissioned officer: 'Very good, your Lordship,' so that his anger abated somewhat. However, the squad, which resented this impious and unofficer-like manner of enforcing subordination, had the spirit to make a butt of the captain. Whenever thereafter he came upon the parade-ground they re-echoed in chorus and in a variety of ridiculous tones: 'I'll make a devil of you, you spawn of Satan.' The other officers, who came to hear of this irregularity and had already rated this young noble-man as more apt for caning his men than for storming half-moons, were not ill-pleased; and before long he found his situation so awkward that he sold his captaincy and left us.

My fellow-corporal, Gentleman Harlowe, always now avoided conversation with me. But in talk with others he used to sneer at me for the increased martiality of my bearing, and himself followed the usual fashion of The Ninth: which was to do well enough to scrape through his duties without disgracing himself or his company, but not well enough to excite admiration among civilian onlookers. 'We are a rough and ready regiment,' the saying was, 'and an old regiment, and we can fight as well as the best.' Upon his appointment to the rank of corporal, Harlowe had this great satisfaction, that his wife was permitted by her father to leave the cottage at Saintfield and enter upon effective rather than merely titular matrimony with him at Dublin.

The jail of Newgate was a small, mean building, and in no degree suited to the respectability of a great city. It stood on the site of ground now known as the Corn Market, a short distance from High Street and contiguous to Thomas Street. It happened once in the range of my duty to have command of a guard there for twenty-four hours beginning on a Friday evening, at the time when a handsome young Papist, a dock labourer, was due for public execution. This was some time towards the end of February 1775. The sympathy of the city was much excited by his fate, for he had 'suffered the misfortune,' as it was vulgarly expressed, to strangle his sweetheart. He had done this as a punishment to her for consorting with one of our drummers.

The guard-house was immediately outside the jail, with a sentry posted before it; and another sentry was posted inside in the entrance-hall. This second man was intended to assist a Mr. Meaghan, who had an apartment there with his wife, and a tap-room next door, being employed in the triple capacity of turnkey, hangman, and ale-house keeper. The criminals were lodged upstairs and only allowed to descend if they could afford to pay for refreshment in Mr. Meaghan's tap-room: and then no more than three at a time. It was a custom of prisoners, then as well as now, to beg from passers-by, by making loud appeals to their pity through the grated upper windows, from which they would let down a bag on a cord to receive alms.

I was passed word by my father, who had heard the noise from a neighbour, that a rescue was planned of the young culprit in my charge. I therefore resolved to omit no precautions against this taking place. As soon as I had relieved the sergeant of the old guard, I desired the turn-key to assist me in searching the prisoners' rooms for weapons or other instruments of escape. This was done, and two small stabbing knives found and confiscated. Next, I made it my personal care that no contraband should be insinuated into the alms-bag, which was most generously filled that night. On my first examining the bag I discovered a small file, which I pocketed; and warned the crowd then that if they had any further donations to make they must use Mr. Meaghan or myself as intermediaries. This announcement excited groans and howls from the dense crowd of Papists who thronged Towns Arch, the entry to Thomas Street; but I assured them with a resolute smile that if they did not remain orderly, I would disperse them with a ball or bayonet. And if this did not content them, I said, their friend the murderer would be refused by me even the money already collected, and thus disabled from 'wetting his throttle, the poor lamb,' as the weeping women termed it. Since I meant precisely what I said, they credited me and subdued themselves.

I then permitted his relatives (whom Mr. and Mrs. Meaghan first searched, according to their sex) to attend his wake in the tap-room. They were eight in number, of whom two were his sisters; but my sentry with a loaded firelock standing at the door was sufficient to overawe them.

The prisoner was now allowed to descend and the stair-door was locked again after him. In short, rescue was impossible with such careful dispositions taken, and the family therefore settled down to merry-making. They had brought in a handsome brass-bound coffin which they placed upon the floor, and set six lighted candles upon it. This ominous furniture served as a board on which to spread a plentiful display of funeral bake-meats. There was punch, wine and spirits, besides beef-steaks, potatoes, cakes, green bacon, and a kettle of Hyson tea; and the murderer, whom they hugged and kissed perpetually, calling him their darling, their jewel, their poor, charming, handsome, disgraced Jimmy, was the heartiest man in the whole hearty assembly. After a time he charitably recollected that his comrades languished upstairs, and sent up two pints of spirits to them, with Mr. Meaghan's permission, and a hamper of potato cakes and butter. This soon set the whole upper story ringing with triumphant song, and the effect upon the crows outside was a happy one. For it assuaged their anger against our men, whom, as comrades of the drummer, they had treated as the accomplices of poor Jimmy's ruin.

A priest, or one who professed to be such, presently came in to confess the murderer. He declared himself insulted when the sentry referred him to Mr. Meaghan to be searched before he was permitted to enter; nevertheless, a horse-pistol was taken from under his frock. He exclaimed in confusion that he had quite forgotten that he carried such a thing, and, rather than aggravate matters, Mr. Meaghan permitted him to enter 'now that his teeth were drawn.' I had seen this priest's sallow face before, but somehow I could not fit it with a priest's cap; and his name, which was given as Father Martin, awoke no memories.

His absolution of the murderer, after confession, was

the signal for long faces, tears, and a sad keening of the sort which Shakespeare likens in one of his tragedies to a pack of Irish wolves howling to the moon. Soon every person in the room, barring the priest, was swaying about pitifully, clutching at his own windpipe in horrid anticipation of the choking in store for their relative when he reached his life's goal at Gallow's Green. Father Martin took his leave about midnight, and I closed this penultimate scene by ordering the removal of all the guests but two. For on the eloquent plea of the murderer's uncle, who quoted his own brother's case as a precedent, I suffered Jimmy to remain in the tap-room until dawn with his two nearest of kin, and there to play cards upon the coffin lid. There is a tale that the uncle cracked a joke out of season by trying to cheat him, and that Jimmy nearly became a double murderer; it may be true, but the same has been told of the last hours of many other culprits. At least, he was kept out of mischief by my indulgence, and although the crowd remained outside, chattering, cheering, and wailing all night, no rescue was attempted by them.

When I had returned to the guard-house from the tap-room, after giving permission to Jimmy's relatives to remain with him, as above described, I found Terry Reeves in a state of the very greatest terror. On my asking what ailed him in Heaven's name, he withheld his reply for a little while; but then, drawing me aside, he inquired, 'Are you acquainted with that person?'

'What person?' I asked.

'The pretended priest,' he replied, shivering again.

'No,' said I, 'I do not know him from Adam.'

'He is a great deal older than Adam,' Terry assured me, 'and only one day younger than Almighty God Himself. That man is the Devil, the Father of Lies. Wouldn't I know that wet, black forelock of his anywhere in the whole world? I first met him when he was in the disguise of a student of physic at the Romish Seminary where I was employed in the coach-house. Ill luck follows him about, and a shivering cold wind.'

'I smelt no sulphur, dear Moon-Curser,' I said, joking to keep up his spirits, though my own spirits began to sink because I had noticed the same cold wind. 'A little diaboli-

cal sulphur would be welcome to fumigate this fetid place.'
But now I felt my own skin creeping on my neck, for I
had remembered where that face had appeared to me before—at the cockpit on the evening of my enlistment. Indeed he was the very man, the one with the little grey
cock, whose challenge had ruined me. I took Terry with
me into the tap-room where we both fortified ourselves
with drink. Terry whispered to me: 'He must have come
to claim poor Jimmy's soul.'

On Sunday morning it was my unpleasant duty to see
the prisoner pinioned and mounted in the criminal cart
or 'humbler' for a procession through the city; and almost
I may say that no task I had subsequently to perform in the
whole course of my service—no, not in any of the six
pitched battles, four sieges, and other hazardous events
in which I took part—was ever so anxious as this. I knew
that I could not count upon the assistance of the city
watchmen who were in general infirm and altogether unfit for that dangerous duty which must occasionally de-
volve on the peace officers and body of the police. To
reach Gallow's Green we must defy the threatening rabble
who had now rushed up in extraordinary numbers from
all the Liberties and suburbs, to fill the whole course of
the High Street through which we must pass. Yet I think
that what Terry had told me comprised the greater part of
my fear.

I was lucky enough to have won the respect of the
crowd at Towns Arch by my frank address to them on
the previous night and by the praise given me by the
mourners at the wake for my politeness and easy bearing.
I disposed my little force with circumspection and spirit,
first publicly examining my men's arms and putting them
through the loading drill in the manner detailed in a
previous chapter. I also was attentive to halt the cart
for a while in Thomas Street, where the High Sheriffs of
the city were awaiting us, while the murderer made an
address of thanks to his sympathizers and benefactors.
Lest he should call for rescue or revenge in his inebriated
state, I sang out to him: 'Courage now, Jimmy, my fine
cock! Soon it will be all over, and you'll find yourself in
Glory and in the company of the Saints.'

This sentiment pleased the crowd as well as it did Jimmy himself; he was good enough to wish me and the guard all good luck, and to confess that he bore us no ill will. But the passage of High Street was most frightful and at many points there was such a jostling and thrusting and such screams of desperate rage from the populace that I thought I should at any moment be obliged to order a volley. Moreover, I discerned among one knot of men armed with cudgels, inciting them to attack, the wild face of Father Martin: which turned me sick, though in effect the attack was not made. We carried our firelocks at the port ready for instant action; Mr. Meaghan, at whom the curses of Dublin were chiefly directed, marching between me and Terry Reeves.

All ended well. We arrived in safety at Gallow's Green, where the victim uttered his last words in so low a tone that nobody could catch them, and the halter being then fastened around his neck, the cart jerked off with his feet and he was dead within ten minutes.

They made a ballad of it, which was hawked about the streets the next day, to the effect that:

> *Poor, pretty, little Jimmy*
> *Was hanged, not for stealing,*
> *But for choking of his honey,*
> *O that was his failing!*
>
> *He drove out from Newgate,*
> *He passed through the city,*
> *His hands were tied behind him*
> *And the ladies wept 'Pity.'*
>
> *etc.*

It was set to an air combining the hilarious and the plaintive in equal measure; while the chorus was nonsensical and comically designed to be sung in a single breath:

> *Is there e'er a pretty lass, now,*
> *From North Wall or South Wall,*
> *Could entice poor pretty little Jimmy from*
> *the sweet green gallow's tree, killa-ma-lee, killa-*
> *ma-loo, whisky, piskey doodle-doo——*
> *Ranty doodle*
> *di do, ring ding fol, lol, lol!*

I give these particulars in some detail, not only for the purpose of exciting surprise at the insecurity of the city in those times, and of waking, by contrast, satisfaction with the present police establishment: but because they are a help to an understanding of the notorious Cunningham affair, in which Gentleman Harlowe was involved when he acted as sergeant of the same guard a few weeks later. Cunningham, a famous highwayman, was confined in Newgate Jail awaiting trial on a capital charge, and it happened that it was I who handed over the guard to Corporal Harlowe. It was my policy never to fail in civility to my former rival, and in this instance I should have thought myself wanting in soldierly duty had I not informed him of all matters affecting the conduct of the guard, which was new to him. I warned him that Cunningham was a very bold fellow and was suspected at this moment of conspiring with his fellow prisoners to break out of jail; and described to him the precautions I had taken on the previous night to forestall any such attempt. He did not answer me offensively, since private soldiers were present and to do so would have occasioned a breach of discipline: however, he was very off-hand in his acknowledgments of my report and plainly intended to pay no attention whatever to it.

That evening Cunningham and a companion obtained a file by means of the alms-bag dangled from the window and contrived to saw the iron bolts of their fetters nearly through. They called down the stairs through the crack under the door for leave to descend, saying that they desired to take punch in the tap-room before the door was finally closed for the night. The inner sentry passed word of this request to the outer sentry; which Corporal Harlowe granted without demur. Mr. Meaghan had the fever in the room adjoining the tap-room, but Mrs. Meaghan unlocked the door, and permitted the two men to descend, locking it again after them. When she had gone into the tap-room to draw the spirits ordered, Cunningham's companion delayed at the foot of the stairs, holding the sentry in talk. Cunningham let fall a coin which rolled behind the sentry, and stooped as if to search for it in the dim light. Instead, he broke off his fetter-bolts and knocked down the soldier, who was armed only with a bayonet, by swinging at him from behind with the fetters.

Mrs. Meaghan, on hearing the noise, rushed out of the tap-room. She was seized by Cunningham and his associate, who tried to force the keys from her, but maintained a stout struggle for several minutes. She bit Cunningham's hand very savagely when he tried to stop her screams with it. In the end, however, they seized the key of the stair-door from her, in order to enlarge a third man, who was undergoing solitary confinement in the punishment cell. When he appeared, the three of them demanded from her the key of the outer door. She fastened it in her clothes, and refused to yield, though already well beaten and bruised. Mrs. Meaghan made, indeed, the most astonishing resistance: the joints of two of her fingers were broken before they wrested the key from her.

By this time, the guard had been alarmed by the cries of the woman and were drawn up in front of the outer door. But notwithstanding the obstacle of an iron chain fastened diagonally across, the criminals unlocked the door, and, what was more amazing, contrived to escape in the face of the guard by darting out through Towns Arch, and without receiving the slightest wound. Cunningham, thus at liberty, was emboldened to resume his career of robbery. He eventually put himself in the way of being again apprehended and imprisoned, and made in the end a capital atonement for his many crimes. But that occurred some months later, and meanwhile the escaping of three prisoners proved disgraceful to Corporal Harlowe who, together with the guard, was confined for it, and became a private soldier again.

I debated with myself whether it would now be proper to offer Mrs. Harlowe assistance, considering on what terms of less than friendship her husband and I had lived since her marriage. I decided in the end that I owed her no malice, seeing that she had not encouraged my suit more warmly than was needed to screen her real intentions from her father. Besides, since my fraud practised upon the minister and Lieutenant Sweetenham was also a fraud practised upon my friend and host, Captain Weldone, I felt it my duty to make provision for his daughter.

I went to her lodgings and told her, with as much delicacy as I could muster, that I would be glad to afford her whatever assistance lay in my power until such time as her husband was released from confinement and could again provide for her.

It has always been a matter of perplexity to me, how far my attitude towards Kate Harlowe sprang from noble causes, and how far there was an admixture of irony because of my scorn for her husband. It would, I think, be just to say that the two motives, namely, that of pleasing and comforting her to the best of my ability, and that of showing her husband by contrastive generosity how shabbily I thought of him, were reconciled and intertwined. In any event, I never (let me swear) planned to coax away her affections from the man she had married, however obnoxious he might be to me, and from a comrade-in-arms too, however lacking in soldierly honour. Nevertheless, the effect of my visit was that her gratitude to me became confused in her heart with yet warmer feelings; and it was as much as I could do to play the virtuous Joseph and, with a cool word or two, disengage myself from her impetuous embrace.

The old passion now stirred again in me, and Kate was soon aware of it. Had not Gentleman Harlowe been released from confinement two days later I do not know to what follies my inclinations might have led me. But the very fact of his now being put under my immediate command proved a sufficient check to my feelings; he was in my power, as any soldier is in the power of a corporal who cares to vent his spite, and I knew that the greatest punishment which I could inflict was to heap coals of fire upon his head, in requital of his former insults and injuries. This I did by treating him no worse than his fellow soldiers, and even a little better, as one who had received training as a non-commissioned officer.

All was not well with me, by any means. Kate Harlowe was seldom out of my thoughts, and whenever I met her in the streets, walking either alone or in her husband's company, the sight of her lovely face and figure was like a stab to me. Because of this preoccupation, I soon slipped back again into my former habits of drinking, gambling, and idleness. Indeed, I so far forfeited the confidence of my officers that I was warned by Major Bolton himself on one occasion that unless I soon sloughed off my negligence I would suffer the same degradation as Richard Harlowe.

In January 1776, when the American War had already been in progress for some months (at a cost so far to us of three million pounds sterling and two or three thousand casualties from wounds or sickness, whereas only one hundred and fifty of the enemy had fallen) I was seized with severe sickness at the Dublin Barracks. I was sent into the general military hospital in James Street (at present used as a barracks) and disabled to march with the Regiment on its receiving the route to the Cove of Cork, where it was to embark for North America. I was the only soldier of The Ninth obliged to stay behind for sickness, and the loneliness of my position, as well as regret for the intemperance which had caused my sickness, made me anxious for a rapid recovery. Early in March I thought myself enough recovered to leave the hospital. I immediately waited on Sir William Montgomery, our Army agent, in Mary Street. Here I was informed that The Ninth was supposed to be already on its voyage, and recommended to join the additional company belonging to us, employed in England on the recruiting service.

My parents and sisters were urgent with me to go with the recruiting parties, in order to detain me from the dangers of foreign service. I had indeed a great curiosity, on the one hand, to visit England, a single country of which seemed of more interest to me than the whole of North America; but on the other hand I considered that remaining aloof from the scene of warfare was not consistent with the manhood of a soldier. I resolved to repair to the Cove of Cork and sail, if possible, with the Regiment; or, if not, then in some later ship bound for the same destination, which was Quebec in Canada. Mrs. Harlowe was among the wives who had elected to follow The Ninth to America, and it was perhaps the thought of standing well in her esteem that swung the balance of my judgment in making my choice.

So to Cork I went and found the Regiment still there, in spite of a delay I had undergone by the desertion of a recruit from Downpatrick, who had been entrusted to my charge and to whom I had advanced a fortnight's pay, knowing that I should be refunded whatever I thus gave him. Incensed and anxious that he should have no cause to plume himself upon 'running the old soldier' so much to my expense, I put up placards in the most public parts of the city, advertising the deserter in minute detail. I had the satisfaction to learn of his arrest, three days later, on the Drogheda Road. This man, by name Casey, was a Papist. Owing to the difficulty of finding recruits to bring our regiments up to full establishment, the rule against the enlistment of Papists had recently been waived. But few enough came forward: for that year and the next were among the most prosperous years for farming that Ireland has ever experienced, and the peasants had an inveterate fear of fire-arms, besides.

My valuable friend, Major Bolton, expressed himself pleased at my joining the Regiment, of which he then again had the command (for Lord Ligonier held too exalted a rank to lead us in person), and characterized me as a volunteer, since I might well have gone to England to beat up recruits. He therefore at once promoted me to the acting rank of sergeant in his own company, and used me occasionally in the capacity of confidential clerk.

On the 26th of April in the same year we embarked in a well-appointed expedition consisting of ourselves, the Twentieth, Twenty-fourth, Thirty-fourth, Fifty-third, and Sixty-second Regiments: with which bare statement I must close this account of my peace-time service in Ireland. Next, I will keep my promise and give some account of the origins of the American War then already in progress; and relate what had so far occurred in it. I will also make it plain why we were being embarked for Canada, which was not in revolt, rather than for the embattled American colonies.

It would not be amiss to mention here that the system of transports is a very bad one; the captains think only of their owners and of themselves, and take whatever liberties they dare with the troops and cargo entrusted to their bottoms. If the Government had sent reinforcements in royal vessels, which it did not, even where the need was most urgent, they would have arrived both more speedily and in better condition, and the course of the war would have changed materially. At least a thousand Highland volunteers sent over later in the war in slow-sailing, unarmed, unescorted transports never reached their destination, being ingloriously captured on the high seas by American privateers. Why did this system continue, to the great hurt of the nation? I fear that the reason preponderating was that certain influential men in the Government drew a commission of three per centum on the hire of these ships, and loved their wives and families too well to relinquish this perquisite.

✿ ✿ ✿ ✿ ✿ ✿ ✿ ✿ ✿ ✿ ✿

CHAPTER

6

I WILL begin my short historical survey of the origins of the American War with a single short sentiment that was freely and continually expressed by all classes and conditions of our people both civil and military, and on either side of the Atlantic Ocean, throughout the conflict: that it was 'a damned business, a very damned ugly business.' Yet I must in honesty add that, though the losses in lives and treasure that it entailed were in every way to be heartily regretted, yet the separation between the Crown and the Colonies must in the nature of things have come about at some time or other, and perhaps it was as well that it came when it did.

America, in her relation to Great Britain, was frequently presented at this time as a froward child who defied an indulgent parent. This figure was, however, in no sense apt: for America as a single consentient nation did not yet exist, and the diverse American provinces had each in turn finished with tutelage and put on the manly gowns.

Now, there is nothing so absurd and so uncomfortable as when grown sons with families of their own are obliged from filial duty to stay under a father's roof, to keep fixed hours, conform to quaint usages, and draw pocket-money instead of wages for whatever labour they perform on his estate. It galls their pride and retards their ambition. The old patriarchs may tell them: 'My sons, surely you are tolerably well off here? You can want for nothing in food, drink, clothing, or other comforts. I allow you each a wing of my mansion to yourself. I pay the tithes and the taxes on your behalf. There is sport enough in my coverts, and the labour that I require of you is light. The authority of my name is sufficient to protect you against all insult and danger. Where else in the world would you and your families find yourselves so well off as here, in this spacious and well-provided mansion? Are you so ungrateful then? Or what more can you want of me that I do not do? What restraint have I ever set upon you? I even—an unheard-of thing—have excused your attendance at family prayers. No, no! Be careful that you do not try my patience, my boys. And see, now it is past ten o'clock. Drink up your quart pots, kiss your mother, and off to bed you go with your wives, and pray let us have no more arguments.'

The sons have no answer to make, unless a low muttering that 'every grown man has the right to live where and how he pleases, in independence.' If they are men of spirit as their father is, sure as fate it will come to a quarrel in the end. This quarrel will blow out of some trifling domestic occurrence and the sons will perhaps have a poor enough case to present to the world. But they will push it to extremes, well knowing that the father must grow exasperated and stand on his authority when he finds that they are deaf to reason. For they fear that, unless they force the issue, they will become confirmed in their dull habit of dependence upon him, and forfeit all dignity of manhood. Their trouble is that a profound admiration for their father makes rebellion alike more difficult and more painful.

It is easy to be wise after the event. For my part I think that where quarrels are due they had best come soon. 'Bear and forbear' is an impossible counsel of domestic perfection. For a certain sort of son, complete independence is the only cure of his moods. Left to himself he will come, in time, to be a polished, respectable citizen of the world, and on civil terms with his father again.

So we come to the quarrel between the Crown and the American colonies, it may be objected that I cannot but be partial in judging the rights and wrongs of this case, seeing that seven of the middle years of my life were spent in America as a loyal soldier of King George after he had quarrelled with his revolted subjects. But I had cause to feel both respect and affection for the better people of America during those seven years, and would not therefore be willingly guilty of making any misrepresentation or suppression of fact that would aggravate an already bitter case. I may observe that I have in my time read a great number of American newspapers and pamphlets—printed in the war years on blue, yellow, brown, and black paper for lack of white—and listened to a large number of political conversations during the year and a half of captivity that I spent among them, and consulted numerous books since published in the United States. Especially I shall beware of sneers and airs of affected superiority as a Briton, in telling my tale. But where things were ill done on the American side I shall be no more ready to conceal them, from false delicacy, than if they had been done on ours.

To begin, then: the people of the colonies planted in North America enjoyed almost every privilege and liberty enjoyed by His Majesty's subjects at home, and were indeed by the various Royal Charters permitted to govern themselves by whatever laws, however odd, that it might please their provincial assemblies to frame—and many of them were mighty odd to our British way of thinking—so long as they did not conclude treaties with a foreign power. The allegiance that the colonists, or all but those of Massachusetts, gave the Crown for two centuries was spontaneous and unquestioning; and the whole American people, you may say roundly, thought it no more than justice that in return for the armed protection afforded their country by the British Army and Fleet, and for the monopoly of tobacco-manufacture, certain trade advantages should be required from them. The English, for example, prohibited the colonists, as they prohibited the Irish, to manufacture various goods in competition with themselves, or to purchase directly from foreign nations certain articles of commerce: England was to remain the sole provider and carrier as she had been at the first.

If any American thought that this bargain was unjust, he could find satisfaction in the thought that on his side it was being persistently evaded. England's claim to engross American trade had not been enforced for a century; there was smuggling done on a vast scale along the whole of the American seaboard. Nor could it be reckoned a hardship that the competition of American manufacturers with the English should be restricted. There were a few small manufactories in the villages of New England that kept hands busy in the long winter months and filled the pedlar's pack; but these were not provided against by the Acts of Trade. Nor were great manufactures for export in the English style ever seriously considered in America. In the first place, the success of such an enterprise must depend on there being a great number of poor people to do the work for small wages and long hours; but in those fortunate colonies there were (and still are) no industrious but unfortunate poor. Where land is cheap and rich, every man of energy who will work with his own hands can soon make an independency for himself as a farmer. Hired labourers or servants are therefore impossible to find but at very big wages; and the few there are know their value so well that the master must treat them most respectfully and indulgently, or down go their tools, on go their hats, and good-bye! As for slave labour, that could only be applied profitably to the raising and manufacture of tobacco in the Southern colonies. In the Northern ones, the severe climate made the clothing, housing, and feeding of Negroes too great a charge on their masters, so that there were few black faces seen north of Maryland. These Acts of Trade had been in force for a century now, and acquiesced in as legally binding upon the colonies.

How was it, then, that the quarrel grew? The paradox that I have drawn above in the case of the restless sons and the patriarchal father holds here: that the quarrel proceeded from an increase rather than a diminution of admiration for Britain on the part of the colonies. One may not call it jealousy, for no American was ever guilty of so servile an emotion, but it was at least keen emulation—a desire to do deeds worthy of their blood, for which they would gain the credit in their own name, not merely as sons and allies of Great Britain.

The Americans were in general exceedingly proud of their British descent, and the name of an Englishman gave them an idea of all that was great and estimable in human nature: by comparison they regarded the rest of the world as little short of barbarian. By a succession of the most brilliant victories by sea and land—for which the bells rang and the people cheered as loudly in America as anywhere—Great Britain had recently subdued the united powers of France and Spain, the former nation outnumbering her in population by nearly four times, and the latter by three, and acquired possession of a vast extent of territory in both the Indies.

Since the contest with France had arisen on their account in 1757, and the Peace of 1763, by securing Canada to the British Crown, freed the colonists from all fear of their ambitious French neighbours, they might well have been expected to add gratitude to respect. But gratitude is spontaneous and not forced, and the English were not always so considerate of the feelings of the freedom-loving American that this generous emotion was stirred.

It is certainly not true, as Dr. Benjamin Franklin pretended, that 'Every man in England seemed to consider himself as a piece of a Sovereign over America, seemed to jostle himself into the Throne with the King, and talked of *Our Subjects in the Colonies.*' But certainly British soldiers would sometimes recall with too great satisfaction that, though a great number of Americans had fought alongside the English in these campaigns, it was only as skirmishers and auxiliaries: there being no American regiments of the line who could successfully oppose the trained forces of the French and Spanish in pitched battle or siege. Some even accused the Americans of cowardice; and there were stories current in the London clubs of a deprecatory and fantastic sort, of which the following will serve as an example. That at the siege of Louisburg, twenty years previously, the Americans placed in the van had run away without firing a shot; and that Sir Peter Warren, the British commander, had then posted them in the rear, assuring them that it was 'the custom of generals to preserve their best troops to the last; especially among the ancient Romans, the only nation that ever resembled the Americans in courage and patriotism.'

Now, the French being gone from Canada, the colonists felt less dependent upon the British than ever before. They believed that they could treat the former savage allies of the French—the Ottawa, Wyandot, and Algonquin Indians—with contempt; and that, because of the degeneracy of the Spanish nation, the Spanish posts in the Havana and New Orleans threatened little danger to themselves. Indeed, they counted themselves the unchallenged masters of the whole American continent and began to cherish large ideas of their coming greatness. My Uncle James, indeed, at the time when the peace terms were published in 1763 greatly lamented that Canada had now passed to the British Crown, for he said that with the removal of the French there would now be no check upon the ambitious and restless Americans; he would have favoured, instead, taking from the French the rich sugar island of Guadaloupe.

The American condition was, in truth, remarkably flourishing. Trade had prospered almost beyond belief in the midst of the distress of a war in which they were so immediately concerned. They had paid themselves in two sorts of money: in English by supplying provisions to our troops, and in French by selling contraband to the enemy. Their population continued on the increase, despite the ravages and depredations of the French and Indians. They were a spirited, active, and inventive people, especially the residents of New England, and saw no limits to their future undertakings. As they entertained the highest opinion of their own value and importance and the immense benefit that the British derived from their connexion with America, they believed themselves entitled to every benefit and mark of respect that could be bestowed on them. And though, as I say, they were permitted to pass what laws they pleased for their own provincial government; though the Church of England exercised no authority over them; and though the existing arrangements of trade between themselves and Great Britain worked greatly to their advantage; they began to view the supremacy of the Crown with a suspicious eye.

So it was that the old game of befooling and thwarting the King's representatives—the regal Governors of the colonies—was taken up with increased zest by many of the Colonial Assemblies, especially in the North. This they were in a position to do, though the Governor had the power of absolute veto upon the laws that the Assemblies would pass, for they held the purse-strings. Unless he assented to their measures they would withhold his salary. There was always great mistrust between the Governor and the Legislature, even when a compromise seemed desirable. The Governors would not pass the laws that were wanted, without being sure of the money, nor the Assemblies give the money, without being sure that the laws would be allowed. The rather indecent bargain-and-sale proceedings that ensued were the rule rather than the exception.

These Governors were accused of being idle and haughty persons and of bringing in their trains a set of worthless rascals who paid their debts with the perquisites of office and gave the colonies nothing of value in return. That we in Great Britain cheerfully bore with the very same concomitants of monarchy did not concern the Americans. My jailers during my captivity were never weary of telling me that their fathers had left the Old World to escape from these monstrous inequalities of fortune and station there prevalent, which they would not allow to be foisted on them in the New. Certainly, America had served for several reigns as a wilderness into which to banish all the factious people who would not conform peaceably to established religious practice—Puritans, Baptists, Quakers, Presbyterians, and Papists—the liberality of the early provincial charters having been baits to these troublesome folk to emigrate. But that some at least of their parents had come over, not of their own free will, but by order of a magistrate and in chains, I was always too delicate or too cautious to observe. (True it is, that in the sixty years preceding the Revolution no fewer than forty thousand felons had been transported to America from Great Britain, besides a number of persons kidnapped by the 'spirits' of the seaport towns and conveyed there against their wills to be sold on arrival as 'redemptioners.')

A deal of loose talk was current in the Northern States about the New World's natural superiority in grandeur to the Old. Dimensions were compared, always favourably to America. Beside the wide Hudson's River, or the wider St. Lawrence, the Severn was no more than a creek and the Thames a poor ditch; the biggest forest in England would seem no more than a coppice if set beside those of the northwestern parts of America; and how many times would the whole United Kingdom fit into the space of a single one of the greater colonies? 'A dwarf claiming sovereignty over a giant,' they said in Boston—Boston being the original seminary of all American malcontents and revolutionaries. Calculations were made as to how soon the population of the American colonies, which doubled itself every thirty years by natural increase, would overtake that of England: this time was expected to be reached about the year 1810. Then how foolish a case that would be, with a great and vigorous nation forced to bow to the superior wisdom of a smaller and weaker, that lived three thousand miles away!

So we come to the hullabaloo raised in America after the Peace of 1763. Then, since the national debt of Great Britain had been much increased by the expenses of the war and a multitude of extraordinary taxes were now being levied at home, as upon window-panes and wagon-wheels, it was thought equitable that Americans should contribute a trifle to the common stock, in the interests of their own security from invasion. Duties were therefore laid on all articles imported into the colonies from the French and other islands of the West Indies, the amounts to be paid in specie to the Exchequer of Great Britain. The colonists warmly remonstrated, asserting that they had hitherto furnished their contingent in men and money by the vote of their Colonial Assemblies; and that the British Parliament, in which they were not represented, had no right to tax them further. No attention was paid to these complaints, and they soon retaliated by forming associations to prevent the use of British manufactures until they should obtain redress.

This agitation was still in progress when the Red Indian, Pontiac, secretly knit up a confederacy of those Northern tribes who had formerly favoured the French, to which were added those of the West who wished for revenge, as having been dispossessed of their hunting-grounds by the sturdy and ruthless American backwoodsmen. Pontiac and his allies made a simultaneous attack upon our weak border posts in the neighbourhood of the Great Lakes and the Ohio River, and took scalps of nearly every one of the defenders. Lord Jeffery Amherst, who commanded our forces in America, found himself woefully short of troops: for after the Peace a quantity of British regiments had been disbanded and the few still stationed in America had fallen very low in strength. There had been costly expeditions sent to the Havana and Martinique, where the fever took off thousands of poor fellows. The Indians therefore were able to continue their ravages upon the borders of Virginia, Maryland, Pennsylvania, and New York, with increasing boldness and violence. Yet when Lord Amherst appealed to each of the colonies for local levies to assist him in his march against Pontiac's main forces, he met with a shabby enough response from almost every Assembly.

Partly it was that Lord Amherst, who soon resigned his command in disgust and sailed home, was held like the rest of our officers in America to have too haughty a way with the provincials. In the Canadian campaign he had seldom or never called the American colonels to a council of war, so that they knew no more of what was afoot than their own sergeants. Partly it was that a long-standing suspicion and jealousy existed between the colonies; so that if one colony held back from contributing to the common interest, the others felt no obligation to be any more active. But the chief reason why the pro-

vincials in general were so lukewarm was that they regarded soldiering as an unprofitable occupation in these
roaring times and best left to the English, should they
be martial-minded enough to undertake it. The provinces
of Massachusetts and Connecticut made conditions which
amounted to a refusal; Rhode Island did not deign to
reply; New Hampshire excused herself; Pennsylvania
would not send a single man; New York and New Jersey
voted a mere thousand men between them—but two-thirds
of these might not pass across their borders; Virginia had
already sent men to her own frontier and could spare no
more, so the Assembly pleaded.

It was two years before Pontiac's power was broken.
By this time the colonies had grudgingly raised between
them something better than two thousand men (of whom
three hundred immediately deserted) to accompany the
British punitive expedition. The most useful fighters were
a few score of frontiersmen from Virginia; but the Virginian Assembly refused to pay their expenses and tried
to fasten the cost personally upon the Colonel of the
Sixtieth Regiment with whom they had marched. The
King's men bore the chief brunt; and won, unsupported,
the only pitched battle of this Indian war, that of Bushy
Run. They felt more than a little resentment when they
recalled that in the days of greatest peril to the colonies
sixty invalids of Montgomery's Highlanders had to be
dragged from hospital and conveyed in carts to the weakly
held frontier forts—because free-born Americans refused
to make the war any concern of theirs.

Now for the famous Stamp Act. It seemed clear enough
that, if left to their own resources, the colonies would be
unable to agree upon secure measures of defence against
depredations of Indians in their rear, or possible naval raids
of French or Spanish upon their front and flanks. Fifteen
thousand men was reckoned by the King's military ad-
visers to be the lowest figure necessary for the protection
of his possessions from Hudson's Bay to the West India
Islands, and it seemed reasonable that the colonies should
pay a part at least of the maintenance of these troops,
having been such great gainers from the late war.

The new First Lord of the Treasury, therefore, Mr.

George Grenville, began considering ways and means. He consulted first with the London agents of the various Colonial Assemblies. He pointed out to them that the Acts of Trade and Navigation were being consistently evaded by the Americans. Even with the addition of the new duties, against which such indignant protests were being raised, the amount of revenue brought in did not pay one-third the cost of its collection! Would not the Colonial Assemblies, since these new duties displeased them, suggest an alternative method of raising money for American defence? But no answer came.

It may be noted that the famous Dr. Benjamin Franklin, agent for Pennsylvania, then privately approved the quartering of British troops in the colonies as a reasonable measure, and as a security not only against foreign invasion but intestine disorder—for armed conflict between the various colonies, in disputes over land, was always threatening. The generality of Americans, however, held that, since no immediate danger seemed to hang over America, and since they had supplied several militia regiments in the late war, for the expulsion of the French from Canada, their obligations were now at an end. It was also held unjust that their militia officers, however extensive their experience of war might be, still ranked junior to the rawest officer from England who held a commission from His Majesty. But the main impediment to a favourable reply, when Mr. Grenville raised this question, was that no two American Colonial Assemblies were ever known to agree, and therefore it would have been impossible, even had the principle of contribution been admitted, to fix the proportions of money that each colony should pay into the common fund for American defence.

The Government then, since the agents did not answer, saw no other alternative but to enforce the Trade and Navigation Acts by a tightening of the preventive system, to pass a Bill for the quartering of troops in America, and to pay the resultant expenses by new imposts in the form of stamp-duties. In the year 1765 the Quartering Act and its more famous companion, the Stamp Act, were passed.

The Stamp Act provided for the annual raising of £100,000, the whole of which was to be spent in America for defraying the costs of that country's defence. Since the population of America was something above two millions all told—exclusive of Negroes and Indians—this amounted to a monthly charge of less than one penny a head. Yet what a howl went up! The loudest mouthed and most energetic dissentients in America were always to be found in Boston and the province of Massachusetts generally. The people of Massachusetts had once enjoyed a far more liberal charter than the present, but it had been withdrawn from them for their frequent defiance of the Crown, and their intolerant killing, whipping, and jailing of harmless Baptists and still more harmless Quakers. Massachusetts was a very litigious province as well, and the numerous irregular lawyers of Boston, who were demagogues to a man, chanced to be hurt in the pocket by this Act: for the new stamp-duties were (as had long been the case in England) applied not only to newspapers, pamphlets, playing cards, and dice but to all legal documents, nor might any but the regular lawyers now ratify documents with the stamps.

These lawyers roused the town mob to the most striking demonstrations of displeasure. On the limb of a large tree, as one came into Boston from the country, were hung two effigies, one designed for the Stamp Master and the other for a jack-boot, with a head and horns peeping out at the top. Great numbers of enthusiasts, both from town and country, flocked to see it. In the evening these poor, foolish effigies were cut down and carried in procession with shouts of 'Liberty and Property for Ever. No Stamps!' But what became of them after, I do not know. The mob went next to the house of Mr. Oliver, the Chief Justice of the colony, beheaded him in effigy, broke his windows and burned down a new building of his which lay adjacent. A few days later they also broke the windows of the Deputy Registrar of the Court of Admiralty, and entering into his house destroyed his official books and papers and much of his furniture. They served the Comptroller of Customs similarly, and drank his cellar dry in addition. As for the Governor himself, Mr. Hutchinson, they wholly wrecked his mansion and not only carried off from it all his plate, furniture, and clothing, but scattered or destroyed the collection of historical documents that he had been thirty years at making. These mobs consisted, not of people of substance, but of a rabble who were as unqualified to vote in their provincial assemblies as the lawyers who stirred them up now were to discharge their assumed profession. They were, in fact, the forerunners and examplars of the *Sans-culotterie* who, guided by a similar school of lawyers, were the smoke and flame of the subsequent Revolution in France.

The mobs of the other colonies did not lag far behind Boston in their excesses. At Newport in Rhode Island they burned the houses of two gentlemen who had in conversation supported the right of Parliament to tax the Americans. In Maryland the effigy of the Stamp Master, on one side of which was written 'Tyranny,' on the other 'Oppression,' and across the breast, 'Damn my Country, I'll get Money,' was carried through the streets from the jail to the whipping-post and from thence to the pillory. After suffering many indignities, this effigy was first hanged and then burned. Similar outrages and frolics took place in New York and Connecticut. On the day that the Act became law there were mock-funerals of Liberty in several towns, church bells tolled mournfully, minute-guns were fired and flags flew at half-mast.

Nor had the mob alone been the instrument of colonial discontent. The respectable General Assembly of Virginia had passed resolutions strongly protesting against the right of England to lay taxes on America. Of this Assembly, the famous George Washington was a member and a zealous speaker on the text: 'No taxation without representation.' But the boldness and novelty of these resolutions, when they were first presented to the Assembly, affected Mr. Randolph, the Speaker, to such a degree that he struck upon the table with his gavel and cried out, 'Treason! Treason!'

It may be thought remarkable that the Virginians, who were the most aristocratic people of America, should have allied themselves with the libertarians of Boston in this protest against taxation. It would indeed have been remarkable, had the flourishing condition continued in which the province found herself when the war ended: for revolution is never made by affluent men. But peace commonly brings unemployment, as the energies that were devoted to destruction are relaxed and cannot at once be converted to constructive ends. Money is scarce, trade stagnates, merchants fail to meet their obligations and men tramp the country in search of employment that is nowhere to be had. All this took place after the Peace of 1763. The prosperity of Virginia was so closely linked to that of England that there were many bankruptcies among the planters; for the London market being glutted with tobacco, which few could afford to smoke or chew, the price of that commodity had fallen alarmingly. The employer of free labour has this advantage over a slave-owner, that he can at least turn his workmen adrift in difficult times: whereas the slave-owner must either house and feed his or sell them in a falling market.

Another cause of great discontent in Virginia and the South in general was that the planters did not receive a proper return for their crop even in the best of times: with British profits, charges for freight, commissions and taxes, the price of British goods sent to America in exchange for tobacco was, it was said, six times their real value. George Washington was just such a planter who had fallen into difficulties from these complicated causes: however, by a rich marriage he was protected against utter ruin. He was also one who, though a Colonel of Militia, and a soldier of experience in the Indian wars, had taken it ill that as an American he could not be granted a higher rank in the British Army than that of Captain, and had quitted the Service in a huff. To a man of his condition the Government's choice of such a time to tax America for the purposes of quartering an army on her soil was, of course, most offensive.

On the matter of taxation and representation the British Government took the following view: owing to the preservation without change of our ancient electoral system, certain decayed Cornish boroughs, for example, of a few houses apiece, still return forty-two members to Parliament between them—while great new cities, such as Birmingham and Manchester, have no members at all. Yet Birmingham and Manchester are *virtually*, it was held, represented by their manufacturers whose interest controls votes in other boroughs; and it was the same with the American merchants, who were indirectly a great power in the British Parliament. Why should Boston and Philadelphia be more tenderly treated than Birmingham and Manchester, cities of rather greater size than themselves?

To which the common American replied: that if the men of Birmingham and Manchester wished to live as slaves, that was their own affair: it did not suit the free populations of America.

To which the answer came again: 'If you would be free, then take concerted measures for your own defence, tax yourselves as you were first requested through your agents —do not burden Great Britain with the business. There can be no more proper a time than now for this mother-country to leave off feeding out of her own vitals the children whom she has nursed up. For, by your own showing, they are arrived at such maturity as to be well able to provide for themselves.'

But the Americans: 'The supposed danger does not exist, or is much exaggerated: if the French or Spanish invade our country we will turn them out easily enough, we reckon, and without your aid.' The hotter-mouthed among them cried, 'We want none of your lazy, foul-mouthed soldiery, hirelings of oppression, quartered upon us, nor of your arrogant, evil-living officers, instruments of a tyranny worse than death itself.'

Mr. Pitt the Elder, who had ruled England in the glorious days of the French wars, was now out of office, suffering from a suppressed but deep-seated gout. This affection prevented him from making any great parliamentary exertions, and was even generally agreed to have impaired his powers of reason, though diminishing little from his fluency as an orator. At the third reading of the Stamp Bill he had warmly taken up the cudgels for the Americans, while tolerantly deprecating the turbulence of the Boston mob. His speech, spoken with great animation, paid witness rather to his continued warmth of heart than to his continued sagacity as a statesman. He declared that he rejoiced that America had resisted the despotic threat to her liberty which this Bill conveyed. Yet he did not suggest by what alternative means the necessary fund for America's defence was to be raised. Nor would he explain in what sense the old-established Acts of Trade, one or two of which he had himself sponsored, were any less despotic in intention than this Stamp Bill—unless it was that they were more easily evaded by the lawless American people than this might prove to be.

The irony of the situation lay in this: that the American boast, to be able to defeat the French and Spanish armies if they invaded the colonies, was taken seriously neither by the British nor by the Americans themselves. Yet it now appears evident that it could have been made good, to judge by the fearful mauling that our armies encountered at their hands when we attempted the same thing.

The Stamp Act was soon repealed, in consequence of a petition to the King and to the Houses of Lords and Commons by a Continental Congress: to which novel institution all the American colonies sent representatives. That the petition was granted was, some will say, evident proof that *virtual* representation in our Parliament was more effective than the actual representation of any English city. Had Old York or Old Boston shown such ill temper over the stamp-duties as their namesakes across the Ocean had done, it would have been a matter for the constabulary and armed forces to settle without delay, nor would any Mr. Pitt have pleaded for indulgence towards them.

The withdrawal of the Stamp Act was presented as a pure act of royal benevolence, and a Declaratory Act was at the same time passed, maintaining the authority of the British Parliament over the colonies, without any reserve.

Yet the mischief was now done, for where England had yielded once she might be expected to yield again. The problem of finding funds for the defence of America and of the West India Islands, on which the colonies were dependent for a great part of their trade, remained unsettled. Mr. Pitt became the Earl of Chatham, accepted power for a while, grew worse of the gout and being unable to attend to colonial affairs, left his Chancellor of the Exchequer to act as he pleased in the matter. Now, the compromise tacitly agreed upon between England and America, at the close of the Stamp Act dispute, was that Parliament would refrain at least from imposing *internal* taxation, which was to be left to the Colonial Assemblies to manage, stamp-duties being counted as internalities. To the principle of *external* taxation, in the sense covered by the Trade Acts, the colonists gave a grudging consent; though to be sure, as an Irish Member of Parliament put it, there seemed but little difference in effect, whether money was to be taken from the coat-pocket or the waistcoat-pocket. This Chancellor of the Exchequer, Mr. Townshend, therefore felt himself at liberty to crack on whatever external duties he pleased, and on various goods, among them tea, that had hitherto passed free of tax. Nor was the expected increase in revenue to be devoted to the quartering of troops in America, but to a fund for the regular payment of colonial governors and judges. Mr. Townshend very properly explained to Parliament that in a country where lawlessness abounded and justice was often a matter of favour, the persons in chief legal authority must now be raised above the temptation to venality. But to the Americans it seemed that these fees were a bribe to the governors and judges to settle all questions to the advantage of the King's friends. The associations formed to refuse English imported goods grew stronger than before, so that the value of such goods fell by a million pounds sterling in a single year. The mob grew still more turbulent, especially that of Boston and New England generally; and even the Loyalists began to think that America should now be treated with the former 'salutary neglect' that gave these low people no excuse for their outrages. To press for the payment of taxes which never could cover the cost of collection seemed like burning down a barn in order to roast an egg.

❀ ❀ ❀ ❀ ❀ ❀ ❀ ❀ ❀ ❀ ❀ ❀

CHAPTER

7

IN THE summer of the year 1768, two regiments of Foot, The Fourteenth and The Twenty-ninth, and one company of Artillery, were sent to Boston to assist the magistrates

and revenue-officers in enforcing the law. This measure
was represented by the Boston politicians as if a great
herd of lions had been let loose on the town to tear and
mangle the inhabitants; but from what I have been told
by men of The Fourteenth who later fought beside me in
Canada and upper New York, the matter was altogether
different—these soldiers felt themselves so many Daniels
in the wild beasts' den. For the lawyers and the Congregational ministers, their allies, controlled the populace, the
most sturdy and intemperate part of which lived in Fish
Street and Battery Marsh. This mob, under the respectable
dress of town-meetings, put terror upon all those who were
accounted friends of England; by beatings, burnings, and
that strange indignity of tar and feathers, the use of which
had been discontinued by our ancestors, so I have read,
about the time of bad King John. No magistrate and no
jury, whatever their real convictions might be, dared
bring in a verdict obnoxious to the real rulers of Boston; it
was endangering his own life and property for any officer
of the law to call assistance of the military; and the individual British soldier accused, however falsely, of a
crime, however trifling, was altogether at the mercy of
these base-minded, facetious, and enthusiastic people.

Constantly soldiers and even officers were arrested on
frivolous charges, refused bail, and kept in jail until the
case came up for trial; when, the prosecutors not coming
forward, the case was dismissed and no explanation or
satisfaction offered. On one occasion a soldier was arrested
in barracks by a constable; since the warrant of arrest did
not particularize the soldier by name, his officers appeared
on his behalf in court to protest against this infringement
of his rights as a citizen. They were thereupon indicted
for riot and rescue and made to pay a heavy fine, while
the magistrate thundered at them from the bench, threatening them with the vengeance of the town! Two soldiers
of The Fourteenth, emerging one day from the hospital
after a bout of fever and scarcely able to walk, were set
upon by the mob and half-killed by sticks, fists, and boots.
They appealed to Major-General Mackay, their commander, for redress and he condoled with them for their
misfortunes. 'But,' said he, 'be advised and seek no revenge.

For even if you can identify your assailants, as you say, there is no justice for soldiers in Boston. Here is half a guinea for each of you, my lads. Drink and forget.'

And it may not be credited, but it actually occurred to my knowledge: a soldier found guilty (I do not know how justly) of a petty theft was condemned to pay damages to the amount of some seventy pounds sterling, but not having so many pence was idented as a slave and sold for a term of years to the highest bidder! For the custom of selling white men into servitude was still oddly common in this land of liberty.

It may be asked, why did not General Mackay proclaim martial law and reduce the mob to reason by a warning shot or two? He was not permitted. Lord Chatham, the Prime Minister, had adjured the House in passionate tones: 'Let affection be the only bond of coercion: pass an amnesty over the errors of the colonists: by measures of lenity allure them to their duty.' The soldiers of the garrison had strict orders never to strike an inhabitant of Boston, whatever the provocation. This the Bostonians knew; and they took every advantage of their knowledge. Soldiers passing peacefully down the street would be saluted from their rear with cries of 'What cheer, lobster scoundrels?' or 'Hallo, you red-herring rascals!' and pelted with stones or filth, the assailants then scuttling away. A sentry standing guard at the entrance to the Custom House or the Magazine would be mobbed by impudent youths, one plucking at his side-arm, another trying to knock off his tall cap with a stick, a third daubing with dirt his white buckskin accoutrements. And these young limbs of mischief would encourage one another: 'Don't be skeered, lads. He dursen't fire. He's a bloody-back coward like the rest.' This term of abuse, 'bloody back,' alluded, like the others, to the scarlet cloth of the infantry uniform; but glanced also at our military custom of flogging delinquents, by which the Americans professed at this time to be greatly shocked. Our men showed a great and disciplined forbearance at Boston.

It was indeed a strange place. The Saints, as the Bostonians were called in fun by the other colonists, were perfectly scandalized by the innocent military music of horns, clarinets, hautboys, and bassoons, especially when played after dark through the streets on the King's birthday, or the anniversary of the Gunpowder Plot, or St. George's Day. Their wives and daughters would shudder and draw their skirts aside if they passed a soldier in the streets. In certain peculiar moral observances, such as the limitation of Sabbath Day travelling, or the abstention from black-puddings, they were near as strict as Jews. Yet for scheming, evading, overreaching, hoodwinking, and, in a favourite phrase of their own, being 'smart men,' the people of Massachusetts in general and of Boston in particular were a byword in the remaining colonies. As for Boston Common—to see the women who sneaked out there at night for clandestine pleasure with the soldiery, you might well (said my informants, with an oath) have believed yourself on Wimbledon Common or Blackheath!

Next came the so-called 'Boston Massacre' of March 1770. A private of the Twenty-ninth Regiment, passing early one Saturday morning along a public rope-walk, was hailed by some ropers there, and asked, 'Would you like to do a job of work?' He replied innocently enough that he would gladly undertake work to supplement his meagre pay. 'Then come and clean out our coffee-house' (as they termed a privy) 'you damned rascal bloody back,' they cried. Says he: 'Boys, I have a prophecy to make. Before much more hemp has been twisted on these walks, your backs will be bloody too.' A fistcuff fight began, three of his comrades running up to defend him, but all these men dutifully refrained from using their side-arms. An officer approaching, the fight was broken off before a decision was reached, but not before the prophetic soldier had engaged the rope-makers in a friendly enough spirit, for he was an Irishman, to fight it out on the Monday morning following—but teeth, nails, and kicking barred. On Sunday the Congregational ministers—the same who used to rant in the pulpits about the Demon Bishops of Britain and how, among other perquisites of episcopacy, every tenth-born child was ravished from its mother's side, along with the tithe-calf and the tithe-pig, for his monstrous appetite—these having got wind of the coming appointment, preached that a massacre of the honest ropers was secretly intended by the British, and that this diabolical plot must be forthwith frustrated. So our four champions, accompanied by a few comrades, all equally unarmed, were astonished on arriving at the agreed place of encounter to find a great number of men drawn up with clubs and sticks to oppose them, the ministers darting among the crowd with cries of exhortation and defiance.

They stood and laughed. At this the mob began to hurl stones, and the bells of a neighbouring church started pealing, setting off all the other peals in Boston. 'Town-born, turn out!' was a cry taken up in all parts of the town.

The mob then moved away from the rope-walk under the influence of a tall, large man, wearing a red cloak and a white wig, and approached Murray's Barracks where they dared the soldiers at the gate to come out and fight like men; at the same time pelting them with snowballs in which stones were wrapped. The soldiers' only answer was a silent contempt; and a passing officer ordered them into barracks. The same ringleader then withdrew them from the barracks and harangued them earnestly. They uttered huzzas and cried: 'On to the Main Guard!' and breaking up into distinct divisions converged on the Custom House in King Street by different routes. Captain Preston, the officer on duty, called out a sergeant and twelve men of the guard with bayonets fixed on their muskets. This order was to protect the sentry, who was now being pelted with snowballs by the rabble. On the appearance of this party, frantic shouts arose of: 'Cowardly bloody-backs! You dursen't fire agin us. Fire, I say, you bloody-back slaves!' The most furious group, composed of sailors who had lost their livelihood by the British interruption of the smuggling trade (the mainstay of this city of Saints) advanced to the very points of the bayonets with most unsaintly oaths and execrations.

Captain Preston pushed his way through the ranks and begged the fellows to go quietly home and play at snowballs among themselves, if they would avoid bloodshed. But the sailors now tried to strike the muskets down with their clubs, and a blow was aimed by one of them at the Captain himself, which he avoided. Among the guard were comrades of the soldier who had been sold into slavery by the miserable action of the magistrates; and one man (the same who gave me this account) had lately been offered by a lawyer the sum of fifty pounds to swear a false affidavit against his own lieutenant, a most humane and excellent officer. Their fingers itched at the triggers.

A sailor struck a soldier on the arm with a club at the moment that the red-cloaked ringleader was shouting back at the Captain. 'Do your worst, damn you! We ain't afeared!' The man's musket went off, but without effect. One of the rabble then happening to shout, 'Fire, my men, fire!' in mimicry of an English officer's tones, this was mistaken for Captain Preston's own order. Several men discharged their pieces. Four sailors fell dead and seven more wounded, two mortally.

To convert an indifferent cause into one that seems to have overwhelming justice on its side, there is nothing so convenient as a martyr: and here was a whole maniple of martyrs. The town broke immediately into full commotion; but, upon the Governor promising to commit Captain Preston and his men to jail and to withdraw the whole of the garrison behind the walls of Castle William, which was a barracks on an island in the harbour, there was no recourse to open fighting. Yet the whole of the colony of Massachusetts threatened to avenge the 'dastardly crime,' as it was described. Fantastically distorted accounts of the occurrences were sent back to England by the penmen of Boston, which the Opposition newspapers published *in extenso* as a means of discrediting the Ministry. Two revolutionary leaders, of whom one was the well-known Mr. John Adams, a self-taught lawyer, then came forward, politically enough, to offer themselves as counsel for the prisoners at their trial. Captain Preston, the sergeant, the sentry, and ten men of the guard were by aid of his eloquence honourably acquitted of the charge of murder. The two remaining men, who were said to have initiated the volley, were found guilty of manslaughter but punished only lightly. Any other verdict would have been plainly scandalous and a damage to the revolutionary cause; yet that these honest soldiers escaped with their lives was advanced as a signal proof of the impartiality of American justice. And at the same time the mob-leaders and ministers did not hesitate to speak of 'the Boston Massacre,' as if there had been a grave miscarriage of justice, the British having secretly overawed the jury by threats.

I have by me an old copy of the Boston *Gazette* of March 1771, referring to the Boston Massacre, in which is mentioned that rancorous Whig, Mr. Paul Revere, whose exploits at the beginning of the Revolution have been very dramatically recounted, but without great relation to the truth:

In the Evening there was a very striking Exhibition at the Dwelling-House of Mr. Paul Revere, fronting the old North Square. At one of the Chamber-Windows was the appearance of the Ghost of the unfortunate young Seider, with one of his Fingers in the Wound, endeavoring to stop the Blood issuing therefrom; near him his Friends were weeping: And at a small distance, a monumental Obelisk, with his Bust in Front:—On the Front of the Pedestal, were the Names of those killed on the Fifth of March: Underneath the following Lines,

> '*Seider's pale Ghost fresh bleeding stands,*
> *And Vengeance for his Death demands.*'

In the next Window were represented the Soldiers drawn up, firing at the People assembled before them—the Dead on the Ground—and the Wounded falling, with the Blood running in Streams from their Wounds; Over which was wrote FOUL PLAY. In the third Window was the Figure of a Woman, representing AMERICA, sitting on the Stump of a Tree, with a Staff in her Hand, and the Cap of Liberty on the Top thereof,—one Foot on the Head of a Grenadier lying prostrate grasping a Serpent—Her Finger pointing to the Tragedy.

The whole was so well executed, that the Spectators which amounted to many Thousands, were struck with solemn Silence, and their Countenances covered with a melancholy Gloom. At nine o'clock the Bells tolled a doleful Peal, until Ten; when the Exhibition was withdrawn, and the People retired to their respective Habitations.

King George, who was at that time in the full vigour of his powers, the sad lunatic strain not having yet revealed itself, chafed at the confusion into which national affairs had fallen. No fewer than three Prime Ministers had resigned office within a space of seven years. He decided that his Kingdom must for a while at least be managed by a Ministry which would pursue a continuous policy and be proof against faction. He therefore instituted a system of personal government—that is, government under his own direction—the parliamentary leadership being given to Lord North, a well-intentioned but slack-minded Tory. Lord North was bound to the King by a stronger tie than mere loyalty, being his near cousin: his mother had been the daughter of one of George II's German mistresses. At the King's gracious desire Lord North removed the vexatious 'Townshend duties' that had occasioned such a falling-off in the American trade, reserving only a single one, namely, the tax on tea, as a token that the King did not waive his sovereign rights. Thus a great landowner, who freely allows the people of a neighbouring village to walk through his park land, nevertheless for one day in the year keeps the great gates shut from sunrise to sundown and admits nobody: lest a 'right of way' be created which might somehow be inconvenient to him or his heirs. The duty on tea was chosen to be retained as one which, after reckoning in the cost of its collection, yielded practically no revenue to the Crown and could therefore not constitute a legitimate grievance. This measure had a good effect upon trade, which soon recovered its former volume, especially since the American associations formed against the importation of English-manufactured goods had now achieved the hidden object for which they had been intended. The shelves of the American merchants were at last cleared, and without loss, of the huge stocks which they had laid in at the close of the French war, before trade had become depressed by the confusions of peace. Yet the two great questions outstanding, that of providing for the external defence of America and that of protecting loyal persons from the molestation of the 'Liberty Boys' (as the revolutionaries now styled themselves) remained unsettled. Matters improved still more in the following year, 1771, there being an alarm of war with Spain. The colonists showed themselves agreeable now to red-coats being quartered among them, and even gave assistance to royal recruiting-parties: our regiments being considerably under strength owing to desertions.

However, in the next year the alarm passed and the agitation against the British continued steadily in New England. It was given substance by an act of the famous and venerable Dr. Benjamin Franklin, already mentioned, the inventor of the lightning conductor for houses, who was then Deputy Postmaster-General of America and resident agent in London of the colony of Massachusetts. Dr. Franklin had by some unknown means possessed himself of certain confidential letters written by Mr. Hutchinson, the Governor of Massachusetts, whose house and collection of historical documents had been destroyed in the Stamp Act riots, and of Mr. Oliver, Lieutenant-Governor, whose house also had been burned on the same occasion: both men very respectable in their private character. In these letters, written to influential friends in England, they had expressed themselves very freely and with pardonable warmth upon the situation of affairs in America, recommending that the Government should adopt more vigorous methods in support of its authority. Let Parliament clap a padlock on the mouths of the over-eloquent orators of Boston, whose one aim was to preserve the remembrance of every disagreeable occurrence that had ever passed between the soldiers and the townsfolk, who ranted ceaselessly on the 'blessings of liberty,' the 'horrors of slavery,' the 'dangers of a standing army,' but only with a view to keeping the popular mind continuously inflamed, and with a fixed aversion to the truth.

These private letters were conveyed by Dr. Franklin to his friends of the Massachusetts Assembly where they were read aloud to one hundred and five members by Mr. Samuel (not John) Adams. This other Adams was an enthusiast by whom the well-known Committees of Correspondence had been founded, which guided particular towns, not only within his colony but scattered throughout all the others, to concerted action against the Crown. These private letters, then, which Dr. Franklin with patriotic and lofty excuses thus mischievously published (some say because of a private pique against the Governor, whose Sabbatarian principles he had offended, and against the Lieutenant-Governor, perhaps in revenge for the rifling of his own private correspondence by secret agents in the British Post Office), threw the Assembly into a violent flame.

By a majority of over twenty to one they voted that the tendency and design of these letters was to subject the Constitution and introduce arbitrary power into the province. They humbly petitioned His Majesty to remove these two men for ever from the government of Massachusetts: asserting that they, being 'no strangers or foreigners but bone of our bone, flesh of our flesh, born and educated among us . . . have alienated from us the affections of our Sovereign, have destroyed the harmony and goodwill which existed between Great Britain and Massachusetts and, having already caused bloodshed in our streets will, if unchecked, plunge our country into all the horrors of civil war.' Dr. Franklin himself conveyed this petition, the sincerity of which may well be questioned, to the King, before whom it was laid in Council. But it became known that the letters on which the petition was grounded had been purloined by this same Dr. Franklin, and the Committee of Lords therefore considered it a somewhat indecent affair. Dr. Franklin, called in evidence, would not reply to interrogation, the petition was thrown out, and Dr. Franklin was dismissed from his Deputy Postmastership. This was thought to be to his satisfaction; for it would prove to the Bostonians that he was ready to suffer from his attachment to their cause—being still somewhat suspect to them as having been a warm supporter of the Quartering Act and the Stamp Act. In the event, he was rewarded by his fellow countrymen, a year or two later, with the Postmaster-Generalship of the United States.

Every one on this side of the Atlantic, as on the other, has heard of the 'Boston Tea-Party' which was the immediate occasion of the American War; but how it came about is not, I find, so generally known.

The East India Company stood on the brink of bankruptcy, one reason being that it had lost many hundreds of thousands of customers in America. Until the new duty had been placed upon it, tea had been, after hard liquor, the favourite beverage not only of the white Americans (especially of the women, who were perfect addicts to it) but of the Indian savages, who boiled it regularly twice a day in the kettles suspended over their wigwam fires. Four million pounds' worth of tea had now accumulated in the London warehouses, and the Cabinet thought to help the East India merchants out of their difficulties by allowing them to sell some of this surplus treasure direct to America at a reduced rate. That is to say, the Company was allowed a drawback of the whole tea duty then payable in England, while the Exchequer continued to claim the duty of threepence on the pound payable by America. This arrangement greatly vexed the Bostonians. It was not only that this slight but aggravating threepence had become a symbol to them of liberties denied—for the watchword, 'No taxation without representation,' was by now made to cover external as well as internal imports; but that it damaged the private interests of their leaders and put many of themselves out of employment. Colonel 'King' Hancock, of the Sons of Liberty, had made a large fortune by smuggling East India tea from Holland, where it was sold at one shilling a pound; having in combination with a few associates handled no fewer than five thousand chests in two years, and engaged a great number of seamen and others in the trade. The new tea being offered for sale far cheaper, even with the duty added, than what Hancock sold (and indeed cheaper than in England, since the English duty was higher than the American) would undercut the profit, amounting to near two hundred per centum, that he was drawing from his venture. It was Colonel Hancock's friend, Mr. Samuel Adams, who personally directed the 'daring action,' as it has been called, of the fifty Boston mobsmen who, on December 16th, 1773, disguised as Mohawk Indians, boarded the British tea-ships on their arrival at Boston harbour, and threw the whole of their cargo, three hundred and forty-two chests, overboard. In the immediate and particular sense it was not daring: Mr. Adams knew well that the troops would not be called out from Castle William to save the tea, since their orders were to intervene in civil disturbances only if blood were shed; nor would the magistrates take any action against him subsequently, for fear of a coat of tar and feathers, even if they were not of his own opinions. But it was a daring action in the sense that it challenged reprisals against the town of Boston as a whole.

This was not the only consignment of tea that was sent to America at that time; and Mr. Adams's Committees of Correspondence in the principal towns of the continent had made preparations for concerted action against its acceptance. The Pennsylvanians greeted a tea-ship on its arrival at Philadelphia, the capital city, with such execrations and threats that the captain turned about and sailed down the Delaware River again and straight home. At Charleston in South Carolina the tea was taken ashore indeed but heaped into a damp cellar, where it was soon utterly spoiled by the mildew.

On being informed of the destruction of the tea, King George considered himself personally affronted, but was considerate that the other cities of America should not suffer for the fault of Boston, where, as he knew, all the present troubles had been fomented. No action was therefore taken against them in the matter of their refusing the tea, but Boston must be sharply punished as a general warning.

In March of the year 1774 'The Boston Port Act' was passed: to 'discontinue the landing and discharging, lading and shipping, of goods, wares, and merchandize at the town of Boston or within the harbour' until such time as the East India Company had been compensated by the city for the loss of the tea, which was valued at £15,000. The business of the Custom House and the seat of Government transferred at the same time to the port of Salem, seventeen miles distant. The unfortunate Mr. Hutchinson was not considered equal to the task of governing Massachusetts in these aggravated conditions: he was instructed to hand over his office to General Gage, a gallant and capable soldier, who had been wounded by Col. Washington's side in the late war, had married an American lady, and was greatly esteemed by the better people of America. It was remembered that on the repeal of the Stamp Act in 1769 his house at New York had been brilliantly illuminated. General Gage had also been appointed Commander-in-Chief of the Force in America.

Let nobody think that the name of Boston figures too importantly in this account. But for Boston, it is difficult to see by what means the necessary separation between England and her colonies would eventually have come about. In Boston alone existed the active resolution to rebel. At the close of the war, a Boston statesman whose name it is not hard to guess wrote of his own part in initiating the general movement (against the inclinations of so many of his countrymen) as follows:

Here in my retreat, like another Catiline, the collar around my neck, in danger of the severest punishment, I laid down the plan of revolt: I endeavoured to persuade my timid accomplices that a most glorious revolution might be the result of our efforts, but I scarcely dared to hope it; and what I have seen realized appears to me like a dream. You know by what obscure intrigues, by what unfaithfulness to the mother-country a powerful party was formed; how the minds of the people were irritated before we could provoke the insurrection.

Can this justification of end by means be admitted as proved, if the end was so little appreciated by the greater part of those for whom it was conceived, even when the war had been for some time in progress? That the end was not generally appreciated does not, of course, argue against its rightness; for in my opinion the American quarrel was inevitable, and in the long run salutary, though a very ugly, damned business while it lasted.

Let me speak more explicitly. I had been told, before I sailed for America, that this was a civil war, a rebellion of recreant Englishmen against their rightful Sovereign. Yet I came to realize before I had been many weeks on the scene of action that it was no civil war. Americans are not merely another sort of English, but are in effect Americans, a nation in their own right. Transplant English roots, herbs, or pulse to America, even to that part of the continent which most nearly resembles England in climate, and in three years what will have occurred? The difference of soil and air will have brought about notable alterations in your plants: in some cases for the better, in others for the worse, but at least a pronounced change. It may be that a crop which was feeble in England and required much care will have grown as rank as a weed over there. Or it may be that after three years there is such a degeneration of seed (as with the cabbage and the turnip) that you will be obliged to send home for fresh. It is the same with fruit, poultry, and cattle. Some varieties thrive enormously, some come to no good at all, all alter. Is it therefore surprising that the English race should also alter on transplantation to this continent? Three, nay, two, generations are sufficient for your Englishman to be transformed (or transmogrified) into a different being. He becomes a native American, who walks, works, plays, speaks, looks, feels, and thinks in a way peculiar to the country; and who, once he becomes aware of these changes in himself, can no longer be ruled by gentlemen, though as learned, eminent, or gracious as you please, sent over from England with royal letters patent.

The town of Boston, however Jesuitical its leaders may appear to our British judgment, however graceless its mob, was right in its main contention; aye, and bold and even, one may say, heroical in maintaining it. Three thousand five hundred able-bodied citizens were not many to challenge so great and powerful an Empire as the British.

The heraldic flag of the American Republic consists of *bars* and *mullets* (vulgarly 'stripes' and 'stars') which commemorate in number the colonies of the Union. It was first hoisted on New Year's Day, 1776. The simple family coat of General Washington, America's saviour and first President, are recalled in this flag: for it consists of the very same bars and mullets, though not so numerous. I consider it remarkable that the young Republic instead of coining the new motto *E pluribus unum* (which is to say, 'One composed of many'), should not have boldly taken over Washington's own, as well as his heraldic charges: for it was EXITUS ACTA PROBAT—'the end justifies the means.'

CHAPTER
8

Tidings of the Port Act were received by the Bostonians with most extravagant tokens of resentment. The text of the Act was printed on mourning paper with a black border and cried about the streets as a 'Barbarous Murder.' The terms 'Whigs' and 'Tories,' for want of better, now being introduced into America (the former covering those who favoured the action of the Bostonians, and the latter those who condemned it as turbulent and unwarrantable) a regular persecution of the Tories throughout New England now began. These Tories were for the most part people of property and education, descendants of the first settlers; but their barns were burned, their cattle driven, their families insulted, their houses broken into, and they themselves forced either to quit or starve. 'A Tory,' the Whigs held, 'is one whose head is in England, whose body is in America, and whose neck should be *stretched*.' If any one of them was caught alone and unarmed he was seized and led for mockery and detestation from township to township—'as by law is provided in the case of strolling idiots, lunatics, and the like.' Soon many hundreds of them had screened themselves in Boston, in the neighbourhood of the barracks. Servants of the Government were most brutally handled, and even ministers of religion whose Toryism was held offensive by their congregations found their cloth no protection to them. One had bullets fired through his windows, another merely had his pulpit nailed up, but a third was put into the village pound, as if he had been a strayed pig; where red herrings were thrown over for him to eat, in mockery of his affection for the redcoats. Only in the case of physicians was a touch of Toryism condoned by the Liberty Boys: from consideration of the ladies whose exigencies could not be denied for a mere political reason.

But a striking discrepancy was discovered by a number of thoughtful Americans between the professions and acts of the Boston agitators. One judicious writer who 'eschewed politics as if they were edged tools' complained about this time that there was something excessively absurd in some men's eternally declaiming on freedom of thought —while not permitting an opponent to open his mouth on the subjects in dispute, without danger of being presented with a coat of tar and feathers, or being obliged to run like a criminal dog into the nearest woods with the hue and cry behind him.

At the instance of the revolutionary party at New York a Congress of Delegates was now called from all the colonies to deliberate on the critical state of their affairs. This Congress, at which Georgia alone of the colonies was unrepresented, met at Philadelphia in the autumn of 1774. The fifty-one delegates declared themselves outright Whigs: urging the Bostonians to persevere in their opposition to the Government until their chartered liberties should be restored to them, engaging to support them in this aim to the best of their powers, and passing various resolutions of American unanimity—in which they even artfully tried to include the French Papists of Canada. They avowed, however, their allegiance to King George and drew up a petition in which they entreated him to grant them peace, liberty, and safety. This civility to the King was added as a sop to the representatives of Pennsylvania and New York, who opposed many of the resolutions and absented themselves from the proceedings for several days. A common front was only marshalled by the energies (to quote an American gentleman who was on the spot) of 'Adams with his crew, and the haughty Sultans of the South, who juggled the whole conclave of delegates.'

The Bostonians had framed an agreement, which they called 'A Solemn League and Covenant,' by which the subscribers engaged in the most sacred manner to 'discontinue commercial intercourse with Great Britain till the late obnoxious Acts are repealed.' This was also taken up by large numbers of people from the other provinces. When General Gage attempted to damp the effect of this covenant by a proclamation against mutiny, they retorted that the law allowed His Majesty's loyal subjects to associate peaceably in defence of their rights; and he could not deny this. Nor could he do anything by legal methods for the proper protection of the Tories, since a Whiggish unanimity had now been forced on all instruments and accessories of the law—magistrates, jurors, and witnesses alike; or even by military means, since the force at his disposal consisted of four weak battalions, which were wholly insufficient to the task of policing so great a province. The men of Massachusetts had now begun secretly to arm themselves and openly to drill; and a rival government to General Gage's, a provincial congress, had resolved to raise the number of these avowed rebels to twelve thousand men, and invited the other New England provinces of Connecticut, Rhode Island, and New Hampshire to assist them with eight thousand more.

To relieve the distress of the people of Boston, liberal gifts were sent in money and kind from other towns of the province, and from so far away as South Carolina. The merchants of Salem and Marblehead, which lay adjacent, placed their wharves at the disposal of their colleagues of Boston; but these towns soon lost the use of their port, from destroying a cargo of tea which arrived in it.

Desertions from the Royal Army became frequent and were due to a variety of causes. In the first place, the daily sixpence which was the pay of a common soldier, was insufficient for his subsistence (because of the heavy stoppages made from it for clothing and other matters, under the title of 'Off-reckonings') even in England. In America, where prices were one-third higher for all European articles, a soldier was never out of debt, unless he happened to be a model of sobriety and thrift. Troops garrisoned in America were always being tempted with offers of employment at high wages by prosperous farmers of the back districts; and with such offers now went an undertaking from the Committee of Correspondence of the township concerned that no sergeant's party of his regiment would be suffered to arrest him as a deserter. If intending deserters could bring their muskets and side-arms with them, so much the better: the sum of twenty dollars apiece was offered by the rebels for Tower muskets in good repair.

Now a new and disgraceful employment was offered to the necessitous soldier: he could count upon fifty pounds sterling in gold money if he consented to become a drill-master and teach the American volunteers their platoon-exercise for use against his King and his comrades. Many soldiers consented, especially those with particular griev-ances against some officer or sergeant; smothering their sense of guilt under a professed concern for the cause of Liberty. Others remarked that they had volunteered as soldiers to fight for King George, and that, though sur-rounded and insulted by hordes of his enemies, they were not permitted to use the arms that had been entrusted to them for this very purpose. If the pride of England had thus decayed, they declared, there was no temptation to remain loyal soldiers, to sweat, shiver, pull off the hat, run into debt, grow decrepit in a thankless service, and every now and then (for some slight dereliction of duty) be tied up to the halberts and helped to two score of lashes laid on by a lusty drummer. They might just as well pass over to the Americans, who for all their uncouthness were men who stood up for their rights, who contrived to eat and drink heartily, to go well clothed and well shod, and were hospitable to new-comers.

The troops were encamped on Boston Common, just outside the town, and, the desertions growing more fre-quent, in spite of the death penalty being ordained for the crime, General Gage was one day heard to remark to his staff: 'We are bleeding to death by damned driblets, gen-tlemen, and I am resolved to stop the flow with a tight bandage.' Whereupon he gave orders for the fortification of Boston Neck, which separated the town from the coun-try behind, and placed his most trustworthy men on guard there to see that no one went out or came in who had no right to do so. But the revolutionary leaders represented this protective bandage rather as a noose tied around the neck of Boston to throttle her. The country people and Bostonians were exceedingly impudent to our sentries as they passed and repassed the lines with their carts. One carter was stopped going out of town with some nineteen thousand ball cartridges, which were taken from him. He had the effrontery to approach Headquarters with a demand for their redelivery, saying that they were for his own use in hunting! The request was of course refused, but, says he: 'Foh, then, it don't matter, I reckon. That was only the last parcel of a very great quantity I have carried out in this cart at different times; and all for my own use in hunting.'

Next, the inhabitants of Newport, in Rhode Island, dismounted forty cannon, which were provided for the protection of the harbour, and carried them off for the use of the revolutionary forces; and the New Hampshire men seized a great quantity of Government stores in the fort of Piscataqua, albeit without bloodshed. Evidently war had grown imminent, and was indeed confidently announced in September 1774, many months before it actually broke out. Then Colonel Israel Putnam of Connecticut, that old hunter of bears and Indians, wrote by express to New York, during the first session of the Continental Congress, that the King's troops and ships had that instant begun an indiscriminate massacre of the wretched people of Boston. He called for aid from every direction. The report caused despair and rage in Philadelphia, to which city it was instantly transmitted, and remained uncontradicted for three days. Colonel Putnam, who was an honest man, was, it is thought, imposed upon by some agent of the political Mr. Samuel Adams, who wished by this false news to force the Congress, by no means unanimous, to declare itself as resolutely as in the event it did. Here I may observe that the most dislikeable man in America, to the English, was this same Sam Adams, with his agued hands and twitching face, his tongue (as was said) alternately dripping honey and venom, his unkempt person, his restless eyes, and ever-empty pockets. He had not long before avoided prison, when charged with defalcation as tax collector, by the interposition of his partisans in office.

General Gage wrote to the Government about this time: 'If force is to be used at length, it must be a considerable one. To begin with small numbers will only

encourage resistance and not terrify.' Since it was esti-
mated that the Americans could raise a force of one hundred and fifty thousand men with knowledge of firelocks,
he asked for fifteen thousand men to be stationed at
Boston, ten thousand at New York, and seven thousand
more to protect Canada against invasion by the Americans.

He had taken what precautions he could against a rising;
removing the powder and arms from magazines in the
vicinity and storing them all in Castle William. He had
also, by the bye, deprived that arch-smuggler, Colonel
'King' Hancock (afterwards President of the Congress) of
his commission as Commander of the Massachusetts Company of Cadets. These cadets were gentlemen who used to
attend the Governor, but since many of them now feared
what the mob might do to themselves and their property
should they continue in this service, the company was disbanded. They returned to the General the Standard that
he had presented to them on succeeding Mr. Hutchinson
as Governor. Mr. Oliver the Lieutenant-Governor and
almost all of the new councillors appointed by a royal
mandamus had by now been obliged to resign by threats
against their lives.

There were some disturbances of a lesser sort in the
town. Mr. Samuel Adams, in the presence of a number of
British officers, during a town-meeting on March 5th in
the Old South Meeting House, moved that the thanks of
the town should be presented to Dr. Warren, who had
just spoken, for his elegant and spirited oration, and that
another should be delivered on March 5th next to commemorate the *Bloody Massacre* of five years previous.
Several officers began to hiss, others cried, 'O fie, fie!' and
an officer dressed in gold lace regimentals with blue
facings, whose name or regiment I cannot learn, advanced
to Mr. Adams and Colonel Hancock, who was also present,
and addressed them in severe terms. He told them that the
Army resented the phrase *Bloody Massacre*, Captain
Preston having been fairly tried and honourably acquitted
by a Boston court of the charge of murder. The Americans
making some reply, the renewed cries of 'Fie! Fie!' were
misheard as an alarm of 'Fire, Fire!' and the whole place
was thrown into a bustle. Women shrieked, men swore,

and many persons leaped headlong out into the street from the lower windows. The drums of the Forty-third Regiment, which happened to be passing, increased the confusion: Mr. Adams, Colonel Hancock, and others present evidently feared that they were about to be apprehended by an officer with a warrant. The meeting was nearly cleared in two minutes, but no lives lost or violence used.

Two days later a man was caught who had attempted to buy from a soldier of The Forty-seventh the lock of his musket. Men of this regiment stripped, tarred and feathered the American and, seating him on a truck, in that manner paraded him through the town for the best part of the afternoon. The officers of The Forty-seventh lent no hand to this excess (which the Americans imputed to them) but turned a blind eye. The affair was much disapproved of by General Gage.

While I was in Dublin, about April of the year 1775, my father showed me the following two letters, copies of which he had been permitted to take by his friend and patron Dean Evelyn of Trim in Meath, whose son, the author, was serving in Boston as a captain in The Fourth, or King's Own Regiment. It expressed so clearly the resentful sentiments of the British forces in America at that time that I take leave to reproduce them here *in extenso*, but omitting personal particulars interesting only to the family.

To the Rev. Doctor Evelyn [his father], *Trim, Ireland*

BOSTON CAMP, *October* 31st 1774

MY DEAR SIR,

It happens so seldom that we have the opportunity of a King's ship going from hence, that we are glad to lay hold of every one that offers to let our friends hear from us; they must be a good deal alarmed for us indeed, if ever they see the bold and desperate resolves of every village in New England, and must conclude that two or three thousand poor fellows of us must have long since been devoured by men of their mighty stomachs; but here we still are in our peaceful camp, and in the same situation as when I last wrote to you; nothing of any consequence has happened, but great preparations for hostilities making on both sides. We, on our part, have fortified the only entrance to the town by land, and thrown up a very extensive work in front of it. We have got General Haldimand, with the 47th Regiment and part of the 18th, from New York, with more artillery and military stores; two other Regiments, the 10th and 52nd, are coming in from Quebec, part of them already in the harbour; and we have a man-of-war, and two companies of the 65th from Newfoundland.

The good people of these provinces are getting ready as fast as they can; they are all provided with arms and ammunition, and every man who is able to use them is obliged to repair at stated times to the place of exercise in order to train; in short, the frenzy with which the people are seized is now got to such a pitch, that it can go but little farther, and they must either soon, very soon break out into civil war or take that turn which the people of England did at the time of the Restoration, and wreak their vengeance on those who have seduced and misled them. I believe never was so much mercy extended to any nation on the face of the earth: they are now in an absolute, open, avowed state of rebellion, and have committed every act of treason which can be devised, but that of openly attacking the troops, which they publicly declare their resolution of doing as soon as they are prepared, and the season will allow them, and they feel bold.

The people of England, in the time of Charles the First, behaved with decency and moderation compared with these. The 'North Briton,' 'Whisperer,' 'Parliamentary Spy,' 'Junius,' etc., are dutiful and respectful addresses compared to the publications here; never before did I see treason and rebellion naked and undisguised; it is the only occasion upon which they lay aside hypocrisy. We expected to have been in barracks by this time, but the sons of liberty have done every thing in their power to prevent our accommodation. As it was found difficult to furnish quarters for so many men, it was resolved (to avoid extremities) to build barracks on the Common, where we are encamped; for some regiments timber was provided, and the frames pretty well advanced, when they thought proper to issue their orders to the carpenters to desist from working for the troops, upon pain of their displeasure. And one man who paid no attention to their order, was waylaid, seized by the mob, and carried off, and narrowly escaped hanging. However, the Government have procured distilleries and vacant warehouses sufficient to hold all the regiments, and our own artificers, with those of the men-of-war, and about 150 from New York and Halifax, are now at work upon them, and we hope to get into them in ten days or a fortnight. They have also forbid all merchants from furnishing their enemies with blankets, tools, or materials of any kind, and have endeavoured to hinder our getting bricks to build chimneys in our barracks, and threatened to prohibit all provisions being brought to market; but the force of English gold no Yankee can withstand, were it offered to purchase his salvation. I can give you no description of the 'holy men of Massachusetts,' by which you can form a just idea of what they are. There are no instances in history to compare them by; the Jews at the time of the siege of Jerusalem seem to come near them, but are injured and disgraced by the comparison.

I beg my best love to all my friends; I should be glad to hear something of them when you have a spare half-hour.

> I am, dear Sir,
> Your ever affectionate,
> W. G. EVELYN

To the Rev. Doctor Evelyn [his father], *Trim, Ireland*

BOSTON, *February* 18th 1775

MY DEAR SIR,

About the 10th of this month, I received your letter (the only one I have got from you) dated the 2nd of November, though it was not opened, as mine to you had been, yet it did not fall short of it in expense, as every letter we receive by the New York Packet costs us three-pence for every pennyweight; for which reason I wish our friends would endeavour to write to us by vessels bound to Salem or Marble Head, or try to have their letters sent in General Gage's bag, as Mr. Butler sends his to his son, and saves him by that means fifteen or twenty shillings a-month. If you would be kind enough to enclose any

nd to urge them on to sedition, treason, and rebellion,
n hopes of profiting by the general distraction.

This is the case of our great patriot and leader, Sam
Adams. Hancock, and those others whose names you hear,
are but his mere tools; though many of them are men of no
mean abilities. Hancock is a poor contemptible fool, led
about by Adams, and has spent a fortune of thirty thousand pounds upon that infamous crew; has sacrificed all
he was worth in the world to the vanity of being admitted
among them, and is now nearly reduced to a state of beggary. The steps by which the *sons of liberty* have proceeded, and the strides with which they are now hasting
to rebellion and civil war, are set forth in a very masterly
manner by a writer (on our side), under the signature of
Massachusettensis; which papers, as far as they have been
hitherto published, I have enclosed to Mr. Butler at the
Castle, directed for you; they will give you a better idea
of the nature of this important contest than any on the
other side, which are composed of sedition, treason, misrepresentation, and falsehood, framed by villains of the
first water, and greedily swallowed with the credulity of
ignorance, and the malignant zeal of inveterate fanatics.

It is but very lately that a Tory writer dare appear, or
that a Printer could be prevailed on to publish any thing
on the side of Government; and nothing now protects
them, but the presence of the troops in Boston. Those who
have remained in the country, whose circumstances and
situation would not admit of their leaving their families,
are hourly in danger. Some are prisoners in their own
houses; a mob constantly mounting guard about them, lest
they should escape; and others have been treated with the
utmost barbarity. Words cannot give you an idea of the
nature of the lower class of people in this province: they
are utterly devoid of every sentiment of truth or common
honesty: they are proscribed throughout the whole Continent, and possess no other human qualities but such as are
the shame and reproach of humanity.

As the event of this very important question depends
upon the determination of the people of Great Britain, and
as they have such unhappy divisions, and so many dangerous enemies to their country among themselves, it is im-

letter for me to him, I am sure he would be
as to send it to the Secretary of State's office ₁
and I should receive it with the General's despat

That lies innumerable should be circulated
papers with regard to what is passing here is
strange, when in this very town, where we are up
spot, the most false, impudent, and incredible re
are every day published concerning us; but the fact i
authors know them to be false, and that not a perso₁
this town (of about twenty thousand inhabitants) belie
a word of them; but they are calculated for the poor d
luded wretches in the country, who are politicians, an₁
swallow everything they see in those seditious papers (and
none other are they allowed to read) with a credulity not
equalled even in old England; and by this means is the
spirit of faction kept alive, and the schemes of a few enterprising, ambitious demagogues made to pass upon the
people for their own act and deed. I said *of a few;* a great
many doubtless appear to be concerned in carrying on the
business; but would you believe it, that this immense continent from New England to Georgia is moved and directed by one man! [1] a man of ordinary birth and desperate fortune, who by his abilities and talent for factious
intrigue, has made himself of some consequence, whose
political existence depends upon the continuance of the
present dispute, and who must sink into insignificancy and
beggary the moment it ceases.

People in general are inclined to attribute the ferment
that at present subsists in this country to a settled plan and
system, formed and prosecuted for some years past by a
few ambitious, enterprising spirits; but in my opinion the
true causes of it are to be found in the nature of mankind;
and I think that it proceeds from a new nation, feeling
itself wealthy, populous, and strong; and that they being
impatient of restraint, are struggling to throw off that
dependency which is so irksome to them. The other seems
to me to be only the consequence; such a time being most
apt for men of abilities, but desperate fortunes, to set themselves forward to practise upon the passions of the people,
foment that spirit of opposition to all law and government,

[1] *scilicet* Samuel Adams.

possible to form any conjecture about it. We who know our own powers, and the helpless situation of the people, consider it as the most fortunate opportunity for Great Britain to establish her superiority over this country; even to reduce it to that state of subjection, which the right of conquest may now give her the fairest title to; at least, to keep it in that state of dependency which they are now avowedly attempting to free themselves from, and which, had they waited for another century, they would probably achieve. Though the point at present in view is, to be independent of Great Britain, and to set up for themselves, yet I do not believe the most sanguine of them have any expectation of accomplishing it at this time; but they hope to make some approaches, and to gain something towards it. In this struggle their great dependence is upon the tenderness and clemency of the English, who they imagine will consider them under infatuation, and will give up some points to them out of humanity, rather than push matters to extremity; and indeed, they may with reason think so, for under no other Government on the face of the earth would they have been suffered to perpetrate so many horrid villainies, as they have done, without being declared in a state of rebellion, and having fire and sword let loose among them. From the accounts given by the faction, people would imagine that the colonies were unanimous to a man in their opposition to Government, but the contrary is the fact; there is a very large party in our favour, and thousands inclined to our side, who dare not openly declare themselves, from an apprehension that Government may leave them in the lurch; this you may depend upon as a certain truth, that those gentlemen who have declared on our side are men of the best property in this country, and those who before these troubles were in the highest esteem, and most respected among the common people.

The hour is now very nigh in which this affair will be brought to a crisis. The resolutions we expect are by this time upon the water, which are to determine the fate of Great Britain and America. We have great confidence in the spirit and pride of our countrymen, that they will not tamely suffer such insolence and disobedience from a set of upstart vagabonds, the dregs and scorn of the human species; and that we shall shortly receive such orders as will authorize us to scourge the rebellion with rods of iron. Under this hope have we been hitherto restrained, and with an unparalleled degree of patience and discipline have we submitted to insults and indignities, from villains who are hired to provoke us to something that may be termed an outrage, and turned to our disadvantage; but these are all treasured up in our memories against that hour in which we shall 'cry havock, and let slip the dogs of war.' Excuse my indignation, I cannot speak with patience of this generation of vipers. If any troops should be ordered from Ireland with officers of distinction, I should beg your interest to procure me some recommendations.

You must not believe implicitly the reports that are spread of the deaths and desertions among the troops; there have been some, and some regiments have been more unlucky than others; but it is very trifling, when you consider that no pains or expenses have been spared to seduce our men. Our regiment, nevertheless, has not lost more than we usually have done in the same length of time in Great Britain. The weather is delightful beyond description, and we are in perfect good health and spirits.

Wishing the same to all friends at home,

I am, dear Sir,

Your ever affectionate,

W. G. E.

Dean Evelyn died in his Dublin residence a few days before I sailed for America and Captain Evelyn did not long survive his parent. On August 27th of the same year he led the British advance in the battle of Long Island, being with the Brigade of Light Infantry, and took five American officers prisoners who were sent in advance to observe the motions of our army in the direction of Jamaica Pass. The overwhelming victory of that day was in great measure due to this capture. He was mortally wounded at the skirmish at Throg's Neck two months later.

CHAPTER

9

THE AMOUNT of troops for which General Gage called staggered the Ministry. They had already voted him a reinforcement of ten thousand men, which had been thought more than handsome: and the troops now actually stationed in Boston amounted to about four thousand. The Earl of Sandwich, the First Lord of the Admiralty, refused to believe that the threat was so serious as was made out. He pronounced the Americans cowards (though unknown to him personally) and regretted that there was no probability of our troops encountering without delay two hundred thousand of such a rabble, armed with old rusty firelocks, pistols, staves, clubs, and broomsticks; and of exterminating them at one blow. Colonel Grant, in the Commons, agreed with the noble Lord 'the colonists possess not a single military trait and would never stand to meet the English bayonet.' He had been in America, he said, and disliked their manner of speaking equally with their way of life, and held them to be 'entirely out of humanity's reach.' Colonel Grant was taken up by Mr. Cruger, an American-born member, and reminded that his own services in the Alleghany mountains had been of no very triumphant character. (The speaker called Mr. Cruger to order before he could say more.) However, Lord North considered these views too sanguine; and since it was impossible to send the troops that General Gage demanded, without stripping the whole Empire, he made a new attempt at conciliating the Americans. He undertook to exempt from taxation any province which would of its own free will make a reasonable contribution to the common defence of America and provision for the support of the civil government.

The Whig Opposition had encouraged their friends in America to believe that England could not or would not make war on them, the country in general being so averse to this, or at least would not venture more than a short campaign. It was true that England stood to lose by the conflict immensely more than she could gain; for the prosperity of the manufacturing towns in the North of England depended largely on the continuance of close relations with the colonies, and the London merchants alone were owed close on a million pounds by their American customers. The chief Opposition speaker, Mr. Fox, now assured the House that the Americans must and would reject Lord North's offer with contempt. To accept exemption from a tax, as an indulgence, and on condition of performing an act equivalent to paying it, would be to admit a principle of liability which every American would oppose with his life's blood. In the Lords, the Earl of Chatham, the gout still heavy on him, spoke of the disdain with which the whole world and Heaven itself regarded the forces entrenched behind Boston Neck: 'An impotent general and a dishonoured army, trusting solely to the pick-axe and the spade for security against the just indignation of an injured and insulted people.'

But Lord North's offer of exemption from taxation came too late in any case; for the first skirmish of the war had already been fought, with the loss of many lives, and from either side complaints of barbarities done contrary to English usage. This was the Lexington affair and it gave an interesting foretaste of the style of fighting that our armies might expect when the campaign began in earnest.

General Gage, having been informed that an important quantity of military stores had been collected by the revolutionaries at Concord, about twenty miles from Boston, decided to seize these by the sudden secret descent of a large body of troops. At ten o'clock on the night of April 18th 1775 a contingent of some seven hundred picked men, namely, the flank companies (the Grenadier and Light Infantry companies) of the twelve or thirteen battalions of the garrison were rowed over in boats with muffled oars from the town, and up Charles River for a mile or two. They were there disembarked and began a silent march on Concord. Though they proceeded with the greatest caution, securing every person whom they met, in order to prevent the alarm being spread, they soon found by the continual firing of guns and ringing of bells that they were discovered. By five o'clock in the morning they had reached Lexington, after a march of fifteen miles: where militia and minute-men (troops so-called from their readiness to rise to arms at a minute's notice, though continuing meanwhile at their ordinary trades) were drawn up on the green to oppose them.

Major Pitcairne, who commanded the advance guard, rode forward and called on them in the King's name to disperse. But they would not. At this moment some shots were fired from a house facing the green, wounding one man and striking the Major's horse in two places. The Americans, however, declare that the Major fired first, with a pistol, and that the English in consequence were to blame for the sequel. Our people at once returned the fire, killing and wounding eighteen of the militiamen, who broke and fled. The march to Concord was then resumed, where the advance guard found no muskets or ammunition, but spoilt some barrels of flour, knocked the trunnions off three old field-pieces, and cut down a Liberty pole—a sort of May pole which was used by the Sons of Liberty as a standard and rallying point of rebellion. There then ensued a sharp skirmish for the possession of a bridge over a river beyond the town. Many Americans and British were killed. It was declared by our people, and furiously denied by the other side, that some of the dead and wounded were scalped by Americans who had adopted this savage and singular custom from the Red Indians. If this was indeed so, it was not remarkable. The Government of Pennsylvania, of which the respectable Governor Penn and Dr. Benjamin Franklin were members, had, but a few years before, offered a bounty for Indian scalps, male and female. Also there was precedent for the taking of white scalps: many had been lifted from Frenchmen in the late war by the Rangers of Connecticut, an act which they glorified.

Here I may interpolate a few remarks upon scalp-taking. The Indians set so much store upon the taking of scalps that it was regarded as of less honour to kill three men in battle and leave them undespoiled than to take the scalp of one, even if he had fallen to another's tomahawk. It was not, as is supposed, the general practice of the scalper to remove the whole fleece of hair, but only the central lock. This, twisted and grasped in the left hand, gave the needed purchase for scoring and scooping from around it, with a knife, a little piece of the skin, about the size of a priest's tonsure. Should the victim be bald, however, or short-haired, the Indians would rip off more, often using their teeth to loosen the skin from the bone. If the scalp were taken in revenge for some injury, as was almost always the case, that of a woman or child was prized more highly than that of a man. A wounded person who has been scalped very often recovers, though the hair never grows again on the crown of the head. I observed one or two scalped men in the back parts of Virginia when I was in captivity there, and lodged with a settler who proudly showed me a pair of scalps that he had himself ripped from Cherokee Indians that he had shot. He had dressed them in Indian fashion by sewing them upon a hoop with deer sinews, and painting them red for the sake of show.

On their retirement from Concord, after a two hours' halt, the British troops were shot at, the whole length of the march, by Americans concealed behind stone walls, of which there were many in the cleared land, or behind trees in the uncleared parts, and taking every advantage that the face of the country afforded them. They never showed themselves in bodies of more than a few men at a time, and immediately retired when any movement was made against them, yet persisted about the column like a swarm of mosquitoes. The column being confined to the road and unable to extend to protect their flanks, because of the continual obstacles of stone walls, dense woods, and morasses to be encountered, suffered very heavily. A minute-man, supported perhaps by a single neighbour or kinsman, would conceal himself behind a bush at fifty paces from the road, and as the tail of the column was passing would discharge his single shot, his companion holding his fire in case there were retaliation. Then they would lie still until the danger had passed.

These countrymen were bred to the musket or rifle-gun from boyhood, and their experience of fighting against the

Indians, or of stalking bears, deer, and other game, had taught them a mode of fighting which to our people seemed mean and skulking; but it certainly caused us much damage and themselves very little and transgressed no rule of civilized warfare. In Europe, to be sure, armies advance towards each other in solid mass, the lines perfectly dressed, with standards flying, drums beating; and tear away at each other with disciplined and simultaneous volleys. But that manner is only a custom of warfare, not a rule; and the Americans saw no reason why they should adopt it to their own disadvantage. Whenever during the war their Continental Line, who were trained in European style, dared to engage our people in a pitched battle they were almost invariably routed; for the British Army was second to none in the formal manner of fighting.

It was surprising that our men escaped as they did. They had already marched twenty-five miles, with smart fighting thrown in, and on empty stomachs, too, for their provision carts were captured. When they reached Lexington again, where a force of eight hundred men, including the main body of the Royal Welch Fusiliers, came hurrying up to their relief, they had expended all their ammunition; and their tongues were hanging out, like dogs', for thirst and weariness. There were two six-pounder field-pieces with the newly arrived troops, which were used with deterrent effect against the Americans; who were by now treading close on the heels of the exhausted column, groaning in derision, 'Britons Strike Home!' and uttering their war-cry of 'King Hancock for Ever!' Despite these guns, the Americans continued with irregular shooting from flanks, front, and rear. Our men threw away their fire very inconsiderately and without being certain of its effect; for many of them were young soldiers, who had been taught that quick firing struck terror into the enemy. But, on the contrary, doing so little execution, it emboldened the Americans to come closer. The noise of battle now brought up fresh reinforcements of Mohairs (as these soldiers without uniforms were contemptuously called in the English ranks) from all the surrounding countryside; and the fatigued column must run the gauntlet of successive companies of cool marksmen, who were often commanded by the Congregational minister of their township, dressed in his preaching clothes. It is said that for want of material these warlike men of God had suffered their religious books to be converted into wadding for their cartridges, especially the hymnals of Dr. Isaac Watts. Then: 'Put a little Watts into 'em, Brethren' was a catchword of the day.

The firing was now heavy from the houses on the road-side, and the British were so enraged at suffering from an unseen enemy that they forced open many of these build-ings and put to death all the defenders; in some cases, seven or eight men. Often they found these houses ap-parently deserted; but soon as the march was resumed, the defenders climbed out of their hiding-places and the pop-ping shots began again from the rear. Before the day was out the enemy numbered some four thousand men, yet no more than fifty were ever seen together at a time, out of respect for the six-pounder guns. No women and chil-dren were, I believe, encountered during the day, all such having doubtless been removed from the neighbourhood at the first warning of battle; certainly none was deliber-ately killed in the houses, as the American leaders alleged against us to incite the vengeance of their followers. It is true that, notwithstanding the efforts of the officers, a few soldiers carried off small articles of plunder from the houses thus broken into; but the day was too hot and the men too weary for the practice to become general.

At length the straggling column reached Charlestown Neck, near Boston, where the guns of the men-of-war anchored close by protected them, and the rebel fire ceased. The Grenadiers and Light Infantry had marched forty miles and eaten nothing for a day and a night; and it was past midnight of the 19th before they reached barracks and bed. Our casualties were near three hundred men killed and wounded, including a number of officers; the Americans lost only a third of that number. Many provi-dential escapes from death were reported. The Earl of Percy, who commanded the relieving force, lost a button shot off his waistcoat; a man of my acquaintance had his cap blown three times off his head and two bullets through his coat, one of these carrying away his bayonet. Lieu-tenant Hawkshaw of the Fifth Fusiliers received a bullet through both cheeks, which also removed several teeth; but did not by any means regard this as a providential escape. He had been accounted the greatest beauty in the Army and was now bitterly mortified in the sad alteration to his appearance.

The affair at Lexington animated the courage of the Americans to the highest degree, insomuch that in a few days their army amounted to twenty thousand men and was continually increasing. Congress appointed George Washington to be Commander-in-Chief of the American armies. His fighting service had ended sixteen years previously, nor had he ever commanded above twelve hundred men. He was chosen chiefly as being a wealthy aristocrat from Virginia, in order to flatter the South into common action with the revolutionary North. John Adams proposed his name. He first enumerated the high qualities that a commander-in-chief should possess, and then remarked that, fortunately, such qualities resided in a member of their own body. At this 'King' Hancock was all satisfaction and smiles, believing that the speaker could only be pointing at him, and Mr. Adams afterwards wrote that never in his life had he seen so sudden a change on any man's face as on John Hancock's when George Washington's name was mentioned in place of his own. Samuel Adams seconded the nomination, which was passed unanimously. General Washington, in accepting, declined to take any payment for his services: which gave him much popularity.

Boston was now completely invested and those critics were confounded who held that a regiment or two could force their way through any part of the continent, and that the very sight of a grenadier's cap would be sufficient to put an American army to flight. The news was especially gratifying to Colonel Hancock, who was to have been charged on the day of the battle with defrauding the customs by smuggling to the tune of half a million dollars. The lawyer he had briefed for his defence was Samuel Adams.

There was worse to come: the battle miscalled that of Bunker's Hill. About the end of May 1775 reinforcements of British troops arrived in Boston under the command of

Generals Howe, Clinton, and Burgoyne whose services in the preceding war had gained them great reputation: bringing up the number of troops in the town to some seven thousand men. A few days later General Gage issued a proclamation to the Americans who 'with a preposterous parade of military arrangement affect to hold the Royal Army besieged': in which he offered pardon to all who would lay down their arms, and thus stand separate and distinct from the parricides of the Constitution. The only persons excepted from this pardon were Colonel Hancock and Mr. Samuel Adams. No revolutionaries offered their submission in reply.

Opposite the city of Boston and separated from it by the Charles River, which was about the breadth of the Thames at London Bridge, another peninsula of much the same size as Boston's jutted towards it, and was similarly joined to the main land by a narrow neck. Charlestown lay at one corner of the flat head of this other peninsula, which was formed mainly of a steep ridge, Charlestown Heights, whose two humps were known as Bunker's Hill and Breed's Pasture; of which Bunker's Hill was both the loftier and the farther from Boston. General Gage, observing that Charlestown Heights commanded the whole of Boston, decided on the precaution of occupying Bunker's Hill. He was, however forestalled by the revolutionaries, who had spies everywhere. Learning of his intention, they decided to seize the hill and fortify it themselves: to show their power and provoke the British to a battle in conditions favouring defence rather than attack.

On the night of June 16th 1775, then, a detachment of some twelve hundred Massachusetts Militia crossed Charlestown Neck with entrenching tools and set hastily to work under the orders of an engineer. Because of some mistake it was the lesser hill, Breed's Pasture, close to Charlestown, that they pitched upon; which was a less defensible position and did not offer so ready an escape over the Neck. Here they worked with such diligence and silence that before dawn they had nearly completed a strong redoubt, mounting ten cannon, and a six-foot-high entrenchment which extended one hundred paces to their left, facing Boston.

When discovered by the British troops at about five o'clock the redoubt was plied with an incessant cannonade from the line-of-battle ships and floating batteries in the river, besides the cannon that could carry across from Boston, three-quarters of a mile distant. Many of the Americans soon ran, including all the gunners, who took four guns off with them, crying that this was murder and that they had been betrayed. However, about five hundred of them coolly continued their work, which they completed about noon; for because of the steep elevation the damage done by our cannonade was not so severe as was predicted.

Meanwhile General Gage as Commander-in-Chief called his Major-Generals together for a council of war. General Sir Henry Clinton, supported by Generals Sir William Howe and John Burgoyne, proposed (very correctly) sending round a picked force of Grenadiers, supported by artillery, to make a landing on the neck of the Charlestown peninsula, which was not two hundred paces wide, and so cut off the retreat of the Americans. This might well have been done without loss. We held command of the water, which was navigable to shallow craft on either side of the Neck, and the Americans encamped on the Neck were in no posture to stand an attack with bayonets. Those on the peninsula must then have chosen between starvation or surrender.

But General Gage opposed this plan. He resolved instead to land a considerable force at Moulton's Point (the right-hand corner of the peninsula, as you look across from Boston) and drive the rebels off the heights by force of arms. He could not resist giving the troops the chance for which they had been so long clamouring: which was to come to grips with the enemy and give them a good drubbing. Boston had lately been a cramped and miserable station, a by-word for high prices and low fever. All longed for a sortie. 'Once let us get into the back country,' cried General Burgoyne, 'and we'll soon find elbow-room!'

Two thousand five hundred troops were therefore landed at Moulton's Point under the command of Major-General Sir William Howe. At three o'clock in the afternoon the advance began, one division deploying against the

enemy's left, intending to turn it and seize Bunker's Hill
in the rear; another making a frontal attack against the
Redoubt on Breed's Pasture.

The day was exceedingly hot, the grass stood knee-high.
Yet the men, dressed in their heavy greatcoats, were bur-
dened, besides their rifles and ammunition, with blankets,
heavy full packs and three days' provisions a man—the
whole weighing above 100 pounds; Mr. Commissary Sted-
man, the historian, rates it at 125 pounds. They advanced
very slowly, the ground being broken by a succession of
high fences; and the ridge, though at its highest point it
rose no more than one hundred and ten feet above the
river, seemed to them like Snowden or the Pyrenees.

The Americans had now been greatly reinforced and,
before the close of the battle, numbered more than three
thousand men. Of these a thousand from New Hampshire
and Connecticut, good men, went to line a long fence, of
stone below and rails above, which protected their left.
This barricade lay 'refused'—that is, somewhat behind the
line of the entrenchment—and along lower ground. They
had stuffed the interstices with grass, and the front was
protected by another rail fence of the zigzag or Virginian
sort. The advance was not supported by artillery as
strongly as it should have been; for at least four reasons.
In the first place, the guns that fired grape, that most
horrific shot, were mired in a soft patch. In the second, the
shot in the side boxes of our six-pounders were, by an
error, twelve-pound balls. In the third, the Chief of
Artillery, Colonel Cleaveland, was not with the batteries,
being absent at a Latin lesson, which is to say that he was
spending his morning in company with pretty Miss Lovell,
daughter of the master of the Latin School. In the fourth,
General Gage had failed to arrange with Admiral Samuel
Graves, with whom he was not on the most cordial terms,
to cover his advance on the right. Gun-boats of light
draught or the *Symmetry* transport, which mounted several eighteen-pounder guns, might have raked the enemy
position from end to end.

The battle was joined near simultaneously along the
whole half-mile of the position, but our men were allowed
to fire their volley too soon—the Americans not yet even

showing their hats above the entrenchments, except for a few look-out men and officers. General Putnam, who was mounted and seemed to be in effective command of the American forces—though there was no hierarchy of rank as yet in this disorderly army—galloped from point to point and swore to shoot any man who fired before the enemy came within point-blank range. The Americans feared and obeyed this violent man, who, by the bye, claimed to have killed and scalped a number of Frenchmen in the previous war. Guided by him, the Massachusetts officers ran very boldly along the parapet, kicking up their men's muskets.

When at length the American volley was permitted, the execution done was terrible. Not only was the general fire well aimed—'Aim at the waist-belt' was their cry—but they had marksmen armed with rifle-guns whose sole charge it was to pick off the royal officers, conspicuous in the bright sun by the glittering gorgets at their throats. The attack was broken all along the line, the front ranks withering away; the remainder, finding themselves leaderless, retired out of range, re-formed and again advanced against the enemy, the companies being now generally commanded by sergeants. The oldest officers and soldiers engaged, among them some who had fought at Minden and other great battles of the Seven Years' War, declared it was the hottest service they had ever seen. The enemy were employing slugs and buckshot in their firelocks, and the wounds that ensued were the despair of our surgeons.

The second attack failed, as the first had done, though personally led by General Howe. It was he who had taken the forlorn-hope up the Heights of Abraham on the glorious day that General Wolfe captured Quebec from the French and made Canada ours. He soon found himself standing alone, before the rail-fence, the whole of his staff of twelve officers having been either killed or wounded, though he was unhurt. He was a tall, large, swarthy man, somewhat of a voluptuary; and very German in appearance, being descended, like Lord North, from George I and a German mistress, though she was a different one from Lord North's grand-dam. His coolness and officer-like behaviour on this occasion cannot be too much ap-

plauded. He went over to the troops who had been flung
back from the Redoubt and ordered them to unbuckle
their packs and remove their greatcoats, together with all
other impediments to action. 'The third try is lucky, my
brave boys,' he is reported to have said, 'and this time we'll
take the bayonet to 'em only.' If he said this, it was a long
speech for him: for he was almost as silent a man as his
brother Admiral Sir Richard Howe, whom the sailors
called 'Black Dick.' He kept his self-possession so wonderfully that when a certain general officer, meeting him
later upon the field of battle, made a teasing remark about
the costliness of 'this new sort of light infantry tactics' he
only grinned in reply.

The British batteries in Boston, and the ships' guns, now
punished Charlestown with red-hot balls and carcasses (or
incendiary shells), for enemy musket-fire from the houses
and the meeting-house steeple had been galling our left.
Soon five hundred wooden houses were in one great blaze.
The smoke and cinders blew into our soldiers' eyes, already sore with the sweat pouring from their brows, and
made them swear loudly; yet they answered General
Howe's summons with a cheer and, for the third time,
advanced intrepidly against the Redoubt. This time the
Americans, who were pretty short of ammunition and
lacked bayonets, would not face the assault, though outnumbering our people by two to one. With their trousers
rolled high above their naked feet and ankles, they scrambled out of the trenches. The majority of them got safe
back across the Neck, which was now swept by the ships'
fire, but many were caught. The Grenadier company of
the Royal Welch Fusiliers, with which in after years I
had the honour to serve, had the post of honour on this
occasion, and lost every man but five of its three-and-
thirty: nevertheless these five managed to make good an
oath of vengeance sworn after the first attack against a
certain sharp-shooter. He stood upon a cask placed on the
banquette of the Redoubt, three feet above his fellows, and
was known to have wounded their company officer, Captain Blakeny, and accounted for three subaltern officers besides. He was perfect at a hundred paces and was kept constantly nourished with loaded rifles by his comrades. This

champion maintained his fire to the last; but the Grenadiers, when they came up with him, and he fought with his rifle-butt, drove their bayonets through his vitals again and again. It was said that three of our officers were in the first assault shot in the back by men behind. This was not deliberately done, the men's loyalty being beyond question: it was, I believe, due to crowding and overlapping at the corner of the Redoubt.

So exhausted were the troops, and their losses so calamitous, that General Howe did not pursue the enemy over Charlestown Neck and on to their headquarters to Cambridge. He contented himself with occupying Bunker's Hill and fortifying it. The Americans thereupon fortified Prospect Hill, at a little distance beyond the Neck (a place with which I was two years later to form a long and miserable acquaintance), and gave our people to understand that they were prepared to sell this eminence at the same price as the last. Our casualties were nearly one thousand men, and ninety-two officers, among these Major Pitcairne, who fell with four balls in his body, the last one fired by a Negro soldier. The Americans lost something more than four hundred killed and wounded, and five guns out of the six that remained.

The general comment among the men was that we had taken the bull by the horns, but would have been better advised to sneak round behind, as mastiffs do in bull-baiting, and fasten upon a softer part. It was also commonly agreed that it had been a mere libel on common sense to take post at Boston of all places in the whole continent, unless in overwhelming strength; for the city was commanded all round—a mere target or Man of the Almanack, with the points of the swords directed at every feature. It was not many weeks before the rebels also seized and fortified Dorchester Heights to the southward, and so served us notice to quit.

There were innumerable other complaints of blunders committed by our generals: for example, that General Gage had permitted all his cabinet papers, Ministers' letters, etc., and private correspondence with Loyalists to be stolen out of a large closet, or wardrobe up one pair of stairs on the landing at Government House, and that his wife was a prime treasoner, in secret communication with the enemy, to whom she disclosed all his military plans and dispositions. It was also urged that we should have lost no time in purchasing the American generals. I have heard Captain Montrésor, an American Loyalist and at this time Chief Engineer in America, declare that even General Israel Putnam could to his certain knowledge have been bought for one dollar a day, or eight shillings New York currency. He added that the following generals could have been obtained at a still more modest expense, viz. Lasher, the New York shoemaker; Heard, the Woodbridge tavern-keeper; Pribble, also a tavern-keeper from Canterbury in England; Seth Pomeroy, the gunsmith, and the other Putnam, namely Rufus, a carpenter of Connecticut. This Captain Montrésor was a bitter man, with a burden of grievances against fate and the British Government: he was six times wounded and six times lost his baggage in twenty-four American campaigns, yet was refused the rank corresponding with his important and extensive command; a restless ball was roaming in his body, resisting excision; he suffered from a hydrocele, a fistula, and a nervous spasm; the revolutionaries had burned to the ground his house and his out-houses, barns, and offices on Montrésor's Island, afterwards Talbot Island, eight miles from New York, for which he could obtain no restitution—and all these troubles were not one-half of his tale of woe. I expect that a modest allowance for exaggeration must therefore be made in his assessment of the venality of these Americans. He hated them so prodigiously for being tradesmen, rebels, and generals all together. I think that he had a grudge against Israel Putnam who had served with him at Niagara in 1764 in the Indian War. Yet he was one of the best-informed men and clearest speakers upon the situation in America to whom I ever had the privilege to listen. I later served under his son, a courageous officer of the Royal Welch Fusiliers, and heard many praises in many quarters of the old Captain and his wife: they kept open table in New York throughout the Revolution, when provisions were excessively dear, and converted their large mansion into a hospital for wounded officers. The whole family was ruined by the war.

CHAPTER

10

I CONCLUDED a previous chapter with an account of how I terminated my peace-time service in Ireland at the Cove of Cork, early in April 1776: by embarking for Quebec with the Ninth Regiment in which I was then a non-commissioned officer. The reason why ourselves and five other regiments of the Line, of which we were the eldest, were being sent to Canada was that news had reached England of a dangerous attempt on the part of the Americans to seize Canada, which was only lightly held by us. The enemy were under the command of Benedict Arnold, of Connecticut, an enterprising militia colonel, and Brigadier-General Montgomery, an Irishman who had formerly held the King's commission. It was commonly feared that our expedition of relief might not reach Quebec in time to prevent an insurrection of the French inhabitants, who numbered about five thousand, or the surrender of the small garrison for some other reason. How strange a war it already appeared! General Montgomery had, twenty years before, played the hero beside Sir William Howe and Sir James Wolfe during the famous capture of Quebec from the French.

It is important to distinguish the motives which prompted this invasion. The Americans' ostensible motive, which was to free the Canadians from British tyranny, must be taken at a heavy discount. A few dozen malcontents in Montreal and elsewhere may have been stirred by the appeal to revolt made by the American Congress of 1776; but in general the Canadians, who were all French, found themselves pretty well off under British rule. They rightly suspected the American offers of help in 'knocking off their chains' as too effusive to be disinterested. The fact was that the Americans wished to secure Canada mainly for reasons of strategy. They feared a British attack by land upon New England, and they wished to deny us naval bases in the St. Lawrence River. There were, besides, powerful Red Indian tribes resident in Canada, which then extended through the central part of what is now New York State, and behind the western boundaries of the other colonies, as far south as the great Mississippi River. These the British might persuade to light the flame of war along the whole inland frontier from New England to Virginia. If the Americans could strike suddenly and victoriously at the Canadian posts and prove that the British were not invincible, they might perhaps swing the Indians across to their own side. However, the more immediate object of their invasion was the capture of military stores from our arsenals at Montreal, St. John's, Quebec, and other places, of which they stood in great need.

In England, no news had been received from Quebec for some months, owing to the freezing of the St. Lawrence River, which cut our communications by sea. The last dispatches that had come were sent in the *Adamant* frigate, together with a few prisoners, on November 12th of the previous year. These told how Colonel Arnold's men had burst into Canada by the back door, that is to say by way of the Kennebec and Chaudière rivers, and, after a march of incredible hardship and exertions over unmapped country, were now within a mile of Quebec. Moreover, General Montgomery's column was knocking at the front door, having moved up by the more familiar route of the Lakes George and Champlain; and the important posts of St. John's and Chambly, with their garrisons, had already fallen to him. Montreal, a city of twelve thousand inhabitants, the largest on the whole American continent, was to be abandoned to this second column for want of troops to defend it; so that in all Canada no place of importance but only Quebec remained in our hands.

It seemed evident that, soon as we disembarked upon the farther shore of the ocean, we would find ourselves hotly engaged with the American colonists, whose fighting abilities the news of Lexington and Bunker's Hill had warned us not to underrate. It was therefore with indescribable emotions that early in the morning of April

8th I stood on the deck of the *Friendship* transport and eyed my native country, as we prepared to leave the harbour. It was bitterly cold for that time of year, though the sun was shining brightly, for a strong north-easterly wind blew. The exit to the cove was by means of a somewhat narrow strait. On the right hand stood the fortifications and the solidly built barracks which we had just quitted; the green hills beyond, spotted with white flocks of sheep, looked delightful as a background to the intervening blue waters. I leaned over the rail, gazing at them. and wondered when, if ever, I should look on them again. There was a certain luxuriousness in my melancholy, which almost drew tears from me, as it did from many of my messmates who were exceedingly drunk. In the *Swallow* transport, which lay a cable's length from us, the military band of The Ninth was playing a lively air, and similar strains proceeded from several other ships of the three hundred which composed our convoy. Two fine frigates were to escort us: we could make out their topsails at the head of the line.

Soon we heard the boom of signal guns, every mast-head broke out with bunting; one by one the ships' crews heaved up their anchors and away slid the ships. The wind was favourable, the tide ran fast, and soon we were racing out through the strait with huzzas and nautical melodies, and the barrack buildings dwindled in the distance. I took a deep tug at my spirit flask, and after one more lingering view of Ireland, went below.

Mr. Lindsay, the Scottish surgeon of The Ninth, who had been pleased to take a kindly interest in me, had given me much useful advice; for he was sailing in another, and larger, transport. I had inquired of him how best to keep myself and the men under my immediate supervision in good health during our passage. He observed, first, that during the first two weeks of sailing there was generally little sickness, except the usual nausea which persons unused to the sea feel and which has no ill effect. Against this sickness, abstinence from fluids was proper, and he recommended magnesia and walking on deck. After this first fortnight, however, a different diet became necessary. The men were given spirits and water instead of small beer, and were obliged to eat salted meat. This diet was not unwholesome, unless the water were putrid, which, however, was common both on the transports and the ship-of-war. Mr. Lindsay recommended sweetening the water for the men of my mess by hoisting the butts out of the hold and pumping the contents with a hand-pump from one butt to another; and continuing this method every day, for three days, before the water was put into the scuttle-butt.

'Above all,' said Mr. Lindsay, "if any of your men be sick, avoid if possible letting them be sent to the sick-bay, which has the worst circulation of air and which breeds disease in those who are confined there for some other cause—such as a broken limb—from the stench of their fellow-patients' evacuations and putrid sweats. This bay is in general dark and its cleanliness but little inspected into. To save life, good air is indispensable.'

On the surgeon's advice, I commenced a regimen of diet and living which was intended to season me for the severities and fatigues in store. I ate and drank sparingly, chose for my berth a place under the main hatchway, and slept on the boards.

Mr. Lindsay had spoken very passionately in my hearing about the negligence which condemned good men to die of disease on ship-board. 'More men by far are lost through injudicious management than by the violence of the most malignant diseases, especially in hot quarters of the globe. Putrid fevers are caught from the smell of the bilge-water lying at the ship's bottom: this becomes dangerously fetid from the soft loam and muddy matter of the ballast, along with the filth thrown down by the crew. This noxious air acts so powerfully that articles of silver taken into the hold are quickly turned to a black colour; and that the men who pump this water from the bilge are often overcome with giddiness, headaches, and fatal fevers. Great heavens, surely in an empire established, as ours is, in the ocean, the inquiry of the Medical Faculty and the constant care of naval officers should be particularly devoted to maintaining cleanliness on board and making arrangements, both in ship-building and general nautical economy, to keep vessels well ventilated! Ill health among troops stowed together in cramped quarters on ship-board promotes riots, quarrels, and ill behaviour: terrible accidents may derive from causes which at first seem insignificant. If only the whole of the Regiment could be transported in one vast ship, so that I might be able to exercise some guiding control over the health of men and officers! But I cannot be everywhere at once in a flotilla of forty craft, and naval surgeons are not provided except on warships; nor will the generality of officers heed me when I impress upon them the graveness of their responsibility for the men's health.'

We experienced rough weather almost as soon as we drew out of sight of land: we split one of our top-sails in a very high wind and broke some of our rigging, in which many sea-fowl became entangled, blown there by the force of the gale. The *Friendship*, in which the celebrated American privateer Paul Jones happened to have served his apprenticeship, was an old, crazy ship and rolled horribly, the gunwales being frequently under green water and the decks awash; so that the Captain was obliged to shut all the hatches. Hardly a soldier or soldier's wife but was overcome by the most dreadful nausea, and since we were all landsmen on board, we fully expected the ship to founder: but most of us were past caring. This ill weather continued for four days, though the hatches were not battened down for more than twenty-four hours, and at the end of that time the greater part of the men were still prostrated. It was not until much later that we recollected an Irishism of one of our recruits sufficiently to laugh as it deserved; he had come down from a visit to the deck in an ecstasy of terror, bawling out: 'O honeys, listen to me! We are all sure to be drowned, for the ship is sinking! Yet we shall be avenged, by my soul, for if she goes to the bottom that rogue of a captain will be accountable for our lives when we reach Quebec!'

At the height of the gale a soldier's wife was brought to bed; on which occasion, as the only person aboard with the least pretence to surgical knowledge and the least affected of any of the troops by sea-sickness, I was called upon to act as man-midwife. Another soldier's wife, who could not rise from her cot for weakness, offered me meanwhile not always coherent advice. I delivered the child creditably within three hours, and it survived the voyage. It will be wondered at, that I had the resolution to attempt this operation, when I tell my readers in what a place it was performed. The poor woman was stowed with two others and their husbands, all prostrated, besides three children (one of whom had a quinsy, from which it subsequently died) in a cabin which was a cube of seven feet—that is, seven feet long, seven feet broad, and seven feet high. Among these others was Mortal Harry and his wife, whom, when I first set eyes upon her and heard her tongue, I judged at once to be God's requital on him for his own wicked character. For one thing only I could feel grateful: that Harlowe and Mrs. Harlowe were not of this number. She was being employed as lady's maid, on another ship, by the wife of the adjutant.

After a week the weather improved, though the sun seldom pierced the clouds, and I was able to spend a deal of my time on deck. Lieutenant Sweetenham, who commanded the troops on the *Friendship*, was desired by the Captain to keep the private soldiers between decks as much as possible, since they interfered with the management of the ship. He consented, though I had already acquainted him with Surgeon Lindsay's views about the healthfulness of fresh air. I now urged that to spend a mere two hours a day on deck, which was all that they were now allowed, and which was occupied by arms drill, was a prejudice to their health; but the Lieutenant continued to defer to the Captain, at whose table he ate, and nothing was done in the matter. Lieutenant Sweetenham was a veteran officer, worn out by the service, to whom a disagreeable voyage was no novelty and who also considered that the men should not be pampered on any account. However, I went to the Mate, who happened to be acquainted with my father and was a good-natured man, and asked permission for the men directly under my charge to be allowed to come up on deck during his daylight watch to perform fatigue duties under his supervision. To this he was pleased to agree, since it saved his own men labour. I would allow no man to plead nausea as an excuse from this duty and was often obliged to tie a rope about some of the lazy ones, and have them hauled out into the fresh air by their more vigorous mess-

mates. As a further precaution against contagious disorders, I made every man wash and comb himself every
morning; and every day, unless it rained, had the beds
brought up on deck to be aired, and the berths sprinkled
with vinegar. In consequence, I had far fewer men on the
sick list in my mess of twenty-five than in the other, which
was Mortal Harry's, or than in messes of other transports.

Brooks the Dipper, on the thirteenth day of the voyage,
so far forgot the promise of good conduct that he had
made to Major Bolton that he stole a linen shirt from
Smutchy Steel's knapsack. Smutchy reported the loss to
me and I knew at once where to seek for the missing
garment, there being no dramshop keepers aboard to act
as receivers of purloined goods: I found Brooks wearing
it under his own.

When Lieutenant Sweetenham was informed of the
crime he decided to flog Brooks on the coming Sunday
after divine service: 'for,' he said, smiling, 'who knows but
that if I defer the penalty until we reach America, we
may all be drowned beforehand and justice cheated? The
King made a pretty hard bargain, Private Brooks, when he
engaged you.'

Brooks decided, on the contrary, that he would rather
drown than suffer another lashing. The next afternoon,
soon as I brought my mess upon deck for our daily
fatigue duty, Brooks broke from the party and, running
forward to the forecastle, leaped headlong into the sea.
The vessel in a moment made her way over him, and he
arose at the stern. We were travelling at a rate which
seemed about that of a man walking fast. I instantly ran
to the cabin where the Captain and the Lieutenant were
dining and crying 'Man overboard!' burst in without a
knock: for which lack of manners I was called a 'damned
insolent rascal' by the Captain, who continued with his
meal unperturbed. He presently complained, in a surly
way, after eating a mouthful or two, that this pother came
of permitting troops to go on deck at irregular hours.
Nevertheless, at Lieutenant Sweetenham's insistence, he
ordered the ship to be put about, and the boat to be
hoisted out and manned.

I then returned anxiously to the deck and was relieved

to make out the form of Brooks, at a little distance ahead of us, swimming strongly. He hoped, I dare say, to be picked up by some other ship of the convoy, at least a dozen sail of which lay astern within half a mile of us. He was soon overhauled and it was with some difficulty that the sailors could force him into the boat. When he was brought back to the ship he was ordered between decks and a sentinel placed over him until the Sunday morning. However, that night he was found to be in a high fever and continued very bad until almost the last day of the voyage, when Lieutenant Sweetenham mitigated the award to forty strokes of the rope's end, which was as much as he was judged capable of enduring. These were duly inflicted.

On the last day of April, at about nine o'clock, a little girl, the elder of the two grown children from the married cabin, came running up to me and, 'O, Mr. Lamb, dear Mr. Lamb,' she cried, 'I believe that mother will murder father. For pity's sake, Mr. Lamb, come at once and unbuckle them.'

I could not, in humanity, assure the child (who was, perhaps, seven years old) that, for all I cared, both her parents, who were Mortal Harry and his wife, Terrible Annie, might tear each other to little shreds and gobbets and be heartily welcome. I therefore hurried to the cabin, where I found the place in indescribable confusion, for breakfast had been in progress when the battle began. On the floor, in the narrow space between the bunks, the two drunken creatures were rolling among the wreckage of their meal, grappled together with the fearful, deadly fury of snake and vulture.

I had once been warned by my father never on any account to intervene in any quarrel or altercation between man and wife; 'Each,' he said, 'will equally resent it and make common cause against you.' But here was an exception to an excellent rule, for, being both beside themselves, neither seemed to notice my presence, not even when with a great effort I disengaged the woman's clutching hands from Mortal Harry's throat, so that he was narrowly preserved from throttling.

They rose—he to a crouching, and she to a kneeling

posture—and glared at each other, without a word. His face was mottled with blood, and one ear torn. At last he said in an odd, pitiful, complaining tone, to curdle the blood—and using no oaths, neither, which was remarkable: 'So you are too fine a lady to eat salted pork, are you, Annie, you touchy, passionate, ill-natured, contradictory woman? You would rather see me drowned first, you say? My dear, is that the truth now? You would rather see your Harry drown?'

'It would make my heart sing psalms, you great Limerick ape,' she replied, 'to know that you were fifty fathoms under the keel.'

Without another word Mortal Harry rushed out of the cabin and up the companion-ladder. The woman went slowly prowling after him, hissing between her teeth. I remained behind, to pacify the children and restore some sort of order to the cabin; for the sake of the poor mother of the child that I had delivered, who lay screaming in an hysterical manner, with a blanket thrown over her face. Suddenly the alarm of 'Man overboard!' was raised, and we felt the jar of the vessel being turned hard about. We were making six knots at the time, and there was a heavy swell. I hurried on deck to find Terrible Annie leaning against the fore-mast, laughing at her loudest. This occasioned great scandal among the seamen who heard her, for Mortal Harry had sunk to the bottom like a plummet and was seen no more. They threatened to throw her after him if she did not cease her cackle; but nothing would make her desist, so I called a drummer and a file of men who forced her below.

Let me here interpose as a remarkable fact that this poor widow had no difficulty at all in finding another mate; but so just were the workings of Providence, or whatever supernatural power regulates these matters, that the man she hit upon was Buchanan, the very same drunken corporal from whose depredations we had suffered so severely as recruits. The conclusion of that story I will not here anticipate.

Accidents are generally found to run in sequences of three, and this was no exception to the rule. Casey, the recruit whom I had been at such trouble to apprehend when he tried to desert in Dublin, was on deck four days later, during the drill hour; I was in charge of the parade. He had been provoked throughout the voyage by his comrades, who taunted him with the name of Jail-hound and with a legend of his having hanged his old mother in order to gain a small legacy by her decease. This he took very ill, and his obvious discomfiture encouraged his messmates to tease him further. It is true that he had been recruited in Downpatrick Jail, where he was confined on suspicion of some crime of violence, but murder was never imputed to him. When I gave the parade an order to stand easy, after the completion of an exercise, they proceeded as usual to chaff Casey. I did not prevent them, because that was outside my range of duty and, besides, the man had treated me very badly in deserting after I had advanced him money from my own pocket. Smutchy Steel now made some blockish remark, which was like a spark in the priming-pan. Casey stood and harangued them all in a high screaming voice, uttering dreadful curses upon them, and wishing that they might all soon become miserable and comfortless captives in the farthest parts of America, and suffer at their enemies' hands all and more than he had lately suffered from his supposed comrades. Then, in his full accoutrements, he ran and leapt off the forecastle from exactly the same spot that Brooks and Mortal Harry had chosen before him. The great deep swallowed him up in a moment.

These deaths greatly sobered the remainder of us, especially Smutchy Steel, who came to me the following day and asked as a favour whether I would instruct him in reading and writing! I readily consented and he learned very quick. There were no further casualties among the troops, in spite of salt-tack, weevil-ridden biscuit, and an increasing foulness of the water with which we mixed our grog. Even of this water there proved to be an insufficiency, the Captain having as a speculation filled a number of our water-butts with porter for sale to the Quebec garrison on his arrival. He prevented me also from sweetening the water for my mess in the manner recommended by Surgeon Lindsay, by withholding the hand-pumps necessary for the task lest we should damage them. I fell back upon the alternative method of scalding the water with irons made red-hot in the galley-furnace. The butts were old wine-butts, improperly cleaned, and in consequence many of us suffered much from dysentery, a miserable complaint for which the only specific we had was to swallow in brandy the rust scraped off an anchor-stock. The captains of transports were in general a set of men who had their own interest far closer at heart than the welfare of their country.

Towards the middle of May we approached the Banks of Newfoundland, which are a surprising range of sunken mountains, extending in a direct line not less than three hundred and thirty miles in length, and about seventy-five in breadth. The top of the ridge, which at its highest reaches within five fathoms of the water's surface, is fre-quented by vast multitudes of lesser fish on which the excellent cod feeds, fattens, and multiplies in inconceivable quantities. Though hundreds of vessels have been laden for centuries past from thence, no scarcity or decrease of cod happens.

During the greater part of our passage across the Banks we never saw the sun, owing to the thick, hazy atmosphere which prevails in that part of the ocean. For two days together a total darkness like midnight covered the sky, so that a continuous firing of guns and beating of drums was needed to enable the ships of the convoy to keep due distance and avoid fouling one another. There was also the danger of running down fishing-vessels, from whose unseen decks hoarse shouts of warning against collision frequently arose. In spite of such risks it was customary for convoys to travel along a depression in the middle of the Banks, which was named the Ditch. The water here was as calm as in a bay, though the winds on either side were extremely impetuous.

At last came a stiff wind and with it a break in the fog. We saw the disc of the sun, dim and red, but gradually blazing with what seemed to us more than its usual splendour. In the welcome light we observed how numer-ous a congregation of fishing-vessels, large and small, lay about us. In times of peace, we were told, more than three thousand sail were annually to be counted there. A vast

flock of sea-fowl was in attendance on the vessels, wheeling above them and ever and again swooping down to
the decks to snatch up a cod's head or some other fishy
prize. Besides the familiar gulls and many larger birds of
the same feather, we observed a flightless, swimming,
knowing sort, called penguins. They were sporting in
pairs here and there, and ducking deep down in the water
in chase of fish. Here the sea was no longer of the usual
azure blue, but of a sandy white colour. We were now
permitted to supplement our diet of salt meat and mag-
gotty biscuit with fresh-caught cod. We baited a hook
first with the entrails of a fowl and soon pulled up a
fish. The hook was then baited with the entrails of this
fish, which was gutted in its turn, and presently we were
hauling in cod as fast as one can imagine. The water mag-
nified the size of them so that it seemed almost impossible
to get them aboard, and their struggles were very obdurate.

The right of fishing on these Banks, though by the law
of nature it should have been common to all nations, had
been appropriated by the French and British, who at this
time had frigates constantly cruising there to prevent
encroachment by ships of other nations. And, by an Act
of the previous year, the revolted colonists of New England had been excluded from the Banks, though it was on
the cod-fishery that their wealth had been founded and
was still largely maintained. The New Englanders took
this very hard, and the fishermen of Marblehead and
Salem who lost their employment because of the Act were,
as privateers, to do us more mischief in the war almost than
any other class of Americans.

We passed close by several of these fishing-vessels, which
had galleries erected on the outside of the rigging from
the mainmast to the stern, and sometimes the whole length
of the ship. On the galleries were ranged barrels with the
tops struck out, into which the fishermen would get to
shelter themselves from the weather. The stay of these
vessels on the Banks was but short, for the method of
curing was as quick as the catching. As soon as the cod
was hauled up, the fisherman cut out its tongue, then
passed it to a mate who struck off its head, plucked out
liver and entrails, and tossed it to a third hand, who drew

out the bone as far as the navel; then down the carcass went into the hold. In the hold stood men who salted and ranged the cod-fish in exact piles, taking care that just sufficient salt was laid between each two rows of fish to prevent them from touching.

It was on this sunny day, May 14th, that we first saw icebergs; but these were small bergs floated down from the St. Lawrence River. Four days later we had a view of the mountains of Newfoundland, covered with snow. We had been forty days at sea without landfall and this dreary island was therefore very pleasant to our eyes. On the following day we entered the noble Bay of St. Lawrence, our fleet being all in sight. We doubled Cape Rosier and found ourselves in the St. Lawrence River itself, which at this place is no less than ninety miles in breadth, with very boisterous water. Soon we were boarded by our first visitors from the New World, at whom we all gazed with the greatest interest, as if to divine from his appearance what sort of fate we were destined to encounter.

He was a French-Canadian pilot, a low-statured, yellow-faced, merry man dressed in seal-skin jacket, well-tarred trousers and stout sea-boots. He affected also a prodigiously long pig-tail, bound with eel-skins, a heavy gilt crucifix about his neck and a round cap of white fox fur.

It was from this person that we heard the first particulars of the recent fighting, which had favoured our arms. The frigate had the day before signalled the fleet the good news that, though Montreal had been in American hands for some months now, the British standard still flew at Quebec. The pilot assured us, it was not to be expected that the Americans would stand their ground much longer, hearing of our approach. It was therefore with relieved minds and no immediate expectation of battle that we continued our voyage up the river.

We passed by Bored Island, so called from an opening in its middle through which a small schooner might pass with her sails up; and Miscon Island with its excellent harbour, in the offing of which a fresh spring spouted up to a considerable height from the salt water; and the Island of Birds, shaped like a sugarloaf, which gave off a most insufferable stench from the droppings of the innumerable sea-fowl that nested upon it—we sent our boat to it, which returned laden with eggs; and the large Island of Anticosti which, upon my inquiry, the pilot represented as absolutely good for nothing.

In the third week of May, we saw, for the first time since we left Ireland, houses and cultivated land: a number of pleasant-looking French plantations upon Mounts Notre Dame and St. Louis. Our navigation grew slow; for, after the river narrowed to about nine miles across at Red Island, shoals, sunken rocks, and whirlpools became frequent. It was here that I caught my first sight of the Indian aboriginals: three of them (of whom one appeared to be a chief by his feathered head-dress) passed within musket-shot of us in a birch-bark canoe, which they paddled downstream with inconceivable celerity. Their faces were painted with green stripes and they paid no attention at all to us when we hailed them.

Before the week was out we had passed by several more islands, but these for the most part well inhabited and cultivated. Stone churches, wayside crucifixes, and neat, whitewashed buildings with boarded roofs were now to be seen almost everywhere; and well-kept woods of red pine-trees, valuable for their profuse yield of turpentine, which we thought very graceful besides. The river-water was sweet to the taste at last, having been brackish for the first three hundred and thirty miles up from the ocean.

In the fourth week we entered a part of the river where the stream was no more than a mile across, and came to our destination—the noble port of Quebec, remarkable for being able to accommodate one hundred ships of the line at four hundred and twenty miles distance from the ocean. The newly arrived troops were not permitted to go ashore, except for a short fatigue-duty across the river at Point Levy, since there was fighting promised for them farther up the river; but disappointment was assuaged by the fresh meat, poultry, and vegetables brought aboard. I was fortunate enough to be an exception to this rule against the allowance of shore-leave; for I was sent to the Upper Town with a detachment of The Ninth, which as the eldest regiment was chosen to provide guards for the day. I had a great curiosity to visit Quebec, if only for the sake of childish memories of the Heights of Abraham (represented by our wood-shed) and the death of that hero, Major-General Sir James Wolfe.

✿ ✿ ✿ ✿ ✿ ✿ ✿ ✿ ✿ ✿ ✿ ✿

CHAPTER

II

WHEN the Americans had entered Canada that autumn, the Governor, Sir Guy Carleton, escaped down the St. Lawrence River from Montreal in a dug-out canoe, by night, and with difficulty reached Quebec. Our pilot described him as 'a man of ten thousand eyes, very courageous.' He was evidently prudent besides, for he had immediately expelled from Quebec, together with their families, all persons of military age who refused to take up arms for the King. On December 1st General Montgomery joined Colonel Benedict Arnold before the city and mounted his cannon for a siege. By a perfect novelty in military science he placed them on platforms of snow and water congealed into solid ice. The shot, however, was too light to make any great impression on the defence; whereupon, after consulting with his officers, General Montgomery determined on a general assault to be delivered simultaneously in two quarters, for the night of December 23rd. He boasted that he would eat his Christmas dinner in Quebec or Hell. Yet he was forced to go back on this undertaking because of the clearness of the weather: since, for a successful assault, he needed the cloak of a snowstorm. Difficult as the situation of the defenders was, with great scarcity of fuel, short rations, a wide circuit of walls to defend and a restless alien citizenry to keep in check, that of the besiegers was far worse. No unanimity existed among these troops, composed of contingents from several colonies, of whom only the Virginian riflemen, being better shod than the rest, did not now have their enthusiasm frozen to death. The temperature had fallen so low that it was found impossible to touch metal with the naked hand lest it should strip off the skin. Even in the city it was sufficient employment for the soldiers to keep their noses from the frost-bite, and several sentries lost the sight of their eyes from the extreme cold.

How any at all of the Americans managed to survive, I do not know. The Virginians wore white linen smocks, which were so obviously unfitted for use in winter that a legend arose among the French peasantry that they were impervious to cold. In the accounts that spread of their exploits the word *toile*, which means 'linen' in the French language, became changed to *tôle*, which is 'sheet-iron,' and a legend will doubtless go down to posterity of ogres clad in white, frost-proof, iron armour, who sought to invade the country. To add to their discomforts, a severe epidemic of smallpox raged in the enemy camp. Desertions from the New England companies were frequent, and many men avoided duty by feigning sick; for which crime they had halters put around their necks and were paraded in derision before their comrades, and then lashed. What made matters yet worse was that sufficient pay in hard money for these troops was wanting. The injunction of the American Congress against alienating the Canadians' affections was so strict, that necessary supplies of food and clothing might not be seized from the country people, nor could they be compelled by any means to accept the new American paper money, termed 'Continental currency.'

General Montgomery had no alternative but either to attack or to retire, for he failed in all attempts to seduce the French population of Quebec to revolt. Messages to that purpose had been shot over the walls tied to arrows, and one emissary, a woman, had somehow contrived to gain admittance: she was seized, tried, jailed, and then drummed out with ignominy.

The distinguishing badge adopted by the Americans, who had no common uniform, was hemlock worn in the hat; but General Montgomery, now deciding on an assault for New Year's Eve, replaced these withered sprigs with a paper badge on which was inscribed, in each soldier's own handwriting: 'Liberty or Death!'

In the words of our French pilot, who appeared greatly tickled by the circumstances—'By Gar, ze General he oblige to try zat day—last day possible.'

'How the last day possible?' we had asked.

'Ze New England militia, zey finish, at finish of year; zey go home goddam quick, finish of year, by Gar.'

The assault was delivered at about five o'clock in the morning of the New Year at 1776 with the aid of a blinding blizzard. The garrison, though warned beforehand that an attack was expected, were distracted by two feints at an escalade made at distant points of the defences, which were no less than three miles in circumference. Many of our men were also incapacitated by having drunk too deeply the health of the New Year. With little opposition the Virginian riflemen, under their gigantic commander Colonel Dan Morgan, forced their way into the Lower Town, which was a large suburb of wooden houses contiguous to the River, and there penetrated to the foot of Mountain Street, which zigzagged upwards to the Upper Town. Here they found the sally port of the lower barrier open, by mistake; and the French levies soon came running down past our well-placed batteries there in whole platoons, to give themselves up as prisoners. This barrier was captured at the first rush. But, instead of pressing on, the Virginians loyally waited: this was their agreed rendezvous with General Montgomery's column, whose attack was being made at some little distance away. They waited in vain, for he was dead, shot through both thighs and the head by a sudden discharge of grape in the moment of assault.

Colonel Benedict Arnold, under whom the Virginians were serving, was adjudged to be the boldest and most skilful soldier in the whole American Army. If he had not had the misfortune, a few minutes before, that his leg was shattered by a musket ball, he would never have permitted the delay and Quebec would doubtless have fallen, for the upper barrier of Mountain Street was only weakly held. But, by the time that the Virginians came to know that they could only count upon their own exertions, the British had rallied and were strongly placed behind the upper barrier. The chance had slipped. The American plan had been to fire the Lower Town, in order to provide a screen of smoke for the storming of the Mountain Street barriers, but this was not effected, and, when morning came, such of the Americans as had not already retreated were surrounded and captured. The enemy lost between six and seven hundred men and officers, more than half their force, in killed, wounded, and prisoners: the British losses were less than twenty. Yet Colonel Arnold had the temerity to encamp within three miles of the city, where smallpox and misery continued to diminish the numbers of his men. Even so, General Carleton was not to be tempted to attack: he lay close in the Upper Town. In April the Americans were reinforced, so that they numbered about two thousand men: but these were insufficient for a renewed assault. On May 3rd three British warships forced their way through the floating ice, to the great encouragement of the garrison. The Americans then broke camp and retired hastily up the River St. Lawrence.

Let me conjure up a picture of Quebec as I saw it from mid-stream of the river, on the morning of May 29th 1776. At the water's edge was a cluster of warehouses and dwellings, the Lower Town, and behind them rose a cliff consisting of slate and marble, upon which, behind batteries and palisades, stands the Upper Town. In the middle of the cliff ran a serpentine road, Mountain Street, and a zigzag footpath with a hand-rail led up past the great grey palace of the Roman Catholic bishop; and, on the left, a little above it, stood Castle St. Louis, the residence of the Governor, a long, irregularly constructed, yellow building of two stories. The Castle was thought to be out of range of guns, because of its elevation, but this proved an error: for one evening of the siege a shot passed through a room next to that where General Carleton sat at cards with his family. Beyond were seen the slate-covered spire of the Cathedral surrounded by the spires of other religious buildings, namely, those of the Jesuits, the Franciscan Recollects, the Ursulines, and the Hotel Dieu, and by many tall and beautiful trees. To the left of Castle St. Louis was a rounded pinnacle of dark slate, known as Cape Diamond, where was a square fort, the

Citadel of Quebec; and on the highest point of the pinnacle a look-out box, an iron cage formerly used to house the bodies of felons. Cape Diamond stood upwards of one thousand feet above the level of the water.

Such a sight was beautiful in the extreme and improved by the numerous ships anchored in the intervening waters; but from a close view, when I went ashore for the Guard, many imperfections appeared. The fortifications, though extensive, wanted much in regularity and solidity, and, the parapet being broken down in many places, the ways of communication betwen the works proved rugged in the extreme. A number of houses, moreover, had been destroyed for fuel by the besieged inhabitants; shot and shells had continually defaced and burned the remainder; and the pavement of Mountain Street had been purposely torn up—in order that the shells might bury themselves in the ground before they burst and so spread less of death—and not yet replaced. Besides this, the streets were very narrow and dirty, and the buildings in general were small, ugly, and inconvenient. But I was delighted with the Canadian women whom I saw as I passed through the town; they were not beautiful but had something to set off this defect, a charm of behaviour and a lively neatness which is more difficult to forget than to describe. I was amused, too, by a curiosity, namely, a great number of broad-shouldered, short-legged dogs yoked in little carts bringing country produce to the market.

The Guard of which I was the Sergeant, under a good-humoured young lieutenant named Kemmis, was a double one: over the St. John's Gate, at the south-east of the city looking across the Charles River, and over the American captives in the solidly built jail near by. Colonel Arnold's attack, which was made at this point, must have been the maddest possible, for the gate and the walls adjoining were stupendous and not to be attempted without heavy artillery.

I was shocked at the appearance of the captives: they had suffered terribly during the siege, though General Carleton had showed them as much humanity and consideration as he could afford. Their living had been salt pork and salt fish, biscuit, rice, and a little butter, but there was no means of providing them with remedies against the scurvy, which many of them, already weakened by the smallpox, took very badly, so that their teeth had loosened and dropped out and their flesh seemed to be rotting on their bones. Their clothing was ragged and verminous, and all their laughter had long forsaken them, giving place to a fixed melancholy. An attempt had been made by them to escape on April 1st, with which was connected a plan for seizing St. John's Gate and admitting Colonel Arnold's forces into the city; but it miscarried. The cause of this failure was that common to almost all American war-like enterprises—the refusal of inexperienced participants to subordinate themselves to the experienced. Towards the completion of their plan only one obstacle still remained to be surmounted: which was the removal of a block of ice that prevented their prison door from opening outwards. Two good men were chosen to creep out and whittle this obstruction silently away with the long knives of which they were possessed; but a pair of meddling know-alls anticipated them by chipping at it with axes—which noise the guards overheard. All was discovered, and the conspirators were thereupon manacled and put in foot-irons. This hindrance to their taking exercise in the prison parade depressed their health further and aided the scurvy, of which many scores of them perished. Governor Carleton, however, had allowed them fresh beef about the middle of April and relieved them of their fetters, soon as the city was relieved. He had also distributed clothing to the naked. Thus I did not see them at their worst, though what I saw was shocking enough.

When I called out one of them, by name James Melville, or perhaps it was Mellon—I disremember—to discourse with me, what he disclosed rang so piercingly in my ears that I could never afterwards forget it. He said: 'If ever I am released from this jail and get home to our people, and fight again—before God I swear that I will never again suffer myself to be taken prisoner in my versal life. I have lost the half of my soul here, seared away by those cold irons. Look at me—you English soldier—I was as hale and stout a man as you in September last when I marched with the rest from Cambridge in Captain Dear-

born's company. Nor was it the Kennebec River that did
this for me, despite the hideous woods and mountains,
and the tarnal hunger and heavy loads; nor the Height of
Land where I wore the flesh from my shoulders at the
Terrible Carry. Nor was it the Chaudière River, where
we waded knee-deep for miles in the icy alder swamps,
the abode only of herons and adders, and fed upon raw
dog-meat and the bark of trees, and I roasted my leather
shot-pouch and ate it; and also had the flux, nation bad
upon me. Nor was it the complicated distress of the campaign before this city, in the coldest winter but one that the
oldest man can recall, and in rags of uniform. It was these
solid prison walls, and the foot-irons.'

He added that, while he could complain of no unkind-
ness on the part of the British, the Canadian militia had
taunted these Americans often and threatened torture and
death, though in effect doing nothing. 'But our worst
enemy proved he who should have been our friend, a
villain named Dewey, chosen from among us to be our
quarter-master sergeant. He defrauded us of a great part
of our provision, so that we had not above three ounces
of pork and not half a pint of rice and two biscuits a day.
Yet the Lord of Hosts delivered us out of his hands. The
villain took the smallpox, which soon swept him off the
face of the earth.'

I asked this soldier, the first native-born American with
whom I ever conversed, a variety of questions. He told me
that he had used his musket at Lexington in April 1775,
marching with his neighbours from Hubbardston in Massachusetts, and that his enthusiasm for the cause of Liberty
had first been fired by a Methodist preacher, lately
arrived from Ireland, a most persuasive speaker. This
preacher had taken from Nehemiah iv. 14: *Be not ye
afraid of them: remember the Lord who is great and
terrible, and fight for your brethren, your sons and your
daughters, your wives and your houses.* 'He had a face
the colour of a biscuit and a black, wet lock hanging over
his eyes. His words were like swords,' this man Melville
said.

I asked him, what quarrel he could possibly have with
King George. He replied that this preacher, along with

the rest, had assured him that the King, not content with forcing him to drink that noxious weed tea, plotted to establish Popery in New England.

'But the King at his Coronation abjured Popery in the most solemn fashion,' said I, smiling. 'He is no more a Papist than you are.'

'Ah,' said he earnestly, 'so you may believe. But I dare swear that he is not the first great person to forswear himself when it was to his convenience. What of the Quebec Act of two years ago? Was that the Act of a Protestant Monarch? It established Popery in Canada as the State Religion, tithes and all. Now missionaries will breed here under the royal protection and spread like flies over our border and seduce all our young people.'

'Well,' said I, 'I see no great harm in granting the French-Canadians permission to continue worshipping God as freely in their ancestral manner as do your allies, the Papists of Maryland; indeed, I consider it a necessary and humane measure. It pleases me to know that on a Sunday, after the Romish service is over, General Carleton with his officers and soldiers resort to the Cathedral for their own worship; and neither party demands the reconsecration of the edifice between whiles.' I would gladly have said much more on this issue, remembering with shame my wretched fellow-countrymen at Timolin, and all along the road from Dublin to Waterford, wishing for humanity's sake that a Quebec Act could be passed by the Irish Parliament, so that the tithes sweated from these poor wretches could at least be paid to priests of their own faith, for the spiritual comfort that would accrue. But I did not wish to make a gratuitous parade or confession before this American of the ills from which Ireland suffered; and kept strictly to the matter in hand.

I am of an inquiring turn of mind and had already been at pains to find out as much as possible about the conditions obtaining in Canada. I was therefore able to tell him: 'As for the other main provision of the Act, against which your Congress has protested as fastening fetters upon the Habitants of Canada—namely, that of re-establishing the French Civil Law except in criminal cases—I am informed that the English-speaking settlers, who are outnumbered as two hundred to one by the French-speaking, have been the only persons to complain. Indeed, I hear that we have forced on the French of this province a greater measure of liberty than they can well digest: they are said to abominate trial by jury, deeming their Seigneurial judges as more likely to give them justice than a parcel of trades-men crowded together in the jury box.'

At that very moment, as we talked together in the main doorway, a tinkle of a bell was heard up the street; and we saw how the people prostrated themselves before the Host conveyed by a robed priest to a dying man in a house near by. Acolytes carried lighted candles before the sacred wafer, which was enclosed in a gilt box laid upon a purple embroidered cushion, and handsome young nuns of the Ursulines walked behind, with their eyes fixed upon the ground. A number of soldiers were in the street, in-cluding Highlanders of the Royal Emigrant Regiment and German mercenaries from Brunswick who had sailed in the convoy that had arrived just ahead of us. But one and all obeyed the Governor's orders and doffed feather bon-net, cocked hat, or grenadier's cap as the procession passed; and, as required, the sentry at the gate presented arms.

'Faugh,' exclaimed this Melville, when they had passed, 'if that is not the dissemination of Scarlet Popery, what tarnal other name would you give it?'

'Good manners,' said I, 'which I am always pleased to witness. I wish we had more of them back in my own country.'

'I watched that same crew perform over a Frenchman in the hospital a month or two ago,' he remarked in a hollow voice. 'The nuns came and read over him, and then the priest entered and they fetched in a table covered with a white cloth, and lighted two wax candles about three feet long and set them on the table. The priest had on his white robe, and the nuns kneeled down, and he stood and read a sentence, and then the nuns a sentence, and so they went on for some time. Then the priest prayed by himself, then the nuns by themselves, and then the priest again. Then all together they read a spell, and finally the priest alone. Then the priest stroked the man's face; then they took away their candles and table. But the man died for all that, I should nation well reckon.'

He described Colonel Benedict Arnold as the most terrible man in America, and said that it was a pity that he was so much of a gentleman.

I pretended not to pay much attention to this, so that his tongue might run on unchecked. 'There was Colonel Easton of Connecticut who disputed the command with Colonel Arnold at Crown Point last year; Colonel Arnold made it a matter of honour and called on him to draw. Colonel Easton pacifically refused, though he had a hanger and a case of pistols on him; so Colonel Arnold kicked his posterior tarnal heartily, which Colonel Easton could not forgive him.'

'You don't like gentlemen, then, in New England?'

'Law for me, no! They are Tories, and enemies of Liberty. But a few are well disposed to us and have military talents, so we employ them. General Montgomery was one such, and a good man in his way. General Philip Schuyler is another, but he gives himself aristocratic airs and was once mighty surly to an honest blacksmith who came uninvited to visit him in his mansion at Stillwater. But General George Washington is a nation worse than all, and if he had his will would put only gentlemen in command of us; we hold him in great suspicion. He is tarnal friendly with Colonel Arnold.'

'I am informed that Colonel Arnold is a druggist and book-seller. How comes he then to rank as a gentleman?'

'Why, he married the High Sheriff's daughter in his town, commanded two companies of the Governor's Guards, and is a pretty considerable merchant. He boasts of his descent from a former Governor of Rhode Island, and he dresses tarnal proud. Well, he took a pet against Colonel Easton, as I have said; and he quarrelled with Colonel Enos, whose three companies later hooked it off from us at the Kennebec River; and with Major Brown, whom he named a damned thief for taking more than his share of the plunder captured at Sorel; and with Colonel Campbell, whom he accused of cowardice; and with Captain Handchett, whom he threatened to arrest for the same thing. Now, I hear he has retired to Montreal because General Wooster, who came up with the reinforcements in April, would not consult his advice.'

'Tell me,' said I. 'Who appoints your officers? Is it General Washington?'

He spat upon the ground. 'Law for me—no, no! We would accept none of his appointment. We want safe men, not men of quality, nary one of 'em.'

I could not resist interjecting sarcastically that quality was sometimes no bad thing, especially when compared with mere quantity. But he did not heed me and continued: 'The Continental Congress appoints generals and colonels and such, and we appoint the rest, from captains down.'

'Whom do you intend by "we"?' I asked in some bewilderment.

'The soldiers who are to serve under him. Our captains and lieutenants are voted for by a show of hands. They are pretty respectable tradesmen—such as hatters, butchers, tanners, shoemakers—and many of them worth several thousand dollars. But, let me tell you, that for all they are very warm men, they resemble our ministers in this —if they do not please us we do not obey, but we bid them hook it off in nation quick time.'

This raised such a ludicrous picture in my mind that I heartily laughed, which offended him. He told me: 'Scoffers will also have their portion in the hell that is prepared for the unrighteous.'

'Who told you that?' I asked, still laughing a little.

'The same preacher of whom I spoke—the Reverend John Martin was his name.'

'The Devil!' I exclaimed involuntarily, at the coincidence of two Irish priests of the name of John Martin, both with sallow faces and a black forelock, the one a Papist and the other a shouting Methodist. With that I dismissed the American; but before the Guard was relieved and we returned to the *Friendship* I gave him an old shirt and a pair of stockings, for which he wrung my hand gratefully.

General Carleton came to inspect us that same afternoon and complimented Lieutenant Kemmins upon our appearance and bearing, which gave us no little satisfaction. Let me describe this famous man who saved Canada for the Crown—not only by his activity and gallantry in this

war but by his considerate framing of the Quebec Act
mentioned above, which consolidated the loyalty of the
French. He was tall, raw-faced, with a very large nose and
a great diffidence in conversation; the best military in-
structor of his day and the most generous man alive.
General Carleton had a quaint humour: when, two months
before Quebec was relieved, the Americans had sent him
a message warning him that the townspeople would revolt
unless he surrendered, he gave no reply, but ordered a
great wooden horse to be placed upon the walls, close to
this Gate of St. John. This was to signify that the treachery
of the wooden horse of Troy would not be repeated by
American emissaries in Quebec. When his staff reproached
him for 'shooting too high for the Americans,' who were
not well read in classical legends and would be nonplussed by the horse, 'O, by God,' he said, 'I'll soon remedy
that. Put a bundle of hay before the beast and write
in bold letters on the wall, using tar: "When this horse
has ate his hay, we surrender." '

After the relief of the city his good nature was such
that he issued the following proclamation:

Whereas I am informed that many of His Majesty's
deluded subjects, of the neighbouring provinces, labouring
under wounds and divers disorders, are dispersed in the
adjacent woods and parishes and in great danger of perish-
ing for want of proper assistance, all captains and other
officers of militia are hereby commanded to make diligent
search for all such distressed persons, and afford them all
necessary relief, and convey them to the general hospital,
where proper care shall be taken of them; all reasonable
expenses which may be incurred in complying with this
order shall be paid by the Receiver-General.

And lest a consciousness of past offences should deter
such miserable wretches from receiving that assistance
which their distressed situation may require: I hereby
make known to them that as soon as their health is restored
they shall have free liberty to return to their respective
provinces.

General Carleton also fed and clothed the sick whom
the Americans, when they broke the siege, had abandoned
in their hospitals. I heard from one of our men who hap-

pened to remain in Quebec during the week following our departure, that General Carleton visited the prison and spoke to the captives there in a very affable and familiar tone.

He asked: 'My lads, why did you come to disturb an honest man in his government, that never did any harm to you in his life? I never invaded your property, nor sent a single soldier to distress you. Come, my boys, you are in a very distressing situation, I see, and not able to go home with any comfort. I must provide you with shoes, stockings, and good warm waistcoats. I must give you some good victuals to carry you home. Take care, my lads, that you do not come here again, lest I should not treat you so kindly.'

He was as good as his word, though owing to the war, and one thing and another, James Melville and his comrades did not sail home until August; they had all voluntarily signed papers promising on their honour never to take up arms again against His Majesty. They sailed in five transports, and the General presented to the officers of each transport a cask of wine and five sheep as ship's stores. Mgr. Briand, the Bishop of Quebec shamed them with a gift of two casks of wine, eight sugar-loaves and a number of pounds of green tea. The tea offended their political consciences and they respectfully refused it; then the good Bishop, to prove that he had not acted with malice, gave them an equal amount of the best coffee in exchange. This set animosity against tea was most violent in the early years of the war. The same James Melville, or Mellon, informed me that his comrade Sergeant Dixon, who lost a leg below the knee with a thirty-six-pounder ball before Quebec, was advised by a surgeon, who had amputated the limb, to drink some tea in default of brandy: for this would stimulate the desired reaction. The lady of the house where he had been brought made a dish of the beverage, which Dixon put away from him with detestation exclaiming: 'No, madam: it is the ruin of my country.' Nor could he be prevailed upon to forgo his resolution and touch this 'nauseous draught of slavery'; but, lock-jaw ensuing, he died.

The Reverend Samuel Seabury, who was to become the first bishop of the Protestant Episcopal Church in America, had recently written a humorous refutation of Congress's commercial policy: they recommended, in retaliation of the tea duty, an agreement against exporting all goods to Great Britain and Ireland. He was a farmer of his own glebe land in Westchester County, near New York, and did not wish to lose his Northern Irish market for flax-seed, of which he had in the previous year threshed and cleaned eleven bushels. He put it thus:

The common price now is at least ten shillings. My seed, then, will fetch me five pounds ten shillings. But I will throw in the ten shillings for expenses. There remain five pounds. In five pounds are four hundred three-pences. Four hundred three-pences, currency, will pay the duty upon two hundred pounds of tea—even reckoning the exchange with London at two hundred per centum. I use in my family about six pounds of tea. Few farmers in my neighbourhood use so much; but I hate to stint my wife and daughters, or my friendly neighbours when they come to see me. Besides, I like a dish of tea too, especially after a little more than ordinary fatigue in hot weather. Now, two hundred pounds of tea, at six pounds a year, will just last thirty-three years and four months; so that, in order to pay this monstrous duty on tea, which has raised all this confounded combustion in the country, I have only to sell the produce of a bushel of flax-seed once in thirty-three years.

But the Reverend Samuel Seabury, as a minister of religion, should have known better than to play the rationalist, confusing substance with symbol. As the elements of the Lord's Supper are held to suffer a divine transformation in the hands of the priest: so Pekoe and Hyson were believed by the Americans to suffer a diabolical transformation when handled by the exciseman.

CHAPTER

12

WE SAILED up the St. Lawrence on the first day of June, our destination being Three Rivers, a village which lay about half-way between Quebec and Montreal and some ninety miles from each; it was so named from the three rivers which joined their current close above it and then fell as one into the St. Lawrence. Here we expected that the enemy would make a stand.

In our passage we were entertained by many beautiful landscapes, the banks being in many places very bold and steep and shaded with lofty trees, now in young leaf. What particularly struck our attention was the beautiful disposition of the towns and villages we passed. Nearly all the settlements in Canada were situated upon the banks of rivers; which was by no means the case in other parts of America, as I afterwards found. The churches appeared frequently and seemed kept in the neatest repair, most of them showing bright spires of tin. It puzzled me why these spires did not rust; but I later discovered that it was from the dryness of the air and from a method they have of nailing on the squares of tin diagonally, the corners folded over the heads of the nails, so as to keep moisture from intruding. The houses were of logs, but much more compact and better built than those which I was to see in the rest of America: the logs were more closely joined and, instead of being left rough and uneven on the out-side, were trimmed with the adze, and whitewashed. It was pleasing beyond description to double a tree-covered headland in the evening and perceive one of these villages opening to view, its houses close upon the river, rosy with the setting sun, and the spire of its church twinkling bright through the leafy trees.

The air became so mild and temperate that we imagined

ourselves transported into another climate; yet I noticed
that hardly a house on the whole river had its windows
thrown open; for the French-Canadians loved a close,
stifling heat as dearly as they loved the tobacco-pipes
which gurgled constantly in their mouths—I once saw a
boy of three years puffing away at one.

The tide still ebbed and flowed in the river as far as
Three Rivers, but not many miles beyond. We disembarked about twenty miles below this place, where the
left-hand bank was flat, and much corn and fruit were
grown. This was June 5th, and we marched along the
river-road all day, with the regimental music ahead of us,
finding great enjoyment in the use of our legs. We remarked upon the extraordinary speed with which the crops
sprouted and the trees leafed, soon as winter had departed,
as also upon the very slovenly manner of farming here in
use. It appeared that manure was seldom put upon the
fields, considered already rich enough by nature, but was
instead thrown into the river. The sandy earth was merely
turned up lightly with a plough and the grain scattered in
furrows which were far from regular. More than half the
fields also had been left without any fences, exposed to
the teeth and hooves of cattle. However, the Habitants
were beginning to be more industrious and better farmers;
because, since the English came, the greed and rapacity
of their feudal landlords, the *Seigneurs*, had been somewhat
curbed. Beforehand, it was not worth their while to ac-
cumulate any surplus of corn or maple-sugar or fuel, because it would all be taken from them under one pretext
or another; but now they counted on the protection of
the Governor and were assured of a steady market for
their produce, owing to the energy of the English merchants of Montreal and Quebec, who sent boats to collect
it on fixed days. Yet for their *Seigneurs* they still had a
habit of reverence, and were bound to them by certain
ties of vassalage, such as being obliged to take their corn
to be ground only at the *Seigneur's* mill, under payment
of a heavy fine, however inconvenient the journey.

The *Seigneurs* lived in a simple style and were often
poorer than their vassals, for they were forbidden by pride
to engage in the tilling of the soil or any mechanical task;

but at the sight of a beaver hat, however shabby, every red night-cap was doffed. This disgust of mechanical employment was shared by the vassal, who was usually related by marriage with a Seigneurial family, and, though he condescended to till the soil, would hold it beneath him to set up as a blacksmith or boot-maker. In consequence, the Canadians had great scorn for the invaders from New England when they were aware that even their officers were tradesmen and artisans.

The women of the Seigneurial class affected long cloaks of scarlet silk, in contrast with those of a similar colour, made of cloth, worn by the plebeians, and a kind of worsted cap with great coloured loops of ribbon. If any woman without a right to these distinctions were to be seen attired in them, they would be torn from her, even in a crowded gathering.

The peasant girls were very pretty, but only the young ones; for their beauty closed prematurely. They wore charming sleeveless bodices in blue or scarlet, petticoats of a different colour and wide-brimmed straw hats. Some sat spinning in the open air outside their house doors. They did most of the farm labour, the men being in general indolent, except when on some adventurous expedition in search of furs. The farms were not in general large, grazing thirty or forty sheep, and about a dozen cows, along with five or six oxen for the plough. The cows were small, but very good for the farmers' use. The people seemed not only immeasurably better circumstanced than the peasants of Ireland, but (a comparison I was able to make in later years) a great deal better than most of the English themselves. Every dwelling-house had a small orchard attached and at evening the return of the herds and flocks from the woods was a very pleasant sight. The swine were also allowed to roam wild in the woods; these were very fierce, and the hardy manner of their life greatly improved the flavour of the flesh and the quality of the bristles for brush-making.

We halted in a small village about an hour after disembarking, and Lieutenant Kemmis, who knew a little French, asked a French farmer, who had come out of his house to watch the troops go by, how far it was to Three

Rivers. 'Oh,' replied he, 'about twenty pipes, sir.' This strange method of computation, which was the common one on the river, represented time rather than distance: the time that it would take to smoke a pipe, according to the element which one used, land or water, and in the latter case according to whether the journey was upstream or down. For men walking along, in the leisurely stroll used by these Frenchman, 'a pipe' was about three-quarters of a mile.

The same farmer, who, in spite of the warmth of the weather, wore a coarse blanket coat tied about his body with a worsted sash, and the habitual red woollen night-cap, invited the Lieutenant and myself into his house for a drink. It was of a single storey, with three or four compartments and a large garret a-top, where in winter he stored his frozen provisions.

I looked about me with interest. The interior of the living-room was neatly boarded and the furniture plain and solid. There was a close iron stove with a long line over it for the drying of dishclouts and clothing. Strips of stout paper were still tightly pasted about the window to keep out the blasts and snow of winter. A crowd of about thirteen people, seated at a long table on stools, were eating their dinner with wooden spoons from wooden bowls (hollowed out from the knots of the curly maple-tree) and drinking cider from tankards of unglazed earthenware. Their bread was sour and black, and the dinner was a great pot of potatoes, cabbage, and beef boiled to shreds. The smell in the room was a curious admixture of sweat, stew, garlic, tobacco, and sulphur. We had not been there above five minutes when we felt our heads beginning to swim, for the stove was roaring hot and giving off noxious fumes.

'Good God, my friend,' exclaimed the Lieutenant, 'do you never open the window even in the hottest day of summer?'

Our host ruminated awhile and then shook his head.

'And why not, pray? Would it not benefit your health?' For the Lieutenant was aware that the French were much subject to the consumption, which these stoves invited.

He puffed at his pipe. 'It is not a custom of the Habitants,' he told us at last; and I was to learn that this same reason was habitually given by his countrymen for many other eccentric refusals to behave in a common-sense manner. So we drank off our cider, which was very rough in the mouth, thanked him, and staggered out again into the road—a very good one too, because the Corvée of France was still in operation hereabouts, which provided forced labour for the maintenance of public works. This road was ditched on both sides and curved in the centre for dryness, and the ruts constantly filled up with stones. A pleasant breeze blew off the river, which was about two miles broad, so that vessels of considerable size sailing in mid-stream appeared like wherries.

We had the luck to observe two sea-wolves sporting in the river, within musket-shot. To have disturbed them by a volley would have been a wanton act, for had we wounded or killed them we should not have been able to recover their bodies; nor did we need fresh meat, being abundantly supplied with very good beef. The sea-wolf, so-called from his howling, is an amphibian creature. His head resembles that of a dog. He has four very short legs, of which the fore ones have nails, but the hind ones terminate in fins. The largest animals weigh upwards of two thousand pounds and are of different colours. Their flesh is good eating, but the profit of it lies in its oil, which is proper for burning and for currying leather. Their skins do excellently for travellers' trunks, and when well-tanned make shoes and boots that do not admit water, and lasting covers for seats. I never saw a sea-cow, though this animal was also found in the river: larger than the sea-wolf but resembling him in figure. The sea-cow is as white as snow and has two teeth, of the thickness and length of a man's arm, that look like horns and are of the finest ivory. These beasts were seldom taken at sea, and on shore only by a stratagem. The people of Nova Scotia used to tie a bull to a stake fixed on the shore to the depth of about two feet of water; they then covertly tormented him by twisting his tail until he roared. As soon as the sea-cows heard this they would take it as a signal from one of their own kind and swim towards the shore; when they reached shallow water they would crawl to the bull on their short, awkward legs and be taken without difficulty.

I later saw several schools of porpoises playing about in

the river: each was said to yield a hogshead of oil, and of their skins were made warm musket-proof waistcoats. They were mostly white and when they rose to the surface had the appearance of hogs. At night, if I may use an Irishism (being Irish born), they often caused beautiful fireworks in the water, especially when two schools crossed each other, a continuous stream of light gliding with each member and curving in and out.

It must not be thought that we were so distracted by the interesting sights of our march that we forgot the purpose for which it was made; namely, to throw back the American invaders out of Canada. We felt indeed an unquestioning assurance that the Americans, fighting not in defence of their homes but as invaders of a foreign country with which they had nothing in common, would have no chance against us. They would lack the opportunity to shoot from behind stone walls at a column in line of march as at Lexington, or to defend a prepared position against frontal attack as at Bunker's Hill; nor could they count upon the assistance or even the neutrality of the Habitants. They were accustomed to fight as individuals not as an army; and in battles in open country, as this was, victory must always attend the side which shows the most perfect discipline and the closest subordination to the instructions of its commander—so long as he be not a perfect fool, as very few of our generals happened to be.

The Americans who opposed us consisted of three several expeditions. First, the two thousand besiegers of Quebec, who upon General Carleton's sortie early in May —'to see,' as he said, 'what these mighty boasters are about' —had fled almost without resistance, abandoning the whole of their artillery and stores. To these were added two thousand new troops under General Tomson, who had been sent up from Boston to assist at the capture of Quebec; they could be spared for the service because General Howe had in March been forced to evacuate Boston, bag and baggage. That they arrived too late was due to mismanagement and dissension. Besides these, three and a half thousand men had arrived under General Sullivan, and Colonel Benedict Arnold from Montreal with his three hundred veterans. This was a respectable force in numbers, but we had thirteen thousand men to set against their eight thousand, and were far better served with artillery. The Americans were reported to be concentrated at Sorel, some forty miles up the river from us and on the other bank. Between them and us lay the broad Lake of St. Peter with its thousand islands, which would be the next stage of our journey up to Montreal.

We arrived at Three Rivers, after being ferried over the intervening stream on *bateaux,* a sort of barge peculiar to Canada, flat-bottomed and with both ends built very sharp and exactly alike. The sides were about four feet high and there were benches and rowlocks for oarsmen; the *bateau* also carried sail, though it was very awkward either to sail or row. Its advantage was that it drew very little water and could be propelled by poles, where there was no wind and where oars would not serve. The poles were about eight feet in length, extremely light and shod with iron. The current in the centre of the St. Lawrence River was to strong that to stem it a crew must keep close to the shore and use their poles in unison. The *bateau* was steered by a man with a pole in the hinder part, who shifted it from side to side to keep the course even.

We found Three Rivers a place of disappointing size, though the third town, in point of importance, in Canada. It contained but two hundred and fifty houses, most of them built of wood and indifferent in appearance, two extinct monasteries, an active convent of Ursuline nuns, and a barrack with capacity for five hundred troops. The town used to be much frequented by Indians who brought furs thither down the rivers after which it is named; but by this time the trade had been diverted to Montreal as being a more accessible market to the Indian trapping-grounds, and Three Rivers was no more than a port of call between Montreal and Quebec.

My company were lodged for the night in a barn belonging to the Ursulines and were shown great kindness by the Chaplain of the sisterhood. He invited Lieutenant Kemmis and myself to enter a part of the convent which could be visited without leave of the Bishop—as the part where the nuns dwelt could not. We were conducted to a handsome parlour with a charming view of the convent gardens, and presently in came gliding the Mother Superior and a bevy of lay-sisters, who were not bound by the same strict vows as the other women. I could only nod and smile, but Lieutenant Kemmis offered a number of gallantries in halting French, which greatly pleased the old woman. The dress of the Order, a poor one, consisted of a black stuff gown, a handkerchief of white linen with rounded corners looped about the throat, a head-piece of the same material which allowed only the centre part of the face to show, a black gauze veil which screened half even of that and overflowed the shoulders, and a heavy silver cross suspended from the breast.

We were shown specimens of the handicrafts of the Sisterhood, by selling which they helped to support themselves; and were expected to purchase some specimens, which we did. It is unusual for soldiers on the eve of a battle to fill their pockets and knapsacks with a heap of keepsakes in fancy-work to send to their friends—but we could not disappoint these poor women. We bought from them two pocket-books, a work-basket, a dressing-box, all of which were made of birch-bark embroidered in elk hair, dyed in various brilliant colours; also some models of Indian tomahawks, scalping-knives, calumets, and those birch-bark canoes for the manufacture of which Three Rivers was famous. They packed them up for us very neatly in little boxes kept for the purpose, of the same bark.

The next day we spent in drill, both by platoons and companies, and Major Bolton impressed upon us that what we had perhaps regarded hitherto as idle ceremony had a practical and deadly purpose. He declared that we must show the same steadiness and unanimity upon the field as upon the parade. In the afternoon I went from curiosity to watch a number of Indians at their canoe-making, a work performed with the utmost neatness. They began with a framework of thick, stout rods of the hickory nut-tree, bound together with remarkably tough strips of elm-bark. Over this they sewed, with deer sinews, large strips of birch-bark, which resembles that of the cork-tree but is of much closer grain and far more pliable. A thick coat of pitch was laid over the seams between the different pieces. The inside was lined with two layers of thin pieces of pine, laid in a contrary direction to each other. A canoe of this sort was so light that two men without fatigue could carry one on their shoulders, with accommodation for six persons. It was wonderful to see with what velocity these canoes might be paddled: in a few minutes a keel-boat rowed by an equal number of men with oars would be left behind, a mere speck on the river. But they were very easily overturned by the least improper movement; and the Habitants preferred more solid canoes hollowed out from a single log of red cedar.

The work was entirely performed by women, who undertook all the labour of the tribe: such as procuring and transporting fuel, planting corn and vegetables, cooking, dressing skins, doctoring, making household instruments and utensils. The men supplied the food and defended the camp, but considered it beneath them to undertake any other labour.

I observed a number of men lounging about on the bank, smoking their calumets, a combination of pipe and axe. One of them, sitting cross-legged in his blanket-coat with a black face and untrimmed locks, which I was told signified mourning and unsatisfied revenge, offered me a handsome otter-skin pouch. I opened it and found inside a lump of tobacco in one compartment and dried leaves in the other. Upon my looking puzzled, he took the pouch from me, extracted the tobacco lump, cut it into shreds in the palm of his hand with his scalping-knife, rubbed it together with the dry leaves, which were of the sumach-tree, and finally, drawing my pipe from my waist-belt, where I had put it, stuffed the bowl with the mixture. He struck fire into a bit of touchwood with his flint and steel, kindled the pipe and put it between my lips. These were simple and familiar actions but performed with indescribable harmony and grace. Except in their war-dances or when they were intoxicated, I never saw an Indian make any movement or gesture that was not beautiful to the eye. I sat for some minutes watching this man, who appeared to be a very sincere and honest smoker. He never removed or replaced his pipe in his mouth without due solemnity, and the act of inhaling the smoke seemed to be closely akin to some religious ceremony. He remained all the time in the profoundest melancholy. A squaw who could speak a little English, of the simple ungrammatical sort used by the Montreal traders, told me his story. He had lost three children from the smallpox, and his brother had been scalped during a fur-getting voyage in the far north. He wished to go to war himself in order to change his luck, but his Sachem had restrained him. His name was Strong Soup, and he wore tied on his legs the furs of pole-cats, which were the insignia of acknowledged valour. The polecat furs he had won for a deed of desperate daring against the Algonquins, undertaken to erase the stigma of a previous misfortune: when he had fled from the same Algonquins weaponless and leaving his breech-clout in their hands. His revenge was to kill three Algonquin warriors, two squaws, and the only infant child of their chief; lifting four scalps in the act. The popular jeer against him in the matter of the lost breech-clout was thereupon forbidden by his war-chief by means of the public crier.

One other incident of interest occurred while I was here. The woman who told me Strong Soup's story had two children with her, an infant and a girl of perhaps seven years old. The infant was swaddled in a blanket and bound tightly to a piece of board somewhat longer than itself. Bent pieces of wood protected the child's face, lest the board should fall, and it was suspended upon the branch of a birch-tree within reach of the mother's hand: she kept it swinging from side to side like a pendulum while still engaged in her canoe-making. The little girl was covered with a loose cotton garment and was very forward. She came behind me and fingered my accoutrements in a way that the mother regarded as unmannerly. The punishment was not a string of curses or a slap, as it would have been in Ireland, but a stern look and a handful of water scooped from the river and flung in her face, which abashed the child so much that she crept away and hid beneath a canoe. To comfort her, I presented her with a sewing-box that I had bought from the nuns; which she gazed at with evident exultation, and said an eloquent speech of thanks.

'What does she say?' I asked the woman.

'She wish you kill plenty bears, plenty deer, take many scalps. Say your hand like a sieve, give very good gifts.'

The woman and the child had most delicate, harmonious voices, which was the rule rather than the exception, I found; whereas every Indian, almost, with whom I ever conversed spoke as if he had a hot potato in his mouth or a heavy weight upon his chest, pronouncing his words laboriously from the lower part of his throat and moving the lips only very slightly.

The women were dressed in moccasins, leggings, and a loose short shirt like the men, but fastened with silver brooches at the neck. They also wore pieces of blue or green cloth folded closely around their middles and reaching to the knees; and silver bangles on their wrists. I shall have more to say later on the subject of these interesting people; but I cannot postpone a record of my astonishment when the squaw with whom I had been conversing took down the cradle from the tree and, unswaddling the young child, hugged it for a while to her tawny bosom— for I perceived that its body was as fair as that of an English child. I was to observe later that even Negro children were not perfectly black when born, but acquired their jetty hue gradually; just as in the vegetable world the first tender blade of spring, on peeping through the soil, turns from white to pale green, and to emerald only when May is come.

We were asleep on straw in the barn of the Ursuline Convent when the drums suddenly began to beat and in came Lieutenant Kemmis, calling for his groom. He appeared to be in great animation.

'Well, my gallant lads,' he cried, 'we are to have a smack at 'em this morning, it seems. See that you fall in quick and without confusion. Sergeant Lamb, pray inspect the men's arms and ammunition. Pay especial attention to the flints. If any appear worn, serve out new from the box —you have the key?'

'Very well, your Honour. . . . Fall in, men, and tumble to it! Your Honour, are they upon us?'

'They crossed over a brigade of fifty *bateaux* last night from Sorel and landed at Point du Lac, about ten miles upstream from here. We are ordered to join the vanguard with the flank companies of the other regiments.'

Soon we were marching out into the darkness along the river-road, in column of route. Our company, being the eldest light infantry company present, had the right to lead the column of route. It was daylight before we came upon their vanguard. They were marching along the river-road in a careless manner, like a congregation coming out of church, as if not expecting to meet with any opposition. They were slender, loose-limbed men dressed in dark green hunting shirts, long mud-coloured breeches, with tan gaiters. They wore tan ruffles around their necks, at the bottom of their coats, on their shoulders, elbows, and about their wrists. Their hats were round and dark with a broad brim folded up in three places, and in one fold was stuck a sprig of green. This colouring, being in perfect imitation of the hues of a forest, made them very inconspicuous in woody country, whereas a red coat showed up like a poppy in a stubblefield. Here, however, in the open land between blue water and the brilliant fresh-green of young corn they were not indifferent targets. We quickly executed one of the new manœuvres that we had learned from The Thirty-third in Dublin, shaking out across a cornfield. There we fired two very disciplined volleys, to the great scandal and grief of the farmer, who tried to head us off with shouts and curses, caring nothing for the bullets which were already whizzing about him. '*Sacré Nom du Grand Archange Saint Michel et de tous ses anges inférieurs—éloignez-vous bien vite de mes putats, assassins, ou je vois le dire au Général Carleton.*' Which, it seems, was to say: 'Sacred Name of the Good Archangel St. Michael and all his inferior angels, get you gone quick from my potatoes, you hired robbers, or I shall go and complain to General Carleton!'

A bullet happened to strike the pipe out of the honest fellow's mouth, and a clay splinter gashed his cheek. Suddenly realizing the hazards of his position between two fires, he leaped like a hare for the ditch, and lay there cursing and shouting. The burden of his song was that he would on the very next day get aboard his boat and descend to Quebec to complain of the outrage to General Carleton, who never failed to give redress.

The Americans did not stay within range, but ran to hold a slight ridge where they began to scoop shallow trenches in the light soil. Reinforcements came up on either side. Our orders were to hold fast and conserve our fire: if they attacked, we were to charge bayonets and meet them as they came.

This being the first skirmish I ever was engaged in, it really appeared to me to be a very serious matter, especially when the bullets came whistling by our ears. There were a few veterans among us who had been well used to this kind of work, among them old Sergeant Fitzpatrick, who went about with a hymn of the Rev. Charles Wesley's upon his lips and a devout anger in his eyes. But Mad Johnny Maguire took it very easy. 'Oh, by the powers, my honeys, take it easy!' he said. 'This is but only the froth of battle. I was with the dear Ninth in Sixty-two when we stormed the Moro Fort at Havannah. That was the real brew, full and deep, by Jesus Christ!'

He had told us all, during my inspection of their arms and pouches that morning: 'Now there's no need to be alarmed if you hear the sound of a bullet fired against you, for that means it isn't there. It's the bullet you don't hear that's the bother, for often you notice afterwards that it has killed you.'

'Did that often happen to you, Johnny Maguire?' we asked him.

'Not to the best of my recollection,' he answered very seriously, 'but I had a devil of a big fright once or twice.'

Soon the cannon from the vessels in the river began to roar, and the field-pieces which accompanied the van shot over our heads. The fire from the river was particularly severe, for the ships stood in close and blazed from the flank at point-blank. In a battle all sense of the passage of time is absent, as in childhood or during play at cards when the stakes are high. It may have been five minutes or half an hour before we observed that the Americans were going away in twos and threes and that their fire was slackening. We charged bayonets and sprang forward at them with a shout. They made no attempt to stand, which would indeed have been folly in their situation. They had suddenly learned that a brigade of British troops had been landed from transports some distance in their rear, and their one thought now was to regain their *bateaux*, lying a matter of three miles away, before they were cut off. A few valiant or obstinate men stayed behind, firing to the last, but singularly little execution was done: in the whole course of the day our army lost no more than a dozen men killed or disabled. The retreating colonists had not far to run before they were in woodland: we pushed so rapidly ahead, to prevent their making a stand on the road, that their laggards took to the trees.

The Americans won the race to the boats, of which only two were taken, and were soon safe away among the islands and shallows of St. Peter's Lake, where our ships could not pursue them. Two generals, several inferior officers, and two hundred men surrendered in the woods. I had no personal adventures to boast of afterwards; the only American whom I shot at, as he ran from me in the forest, I missed. So ended the brief, glorious, and unremarkable battle of Three Rivers: of which the Americans later spoke as if it had been a great victory, declaring that as many of our people had fallen as at Bunker's Hill, while their own losses were insignificant.

On the day following, we left Three Rivers and were put aboard our transports with all expedition; the wind springing up fair, the fleet sailed towards Sorel. The greatest breadth of St. Peter's Lake, through which we were now sailing, was about fourteen miles, and its length about eighteen. The number of islands here was so extraordinary that it was impossible not to feel astonishment that such large vessels as visited Montreal could pass between them; and indeed the channel was very intricate. Lieutenant Kemmis found the prospect highly romantic, especially since many islands were peopled with camps of Indians dressed in their festival clothes to salute the convoy as it passed, and birch-bark canoes were continually speeding in and out of the vessels, the Indians shouting lengthy exhortations and greetings. The only intelligible part of these was an insistent demand for Christians' fire-water, as spirits were called; for, until the English landed on the American continent, no intoxicating liquors were known to these happy people.

The *Friendship* grounded on a sand-bank in the very

middle of the lake. Some men were sent out in a boat with an anchor, which they dropped in deep water; this gave us purchase to heave the vessel clear so, that we were only stuck fast for two hours. However, it was found impossible to recover the anchor, which loss caused such grief and vexation to the Captain as I should not have expected him to express for that of the whole ship's burden and company. With captains of hired transports, it was evident that the crew, the cargo, and the welfare of their country were but secondary objects. One of them about this time gave the frigate guarding a convoy the slip, and got safe into Boston with a cargo of fifteen hundred barrels of gunpowder, which he sold to the Americans for a sum which made him rich for life.

Our journey from Three Rivers to Sorel at the head of the lake took five days, which was one too many, for upon our disembarking we found the fires of the American encampment still burning, but the men gone. It was here that we saw the last of the *Friendship*. We disembarked with all our baggage and, leaving the St. Lawrence (which runs eight miles an hour at this point), marched south up the Sorel River towards Lake Champlain. A second column pursued another part of the American forces towards Montreal. We began our march in three columns under the command of Lieutenant-General John Burgoyne, M.P., an officer of the greatest experience and universally esteemed by his men, yet somewhat of a grumbler and too easily carried away by his natural eloquence into an exaggeration of injuries received from, and faults committed by, those in authority over him. It was an excellent army, and a great many men served in it who had fought against the French and Spanish. The mistakes that we committed were therefore totally different from those of the Americans: accustomed only to warfare in Indian fashion, they erred in too little regularity of organization and discipline, we often in too great rigidity. Our arrangements for the march, for bivouacking, for reconnaissance of ground, for the placing of outposts, and for the supply of ammunition, victuals, and forage, were admirable; as they were throughout the war, consistent with circumstances. But we were always a few hours' march behind the retreating enemy, who, notwithstanding their haste, took care to destroy by fire all *bateaux*, ships and military stores that they could not take with them, and many houses besides.

Their distresses were very great: a British army of superior strength hanging close on their rear, their men obliged to haul loaded *bateaux* up the rapids by main strength, often to their middles in water. They were likewise very short of lead for running their bullets, of paper and thread for cartridge-making, and of every sort of medicament. This last was the most serious lack of all, since great numbers of them were labouring under that terrible disease, the smallpox, which always struck so fatally in America. We had orders not to handle any belongings left behind by them in their flight, nor to occupy any dwellings where they had lodged. Their dead and dying being left behind in considerable numbers, we provided regular burial squads, consisting of men who had already suffered from the disease.

The sickly season of the year had come, and the Americans felt such terror of death by smallpox that they suffered themselves to be inoculated against it by their surgeons—that is, the fetid matter from one suffering from the disease was pushed under the fingernails of a healthy man. The intention was that he should take the disease, but not badly, and thereafter be immune against the natural infection. In America, ever since the great epidemic of 1764, it had been the custom to have inoculation frolics: to make up a cheerful party of persons of both sexes, in a spacious house with an enclosed garden, for all to be infected together. They could count on two or three days in bed, and six weeks of quarantine spent in pleasant lounging, drinking, amatory and political discourse, cards, prayers, and horse-play. In these conditions, a few were seriously sick, some died, but very many lives were saved. However, the present was no time for such a frolic; the poor creatures being already worn out with the hardships of war and unable to endure the poison. Moreover, no quarantine was possible and those who were inoculated passed on the disease to their comrades. The surgeons were ordered to discontinue the practice, but this did not hinder the men from inoculating one another and performing the operation in a very dirty manner. Though the fatigues of our march were great, we could, I am sure, have overtaken the Americans had instinct not kept our men from increased exertions: we slackened our pace sufficiently to avoid infection from our sick adversaries.

The Canadians showed violent resentment against the invaders for bringing so much ill luck and so little real money into the country. Many of them had been influenced by hopes of gain or by prophecies of a British defeat to take a decided part in the Americans' favour; and this against the warnings of their priests, who refused to confess any rebel. Nor could the clergy have well been expected to adopt any other course of action, Congress having been so highly indiscreet, not to say double-faced; for while pretending great attachment to the Habitants in their struggle against British oppression, they had at the same time published an address to the people of England, which totally contradicted this. The address warmly indicted Parliament for the countenance it had given to Popery in Canada, which they declared to be the dissemination of impiety, persecution, and murder in every part of the globe. Now, though Congress had assured these Canadian rebels, but a few months before, that 'we will never abandon our Canadian friends to the fury of our common enemies,' they were left exposed to the heavy penalties annexed to the crime of aiding or comforting His Majesty's foes. The retreating army could only recommend the rebel Habitants to throw themselves on the mercy of the Government; and this, though ironically intended, proved to be good advice. To the best of my knowledge (I was in Canada for twelve months after this) none of them was either imprisoned or otherwise punished by General Carleton.

On June 17th we came to the hills of Chambly, some forty miles beyond Sorel and there took possession of the old French castle. We found that all the wooden buildings of the place, and all the boats too large to be dragged up the rapids, had been reduced to ashes. The French people hereabouts were greatly relieved that in this new war they were not to be called up for forced labour, as in the old days. We were told that General Montcalm had once visited the Castle in the last war to assure himself that it was in a correct posture of defence; the peasants came dropping on their knees about him to implore him to abate the oppression and tyranny of their militia captains. Among others, the owner of the saw-mill complained that, loyal subject of King Louis though he was, he had been reduced to extremities by the Corvée—his harvest was lost, his family starving, and his two remaining horses had perished of overwork that very day. Monsieur Montcalm looked sternly at him and then, thoughtfully twirling his Cross of St. Louis, remarked: 'But you have the hides still, have you not? That's a deal, a great deal!'

It was at Chambly that our General Prescott had been captured by General Montgomery in the preceding year, together with eleven ships and several companies of men of the Seventh and Twenty-sixth Regiments. He was soon exchanged with the Americans for General Sullivan, who was now opposing us, and put in command of Newport, Rhode Island; but there he was again captured by a party of raiders as he slept, and carried off without his breeches. He was a very peevish, foolish man and suffered tortures from the gout. Our people then brought him back in exchange for another American general, Charles Lee; not so much because they needed poor General Prescott as because the return of General Lee to an enemy command would embarrass General Washington, to whom he was openly hostile. General Prescott won the jocular title of 'Continental Currency.'

On the next day we occupied the redoubts at St. John's; where the enemy in their precipitation had left behind twenty-two pieces of cannon, unspiked and with their ammunition unexploded. The country that we had marched through until we came to Chambly was flat and without interest except for the unusual birds, flowers, trees, and animals. We saw grey squirrels, and deer; and Smutchy Steel had the misfortune to catch a creature resembling a bushy-tailed grey cat streaked with white, which was pursued towards us by a pair of our dogs. This animal, which the Canadians called Devil's Child, discharges its urine when attacked, which infects the air with an intolerable stench. Smutchy had his black linen gaiters soiled and was fain to strip them off and abandon them. There were sweet wild raspberries in plenty beside our route.

A bear crossed a clearing and I had a snapping shot at him, but missed. This animal was rather shy than fierce; he would seldom attack a man, and fled in terror from a yapping dog. Only in July was he dangerous, for this was his mating season and he was abominably jealous. Then he grew very lean for passion and rage, and abstained from eating. His flesh acquired so disagreeable a relish that the Indians would not eat him; but, this season over, he became fat again and ate his fill of honey, and of wild grapes and other autumnal fruit.

Of trees there were an infinite and delightful variety, many of them excessively tall, and very few exactly corresponding in foliage or bark to British trees. For example, there were three different sorts of walnut-tree—the hard, the tender, and the bitter. Of the tender, the wood of which was almost incorruptible in water on the ground, the Canadians made their coffins; the nut of the bitter yielded a very good sort of lamp-oil; the nut of the hard was the best to eat, but caused costiveness. There were beech and elm in great abundance, and the sugar-bearing maple, and cedars, and wild plum, and cherry.

But every local advantage is set off by disadvantages. When we camped at evening we were obliged to clear off the underwood and cut away the small trees from about us: on such occasions we were constantly assailed by enormous swarms of mosquitoes. They could not be kept from attacking us even by the smoke or flame of large fires, which we were always obliged to kindle. The fine perfumes and blooming abundance of such luxuriant regions as these are thus lost from enjoyment by man. For the loss of peace and comfort caused by angry and odious vermin nothing can compensate; and an Englishman's blood being richer or less hardened against mosquito bites than the American's, he suffers almost to madness.

We pressed on for a week past the swamp of St. John's and Nut Island, until we reached the northern reaches of Lake Champlain, which was narrow and long, running south for a hundred miles to Crown Point, where it was linked with the smaller waters of Lake George. For want of boats we could not pursue the enemy farther, and they had several armed vessels on the lake besides. But we had seen them safe out of Canada, and between the smallpox and the fighting they had in a month lost five thousand men. The smallpox accounted for by far the greater number of these. We heard that at one time two of their regiments had not a single man in health, another only six, a fourth only forty—two more were nearly in the same condition. If the rest of the war were to take the same course, we would soon be home again. However, we were obliged to pause now in order to transport a fleet up to Lake Champlain sufficiently strong to out-gun the enemy's schooners which patrolled it and prevented our further advance.

❁ ❁ ❁ ❁ ❁ ❁ ❁ ❁ ❁ ❁ ❁ ❁

CHAPTER

13

THIS highly important task of shipbuilding was commenced on July 4th, the very day that the United Provinces signed the famous Declaration of Independence, formally breaking their ancient connexion with the Crown and people of Great Britain. This declaration anticipated by a few days the arrival of Admiral Howe at Staten Island, close to New York (where his brother, the General, was in command of an expeditionary force that had landed there) with orders from King George for the pair of them to act as Commissioners for restoring peace, though at the eleventh hour. Colonel Paterson, the Adjutant-General of the Forces, was sent with a letter to General Washington as the Commander-in-Chief of the American armies, stating that the Commissioners were invested with powers of reconciliation, and that they wished their visit to be considered as the first advance towards that desirable object.

After the usual compliments, in which, as well as through the whole conversation, he addressed General Washington by the title of 'Excellency,' Colonel Paterson entered upon the business by saying that General Howe much regretted the difficulties which had arisen, respecting the address of the letters to General Washington. For, a few days before this interview, General Howe had sent a letter directed 'To George Washington, Esquire,' which the latter refused to receive, as not being addressed to him in his official capacity. Colonel Paterson explained that the address was deemed consistent with propriety, and founded upon precedents of the like nature, by ambassadors and plenipotentiaries, where disputes of difficulties of rank had arisen. He added that General Washington might recollect he had himself last summer addressed a letter to General Howe, 'To the Honourable William Howe, Esquire.' Lord Howe and General Howe, he said, did not mean to derogate from the respect or rank of General Washington, for they held his person and character in the highest esteem; and the direction, with the addition of '&c., &c., &c.,' implied everything that ought to follow. The Colonel then produced a letter, which he did not directly offer to General Washington, but observed that it was the same letter which had been sent, and laid it on the table with the superscription 'To George Washington, &c., &c., &c.'

The General declined the letter. He said that a letter directed to a person in a public character should have some description or indication of it, otherwise it would appear a mere private letter. It was true that '&c., &c., &c.,' implied everything, but they also implied anything. The letter to General Howe, now alluded to, was an answer to one received, under a like address from him, which the officer on duty having taken, he did not think proper to return, but answered it in the same mode of address. He should absolutely decline any letter directed to him as a private person, when it related to his public station.

Colonel Paterson then said that General Howe would not urge his delicacy any further, and repeated his assertions that no failure of respect was intended.

After an exchange of views on the subject of the treatment of prisoners on both sides, Colonel Paterson proceeded to say that the goodness and benevolence of the King had induced him to appoint Admiral Lord Howe and General Howe, his Commissioners, to accommodate this unhappy dispute; that they had wide powers and would derive the greatest pleasure from effecting an accommodation, and that he (Colonel Paterson) wished to have this visit considered as marking the first advances to this desirable object.

General Washington replied that he was not invested with any powers on this subject by those from whom he derived his authority. But, he said, from what had appeared or transpired on this head, Lord Howe and General Howe were only to grant pardons. Those who had committed no fault, wanted no pardon. The Americans were only defending what they deemed their indisputable right.

Colonel Paterson said, 'That, your Excellency, would open a very wide field for argument.' He confessed his apprehensions that an adherence to forms was likely to obstruct business of the greatest moment and concern.

Colonel Paterson was treated with the greatest attention and politeness during the whole business, and expressed acknowledgments that the usual ceremony of blinding his eyes had been dispensed with. At the breaking up of the conference, General Washington strongly invited him to partake of a small collation provided for him, which he politely declined, alleging his late breakfast, and an impatience to return to General Howe, though he had not executed his commission amply as he wished.

While these two royal Commissioners, the Admiral and the General, were endeavouring in their civil capacity to effect a reunion between Great Britain and the Colonies, in order to avert the calamities of war, Congress seemed more determined in opposition. They ridiculed the power with which the Commissioners were invested 'of granting general and particular pardons to all those who, though they had deviated from their allegiance, were willing to return to their duty.' Their general answer to this was that 'they who have committed no fault want no pardon'; and immediately entered into a resolution to the effect that 'the good people of the United States might be informed of the plan of the Commissioners, and what the terms were with which the insidious Court of Great Britain had endeavoured to amuse and disarm them, and that the few Americans who still remained suspended by a hope, founded either in the justice or moderation of their late King, might now at length be convinced that the valour alone of the country was to save its liberties.'

This was immediately followed by another resolution, in order to detach the Germans who had entered into the service of Britain. It was penned in these words:

'Resolved, that these States will receive all such foreigners who shall leave the armies of His Britannic Majesty in America, and shall choose to become members of any of these States, and they shall be protected in the free exercise of their respective religions, and be invested with the rights, privileges, and immunities of natives, as established by the laws of these States; and moreover, that this Congress will provide for every such person, fifty acres of unappropriated lands in some of these States, to be held by him and his heirs as absolute property.'

So there was clearly no other course to be followed but to prosecute the war with energy: and the campaign began with an attack upon Long Island and the capture of New York. Yet the same aggrieved Captain Montrésor, whose remarks upon the supposed blunders of the British I have already quoted, was very hot against this attempted reconciliation. He stigmatized as a greater blunder than any: 'The sending of the two Howes out as Commanders-in-Chief and Commissioners for restoring peace, with the sword in one hand and the olive-branch in the other; and these two at the same time avowedly in the Opposition and friends to the Americans!' It is true that General Howe did not prosecute the war with remarkable energy, and that the memory of his elder brother who had died in America in the previous campaign, greatly beloved by the colonists, made him more tender than he otherwise might have been towards them. He rejected the view common to most of his subordinates that 'we must be permitted to restore to the King his dominion of the country by laying it waste and almost extirpating the present rebellious race, and upon no other terms will he ever possess it in peace.' Yet Captain Montrésor's hint of General Howe's disloyalty to the royal cause cannot be readily accepted; nor the story that was current in the barrack-rooms that the King had warned both General Howe and General Clinton, when they evinced reluctance to serve in America, that they must either do so or starve. It was, I believe, more sloth than disloyalty that kept General Howe from pressing his advantage at the close of this year, when General Washington was almost beat and the war only kept alive by this eminent soldier's peculiar courage and by the steadfastness of a handful of his adherents, to whom Congress showed itself a worse enemy than any officer of the Crown.

Mention has been made of German mercenaries serving with our forces. To their participation in the war and to that of our Indian allies, the strongest objection was raised both by the Americans themselves and by the Whig Opposition in Great Britain; though hardly with reason, granted the propriety of fighting a war at all. Was there any novelty in the hiring of German mercenaries either by ourselves or by any other nation? There was not. In the Seven Years' War we had employed great numbers of them upon the battlefields of Europe, where the war was won that freed America from the power of the French. Protestant Germans had been called into Great Britain itself to help in the suppression of the Jacobite rebellions of 1715 and 1745: as was natural, seeing that we had set a German Protestant dynasty upon the throne of England, while the defeated Papist dynasty had been Scottish. The Sixtieth Regiment, or Royal Americans, consisting of four battalions who were foreigners almost to a man, had not only protected the colonies from the incursions of the Indians under Pontiac but had been used as a police force against the turbulent border of Virginia and Pennsylvania, to the great gratification of the provincial Assemblies of those colonies. Or was the consideration that these mercenaries were Germans, rather than Swiss or members of some other nation, a source of irritation to the Americans? Again, no. Great numbers of Germans were already residing in America and had been welcomed as the most peaceful, industrious, and valuable immigrants of all; and I have already quoted the resolution of Congress offering citizenship and land to every German soldier who cared to desert. (The ingenious Dr. Franklin made sure that this offer came to the notice of those for whom it was intended, by printing it in German and wrapping it around a large number of packages of tobacco, which he allowed to be captured by Hessian foragers; it had a magnetic effect upon intending deserters.) When the question was later raised of a common language, other than English, to unite all the States under a Federal Government, the German was very favourably considered and, but for the opposition of those who favoured the Hebrew, would, I believe, have been adopted.

Or was the vexation that the Americans felt caused by a sense that the Germans should never have been employed in a civil war of British against British? Then the Americans should certainly have refrained from an appeal to the Canadian-French to rise against us, and should never have sent an army to annex Canada; since this was a war of aggression and not to be represented as one fought in defence of their own liberties.

The fact was, the Americans were aware of the very low point to which the war establishment of Great Britain and the Empire had been reduced, and believed that the regiments that could be spared for the purpose of suppressing the Revolution would be totally insufficient for the purpose. A number of Highland clansmen forced to leave their homes because of elevated rents and the poverty of the soil were glad to enlist in our Army; but few other recruits could be beaten up, even among Irish Papists, notwithstanding the increased value of the bounty paid on enlistment and a dangerous leniency in assessing the requisites of height, age, and health in a serving soldier. Nor was the militia of Great Britain in a fit state to be called out for the defence of their country, to take the place of troops sent abroad. The Americans did not reckon on our raising mercenaries at the tremendous expense that was clearly necessary. They believed we would consider that the wisest course was to cut our losses at once: for the cost of the war had already enormously outweighed the possible financial gains to be won by victory. But Great Britain never reckons profit and loss in a monetary sense when she considers her national honour at stake. There was talk of supplementing our forces in America by the hire of twenty thousand barbarous and hardy Russians from the Empress Catherine, and almost they were sent; but the Empress was in the end persuaded to refuse by her friend King Frederick of Prussia. She wrote to King George in her own hand, somewhat impertinently, to the effect that she had not only her own dignity to consider, but his also. To lend him troops in such numbers would be to imply that he was one of those monarchs who could not suppress with his own armies a rebellion in his own domains. Besides, she would not risk the loss of her brave subjects in another hemisphere of the globe, and so far removed from all contact with herself. This was a great disappointment to our people in America, who considered that the employment of the Russians would be in the highest degree politic; not only were they good soldiers and accustomed to extremes of cold and heat but, not having any connexion with America, nor understanding the language, were 'less likely to be seduced by the artifice and intrigue of those holy hypocrites in Congress.'

However, there are always solders to be bought somewhere on the Continent, if the price offered be high enough: for in Germany especially soldiers are like cattle, and, in loyalty to the rulers whose property they are, and in hope of plunder, will go wherever they are led or driven. They are trained, like spaniels, by the stick. The Duke of Brunswick had a few soldiers to sell. He was a relative by marriage of King George and undertook to provide four thousand infantry and three hundred dragoons in return for fifteen thousand pounds a year paid into his Treasury during their absence abroad, and thirty thousand a year during the two years following their return to Germany. They themselves were to receive the English pay corresponding with their ranks. As a Prince who professed to study the interests of his country, the Duke only detached from his regular forces two battalions of infantry and the dragoons, nor did he supply any horses with the latter. The remainder of the contingent were make-weights of an extreme wretchedness, young boys and wornout old men unprovided with any material of war or the simplest soldier's necessaries: they must be clothed and armed on their arrival at Portsmouth. The officers were veterans, living on half-pay which the Duke now threatened to withhold from them if they would not march at his orders.

The Landgrave of Hesse drove a harder bargain with King George, for he had better troops to offer and was well informed of our exigencies. The Hessians were tall, vigorous, well-trained men and so docile that it has always been a proverb in Germany that Hessians and cats are alike born with their eyes closed. He had twelve thousand of them disposable, and thirty-two pieces of artillery. The pay was to be English pay, but a bounty of £110,000 a year was also to be given the Landgrave so long as the troops remained out of his Principality, and for a twelve month afterwards. For ever soldier killed in action a compensation of thirty dollars was also agreed upon. Moreover, England was to pay for clothing and equipping these troops, and the manufacturers of Hesse were to enjoy the profitable contracts. The Landgrave followed the grocer's fashion of his cousin of Brunswick in, as it were, sanding his sugar and adulterating his tea: he mixed in with his Hessian subjects the off-scouring and scum of every barrack-room in Europe. By these means he raised his country from squalor to affluence, built roads, libraries, museums, seminaries, an opera house, and I do not know what else for the comfort and delight of his remaining subjects.

As for the troops sold to King George by the Margrave of Anspach, they were a bad case; they were forced aboard the transports that were to take them overseas by the use of heavy whips and volleys of musketry. Yet this was not a numerous contingent, and for the most part the Germans were as ready to do what was required of them as our own sailors forced to serve by the press-gang—which, by the bye, was exceedingly active at this time. We served beside the Brunswickers on several occasions during the campaign in the North but seldom with any sense of pleasure or security in their companionship. Except for

'Old Red Hazel,' as our soldiers named General Riedesel, their commander, his two well-trained regular battalions, and the dragoons, they were like a stone round our necks. There seemed no intermediate age among them between grandparents and grandchildren, with the grandparents in the majority; they marched ill, worked slowly, complained much, were ridden with terror of death and were, in brief, wholly unfitted for an active and stern campaign in the frightful woods and deserts that we were to pass through. The famous Prince de Ligne has remarked that a soldier is not at his best when the sap has ceased to mount; most of these poor fellows were already withered—leaf, branch, and root.

A great outcry was also made when it was learned that we were employing Indian warriors against the colonists. It is true that the Indians were cunning, savage, and relentless, but if one side thought fit to employ them as scouts and skirmishers, the other would have been mad to forgo the same military advantages—for they were unequalled in this sort of warfare. It must be noted that the Americans were the first to invite the savages' assistance in their war against us; for in 1775, while we hesitated, Congress had determined to purchase and distribute among them a suitable assortment of goods to the amount of forty thousand pounds sterling to gain their favour. They also sent a speech to them, couched in the simple language always used on such occasions:

Brothers, Sachems and Warriors! We, the delegates from the twelve United Provinces, now sitting in general congress at Philadelphia, send their talk to you, our brothers.

Brothers and Friends, now attend! When our fathers crossed the great water, and came over to this land, the King of England gave them a talk, assuring them that they and their children should be his children; and that if they would leave their native country, and make settlements and live here, and buy and sell and trade with their brethren beyond the water, they should still keep hold of the same covenant chain, and enjoy peace; and it was covenanted that the fields, houses, goods, and possessions, which our fathers should acquire, should remain to them, as their own, and be their children's for ever and at their sole disposal.

Brothers and Friends, open a kind ear! We will now tell you of the quarrel between the counsellors of King George and the inhabitants of the colonies of America. Many of his counsellors have persuaded him to break the covenant chain, and not to send us any more good talks. They have prevailed upon him to enter into a covenant against us; and have torn asunder, and cast behind their back, the good old covenant, which their ancestors and ours entered into and took strong hold of. They now tell us they will put their hands into our pockets without asking, as though it were their own; and at their pleasure they will take from us our charters, or written civil constitution, which we love as our lives; also our plantations, our houses and goods, whenever they please, without asking our leave. They will tell us that our vessels may go to this or that island in the sea, but to this or that particular island we shall not trade any more; and in case of our non-compliance with these new orders they shut up our harbours.

Brothers, we live on the same ground with you; the same land is our common birthplace; we desire to sit down under the same tree of peace with you; let us water its roots, and cherish its growth, till the large leaves and branches shall extend to the setting sun and reach the skies. If anything disagreeable should ever fall out between us, the twelve United Colonies, and you, the Six Nations, to wound our peace, let us immediately seek measures for healing the breach. From the present situation of our affairs, we judge it expedient to kindle up a small fire at Albany, where we may hear each other's voice, and disclose our minds fully to one another.

Subsequently they besought the Mohawk nation to whet their hatchets against us, on the curious ground—among others—of the probable increase of Popery in Canada! They also persuaded Jehoiakin Mothskin of the Stockbridge Indians to take up the hatchet, who warned 'King' Hancock, as the President of Congress, that they must expect him to fight not in the English, but in Indian fashion. All that he desired was to be informed where his enemy lay. He was regularly enrolled in the Army of

Massachusetts. Sir Guy Carleton had attempted in that same year to win over the Six Nations from the seductions of Congress; and had accordingly invited their chiefs, in a language they understood, to 'feast on a Bostonian and drink his blood.' This meant no more than to partake of a roasted ox, of the sort brought up from New England by the drovers, and to wash the meat down with a pipe of wine. The American patriots, however, affected to understand this speech in a literal sense. It furnished a convenient instrument for operating upon the passions of the people, the more so as it was well known that the Mohawks were not by any means averse to eating the flesh of their foes. This they did (as also the Ottawa, Tonkawa, Kickapoo, and Twighee tribes), not from bestial gluttony but from a belief that the estimable qualities of the man they had slain, which centred chiefly in the heart, could be absorbed by the victor who partook of that organ roasted. Most Indians, however, looked upon cannibalism with the same horror that we Europeans do.

How to look upon our Indian allies was a question which greatly puzzled us. It was said that at one period the Indian had not been ready to pick quarrels and perform wanton barbarities as then; and that Penn the Quaker, who founded the Commonwealth of Pennsylvania, proved that his policy of fair, generous, and pacific dealings with the Indian chiefs was never disappointed by any act of spite or ingratitude on their part. He went unarmed in their midst, ate of roast acorns and stirabout with them, and even on occasion shook a leg at their dances. When the first English settlers arrived in New England they were at pains to cultivate the friendship of the Indians of those parts, who often succoured them in their worst need, when nearly dead of cold and starvation. It was only a hundred years later that wars arose. The cupidity or cruelty of individual colonists had excited the communal vengeance of the Indians. Similarly, the Quakers did not forfeit the affectionate respect of the tribes until overreaching them in the purchase of lands: they had covenanted to buy from them as much land as could be walked in a day, but ran rather than walked, and quite omitted the usual custom of sitting down now and then, for good manners, for a smoke and a meal.

Gradually a very evil view came to be adopted by the colonists as a means of stilling the prick of conscience: namely, that the Indians, being heathen, had no claim upon the Christians for fair treatment. In the frontier districts of America, such was the readiness with which offence was taken against an Indian, that should a warrior so much as slap a white man for committing a criminal offence, the act would be eagerly seized upon and exaggerated, the whole white population would rush to war and the tawny men be hunted from their homes like wild beasts. Nor did even the adoption of Christianity serve to protect Indians from the animosity of the Americans: as witness the massacre in 1763 of the twenty peaceful, psalm-singing Conestogas at Lancaster in Pennsylvania by a mob known as the Paxtang Boys—the first burned the Indian houses early one morning and killed six, and later broke into the workhouse where the magistrates had put the fourteen survivors for safe keeping and killed them all—man, woman, and child. They scalped them too, in order to collect the bounty offered by the Government of Pennsylvania for Indian scalps of either sex. The Paxtang rascals were not grudged this blood-money or in any way punished for their wicked action.

There was no peace possible on the frontier, since agriculture, by which the settlers lived, and hunting, by which the Indians lived, are trades that cannot be practised compatibly in the same district; the plough and axe are always the victors. The Indians naturally resented being driven from their ancestral hunting-grounds, without compensation, and from the tombs of their ancestors, and were at their wits' end how to act, for the American pioneers were terrible men and avenged their own losses, ten lives for one. These pioneers, being of a restless and dissatisfied turn of mind, not untainted with greed, instead of keeping within provincial territories where millions of acres remained unoccupied (but all had to be paid for), crossed the boundary lines into Indian territory with no by-your-leave and began to behave in a most proprietary manner. The

Indians' only hope now was to recover some of their losses at least by profiting from the disagreements of the white men. They sold their military services to the French, the English, the Americans in turn at the highest price obtainable.

They became, in effect, banditti and made war not for glory or for any generous motive but only in order to obtain money, rum, guns and powder—necessities of which they had once never even known the name. Many of them were now regular camp-followers, and periodical beggars at the gates of forts and trading-houses; and the alms or stipends given them to avert their hostility were sufficient, wretched as they were, to destroy their self-dependence. Supplied with munitions of war, their propensity for mischief was quickened by the increased means of gratifying it; and they knew their power to enforce tribute by intimidation.

Thus the Indian, who in his natural state was generous and hospitable and expected generosity and hospitality, had been to such a degree spoilt by his dealings with the white races that to expect him either to forget his wrongs suffered at their hands, or to relinquish new appetites that he had acquired and return to his simple state, was manifestly foolish. Even Dr. Franklin, who had disapproved of the Paxtang Boys and who had joined in the 'good talk' quoted above between Congress and the Six Nations, believed firmly that the only solution to the problem of how to deal with the Indian was a gradual extermination of all the tribes.

Revenge is the emotion that burns most hotly in a savage's breast, nor is he careful to distinguish between a particular wrongdoer and the wrongdoer's associates. Let me take an example from the abuses of the fur trade, which were almost incredibly enormous. The Indians assembled at Montreal, Three Rivers, or some other trading-place in the autumn, to exchange the skins taken in the past season for arms, ammunition, blankets, and other articles needed for their support. For two or three hundred pounds' worth of peltry, the product of a whole year's hunting with all its concurrent fatigues and dangers, the hunter was plied with brandy and then given a kettle, a handsome firelock, a few pounds of powder, a knife, a duffel-blanket, some paltry ornaments of tin for his arms and nose, together with paints, a looking-glass, and a little scarlet cloth and cheap calico to make a dress for his squaw. The whole was not worth one twentieth part of the furs which the Indian had brought in. If then the firelock which he had been given proved as unserviceable a weapon as it too often was, despite its showy appearance, and burst at the first discharge, wounding him, he would be like to seek revenge, not on the fraudulent trader who supplied the weapon, but indiscriminately on the first party of white men whom he encountered.

❁ ❁ ❁ ❁ ❁ ❁ ❁ ❁ ❁ ❁ ❁ ❁

CHAPTER

14

In the journal of occurrences that I kept posted throughout this Northern campaign, a gap occurs between June 26th 1776 and the last day of September in the same year. These three months were among the busiest and happiest in my life. In company with all the rest of the Army under the command of General Sir Guy Carleton I was busy shipbuilding. As has already been remarked on an earlier page, vessels were needed on Lake Champlain to oppose the American fleet now cruising up and down upon its waters and hindering our advance, for on either side of the lake the virgin forests presented an impenetrable barrier to invasion. Sir Guy had sent in haste to England for a number of gunboats, in sections. These could be reconstructed in the dockyard at St. John's which lay, as I have said, well above the rapids of Chambly that hindered direct navigation between Lake Champlain and the St. Lawrence River. There was a vessel of one hundred and eighty tons, the *Inflexible*, in building at Quebec; Sir Guy ordered her to be taken to pieces and shipped up the river in *bateaux* together with the carpenters who had been engaged upon her construction—she was likewise to be completed in the dockyard at St. John's. The *Inflexible* carried eighteen twelve-pounders and was ship-rigged. Two schooners lay at Montreal, the *Maria* armed with fourteen six-pounders, and the *Carleton* with twelve. These were sailed at once to Chambly and, rather than lose the time of taking them to pieces, it was proposed by the naval lieutenant who commanded the *Inflexible*, to convoy them upon a cradle overland to St. John's; and the troops should be called upon to build a road for them. General Carleton acquiesced and we set to.

This was a very slow and tedious business, for it meant felling thousands of trees and levelling off the stumps, and hauling the vessels forward by means of cables fixed to windlasses at every twenty yards. Our men lost a great deal of weight by sweating, and much skin from their hands; but this hard work was on the whole beneficial to their health, as was also the copious ration of spruce beer now served out to us as a preventive of scurvy, for we were again living mainly on salt meat and biscuit. At the end of a week, in spite of all we could do, we had advanced the *Maria* no more than a half mile. The General, perceiving that this mode of conveyance would engross more time than the other, ordered the two schooners to be taken to pieces and reconstructed at St. John's in the same manner as the *Inflexible* and the gunboats. Some of us were then employed in the hauling of two hundred laden *bateaux* up the Chambly rapids, which demanded almost incredible exertions; others at the ropewalk at St. John's in making rigging; others in assisting the Royal Marines to improvise stocks and slipways, to reconstruct the schooners and the gunboats (which carried one brass field-piece apiece, varying from nine-pounders to twenty-pounders), and to build, besides the *Inflexible*, a flat-bottomed *radeau* or raft, to mount twelve guns and a number of howitzers, also a gondola with seven nine-pounders, numerous long-boats and a whole fleet of *bateaux*.

My company happened to be employed at first in out-post duty, three miles into the forest from St. John's, where we occupied a block-house protected by a screen

of Indian scouts. It was very pleasant thereabouts. As well
as the other Canadian trees before mentioned, the paper
birch grew plentifully around us, and that rich shrub,
the aralia, with numerous flowers and a high pink fra-
grance, also a wild gooseberry, the honeysuckle of the
garden and strawberries in abundance. We were next set
to building barracks for the troops and artificers. American blockhouses never varied in plan. They were constructed of roughly trimmed logs, placed one on the other
and overlapping at the corners. Each length of timber in
roof and walls was so jointed as to be independent of the
length next to it; so that if a piece of artillery were played
upon the house only that timber which was struck would
be displaced; indeed if one half of the construction were
completely shot away, the remainder would stand firm.
There were two storeys, a shingle-roofed loft, and a chim-
ney constructed of brick or dressed stone; the upper
storey, reached by a ladder, projected two or three feet
beyond the walls of the lower one. Each of these storeys
was supplied with a couple of pieces of cannon and four
port-holes, so that the cannon could be trained in any
direction to resist attack. There were also loop-holes for
musket-fire in all the walls, and holes in the floor of the
upper storey—both at the projected sides, to fire down
upon the enemy if he attempted to storm the lower part,
and in the centre should he succeed in gaining an entrance.
Each block-house served to lodge a hundred men, and
there was an apartment in the upper storey for the officers.
The building was made weatherproof by clay daubed
in the interstices of the timber, and proved snug enough
in winter if the two fireplaces were well supplied with dry
fuel. A block-house was a very strong defence, unless
the enemy succeeded in firing it by incendiary shells, especially when placed on a little knoll in a clearing, as ours
was. The barracks that we built were only rough affairs,
of untrimmed logs, but sufficient to the purpose; it was
not to be expected that they would be needed for more
than short use. Some of our men became handy with the
axe, though it would have needed years more at the task
to make them equal in expertness with the Canadians or
with our American foes.

On one of the rare days when I was free to leave my duty for an hour or so and visit the dockyard I found that the two schooners, *Maria* and *Carleton*, had been reconstructed in a mere ten days; but even this prodigy of expedition was surpassed by the building of the frigate *Inflexible*. Her parts only arrived at St. John's on September 4th, her keel was laid on September 7th, and she was all rigged, armed, and ready to sail by the end of that month. Only sixteen shipwrights built her, and one of these was so badly wounded by an adze on the third day as to be of little service.

One evening at the block-house, where I happened to be in command since the two company commanders were absent at a general conference of officers, and the other officers were out hunting with their dogs, I visited my chain of sentries. I heard a challenge at some distance away and a deal of argument. Presently Mad Johnny Maguire and another soldier brought along for my examination two persons who wished to pass through the posts.

'Who are they, Maguire?' I asked. There was only a feeble light and they had halted at a few paces from me.

'That I do not know, Sergeant,' he grumbled. 'I have had many and various customers pass through my post since first I stood sentry, but here's a pair of queer fish that beat and bewilder me entirely. There's one who says he's a warrior, though, by Jesus, he's a squaw unless my two eyes are liars; and the other calls himself Captain Brant and speaks better English than I do, yet he's a rogue of an Indian for all that. Who knows that they an't a couple of Yankee spies, such fancy fellows as they are, upon my soul!'

I brought them into the officers' apartment at the block-house, where I could question them at greater convenience and without the inquisitive stares of the men. Maguire had not deceived me as to their appearance. The person describing himself as Captain Brant was clearly an Indian of blood, tall, slender, and of commanding appearance. He wore elegant deerskin leggings trimmed with gold lace, moccasins with diamond buckles, a blue military top-coat with tarnished silver buttons, good lace at his cuffs and throat, a pair of excellent duelling pistols in a holster at his side, and several strings of wampum about his neck. His head was bare and shaved clean, but for his scalp-lock which was dyed vermilion. His face was streaked with war-paint.

The other, introduced as Sweet Yellow Head, wore a red velvet dress with a silver girdle, bangles, and long Spanish earrings, a necklace of garnets and small white beads, a wrapper of white fox fur, and a fusil slung on his shoulder. His face was delicately powdered and rouged, and his long, braided hair, with its vermilion streaked parting, was dyed bright yellow. He walked in an exaggerated mincing manner, rolled his eyes coyly about, constantly tossed his hair, and in a word behaved exactly as a gay young ensign would do at a regimental theatrical performance when called upon to play the heroine in a farce.

Captain Brant spoke severely to this creature in the Mohawk language, which I did not understand, and evidently bade him conduct himself in a more seemly fashion. Then he asked me in a deep voice: 'Sergeant, where are your officers?'

I told him that I was in command at the block-house and asked him his business. He replied: 'I am a great man of your allies, the Six Iroquois Nations. I am Thayen-danegea, the Mohican war-chief. My English name is Captain Brant. In the month of May last I fought in the company of Captain Forster at the engagement of The Cedars, thirty miles from Montreal. We took near five hundred Yankees as prisoners; it was great glory. Yet for the love of Jesus Christ, who died for us all, I restrained my warriors from taking scalps and from burning alive a Yankee captain whom they had secured.'

'That was a noble action on your part,' I remarked dryly, 'and I applaud you for it.'

'I thank you, Sergeant,' said he. 'I persuaded my people to do no more than nick a few of their ears, as we do with cattle, to claim possession.'

'That must have angered them excessively,' said I, and he nodded.

'But,' said he, 'they were revenged upon our people for this indignity, for when some of our warriors stripped them of their military finery to wear themselves, the small-pox infected them, and many died.'

He told me that the American Congress had not only refused to ratify a cartel for an exchange of prisoners made between Captain Forster and Colonel Arnold, on the ground of Captain Forster's inhumanity in the matter of the nicked ears, but had demanded him to be delivered up to them by General Carleton to answer for his conduct in this 'atrocious massacre.' Congress, Thayendanegea conjectured, took this unheard-of course to spite Colonel Arnold—though why they did not rather fulfil the agreement than leave their hostages in the hands of so merciless an enemy, only Mr. Samuel Adams perhaps could explain.

Said I: 'No doubt Mr. Adams and his kind regard their troops only when Heaven makes them victorious.' I continued: 'Yet I find it a little singular that you speak English so well, and that the name of the Saviour is on your lips. How does that come about?'

'Easily answered,' replied Thayendanegea (which means, in the Indian tongue, 'holder-of-the-stakes-made-by-the-parties-in-a-wager,' or 'mediator'). 'As a youth I attended the missionary school of the Reverend Doctor Wheelock at Lebanon in the colony of Connecticut, and embraced the Christian religion. I am a well-read man. I assisted Doctor Barclay in revising the Prayer Book as translated into the Mohawk tongue, and Doctor Stewart in translating the Acts of the Apostles. I have myself made a translation of the Gospel of Saint Matthew and have converted numbers of my people. I am acquainted with many English men of letters, including your famous Doctor Samuel Johnson, the lexicographer and author of that pertinent pamphlet, *Taxation no Tyranny*; to whom his *fidus Achates*, Mr. James Boswell, introduced me.'

'From whence do you come now? I had no notification of your approach.'

'From General Herkimer of the New York Militia at Unadilla, in New York Colony, one hundred and fifty miles to the southwest of this place. He called me to a conference.'

'You have been treating with the enemy!' I exclaimed. 'Do you dare tell me so?'

'He had been my friend and neighbour on the Mohawk River and I could not refuse to parley with him. It might be that he wished me to take a letter to Sir Guy Carleton, offering his submission to the King. I agreed to a rendez-vous at Unadilla, where a large hut was to be erected in an open space between his encampment and ours, a mile apart from each. We covenanted to leave our arms behind us, and to meet with only ten men in the suite of each. This was done.

'We shook hands and exchanged general talk, he seeking to know my mind, I to know his. The old man spoke much about peace and how greatly to the advantage of the Mohawk nation it would be if we embraced the sacred cause of Liberty, or at least remained neuter. I spoke to him like a brother, warning him that the cause of rebellion was one accursed of God. He grew impatient. He asked me how much money Sir Guy Carleton had paid me for my services in the cause of tyranny, and undertook to double this sum and to give every member of my suite a rifle-gun and other gifts if we would join his forces. I was offended. I asked, did he take us for dogs? I sent my warriors running back for their rifle-guns to show him that we were not beggars. They discharged a volley in the air and uttered a war-whoop, to his great consterna-tion. He said: "You have broken the covenant," and he was right. For in my impetuosity I had forgotten that no weapons were to be brought to the hut. Then he said: "To-morrow let us meet again, to-morrow in the morn-ing, and talk quietly without anger on these matters." We agreed that only four of us were to be present at the meeting.

'That evening a squaw, who was living as the wife of an American named Waggoner, came secretly to me; she made me swear to spare her husband if she disclosed a plot to take my life. I swore. She was a good woman and to be trusted. "Father," she said, "to-morrow the General and his three men, my husband among them, will have pistols concealed in their shirts. When he proffers you his snuff-box and you go forward to take a pinch, it will be the signal to them to murder you with a volley."

'The next day I went to the hut with my three men, all

unarmed. The General spoke to me very mildly, like a dove, and asked me whether it would be the act of a Christian to permit savages to fall upon my co-religionists, to burn, kill, and destroy them. I replied: "When I was at Lebanon, learning at the feet of the Rev. Dr. Wheelock, he told me that war was evil. But, Neighbour Herkimer, were not your people the first to take up arms in this war?" "Never mind about that," said he hotly. "God damn it, my friend, we were but defending our liberties." I said: "The Rev. Dr. Wheelock, that excellent man, taught me and my friends that the first duty of a Christian was to fear God, and the second to honour the King. Now you both blaspheme God and try to win me, by bribery, to take up arms against your King." He turned pale with rage and said to me: "Let us not bandy arguments, Captain Brant, but know each other for open foes, since you will not listen to the voice of conscience. Let me offer you a pinch . . ."

'I interrupted him: "No, General Herkimer, I will have none of your SNUFF." At that word, which was a signal, five hundred of my warriors sprang from the long grass where they had lain concealed, dressed in their war-paint and brandishing their arms. "Now," says I, "you see, Neighbour Herkimer, how unwise it would have been for me to accept your snuff. I would have sneezed you into your graves. You are in my power, but since we have been friends and neighbours, I will not take advantage of you. We have both been at fault, I to forget yesterday that rifles were not to be brought near to the hut; you to come here to-day with a pistol concealed in the bosom of your shirt. But let me assure you of this, that if ever we meet again before the hatchet is buried, I know well which scalp, of our two, will adorn the other's wigwam." So we came away through the woods, and here I am.'

'Can such treachery be possible?' I asked. 'I have heard that General Herkimer is much regarded among the Americans as a gentleman of honour.'

'That may be,' he replied. 'But with American gentlemen there is this reservation to their code of honour: as none would ever believe the oath either of a whore or an

Indian, so one would not hold oneself bound by any oath
sworn to a whore or an Indian. They seldom cloak their
sentiments, either. I would rather a thousand times deal
with a poor French farmer or a raw British subaltern
officer than with General Washington himself, who is the
most honourable man in their whole army, barring only
Philip Schuyler.'

It came into my mind to ask him what his opinion was
upon Negro slavery, which I regarded as a detestable
practice and incompatible with the Americans' claim in
their Declaration of Independence that all men have an
inalienable right to be free. Says he: 'That is a matter for
their consciences. The Congress of Massachusetts raised the
subject two years ago, but upon their considering the ill
effect that a motion condemning slavery would have upon
their friends in the South, the matter was allowed to sub-
side. I am told that General Washington is an attentive
and just master to his slaves, and there are many like him
in this respect. Should I settle down to farm an estate when
this war is over, I should assuredly employ Negro slaves.
No Indian is apt to the labour of farming, and no white
man would care to work for an Indian. Besides, the blessed
Bible countenances slavery, saying, "Ham shall serve his
brethren." '

I objected to this conclusion, declaring that there was a
world of difference between service and slavery. Then he
told me a fable current among the Indians, which I consider not unworthy of repetition here.

The Great Spirit, God, made the world. It was solitary
and very lovely to look upon. The forests were rich in
game and fruit, the prairies abounded in deer, elk, and
buffalo, the rivers were well stocked with fish. There were
also countless bears, beavers, and other fat animals, but no
sentient being was present to enjoy these good things.
God then spoke: 'Let us make man.' And man was made;
but when he came up before his Maker he was of a pale,
whitish colour. God was sorry, He had pity on the poor
pale creature and did not resolve him into his original
elements, but permitted him to live. God tried once more,
determined to improve upon his handsel task, but inadvertently ran to the other extreme, making his second

man of a black colour. He liked this black man even less than the white, but at the third trial he was fortunate enough to accomplish his design: he made a red man, and was content.

These three men were very poor at the first. They had no lodges, no houses, no tools, no traps—nothing. All of a sudden down came three large chests from the sky on ropes; and the three men, the red, the white, and the black, watched their gradual descent. They landed in a meadow. God said: 'My poor white eldest-begotten, you shall have the privilege of first choice from these boxes. Open them, examine them, choose your portion.' The white man opened, looked, chose. The chest was filled with pens, ink, paper, sand-castors, spectacles, nightcaps, chairs and tables. He put spectacles on his nose, a nightcap on his head, took a pen in hand, sat down on a chair at a table, and began writing out his accounts; nor did he pay any further attention to the proceedings. God thrust the black man aside and said, 'I do not like you, the red man has the next choice.' The red man chose a box filled with tomahawks, war-clubs, traps, knives, calumets, and a variety of other useful objects. He thanked his Maker and went off proudly into the wilderness. God laughed with pleasure. The black man had what was left. It was a chest full of hoes, sickles, water-buckets, ox-whips and shackles; and this slavish lot has been the lot of the Negro ever since, and so will ever be.

I should add to this that the Indian would slay a Negro with as much unconcern as a dog or a cat. I heard of an Indian woman of rank who had a Negro slave captured in a raid from an estate in Virginia; application was made to her for the return of this Negro, who was a remarkably tall, handsome fellow. She listened quietly to the American officers who came after their property, but was determined not to gratify them. Instead, she stepped inside her lodge, fetched a large knife and walking up to her slave, without any sign of emotion plunged it into his belly. 'Now,' she said to the Virginians, 'you can have him if you wish.' The Negro lay writhing on the ground in agony until one of the warriors compassionately put him out of his pain with a blow of a tomahawk.

While I was thus agreeably conversing with Captain

Brant, his companion had sidled out of the room and begun conversing with the men in the lower apartment. Hearing angry oaths, loud laughter, and shrill falsetto cries, I hastily drew out the wedge, or stopper, from a musket-hole in the floor and gazed down. Sweet Yellow Head had taken a fancy to Sergeant Buchanan, who had just entered the room, and now pursued him with disgusting advances, which the troops found very ludicrous but which enraged the Sergeant beyond measure. He flung the Indian from him, seized a musket and would have shot him had I not loudly bawled out: 'No, no!' from above him. This prompted Corporal Terry Reeves, who stood by, to knock up the musket and disarm him; and I then hurriedly descended the ladder by way of the trap-door.

Thayendanegea came after me, and thanked Terry and myself for our good services. Said he: 'If this sergeant had killed my poor cousin, I should have been obliged in honour to avenge the death, as his nearest relation. I am deeply grateful that no blood has been shed. My poor cousin is a *bardash*, born neither one thing nor the other; God knows the reason but not I. He is a brave man and the fleetest on his feet of our whole nation. He has married three men and been faithless to all. I should not have let him out of my sight.'

He called his cousin to him, and publicly chastised him, to the great amusement of the barrack-room. Thereupon, bidding me good-day and assuring me that I could always call upon his services were I ever in need of them, he went off under the escort of Terry Reeves and another soldier in the direction of the camp, taking Sweet Yellow Head with him. On the following day another Indian arrived at the block-house with a fine buck upon his shoulders and a great basket of cranberries in his hand, as a present from Thayendanegea for myself. I recognized the Indian as Strong Soup, his locks still untrimmed, his face still black in mourning. He told me that his squaw having died, his Sachem had at length permitted him to join the war-party; soon his luck would change. I would have given him a present; but he refused, saying that Thayendanegea had forbidden him either to ask for or accept anything, unless it were a fill for his pipe. The fresh meat was so seasonable that I filled his pouch with tobacco, and he appeared gratified. He skinned the buck for me very dexterously and cut it into steaks. The cranberries we boiled in maple sugar.

❁ ❁ ❁ ❁ ❁ ❁ ❁ ❁ ❁ ❁ ❁ ❁

CHAPTER

15

To JUDGE from reports that reached us, the American armies were a most haphazard and disorderly assemblage of men. They could be roused to desperate and courageous action in defence of their homes, but were altogether impatient of discipline. The regimental officers were often the servants, not the masters, of the men, and known for their obsequiousness and easy humour rather than for military qualities; they were also constantly engaged in struggles among themselves as to who should be the highest in office. We all heartily laughed at a report which our informant, an American volunteer in the transport service, swore was true, of a Connecticut captain shaving one of his men, for a fee, on the parade-ground; and how another was cashiered for stealing and selling his men's blankets, which he did as a revenge for their having insisted that he throw his pay into the common stock! However, one of our people who had served in 1762 upon the Spanish Peninsula told me that this very sort of thing was known in Europe also: at Lisbon a Portuguese officer would supplement his meagre pay with journeyman tailoring and cobbling, and his lady would take in washing—nor was he above asking alms of passers-by as he mounted the guard at the gates of the Royal Palace at Lisbon. Yet at least, our man said, the Portuguese service had never suffered from the spirit of insubordination that reigned in the American. There it was so strong that, as we now know, General Philip Schuyler resigned his command rather than be forced to 'coax, to wheedle and even to lie to carry on the service'; and that General Montgomery had on more than one occasion informed his officers that unless they would obey his orders he would quit the service and leave them to cut one another's throats at their pleasure. General Washington himself declared that, had he seen what was before him, no earthly consideration should have wooed him to accept the chief command; for discipline was impossible while men considered themselves the equals of their officers and regarded them no more than a broomstick. These three were all generals in the aristocratic way, and were greatly hindered in their efforts to improve the fighting efficacy of the forces: by two or three humbly born colleagues who had won general's rank, not because of proved military experience or talent but because of their known inveterate rancour against the British and a talent for ingratiating themselves with members of Congress. General Washington made many enemies in Congress by his too ingenuous plea that gentlemen and men of character should be given the preference in the allotment of commissions.

The length of service fixed by the various provincial Assemblies for their militia varied greatly, but more than a year was never required of them. Volunteers might engage themselves to serve for six months or a year, for six weeks or four weeks, or for as long as it pleased them. A militiaman might buy a substitute and many did so, from the dregs of the population; the American Army contained numbers of ruffians so hired, transported felons and such, to whom the Mosaic allowance of thirty-nine lashes was a contemptible punishment—they would offer, after receiving it, to suffer as much again for the fee of a pint of rum. These regiments were continually fluctuating between camp and farm. A soldier would announce unceremoniously to his captain: 'See here, Neighbour Hezekiah, my old woman writes to tell me that she has but one nigger and my boy left on the farm, since the hired man was called. She has all the ploughing to do yet for the winter grain, and ten loads of hay to get in. Within ten days she'll be lying in, and my elder daughter is tarnal sick with fever. I believe now, I must make my way home to Waterbury to-morrow, battle or no battle.' When he went, he took his firelock and the powder and shot served out to him, and seldom returned. The Connecticut men were the worst offenders in this respect; but the staunch Virginians accused the New Englanders in general of having an 'ardent desire to be chimney-corner heroes.'

When we British enlist, we know what to expect from a soldier's life; but with the Americans the motive of Liberty, which spurred a peaceful man to take up arms on an impulse, was often insufficient to nourish him as a soldier. Washington is reported to have written to Congress at this very time that: 'Men just dragged from the tender scenes of domestic life, unaccustomed to the din of arms, and totally unacquainted with every kind of military drill are timid and ready to fly from their own shadows. The sudden change in their manner of living, particularly in their lodging, brings on sickness in many, impatience in all, and such an unconquerable desire of returning to their respective homes that it not only produces shameful deserters among themselves, but infuses the like spirit into others.'

There was a great shortage among them of arms and ammunition, the commissariat service was irregular and often the men went hungry; for Congress had little force of authority and could only request, not compel, the States of the Unions to provide rations for the troops stationed on their soil. Much meat and flour was lost by careless transport; for example, wagoners with a load of pickled pork would broach the casks and let the liquid escape in order to lighten their load, so that the meat would be rotten before it could be issued.

There was great quarrelling and jealousy among regiments sent from different parts of America. The 'Buckskins' of the South railed against the 'scurvy damned Yankees' of the North, the Yankees against 'the haughty coxcombical Buckskins'; but these enemies were united in their dislike of the people of the middle provinces, who seemed to them undisguised Tories and rank Britainers. How they fought the war out together to a successful issue is a standing mystery to us all; despite the gross errors and treacheries of our fellow-countrymen in England, and the aid that the French, Dutch and Spanish afterwards provided.

While we were completing our fleet, the Americans at the foot of the lake were attempting to strengthen theirs; though in addition to all the other disagreeables enumerated above, the continuance of the smallpox among them, the increasing sickliness of the season and an utter destitution of all necessaries and comforts made it almost impossible for them to hold their ground. An average of thirty new graves a day were dug at Crown Point. Had it not been for the reckless and indomitable spirit of Brigadier-General Benedict Arnold, their commander, they were already vanquished. General Arnold, who had considerable maritime experience from his trading voyages to the West Indies, asked Congress for three hundred shipwrights to be sent at once to help his men construct thirty gondolas and row-galleys, to reinforce the three schooners and the sloop already under his command. The gondolas were a large sort of *bateau* manned by a crew of forty-five; the row-galleys were keeled and carried a sail, their complement being eighty men, and were both faster and handier than gondolas in open water. He also desired a frigate of thirty-six guns to be constructed, but the carpenters did not appear in the numbers expected. By the end of September, when we were ready with our fleet, the newly constructed American boats numbered only four galleys and eight gondolas. These were, however, not vessels to be despised, being very well-gunned. Their fleet could at any single time bring thirty-two of their eighty-four pieces to bear on any quarter; ours disposed of only forty-two guns in all, if I leave out of computation the radeau *Thunderer* and our single gondola, both of which proved unmanageable. Our advantage lay in the frigate *Inflexible*, which was better than any vessel they could boast, and in our crews. For not only had a number of regular naval officers offered themselves for lake service, from the royal squadron that lay at Quebec, but two hundred prime seamen from the transports had come forward too. Arnold's fleet was manned by landsmen, the three hundred mariners from Marblehead that he expected not arriving until after the engagement.

On October 4th, our little squadron sailed out under the command of Captain Pringle, with General Carleton aboard the schooner *Maria*, our flagship. That same day my company, with the rest of the Light Infantry, had orders to draw a week's rations and move along the western shore of the lake, a screen of Indian scouts protecting us. This we did, and strove to keep abreast of the fleet. The woods were very dense and because of quags and other difficulties we could make no more than a few miles a day before bivouacking at night. General Carleton had expected to find the enemy on the eastern side of the lake, and in consequence we had no hope of witnessing a sea-battle. However, we were lucky enough to come within sight of Valcour Island, some forty miles on our way, at the moment when General Arnold's fleet, which was sheltering in a small bay within full view of the shore, no more than a half mile from us, was engaged by our ships. Valcour Island was two miles in length and had high cliffs. There were many Indians friendly to us encamped upon it at the time. The Americans lay in a half-moon formation, close together. They were so disposed, we observed, that few vessels could attack them at the same time, and these would be exposed to the fire of the whole fleet. Our ships, driving with a strong north-easterly wind, had overshot the island, before discovering the enemy, and were under the disadvantage of attacking from the leeward.

We were spectators of the whole battle, taking post on the shore, each company digging itself an entrenchment, from behind which it could prevent the Americans from landing if they were forced ashore by the cannonade of our ships. It was an awful and glorious sight. A little before noon, Arnold's flagship, the *Royal Savage* schooner, and four galleys got under way. They ran down with the wind against the *Inflexible* frigate as she drew slowly under the lee of the island. But the *Royal Savage* was mishandled and dropped to leeward, coming unsupported under the fire of the *Inflexible*, which headed our line. Three heavy shot struck her and she ran ashore on the southern point of the island, where a great number of our gunboats came up and silenced her from short range. One of them was sunk. As an Irishman, I was proud to know, watching this fine fight, that the matrosses who served in the gunboats were drafts from the Irish Artillery in Chapelizod. General Arnold abandoned the ship and transferred himself and his flag to the *Congress* galley; where for want of trained artillerymen he was obliged to point and discharge every gun himself, stepping rapidly from one to the other, like a person touching off fireworks on the King's birthday.

The *Inflexible* could not make any headway, because the wind was blowing from the north, but the schooner *Carleton*, which followed, caught a flaw from the cliffs which fetched her nearly into the middle of the American fleet. There her commander intrepidly anchored with a spring on her cable; which is to say, a rope attached from one side of the stern to the anchor, by hauling on which a broadside could be fired at the foe alternately from starboard and larboard. There she did much execution among the Americans, sinking a gondola, but suffered severely herself. Half of her crew were killed or wounded, her commander was knocked senseless, another officer lost his arm and only Mr. Edward Pellew, a lad of nineteen, remained fit for duty. (He was to become Admiral Sir Edward Pellew, now Commander-in-Chief of our Forces in the Mediterranean, and the most famous of all our frigate-captains in the French Wars.) The spring being shot away, the *Carleton* swung bows on to the enemy and her fire was silenced. Captain Pringle in the *Maria* signalled to her to retire, but she could not, and two gunboats came to tow her off; her hull had been pierced in many places and she had two foot of water in her hold. Meanwhile the commander of our radeau *Thunderer*, not being able to come into action, went with a boat's crew aboard the *Royal Savage* and turned her guns on the two larger enemy galleys, *Congress* and *Washington*, who returned the fire.

The noise of the cannonade was tremendous and was tossed back and forth in echoes across the water between cliffs and woods. Our men held their fire, for the enemy were out of range; but the Indians, who had rushed up on hearing the noise and were dancing about and yelling in their excitement, fired a great number of useless shots across the strait. We also distinguished musket-fire from the cliffs of Valcour where a large number of Indians were congregated. Two enemy boats were now seen making for the *Royal Savage* in an endeavour to retake her; but in good time our people set her on fire, and before the boarding-party could arrive she was blazing hotly and soon blew up with an awful roar.

There was a lull in the fighting, of which we took advantage to eat our biscuit and dressed meat, and some of us even slept awhile. As the afternoon wore on, the breeze changed direction, and to our great satisfaction we saw the *Inflexible* slowly tacking up the strait, followed by the *Maria*. By evening she had worked to within point-blank range of the American squadron and with five heavy broadsides silenced the whole line.

It was growing too dark to distinguish friend from foe, and to avoid being rammed or boarded, the *Inflexible* fell back; the whole squadron thereupon anchored in a line across the strait. The Americans had suffered severely. Two gondolas and the *Congress* galley had been badly holed, most of the officers had been killed or wounded, and they had blown away nearly all their ammunition. We had orders to keep a strict watch all night lest the Americans attempted to land on our coast; for that seemed their only hope of escape from this predicament. The breeze fell and a thick mist overspread the lake. We were very cold that night and crowded near our camp-fires.

When at about eight o'clock in the morning a southerly wind sprang up and the view cleared, we were surprised to find the Americans gone. General Arnold had contrived to bring the whole fleet away safely under cover of the mist and the extreme obscurity of the night. They had stolen out 'in Indian file,' as it were, through a gap in the British line, with a dark-lantern on the counter of each vessel to guide the one following. The *Congress* brought up the rear of the column, for Arnold was always a laggard in any retirement. Three months before he had been the very last man to quit Canada in the retreat, riding back for a view of our vanguard and with difficulty escaping capture by our Light Infantry. For his beaked face, angry eye, and towering ambition the Indians named him 'Dark Eagle.'

General Carleton was enraged to find that his prey had escaped, and was in such a haste to take up the pursuit that he sailed off without leaving us orders; so we kept our posts for another day but sent out scouts, north and south.

That evening he returned again, believing that the Americans had gone up the lake, after all; but we brought him word from the Indians that the vessels had been seen hiding behind Schuyler's Island, eight miles down; they were weaker by two gondolas, which could not be patched into sea-worthiness, or lake-worthiness rather, and had been scuttled.

The wind had now turned round and was blowing up the lake. It hindered both the Americans' retreat to Crown Point and our pursuit. Their remaining six gondolas were slow and delayed the rest of the fleet, so that though they had a start of fifteen miles, from the moment when General Carleton once more turned about, he had a hope of catching them. Our orders were to continue down the lake so soon as daybreak came. We could not move rapidly enough to be present at the coming battle. It took place at noon that day, October 13th, in the lower narrows of the lake, at a place called Split Rock, about twelve miles above Crown Point and thirty from Valcour Island. The wind was now north-east. Here the *Maria* schooner, with the *Inflexible* and *Carleton* close astern, having greatly outdistanced our gunboats and the rest of the fleet, came up with the Americans. Split Rock was a strait between two rocks, just wide enough for our large ships to pass through, and with a very rapid current. The action lasted two hours; we could hear the noise of the cannonade brought down the wind, and mended our pace; though we knew that this was to no purpose.

Our ships were victorious; but General Arnold by fighting a delaying battle contrived to save part of his fleet, which got safely away, viz. two schooners, the sloop, two galleys, and one gondola. But the *Washington* galley struck early in the action was taken with a general aboard, General Arnold's second-in-command; and, as for the *Congress* galley and the four remaining gondolas, they were lost. By General Arnold's orders they were pulled to windward where our men could not pursue, except in small boats, then steered into a creek about ten miles from Crown Point, but on the other side of the lake from us, run ashore and set on fire.

As usual, General Arnold was the last man to leave the post of danger. He stayed aboard the *Congress* until the flames had fairly caught her, whereupon he clambered along the bowsprit and leaped down to the beach. He and his men came safe back through the woods opposite Crown Point, after a skirmish with the Indians; then he saw a great smoke across the water, and learned that the Americans, on hearing the noise of gunfire from up the lake, had at once sent off their sick and baggage from Crown Point, set all the buildings there a-fire, and were now falling back on the fortress of Ticonderoga. So General Arnold went there likewise. Ticonderoga was fifteen miles below Crown Point, and its newly built fortifications were reputedly of great strength: they had been laid out for the Americans by a Polish military engineer who has since become famous on other fields of action—the patriot Thaddeus Kosciusko.

It was three days before we rejoined General Carleton, who had landed at Crown Point, and four more before the main body of our army appeared, transported on a fleet of *bateaux*. Meanwhile we encamped in a place called Button-Mould Bay, after the abundance of pebbles, thrown up on the shores, of the exact form of a button mould. Where those of wood or horn could not be procured, they would make excellent substitutes. When the Army came ashore we continued towards Ticonderoga, with our light infantry companies to the front as usual, in two columns, one on either side of the lake. Some of our vessels approached within cannon-shot of the enemy works, but the attack was not pressed. General Carleton judged it too late in the year to continue the campaign, even if we could quickly reduce Ticonderoga, which appeared doubtful. The intention had been to push on into the heart of New York State and to take the town of Albany on Hudson's River, where there was an important arms manufactory. General Carleton foresaw that communications with our base in Canada would be long and difficult, and now that the Americans had their harvest in, great forces of frontiersmen and militiamen from every part of New England would be free to beset us on all sides. It was no light task to march an army, of inferior strength to the enemy, through one hundred miles of tangled forest in the American winter. Old General Phillips, of the Artillery, was for taking a crack at the defences of Ticonderoga, which he swore were easily taken, and wintering there. General

Phillips had gained great glory at the battle of Minden, by galloping his guns ahead to harass the broken French; General Riedesel, who had also been present at this battle, in the service of Prince Ferdinand of Brunswick, agreed with him now that the enemy redoubts were more pretentious than strong. But General Carleton would not heed. 'Let us leave the Americans alone,' he said, 'and they will destroy themselves more effectively than could we: if the events of the past year have been any indication of their quality as soldiers.'

On the last day of October we were withdrawn up the lake, on *bateaux*, much to the relief of the Americans.

The colonies were now in the way to lose the war, largely from their common tendency to set the desire of personal irresponsibility before the ideal of national independence. Boston had been abandoned by us, but New York City and the seaward ports of New Jersey occupied by very large forces. General Howe had beaten General Washington's army in several engagements; and, before the year was out, forced him across the Delaware River into Pennsylvania. Moreover, we had occupied Rhode Island, one hundred and fifty miles farther up the coast towards Boston, and in the coming year a converging attack was to be made simultaneously on the revolutionaries by three armies—ours from the northward, by way of the lakes; the New York army from the southward, up the valley of Hudson's River, and another army from the eastward, with Newport, Rhode Island, as its base, marching through Massachusetts. The King very sensibly decided that the tinder and dry fuel of rebellion lay in the Northern provinces. If the conflagration could be stamped out there, it would die out elsewhere for want of nourishment. The South was green wood, slow to catch, and the Middle provinces were damp straw. It was unfortunate, however, and shameful too, that this plan of campaign, which was a Ministerial secret, should have been disclosed to members of the Opposition and published by them in the newspapers, copies of which reached America. The enemy were thus forewarned, many months in advance.

Our return up the lake to Canada was without adventures, and the beauties of Nature that unfolded themselves before us seemed the more fascinating now that for some months at least the hideous spirit of war need not hover between. The autumnal hues of the woods surpassed language, for their variety, and afforded infinitely more satisfaction, than when all had been uniformly green. Sunsets and rainbows appeared tumbled among the forests. The gaudy reds and yellows intermingling with the dark green of the pines and the shadows of the rocks, as we threaded our way between the islands, were reflected in the placid blue waters of the lake. At some points the mountains were in a blaze of glory, and yet as Sergeant Fitzpatrick remarked, 'like the Burning Bush that astonished Moses, they are not consumed.'

I had brought a fishing-line on the campaign and amused myself by baiting a hook with a shred of ration beef and seeing what I could pull up. One morning I had a bite; I struck, and pulled up a singular dark-brown fish with horns like a snail's and a cat's visage. As it lay struggling in the bottom of the boat, I observed that it could lift or retract these horns at pleasure. I had the curiosity to touch one of them, to see whether it would draw them completely into its head, but I was punished by a severe numbing sensation, passing right up my arm, which stung so painfully all that day that I was incapacitated for duty. It was explained to me by Lieutenant Sweetenham, who was in our boat, that the horns of this creature, which was called a catfish, were naturally charged with the electric fire or principle which the celebrated Dr. Franklin first drew down from heaven by a kite-string. Its flesh proved fat and luscious, very much like that of the common eel; the fins were bony and strong.

On November 2nd we disembarked at St. John's again and were marched for two days through the woods till we came to Montreal, the first inland city of the American continent. It was built upon an island thirty miles in length and about twelve in breadth, formed by a divarication of the River St. Lawrence, and containing two large mounttains. The Ninth were to be quartered upon the Isle of Jesus, which was an island within this island, being about three miles in length and a little less in breadth and contained by two inlets of the river. The Isle of Jesus was cleared of woods and had a church and a number of farm-houses, as well as the barracks put up for our accommoda-tion, and provided us with a very agreeable place of repose after our labours of the summer. The troops were rarely given leave of absence to visit Montreal, but we were one day marched by Lieutenant Kemmis to the top of the higher mountain of Montreal island in order to enjoy what he described as the most sublime view in all North America.

This was a most fatiguing journey, for there was no regular path to be discovered, and we were in full march-ing order for the exercise; but even the greatest grumblers of the company confessed, when we gained the summit and had well eaten and drunk of what we brought with us, that the prospect was an ample compensation. A vast coloured sea of woods stretched out before us, through which whirled the huge stream of the St. Lawrence. Far below us in the near distance we could descry the city of Montreal in the sunlight. It made a narrow oblong square, on a low ridge parallel with the river, sloping down evenly to the water-front and divided by regular well-formed streets. All the houses, almost, were whitewashed. A high plastered stone wall surrounded the city, consisting of cur-tains and bastions; and beyond, except on the waterside, were a dry ditch and a sort of glacis surmounted by a parapet loopholed for musketry. These defences were not strong and had been raised by the French long ago as a protection against Indians armed with bows and arrows, rather than a European enemy. The city was so situated, as we could see, that no works could be raised to enable it to stand a regular siege: for it was commanded by many eminences near by. There were numerous elegant houses in the suburbs, but these did not catch the sun so hand-somely as those inside the city, which were covered with tin-plates, instead of shingles, for fear of fire. Fires, due to the inhabitants' attachment to red-hot stoves kept burn-ing all night, had so often destroyed the city that it was now built wholly of stone with sheet-iron shutters to the doors and windows; which gave it, as one walked down the street after dark, the appearance of an assemblage of prisons. We lifted our eyes from the city and looked

south-east across the river to the distant hills of Chambly;
and beyond them to the Green Mountains of Vermont,
about sixty miles away, capped with snow—the residence
of our enemies.

Our English-speaking guide bade us beware of serpents,
which abounded in these woods, but he confessed that they
were frightened off by the regular tramp of marching
boots and would not bite unless surprised by the stealthy
approach of a single person in moccasins. Only the cop-
perhead snake, he said, was so torpid and sulky that he
would not move out of the path though an elephant approached, but would infallibly strike at him as he passed.
I may add, however, that no elephant had as yet visited the
American continent; nor was one brought there for a show
until some years after the Revolution.

This guide discoursed much upon snakes—the rattlesnake, whose skin, when the animal is enraged, exhibits a
variety of beautiful tints, and who gains a new rattle to his
tail for every year of his noxious life. Later, I saw two
or three of them scuttling from me in the woods. This
creature is greenish-yellow in colour, as thick as a man's
wrist and about four feet in length. The Indians esteem
his flesh as whiter and more delicate than the best fish. His
sloughed skin, charred, pulverized, and swallowed with
brandy is the best-known specific against rheumatism.

The guide told us a very deplorable story of an American farmer of the Minisink who one day went to mowing
with his Negroes, but wore boots as a precaution against
being stung. Inadvertently he trod on a snake, which immediately attacked his legs, but, as it drew back in order
to renew its blow, one of his Negroes cut it in two with
his scythe. They prosecuted their work all day, and returned home when the sun set. After dinner, the farmer
pulled off his boots and went to bed. He was soon after
seized with a strange sickness at his stomach. He swelled
up and died before a physician could be procured. A few
days after his decease his son put on the same boots, and
likewise went to the meadow to work. At night he pulled
them off, went to bed, and experienced similar sufferings
of sickness as took off his father. A little before he expired
a doctor came, but, not being able to assign the cause of

so singular a disorder, he pronounced both men to have died by witchcraft. Some weeks after, the widow sold all the movables for the benefit of the younger children, and the farm was leased. One of the neighbours who bought the boots, presently put them on, and fell sick, as had happened in the case of the other two. But this man's wife, being alarmed by what befell the former family, dispatched one of her Negroes for an eminent physician who, fortunately having heard of the dreadful affair, divined the cause, and applied medicines which recovered the man. The boots which had been so fatal were then carefully examined, and he found that the two fangs of the snake had been left in the leather, after being wrenched out of their sockets by the strength with which the snake had drawn back its head. The bladders which contained the poison, and several of the small nerves, were still fresh and adhered to the boot. The unfortunate father and son had both been poisoned by wearing these boots, in which action they imperceptibly scratched their legs with the points of the fangs—through the hollow of which some of the astonishing venom was conveyed.

The best specific against rattlesnake bite is the juice of a sort of plantain-leaf: it was accidentally discovered by a Virginian Negro who desperately rubbed it upon his leg to soothe the agonies of a bite, as he lay by the wayside. The Negro not only recovered from the poison, but was emancipated by his master as a reward for this service to humanity.

The same guide told us also of a small, speckled, hissing snake with spots which glow with a variety of colours when he is enraged; at the same time he blows from his mouth a subtile and nauseous wind that if drawn into the mouth of an unwary traveller will infallibly bring on a mortal decline; for there is no remedy against it. He tried our credulity further with an account of the whip-snake which, he said, pursues cattle through wood and meadow, lashing them with his tail, until overcome with the fatigue of the chase they drop exhausted to the ground, where the whip-snake preys upon their flesh. This was perhaps true, but we could not accept his account of the hoop-snake which thrusts the extremity of his tail into a cavity of his mouth, where it catches fast with an arrangement like a pawl and ratchet, and then rolls forward like a boy's hoop with such extreme velocity that neither man nor beast can hope to escape from his devouring jaws.

There was a silence of a few moments after this tale, which Mad Johnny Maguire took the privilege of breaking, as he was the oldest soldier among us. 'Oh, what a darling monster that must be, from which nobody has ever escaped alive to give so sensible an account of his habits! But he's nothing at all compared with the serpents of Killaloo that Saint Patrick drove out of my country when he first came. They banged all: they could wrap their necks about a rifle-gun and squint along the barrel, and both load and fire it with their tails! But the Saint prayed at them, and waved his staff at them, and told them to quit before the Sunday following, and off they went, howling. The proof that I'm not codding you is that not a single specimen of the breed is still to be found on the shores of Ireland. Let us hope, by Jesus God, that they did not take ship to Canada.'

❀ ❀ ❀ ❀ ❀ ❀ ❀ ❀ ❀ ❀ ❀ ❀

CHAPTER

16

MAJOR BOLTON was taken from us to command the Eighth Regiment; they were stationed partly at Niagara, by the world-renowned waterfalls which lie between the Great Lakes of Ontario and Erie, and partly at Detroit on the waterway joining Lakes Erie and Huron. We were sorry to lose so considerate an officer, but my private feelings were the more affected by the news of his removal when I learned that Private Harlowe, who was now his orderly, was going along with him. I did not care two-pence whether or not I ever beheld Harlowe himself again in the whole future course of 'my versal life,' but his wife would naturally accompany him; and let me here confess that for months past I had been tormented by longing thoughts of her. Struggle as I might against the spell that she had cast upon me, her face invaded my dreams and constantly stood before my imagination at all hours of the day, especially when I was in a relaxed condition of body after some heavy duty. I had not set eyes on her since we sailed from Ireland, for the women and children had remained behind with the baggage-guard during our advance to St. John's and had been removed to Montreal when we proceeded up the lake. Now, at the first consideration, I was deeply grieved that I should not see her about the camp in the Isle of Jesus, as I had imagined that I would; but, at the second, there came a feeling of relief. For the sick temptation to run on evil courses, as well as the innocent pleasure of looking upon a face that I heartily loved, would be removed by her residence at Niagara. I busied myself in my military duties and began to look forward with keen expectation to the winter, which was the social season in Canada and always passed with great good cheer and merriment—especially in the neighbourhood of Montreal, where there were numerous sports performed in the ice and snow every day, and dances near every night in the better sort of houses. But first came the time called the Indian Summer, marked by a reddish, hazy, quiet atmosphere; the woods were close and warm with the exhalations of fallen and rotting leaves, which bred melancholy thoughts.

However, I was to be absent for some time from my comrades. We had not been in our new quarters above three weeks, during the last few days of which it snowed almost incessantly, so that the ground was covered to a depth of about four feet, when Captain Sweetenham, as he now was, sent for me. 'Sergeant Lamb,' he said, 'Colonel Guy Johnson is inquiring after you, and Corporal Reeves and yourself are to wait upon him this afternoon at his residence near the Place des Armes in Montreal.'

'I do not know the gentleman, your Honour,' said I.

'He is an Irishman, the Superintendent of the Indian Department of our Government and a person of great consequence among the tribes. Colonel Johnson has asked for three months' leave of absence to be given you for a special mission, in case you wish to accept it.'

'I shall be glad to go on any mission,' I answered, 'and the more adventurous the better it will please me. In Corporal Reeves's company I would dare go anywhere.'

'You will hand over your duties to Sergeant Buchanan,' the Captain said. 'Inform him so.'

I touched my tall cap and departed, with a pleasurable sense that my friend Thayendanegea was at the bottom of this business; and, upon my arrival at Montreal with Terry Reeves, I found that it was so. Terry and I made the journey in a hired cariole, a sort of carriage upon runners which the horses of the country could draw with ease, through ice or snow, at the rate of fifteen miles an hour. The people of Montreal were very curious in the way that they fashioned their carioles in every possible variety of design, such as the representation of some beast or fowl, a Venetian gondola, a Quaker shoe, a whale, or a monster goldfish. This one simulated a black swan, and was well provided with blankets. The cold was so severe that the St. Lawrence itself was now nearly all frozen over, though there is a ten-knot current at Montreal; but Terry and I were surprised that we felt so little inconvenience from it. The reason was the superior dryness of the air. Perhaps this dryness excused a habit of the Canadian which seemed barbarous to us, namely, of allowing his horses, sweating after a journey of perhaps twenty or thirty miles, to stand for hours on end, without any covering at all, outside the door where he had gone visiting.

The journey into Montreal was doubled in length by our driver constantly stopping, whenever he came to a wayside shrine or crucifix, to climb down and say a prayer. He was not to be deterred from this practice even by Terry's threats to cut off his treasured queue with a jack-knife, did he not shorten his orisons. It then occurred to me that the word of command, '*Marche-donc*,' spoken to the horse in tones, simulating those of his master, would likely enough set our chariot in motion. The plan succeeded, and the driver, hearing our loud farewells, leapt up, cursing, from his knees and rushed after us. It was fortunate that the horses recognized his voice and presently pulled up, for neither Terry nor I knew the word for 'Whoa,' and might well have been arrested for the theft of a cariole. The fur-clad driver was quite breathless from his long run when he climbed up into his seat, which enabled me to anticipate the French sentence which I knew was choking in his throat. '*Je vais le dire au Général Carleton,*' said I, very severely.

Then I offered him a drink of spirits and presently we were good friends again. He only descended for a short prayer at one more shrine, where was represented the sponge, vinegar-bottle, spear, and various other instruments mentioned in the Gospel chapters concerning the crucifixion of Jesus Christ; the whole assemblage surmounted by St. Peter's cock.

Montreal presented a very animated appearance, for this was the season when the Indian fur-trappers assembled with their peltry to sell to the resident merchants. The city then took on the appearance of a great fair, with booths adorned with fir-branches set up in all public places for the sale of every conceivable object of utility or luxury. We saw numerous painted, pipe-smoking Indians, with capes over their heads and shoulders wadded with feathers, and the squaws dressed in their finest clothes with jewellery, ribbons, and dyed plumes; British officers on horseback in full regimentals of flashing gold, silver, blue and scarlet; merchants whose Parisian extravagance of dress was intended to impress the Indians with an idea of their consequence; priests, friars, lay-sisters; armed parties of British soldiers in travel-worn greatcoats, marching to fife and drum; groups of animated French Habitants of both sexes—the women in long scarlet cloaks, the men in their sleekest furs, and swarms of warmly muffled, exuberant children; fantastic carioles jingling and whirling up and down the narrow streets; and, in the squares, frequent statues of men, monsters, beasts, and birds fashioned of heaped snow and glazed to perfection by pails of coloured water dashed over them.

At the Place des Armes, a sort of square which was used before the Conquest as a parade-ground for French soldiers, we were directed to the house of Colonel Guy Johnson, who had succeeded his recently deceased father-in-law, Sir William Johnson, in his Superintendency. We were given rum in an anteroom, where stood glass cases full of curiosities of Indian domestic manufacture—such as embroidered wampum-belts, pouches and tobacco-pipes of intricate manufacture, weapons of various sorts, and ceremonious head-dresses. The corporal on duty gave us an account of them, and told us among other surprising things that the 'wampum' or shell-beads, strung on leather, which are universal currency as money among the Indian tribes, are coined in Old England: wampum was formerly made by the Indians themselves in the form of crude beads of baked white clay, but then of sea-shell, which we could cut by machinery much more expeditiously and regularly than they by hand, to the shape and size of the glass bugles worn on ladies' dresses. The shell used was that of the clam, a large sort of scallop found on the coasts of New England and Virginia, and the purple sort was more esteemed by the Indians than the white: they would pay an equal weight in silver for it.

This corporal was one of the armourers employed by the Indian Department for mending the firelocks of friendly Indians; but he had the week before been wounded in the hand by a drunken Indian and withdrawn from his employment until it healed.

Colonel Johnson presently sent for us, and was most affable. He said, 'My friend Thayendanegea has an invitation to offer you.'

Thayendanegea was at table with him, in a company of several other war-chiefs of the Six Nations—Senecas, Oneidas, Onondagas, Cayugas, Tuscaroras, and Mohawks —among them the Chief Sachem of the Mohawks himself, by name Little Abraham. This venerable person, it seems, secretly favored an alliance of the Confederacy with the revolted colonists, and was now doing what he could to incline his inferior chiefs to that course. But Thayendanegea and his very active wife Miss Molly, with whom he lived in monogamous union on account of his Christian faith, were leaders of the opposition to Little Abraham; and their influence seemed to be preponderant at the table. The cloth was spread with beef-steaks, salted bear's-legs, dressed capons, and a number of fricassees and complicated confections in the French style which the Indians universally preferred to our English style of cooking.

They were all to some degree intoxicated and had, as was their wont before sitting down to drink, given their weapons into the safe keeping of one of their number, who was pledged for the occasion to keg himself. However, on so ceremonious an occasion it was not to be expected that they would risk their dignity by any recourse to violence. For Indians of rank deemed it highly becoming to accommodate their manners to those of a distinguished stranger, especially a host, and they were wonderfully observant; so that you would seldom find a well-born Indian behaving other than with ease and gentility in the most select company, if a hint were but supplied him, before his entry, of the forms expected. Yet the Colonel was visibly restraining his impatience with the unusual and unexpected ill manners which one or two of his guests were showing. I was told later that the offenders on this occasion had recently been the guests of a Brunswick officers' mess at Three Rivers, and the greater licence for horse-play and raillery there permitted to the intoxicated had given them an incorrect notion of what would be fashionable in Montreal at the residence of a British officer of rank.

Just as we entered, Thayendanegea was addressing in English a Seneca chief named Gyantwaia, or 'Cornplanter,' who was gravely balancing a bottle of Madeira upon his nose (distinguished for a gold nose-ring with a little gold bell-pendant dropping to his upper lip). Thayendanegea said very civilly to him: 'My courageous ally and brother, it impresses me vastly to observe your feats of *leger de nez*, but perhaps the hilarity of the occasion has blinded your eye to the fact that *a lady is present!*'—indicating Miss Molly, who modestly turned away. Then improving upon the occasion, for Cornplanter (whose father, by the way, was a Dutch settler from Albany in New York) seemed somewhat abashed, Thayendanegea added: 'And if our generous host will permit it, we will now cease our potations of his very fine liquors, which have somewhat disequilibriated our judgment. Instead, we will keep my wife, Miss Molly, company in a dish of tea, which as the rebellious colonists regard as noxious to all disloyal persons, so we may well drink with pride and gratification in honour of our ally and father, King George.'

Little Abraham was put in a cleft stick by this artful orator. He could not refuse to drink tea without discourtesy to Miss Molly, who was sitting there in the quality of a Christian matron, not an Indian squaw; yet he feared that to partake of the beverage would constitute a declaration in favour of the British side in the conflict, and that the Americans would have news of it, and cease to give him presents.

He said, in halting English, that the Madeira wine had so confused his wits that he did not know with which part of his face to drink, and that therefore he would abstain.

Thayendanegea pressed his advantage—and it was remarkable that, from courtesy to his overlord, he never failed to rise from his chair whenever he spoke so much as a word in his presence: 'My father, were you to embrace the Christian faith and read our Scriptures, you would learn into what shameful dangers the sin of intemperance is apt to lead such venerable old men as the patriarch Noah and yourself; nor would you drink anything but tea, avoiding the fermented juice of the grape. I will send you a present, to-morrow, of fifty pounds weight of superior tea, to refresh your whole household.'

Cornplanter, who was of Little Abraham's way of thinking, spoke up in his behalf; he had not Thayendanegea's command of English, but was not without eloquence. He said, in substance: 'My brother and ally, I thank you. Your words are very pretty. But we would not wish the Colonel to think that his wines are either so worthless or so injurious to us that we reject them and call for tea; which is no more than boiling water poured upon a dried herb. To call upon him for tea at such a social time would be to violate the custom of the white officers, with which I am well acquainted.'

Thayendanegea smiled pleasantly: 'My dear friend, do as you think fit, and no doubt my revered father, Little Abraham, will do likewise. But avoid provoking the Colonel to laughter. You talk of your knowledge of the white officer's customs, yet know no better than to *eat that peach unpeeled*!'

Leaving his two opponents, both now thoroughly disconcerted, to please themselves whether they drank tea or no, Thayendanegea dismissed the matter as settled. He waved a greeting to Corporal Reeves and myself with his pipe and asked us directly, without preamble, whether we would care to accompany a hunting expedition of his tribe towards the south-west. He said that General Carleton had wished aloud, in his presence, that our light infantry could be acclimatized to American forest life, especially in winter-time, so that they could contend on equal terms with the revolutionaries. Thereupon, said Thayendanegea, he had offered the General to act as schoolmaster to one or two of them at last, who could pass the lesson on to the rest—as in the monitor system now in use in the popular schools of Great Britain. Remembering our names and his debt to us in the matter of Sweet Yellow Head, he had then asked the General whether Colonel Johnson might apply for our temporary release from The Ninth for the purpose of accompanying him; and the General had consented.

Few invitations could have given me keener pleasure, but I had observed that it was regarded as a virtue among the Indians to appear indifferent to good news or bad; that no man would be esteemed a good warrior or a dignified character who openly betrayed any extravagant emotions of surprise, joy, sorrow, or fear on any occasion whatsoever. I replied calmly that if the General approved the plan, it would please me well; and that I and my comrade would be ready to set forth at whatever time was most convenient to him on the following day. Thayendanegea named a rendezvous on the road half-way between Montreal and our barracks, and after the exchange of a few civilities we took our leave.

Colonel Johnson went with us into the ante-room and advised us, if we would have an interesting and prosperous journey, to live as nearly as possible in the Indian style: in which we would find, if we were philosophers, more matter for admiration than for disgust. He said: 'They are, contrary to what is usually said of them, a sensitive, generous, and poetical people. Their apathy is only assumed, and proceeds from no real want of feeling. No people on earth are more alive to the calls of friendship or more ready to sacrifice everything they possess to help an ally in distress. If they appear greedy, that is no more than the reverse side of their generosity. Do you dress Indian fashion, observe their ways, cultivate their goodwill and forget nothing you learn. The hunting expedition on which you are going is, in reality, a missionary tour undertaken by Thayendanegea to excite the whole confederacy of the Six Nations to take up the hatchet for us in the coming campaign.'

The Colonel was then obliging enough to put us in the hands of his clerk, who undertook to provide us with Indian clothes and necessaries, which we signed for, and to claim the amount thus expended from the paymaster of the Regiment. We both chose to wear round beaver caps with flaps for our ears; deerskin leggings, dark-blue cloth breech-clouts, red riding-frocks, and furlined half-boots; also whitish capes of buffalo-skin, reduced to silky softness by a laborious process of dressing them with the brains of the dead beast. Terry fixed in his cap a little silver badge of Britannia seated, which was the device verbally conferred on The Ninth by Queen Anne. This later won him an Indian name which I have forgotten, the signification of which was, at all events, 'husband-of-the-woman-with-a-fork.' I may here mention that I was complimented for my willingness to indulge in any adventure or prank that was on foot, with the name *Otetiani*, or 'always ready.' But often we were called 'Teri' and 'Geri.' Both of us had rifle-guns, that we had picked up during the American retreat from Three Rivers, and which were weapons of precision. With a little practice I could hit a board the size of a man's head at two hundred and fifty paces.

'Remember,' said Colonel Johnson to us in parting, 'this invitation is a great honour to you, and I would have you remember that your behaviour and bearing will everywhere be remarked, and that if you win the esteem of your hosts this will reflect well upon the British Army as a whole. I may say that I have satisfied myself by inquiries from your commanding officer that you are worthy of the choice.'

The party, who were at the rendezvous the next day, consisted of Thayendanegea, Strong Soup, and four young warriors of rank, with their squaws. Were I to recount our adventures and wanderings of the next three months it would make a volume in itself. I will be brief then, and confine my account to a few particulars. Thayendanegea took us for a tour of the whole territory of the Six Nations, which lies between Lake Ontario and the headwaters of the Susquehanna and Delaware Rivers. We proceeded first along the shores of Lake Ontario until we came to the Falls of Niagara, and then striking south-west, below Lake Erie, for a short excursion into Wyandot territory, made a circuit through the northern borders of Pennsylvania and so back by the Susquehanna River, the Mohawk valley, and the hills to the westward of Lake Champlain. I was surprised at the high degree of civilization in the several Indian settlements that we visited in the fertile region of the Susquehanna, which must have been very beautiful in the summer. We were everywhere welcomed and feasted and Thayendanegea succeeded by his oratory in persuading many hundreds of warriors to join our standard.

The winter was not expected to be an intensely cold one, nor did it prove so. The approach of intense cold was always known in advance to the Indians by the behaviour of the birds and beasts that migrated in great flocks and droves in the autumn before: bears and pigeons coming down from the northern regions of Canada and swimming or flying over the St. Lawrence River into the province of New York, black squirrels, on the contrary, crossing over into Canada at a narrow piece of water just above the Falls of Niagara. Nevertheless, it froze very hard already; and on the first night when we encamped in the snowy woods far from any human habitation, Terry Reeves and I stared at each other in fearful surmise, wondering how we should live through the night. The Indians, however, soon cleared away the snow from a place under the shelter of an overhanging rock and piled it up high to form the walls of a hut. The squaws cut and plaited together brushwood hurdles which made the foundation of a roof, over which more snow was heaped, but a small orifice was left to allow the smoke of our camp-fire to escape. The interior of this dwelling soon became extremely warm and after dining well upon the fresh pork we had brought with us from the city, seethed with potatoes in an iron kettle suspended above the blaze, we wrapped ourselves in our buffalo capes with our feet to the fire and slept in great comfort until dawn; the squaws taking turns to watch and mend the fire.

Thayendanegea amused us with tales of his first experience of life among the white men at Lebanon; how he was frightened by the way that the family gazed at him as if they wished to kill him, and disconcerted by the fire being built at one end of the house and not in the middle, and scandalized by the wife of the Rev. Dr. Wheelock when she ordered her husband to go outside and feed the chickens for her, for she was busy. He blacked his face as a sign of affliction and sat apart from them in the barn for two days; but to please his father, who had sent him to this place, he did not run away, and soon he became reconciled to the white man's ways. He told us an anecdote of another young Indian, a chief's son, who had come with him to Lebanon, and was directed by Dr. Wheelock's son to saddle his horse. The Indian refused to do so on the ground that this was a menial office, unbefitting a gentleman's son. 'Pray, do you know what a gentleman is?' young Wheelock had asked. He replied, 'I do. A gentleman keeps race-horses and drinks Madeira wine. You do neither, nor does your father. Saddle the horse yourself.'

It was fortunate for us that Thayendanegea could speak English perfectly and could teach us a little of the Mohawk tongue. We learned more for ourselves by a study of the Book of Common Prayer, a copy of which he presented to me, printed at New York seven years previously: which we could compare in memory with the English liturgy. It is not generally understood that there is no language common to all the Indians and that often neighbouring tribes speak in a manner as little intelligible one to the other as the English and French. Nor is it always possible to learn by the use of gestures the name of common things, because of misunderstandings. If a savage wishes to teach a traveller the word for 'head,' and puts his hand upon his crown, it is possible to mistake him: he may be wishing to indicate 'top,' or 'hair,' or 'thought' as resident in the head. When I offered one of my companions, who enjoyed the peculiar appellation of 'Kiss Me,' some tobacco from my pouch, and he put out his hand for more, uttering a word which I took to mean 'give me more,' it proved later that the significance was 'only a little, please.'

It is said that the very word 'Canada' derived from a misunderstanding. It was the reply given by an Indian to the original European discoverer of the mainland, who haughtily asked, 'What is the name of this desolate country?' When the first settlers came to study the language, the word proved not to be the name of the country at all, but an injurious expletive.

It was a habit of our hosts upon a march to keep perfectly silent and follow one behind the other, constantly glancing from side to side. To this habit we naturally conformed, and soon I came to understand it as not merely due to caution, the constant fear of being surprised by an enemy, but to a concentration of attention upon the natural features of the landscape; so that Indians never lose themselves in a country through which they have once passed. To a European eye, one wild stretch of forest is much the same as another; to the Indian, a rock, or a withered branch, or a knotted bole, is noted for its unique shape, and its relation to neighbouring objects, and becomes an unforgettable landmark.

This was the season when bear, squirrel, wild-cat, and many other beasts of the forest take to their long winter rest in hollow trees or caves, and remain there asleep until the snows melt and the warmth of the sun awakens them. The Indians took pleasure in awakening the beasts before their time, and startling them from their hiding-places to kill them for their fur and flesh. Into such a method of hunting we were soon initiated. One of the party came upon the trail of a bear, which they all agreed was not above three days old; and we followed it for perhaps fifteen miles, though in places it was obliterated by new snow and we had to cast about until we hit it once more. We had three bear-dogs with us, a breed between the blood-hound and mastiff, and when we reached the hollow white-oak where our quarry was concealed they set up a dismal barking and howling.

We formed a circle around the tree, where the bear's claw-marks were clearly distinguishable on the bark, and waited for the emergence of our quarry. To rouse him out, the Indians had applied a blazing torch to the hole, at the height of a man's head, by which he had entered. Soon thick clouds of smoke could be seen, issuing from a small hole a good deal higher up; the fire having caught the pine-branches that the bear had drawn together to stop the lower hole as a protection from the cold. We heard a choking, a coughing, and a grumbling noise. The bear emerged, a large, reddish brute, half-stifled by the smoke, and scrambled out from the upper hole. The Indians all fired at once, but they are as wretched marksmen with a gun as they are wonderful with the blow-pipe or the bow, and the bear was not even wounded. He descended at his ease, and while his enemies darted away behind trees, he stood blinking stupidly. Then Terry, who was posted on the other side of the tree from him, came around and shot him in the shoulder. This roused the bear to fury, and he made a rush for the warrior Kiss Me, whose head he espied behind a bush, but Kiss Me avoided him by springing nimbly aside. The dogs now set upon Bruin. He killed one with a blow of his paw and hugged another to his breast, but was struck down with a dexterously hurled tomahawk from Thayendanegea's hand, that caught him on the side of the head. I stepped up swiftly and put him out of action with a bullet through his head. The ball that the Canadians used for bear is a very heavy one, of the size of thirty to a pound; but the frontiersmen of New York and Pennsylvania preferred one of half that weight.

The killing of the bear caused much satisfaction, and he was soon flayed with skinning knives, and cut up with tomahawks. The choicest parts were taken off with us, but the rest left where it lay. I noticed that the paws, which are held in great estimation as a delicacy, were gashed with a knife, and were hung in the smoke-hole of our hut that night to dry. Later, we ate them stewed with young puppies, which is a traditional dish on all festive occasions; and not to be despised by Europeans.

It is said that the bear, who never lays in any store of

provisions and yet is as fat when the thaw comes in May as when he began his sleep in the previous November, is a good deal subsisted by licking his own greasy paws; but this is an unlikely tale. Natural philosophers believe the bear, by discontinuing the process of sweating when in this lethargic state, is saved from those losses of the constitution which other animals, not similarly gifted, repair by regular eating and drinking.

When we came into Seneca territory I was greatly astonished with the precision with which the young men of this nation would kill little red squirrels or big black squirrels, such as were not yet a-bed for the winter, with their long blow-pipes, of cane reed. The arrows were not much thicker than the lower string of a violin, headed with tin, and feathered with thistledown. They were propelled through the tube by a sharp puff of the breath, and at fifteen yards these marksmen never missed, but drove them through and through the squirrels' heads. The effect of these weapons was at first like magic: the tube was placed to the mouth, and the next instant the skipping squirrel on the bough fell lifeless to the ground. North America is remarkable for its variety of squirrels, among which are many that burrow and some that fly.

On one occasion, when we were in need of fresh meat, a number of squirrels were seen at the top of a hollow tree; the trunk was hewn at with tomahawks and the squirrels presently slain as they jumped clear of the toppling tree. We were told that such a practice was permitted by the Great Spirit, but not the felling of a tree for the sake of wild honey, which was unlucky and would result in death.

We hunted a great variety of animals—the stag, the caribou, the elk—and came one day to a colony of beavers, where the Indians, with no thought of compassion for these harmless and social creatures, broke down their dam and so drained the water from the artificial lake that they had made in a stream, and left their cabins high and dry. The beavers, hearing a barking from the lake-side, tried to escape from the back doors of the cabins, which led to the woods; where the Indians shot them. The cabins were built upon piles and divided into apartments spread with fir-boughs, each large enough to contain a male and a female. There were also storehouses in each hut proportionate to the number of the company that built it; it is said that each member knows his own store and would scorn to steal from his neighbour. The apartments were very fresh and clean. Beavers are big creatures, weighing from forty to sixty pounds, with a flat, oval tail, rat-like head, and webbed hind-feet. How they sink the piles for the cabins is as absurd a tale as any, but true, nevertheless. Four or five of them gnaw a stake through with their teeth, sharpening one end; with their nailed fore-feet they dig a hole in the bottom of the stream; with their teeth they rest the stake against the bank; with their feet again they raise it and sink it in the hole; and with their tails they whisk clay about it to make it secure. They also interweave branches between the piles to secure them.

The Indians have never considered, as British sportsmen do, the propriety of sparing an occasional pair of any kind of animal for breeding purposes; but have killed all indiscriminately, so that many of the rarer fur-bearing animals are in danger of one day becoming extinct. The most beautiful animal that I saw was the ermine; a squirrel-like creature with fine white fur and a jetty spot at the end of his long, bushy tail. In the summer his tail-tip only would remain unaltered in hue, the rest of his fur turning as yellow as gold. I was shown the track of a marten, which appeared the footstep of a larger animal; but this was occasioned by his jumping along in his pursuit of small birds and giving the marks of both feet at once.

The Indians concentrated their minds so closely upon the chase as hardly to have time for any other topic of interest, though I was occasionally questioned upon life in Europe. I took pains, in answering through the mouth of Thayendanegea, to present my own former condition, and that of my fellow countrymen in Ireland, as far more splendid and prosperous than it was. My father, I told them (may God forgive me!) was a merchant who owned a number of vessels and a great warehouse full of scarlet cloth, looking-glasses, guns, beads, kettles, compasses, and all useful things. He daily took out a great map of the world and told his captains where to send his goods for trading purposes.

The Indians did not dispute the first part of the story, but disbelieved in the map, when Thayendanegea informed them that the design of the whole world could be reduced to little upon a single sheet of paper. However, they are never so indelicate as to give a person the lie: they said, 'We dare say, brother, that you yourself believe this to be true, but it appears so improbable to us that to assent to it would confuse our minds in respect to other related subjects.' I had with me, in an oiled silk bag, a map of the River St. Lawrence and the Great Lakes. They understood the principle of a map: for in giving directions to a traveller, they would often trace on the ground with a stick the course of a river and indicate the natural features of the surrounding country. I showed them Buffalo Creek, down which we were travelling at the time, and 'There are the Falls of Niagara,' I said, 'and there is Lake Erie, and, if you cross the water at this point, in a matter of ten days or so in a canoe you will reach Detroit, and so upwards to Lake Huron.' They were fascinated, and exclaimed 'Wa-wa!' in astonishment.

'Then,' said I, 'if you shrink this map to a tenth the size, the directions and shapes remain the same, and there is room on the paper for my home in Ireland, and for the hot lands in the south, and for all the rest of the world.'

They confessed that they had been at fault and begged my pardon; so that the lie about my father, which I told in order to enhance my consequentiality among them—for they have a great scorn of indigent and ill-born persons—passed as Gospel truth.

Terry and I were in perfect health. He had a flux on the third day, but this was soon cured by a medicine that they gave him, decocted from a sort of fungus that grows on the pine. The squaws are the physicians of the tribe and carry medicine bags containing herbal remedies for wounds, snake-bite, and the commoner ailments. So healthy is the blood of these Indians (and I may say that they have the best teeth and sweetest breath of any people I know—by the bye, the cigar-smoking New York Dutch have the worst) that they recover rapidly from the effects of wounds that would be fatal in a European. I inquired closely into the appearance and properties of these herbs, many of which I was able to recognize in their green state when the summer came again, and add to my military *pharmacopœia*.

Near Lake Seneca there was a solemn conference of chiefs in a fine grove of butter-nut trees upon a hill, where it was resolved to support the British cause to the utmost. As we approached the Senecan village of Buffalo, Terry was accidentally shot in the leg by a *feu de joie* of welcome to us. He remained there in Cornplanter's lodge to recover of his wound, much to my regret. Terry took an Indian girl to wife, which was an inconsiderate action on his part, for these women are remarkably faithful, and he could not hope to keep her with him on his return to the Regiment; the life of a soldier's wife in a crowded barrack would be death to a girl trained in the freedom of the woods and lakes. However, who am I to judge of Terry? For, on my resuming the journey, I fell into what will be judged by my readers to be still graver error.

❁ ❁ ❁ ❁ ❁ ❁ ❁ ❁ ❁ ❁ ❁ ❁

CHAPTER

17

WE WERE passing through the territory of the Wyandots, who are in general hostile to the Six Nations, being allied with their principal foes, the Algonquins and Ottawas; but in the words of one of our warriors, by name Bear-Whose-Screams-Disturb-Sleep, the war-hatchet was 'now buried under a few leaves and sticks, and though restless was not showing its edge to the light of the sun.' In other words, we could count upon passing safely through the territory unless we happened to encounter some Indian who had a private blood-feud against a member of our party. One afternoon, as we were gliding through a forest fifty miles

to the south of Lake Erie, close to French Creek, Kiss
Me told us: 'I smell a camp-fire. Fish is frying. Let us go
to it.' So marvellously keen was his smell that we followed
up the wind for a distance of five miles before we came to
the encampment; which we approached, weapons in hand,
with extreme caution in order to assure ourselves that the
strangers were friendly.

We came upon a scene of great animation; two warriors
were strutting about in the circle of the fire. They were
making speeches and counter-speeches in a resentful tone,
with a great amount of descriptive gesture of a very vivid
and graceful variety. Though they were clearly incensed,
one with another, the common forms of politeness were
not outraged: each waited patiently without interruption,
though with a mocking smile upon his lips, for the other
to finish his say. They continually referred to a woman,
the evident subject of their quarrel, who was seated before
the fire, with her back turned to me, at a point equidistant
from the two disputants. She was dressed in a soldier's
jacket and her hair was tied with a coloured handkerchief.
She appeared from her posture to be weeping.

I did not understand a word of their language, yet my
heart swelled and shrank to the rhythm of their eloquence,
and I had a strange sense that it was my fate, not the
squaw's, that was being debated. Suddenly one of the orators who, to judge from the murmurs of the onlookers,
appeared to be having the worst of the encounter, rolled
his eyes, uttered an exclamation of defiance, and rushed at
the woman with upraised tomahawk. It was as if to say in
the plainest language: "Sir, if I do not win this prize from
you, why, you shall not enjoy her, neither.' The unfortunate creature would infallibly have perished, had not some
one at my side uttered the ceremonious word in the
Mohawk tongue which signifies 'I am revenged,' and fired
at point-blank range with his firelock. The Indian dropped
with a bullet in his breast, his tomahawk flying high into
the air and lodging in the branch of a tree; instantly,
Strong Soup, who was the murderer, sprang into the circle,
struck the dying man with his club (as symbolically claiming the victory) and began scalping him before the eyes of
all. The assembly sat dumbfounded, but doubtless a fierce

battle would have ensued a moment later had not Thayen-danegea, with a shout to our party to hold their hand, darted forward, pipe in hand and stood smiling in the friendliest manner imaginable at the company.

The pipe to the Indian is as the white flag to civilized people, and universally respected among them. They did not stir from their pacific postures, but listened to him attentively. It seems that these were a delegation of Otta-was passing through Wyandot territory on a visit to our American adversaries at Ticonderoga. The dead man was the very person who had killed Strong Soup's brother in the previous year and initiated his run of ill luck: his name was Mad Dog, and the murder had been committed in wantonness and in a time of supposed peace. Thayen-danegea assured the Ottawas that his own intentions to them were perfectly peaceful; let the nearest of kin to the murdered man charge himself with the continuance of the private feud, but let no new public war be set on foot.

The Indians, who were aware that they were surrounded and at our mercy, were glad to agree to Thayendanegea's proposal. It so happened that no kinsman of Mad Dog was present in the delegation, and though any person might, if he care, assume the burden of a feud by a public declara-tion to that effect, nobody loved the dead man well enough to risk avenging him. We all now came from behind our trees, pipe in hand, to join the gathering as guests. I had the curiosity, as I was passing, to glance at the face of the squaw who had so nearly played the Helen to a savage war of Trojans and Greeks—but started back with so pro-found a shock of astonishment that I was hardly sensible what I did or said in the succeeding moments. The woman was none other than Kate Harlowe. I caught her up in my arms and pressed her to my bosom with a thousand expres-sions of love, joy, anxiety, and amazement; nor did she resist these endearments, but clung close to me and mut-tered in a broken voice that she was happy at last.

Kate Harlowe had run from her husband at Fort Chippeway, which lay three miles above the Falls of Niagara, in a fit of vexation. If her account was true, as I have no reason to doubt, she had reproached him for in-

fidelity with a half-breed Indian woman, and he had retaliated by calling her a name which, once spoken by a
husband to a wife, is never either forgotten or forgiven. He
had then named me as her paramour and she, while deny-
ing this, declared that she wished, nevertheless, that it
had been so: that she had learned from Johnny Maguire
the full story of what had happened at Saintfield. He had
thought to cheat me into forging the marriage licence for
them, she said, but I had already undertaken to do so in
pure chivalry of spirit, etc., etc., and she now heartily regretted her infatuation for a cruel, treacherous, good-for-
nothing, prating, Papistical, *hedge-gentleman*. 'Ah, now!'
she said, 'between the hedge-gentleman and the gentleman,
what a great gulf is fixed—over that no horse can leap or
bridge be thrown! Gerry Lamb is a true gentleman and the
shame is on you. So good-bye, Hedge-gentleman Harlowe,
and be damned to you, body and soul!'

He replied briefly and scornfully that it was a good rid-
dance for him, since Marie Jeanne (the Canadian woman)
was worth fifty of her sort of woman; and that the faster
she went, the better he would be pleased.

It was her intention to take her life by throwing herself
into the river above the Falls aforementioned. We had
lately passed by this prodigious cascade and I now shuddered to think of the death to which she had so nearly consigned herself. The pitch which the stupendous volume
of water acquired was horrific beyond any previous idea
that could be entertained of it. A stupefaction seized me
when I beheld an entire furious river, half a mile wide,
precipitating itself into so dreadful a chasm. The huge
hollow roar of descending waters could be heard at a distance of twenty miles on all sides, and more than forty
miles in the current of a favouring wind. From the shock
occasioned by it a tremulous motion was communicated to
the earth for several rods around, and a constant mist be-
clouded the horizon, in which rainbows appeared from the
shining of the sun. The foliage of the neighbouring pines
was besprinkled with the spray, which depended upon the
branches in thousands of little icicles. Below this terrible
cataract were always to be found the bruised and lacerated
bodies of fishes and land animals which had been arrested

by the suction of the voracious waves, as also shattered beams and timbers. Yet so strange is the mind of woman that (as Kate assured me) the reason that she did not plunge in and allow herself to be drawn down to death in the Falls was that the water, in which large masses of ice were whirling, appeared to her too cold by far!

As she was hesitating on the bank she was approached by a womanish person, who from Kate's description, can have been none other than the *bardash* Sweet Yellow Head —though what his business in those parts could have been, I have no guess—and spoke very sympathetically with her, evidently divining the circumstances in which she was placed. He told her in broken English, mixed with French, that he was often unfortunate too, that unrequited passion and the cruelty of men made him long for suicide; but that he always refrained, in the confidence that his luck would change if he preserved his equanimity. Kate laughed to be sister in distress to so extraordinary a person, who undertook to help her, if she wished. He would use his influence with a friend among the Ottawas, who was crossing the river that day, to take her with him into the State of New York, where she would no doubt find a new lover among the white settlers of the border, where women were scarce, and there initiate a new and happy life. Sweet Yellow Head assured Kate that her virtue would not be assailed against her will. The Indians were never a lecherous people, as are the Negroes, and there is no record of a white woman being violated by one of them, though many have lost their lives and scalps.

The man-woman was as good as his word. Kate returned to Fort Chippeway, where she provided herself with money and clothing suitable for a long journey through the wintry forest, and was soon under the protection of this Ottawa delegation, consisting of twenty persons. Two young chiefs of the party fell in love with her, for white women exercise a certain fascination for tawny men, and each had in turn pressed his suit. She had no liking for either of them and was obliged to adopt the character of a coquette, for fear of offending both. At last it was decreed by the leader of the party that since she had not said plainly, as she should have done, that she would have neither, to avoid dissension in the camp she must plainly declare for one, and be his. So began the dispute which ended in the death of the unsuccessful suitor.

It thus remained to settle with the other chief, to whom Kate now by decree belonged; but that was an easy matter. The Indian, being guilefully informed by Thayendanegea that I was her husband and that perfect love existed between herself and me, was content to relinquish his claim. He was highly gratified when I gave him, in quittance of my obligation to him, the map which had excited so much interest among my companions. The spot where we were now standing I marked upon the map with an allegorical scene in lead pencil: Feathered Turtle (for that was his name) shaking hands with, or rather presenting a flipper to, myself. I was represented as a lamb holding a firelock in the Make Ready position. He shook hands very warmly with me, and wished me long life and many sons.

We spent the evening very pleasantly in the company of these Ottawas, and Kate and I slept together that night, with her blanket beneath and my buffalo-skin above, in the character of man and wife. The ecclesiastical forms of marriage seemed so remote from us here in the wilderness that the invidious word 'adultery' never sounded in the conscience of either. Harlowe had repudiated her, and she him; she and I were now living Indian-fashion, and in Indian-fashion I had won her by purchase. Our reciprocal desires smothered all consideration of the future, for both of us, having been in the company of savages for so many weeks and obliged to conform exactly to their ways, dwelt like them carelessly in the present. But in order to justify myself formally, I permitted myself to be enrolled as a member of the Mohican nation.

Thayendanegea performed the ceremony in the presence of my fellow warriors. He bade me strip myself naked, and with the bone of a wolf, the knuckle-end of which was cut to tooth-like points, he scratched me from the palm of one hand along the upper part of the fore-arm, across the breast and across the other arm to the palm again. In like manner he scratched me from my heels upward to the shoulders, and from the shoulders again to the feet over the breast, and again up the reverse part of my arms and across the back. The lines drew blood from me along their entire extent, but I knew better than to flinch or cry out. He told me then, 'I have made you dreadful,' and desired me to roll in the snow; which I did. Then he washed my wounds with a decoction of medicinal herbs and bade me keep apart from my wife for the space of seven days. He also set before me a spruce-partridge roasted in bear's grease. This food was symbolical of the qualities of a warrior; for the spruce-partridge makes a thunderous noise with its wings when in flight, and when hiding from a foe is remarkably difficult to discover. Thus I was to be endued with fury for the onset of battle; with patient cunning for the ambush; and with the strength and courage of a bear at bay. In conclusion, Thayendanegea presented me with a small stick whittled in the shape of a war-club, as a talisman.

Other white men have been adopted into the tribe as a mark of honour, notably Lord Percy and the American General, Charles Lee; but none, I believe, with the full native ceremony which made me a Mohawk in fact, not merely in name. Thayendanegea then took me in his arms and embraced me tenderly. While my wounds still smarted I allowed myself to suffer another operation, for which I have ever since had every reason to be thankful. Hair on the face is considered very unsightly by the Indians, and they remove it, roots and all, with the help of a small pliable worm made of flattened brass wire. Though I would not, merely to please them, allow them to remove my eyebrows and lashes, I suffered them to pluck out my beard. The instrument was closely applied in its flat state to my chin, where the hair was already growing luxuriantly, and compressed between finger and thumb; a number of hairs caught in the spirals were then drawn out with a sudden twitch. The operation, though exquisitely painful, was not a lengthy one; and when I consider how much fatigue and pain are caused in a lifetime by the daily operation of shaving, I wonder that more people, soldiers especially, do not summon up resolution and submit patiently to depilation in this manner.

Of the feasts that we attended in our journey the greatest was given to us by the Cayugas, who were the most violent in their desire for a war against the Americans. The festivities were attended by hundreds of persons. In this religious ceremony—it was this rather than a social occasion—each warrior appeared dressed and painted in simulation of the animal sacred to his family: for the tribes are divided into families named the Bears, Buffaloes, Stags, Pigeons, Eagles, Frogs, and so forth. Some therefore were covered with a buffalo's or a stag's hide, having the horns extended; others wore dresses of feathers in a variety of grotesque devices; the Frogs' bodies were entirely naked but painted with green and yellow. I had been adopted by Thayendanegea into his family, the Wolves, and dressed accordingly with a wolf's head and his bushy tail. All our faces were daubed with vermilion and black, since this was a war-dance, laid upon a coating of bear's grease. In his preparations for the masquerade each warrior was most sedulous to make the ferocity of his face the most ghastly and glaring possible; for this he used a small looking-glass, which enabled him to apply the colours with great nicety, but, frequently growing impatient with the result, he would wipe off the whole picture with a cloth and recommence from his natural skin.

When all was ready, we sat down on our hams in a circle around a great fire, near which a large stake was fixed. After a while the war-chief of the Cayugas arose, as the person of greatest respectability present, and, placing himself in the centre, by the stake, began rehearsing all the gallant exploits of his life. He dwelt upon the number of enemies he had killed, describing with gestures how he stalked them, struck them down, scalped them—how he stole horses, ripped open enemies' lodges as an insult, did this and that atrocious deed. His recital, which was spoken with great fluency and dramatic earnestness, cannot have lasted less than three hours. He was greeted with great acclamation and cries of *Etow! Etow!* He continually knocked against the stake with his war-club, making it the witness to the truth of his boasts. I could follow the whole tale by his pantomime gestures. Especially I enjoyed his stealing of the horses of the Wyandots: how after much waiting and watching he had crept up to the horses, stooped down to cut their hopples, mounted the finest, seized another by the forelock and galloped off with both. He rode his tomahawk during this account, as children do broomsticks, making use of an imaginary whip to indicate the necessity of rapid movement, and glancing continuously over his shoulder at the pursuing foe. When he had done, we all arose and joined in a hopping dance, leaping about and brandishing our weapons; I should have preferred a fiddle to the monotonous beating of the drums, but the exercise after so long waiting in the cold was grateful. The Indian war-drum was a piece of hollow tree over which a skin was stretched, with kettles formed of dried gourds filled with peas. We passed around the fire in a circle with our bodies bent uncouthly forward, and uttered the same low dismal sounds, without variation, being the words '*blood, blood,*' '*kill, kill*'; and ever and again raised the famous Indian war-whoop. This ferocious cry consisted in the sound *whoo-oo-oop!* which was continued so long as the breath lasted, and then broken off with a sudden lifting of the voice. A few modulated the cry with howling notes, placing the hand before the mouth to effect this. In either case, the whoop carried for an immense distance.

'Thayendanegea was next, and he went through the same performance, though in a somewhat different manner. He told of his martial exploits, but also of his travels across the Great Water, and threw a rich humour into his tale with imitations of the strutting lords, fashionable ladies, snuff-taking bishops and other London notables he had encountered, to the infinite delight of the gathering. He concluded with a passionate invective against the rebellious Yankees who had taken up arms against their long-suffering father, King George. He finished, and we all danced again. Two fat bucks had been put to roast at the great fire and whenever a man felt so disposed he would glide to the nearest carcass and cut off a great slice of meat for his own use. So the performance continued, Mohicans and Cayugans taking the floor alternately, until I thought it would never end. There was a person appointed to stand outside the circle and rouse any member of the audience who showed the least signs of sleep.

The celebration went on for no less than four whole days and nights. The speeches and dances persisted with unabated energy, fresh meat was continually put upon the spit, and the fire ever and again replenished. On the second day I was called upon to recount my own deeds of valour. I had not much to relate; but not wishing to lower myself in the estimation of my hosts and comrades I told resounding tales in English of the exploits of my regiment at the Battle of the Boyne and the assault of Athlone, and its service in many important fights in Spain during the War of the Spanish Succession, concluding with a dramatic recitation from Shakespeare's *Hamlet*, which I had by heart, in the course of which, in the character of the mad Prince, I was able to exhibit my skill at lunging and parrying with a small-sword, in contest with an imaginary foe. My performance was greeted with prolonged applause and Thayendanegea was good enough not to betray the cheat to the company.

It was February before we approached Montreal once more, and at each step I took my heart grew heavier. I had been living with Kate in a fantastic fairyland in which I would willingly have continued for the remainder of my life, so much did forest-life please me; but that the small insistent voice of Duty began to speak in my ear and to remind me of my service to my Sovereign. The parting from my new but well-tried friends would not have been so painful, had it not meant equally a separation from my squaw (as I had affectionately named her); and my squaw, to judge from certain infallible signs, would before the summer was out seal her union with me by the birth of a child. We were at a loss what course to take. Kate could not return in my company to The Ninth, where she was well known, nor go to The Eighth without me, bringing her husband the gift of a bastard. We both felt with bitterness the irony of fate in condemning our separation, who loved each other so tenderly. And why must this be? Because I was but a sergeant, and she a soldier's wife. That General Howe and General Burgoyne each openly consorted with the wife of one of his commissaries was condoned as a fashionable peccadillo, but the same fault in us would be regarded as heinous and vulgar. We shed tears when we perceived to what a strait our thoughtlessness had brought us. Indian women have certain simples, such as the sumach flower, which they use to procure abortion, but Kate would have none of them, saying that she wished to abide by what she had done, nor add the crime of murder to what had but been loving folly.

Thayendanegea, seeing me sitting very pensively apart one day, asked me gently what trouble was eating at me, and I told him the whole story. He continued thoughtful for a while and then begged me not to despair: he would arrange the matter for us both without scandal. And so in the event he did.

I will never forget our last discourse together. Kate was not fretful or passionate, but spoke reasonably with me. I had the chance, she said, to remain with her and with the fruit of our love, either wandering through the forests in the company of these good friends of ours—whose ways, though savage, were gentlemanly and considerate— or settling in a cote which we might build for ourselves in the wilderness under their protection. Surely that was in every way better than to return alone to my military life? Did I choose the former case, she promised me as faithful duty in the capacity of wife as if the ceremony performed at Newton Breda had been between herself and me, and not between herself and Richard Harlowe. In the latter case, she would harbour no ill feelings against me; but I must clearly understand that, saying good-bye to her now, I would say a perpetual good-bye. If ever afterwards we happened to meet she would feign not to know me, and would not address a single affectionate word to me; and, as for the child, I must renounce my paternity of it—what became of it need not interest me. She would take full responsibility for its birth and upbringing.

What can I say? What could I say then to her? As we spoke together in the snow, under the shadow of a tall white-pine behind which the sunset shed a glorious dying glow over the wide St. Lawrence valley, I heard the music of the bugles from the British camp and the boom of the evening gun, and I knew that I could never choose as she wished me to choose. My skin was white, not

tawny; my weapon of assault the bayonet, not the tomahawk; my birth British, not Mohican. As I kissed Kate
adieu, my heart was heavy as a stone and I told her that
I could not ask her forgiveness, since I did not deserve it.
But I begged her to accept, as a token to tie around the
neck of the child, a pierced silver groat of King Charles II
that my father had given me in my boyhood and that
had ever since hung about my neck on a string. She accepted it; then, taking me solemnly by the hand, she made
me swear, by the name of God, never so long as she
lived to divulge to a soul what had passed between us.
She went back to the camp-fire of the Indians without
another word.

✺ ✺ ✺ ✺ ✺ ✺ ✺ ✺ ✺ ✺ ✺ ✺

CHAPTER
18

ON MY return to barracks at the Isle of Jesus, I found it
difficult to accommodate myself immediately to civilized
customs, and was glad to be told that in ten days' time I
would be sent out in an officers' party to train twenty non-
commissioned officers in the arts that I had learned from
the Indians. Meanwhile I detested the disorder and quarrelsomeness of barrack life. Since Major Bolton went, there
was little care shown for the well-being of the men: they
were not regularly and usefully employed, and preferred
idleness and drinking to that healthful indulgence in sport
which kept the Canadian merry. A whimsical notion occurred to me: how salutary it would be if a Colonel,
with a perfect indifference to precedent, were to put the
men under his command to school during such periods of
enforced idleness! It would be vain, of course, to hope for
signs of genius in the pupils, but at least all could be
taught to read and write a fair hand, and to state a plain
matter intelligibly upon paper, which so few were able
to do, even among the sergeants. Nor would it be ill for

such an innovator also to instruct his young officers in the military science, in which on the whole they were dangerously deficient, especially in that of military engineering.

The quarrelsomeness of which I complained was not confined to the ranks, for officers frequently called one another out to avenge imagined affronts. One ludicrous case occurred. A Captain Montgomery of The Ninth, who had a very prominent nose, happened to leave his lodging to go to the Mess, not four doors away, when he met with Lieutenant Murray emerging from thence. 'God bless me!' cries the Lieutenant, 'your nose is frostbit.'

The Captain was very tender on the subject of his nose and because it was not half a minute since he had stepped into the street, believed that he was being bantered. 'God damn you, sir, for your impertinence!' he cried.

Lieutenant Murray could not let this pass, and says he: 'Sir, let me repeat in all civility that you have a large nose that is frostbit. Go, rub it in snow to make the blood circulate and keep away from a fire, else you will have but a short nose.'

Captain Montgomery very fiercely: 'Mr. Murray, my second will wait upon you to-morrow morning to arrange a rendezvous.'

Lieutenant Murray: 'Sir, frostbite occasions no sort of pain, and you are therefore unaware that what I say is true. Rub your nose at once with snow, or mortification will ensue. Or, perhaps, get your second to perform the service for you.'

The Captain went blustering into the mess, and 'God bless me!' every one cried, 'Your nose is frostbit! Keep away from the fire in heaven's name! Outside at once, and rub it well with snow, else you will lose it for sure.'

So out he went, to rub his nose with snow, and though a greedy man and sharp set with hunger missed a very good meal; exactly as Lieutenant Murray, that waggish Irishman, had intended when he had rehearsed the scene beforehand with his brother-officers. And the Captain that same evening made the Lieutenant a handsome apology.

It was remarkable to me that none of the men attempted

to learn how to glide along the frozen river on skates. Perhaps they thought that to do so would be presumptuous, for several of the officers had provided themselves with skates and had instituted a skating club. I had myself learned the sport from the Indians, who could cover immense distances by this means of progression; it may not be credited but, for a wager, three Indians not long before had skated in a single day, between dawn and dusk, all the way from Montreal to Quebec—a distance of one hundred and eighty miles! However, this glory was purchased with death, for two instantly expired on reaching their goal and the third did not survive above a week. Contiguous to the frozen river's sides, the ice supplied a flat and level ground to go on, but in the mid-current the passage was rugged and hilly. This was occasioned by the powerful force and rapidity of the water underneath, throwing up fragments of broken ice. Standing upon a rising ground of ice thus formed, you might perceive the most grotesque appearances and figures, sometimes of human beings, beasts and birds and of almost every object which the earth offers the eye.

My journey with the non-commissioned officers proved uneventful and pleasant; Lieutenant Kemmis conducted us. He was a gentleman who never affected, as many young coxcombs do, that the epaulettes upon his shoulders had given him the power of knowing better than his subordinates in rank upon every conceivable subject. While avoiding to appear publicly in the character of my pupil, he inquired beforehand from me how marching, cooking, sleeping, and other matters were regulated among the Indians, and gave his orders accordingly; whenever an occasion arose where he was at a loss, he had no false shame in asking my advice.

Our tour was to Three Rivers, through the woods on the northern side of the river and back through the woods on the opposing side. We stopped for a night at Three Rivers and drank with the Brunswick Grenadiers at the barrack. The Germans I found a very strange people, combining fortitude with superstitious panic, kindliness with brutality, mechanical skill with sheer stupidity, erudition with a plentiful lack of wit. Those with whom we spoke seemed to have no notion of the cause they were engaged in, or of the probable course of the campaign, nor had they any curiosity to inform themselves. Their thoughts ran on pay, plunder, their families in Germany, and God. They were for ever singing psalms and hymns, and had less idea of diverting themselves with sport even than our men. Their attention to religion had, in a manner of speaking, been their downfall, for the Duke of Brunswick's press-gang had caught most of them as they emerged from their parish churches one fine Sunday morning.

I have heard it said that if one is acquainted with five Britons, one is acquainted merely with five several Britons; whereas to be acquainted with a similar number of Germans, from whatever principality or walk of life they might be taken, is to know all Germans. Their humours and character are said to vary but little between whole multitudes, and Lieutenant Kemmis informed us that a Roman historian who lived about the time of the Emperor Nero had remarked, even at that early date, that the German tribes known to him exhibited a remarkable sameness of behaviour. Thus it is that they are more subject to sympathetic infection by joy, fear, or any other emotion than any nation in the world: let ten men go weeping through a street in a German town and soon the entire countryside will be in tears; or let them dance, and a long procession will follow them of passionate dancers. At Three Rivers the emotion was melancholy and the word: '*Werd ich meine armen Kinder nimmer wieder sehen?*' 'Am I ne'er to see my poor children again?' From this they proceeded to a conviction that, no, they would never live to revisit their homes. Parties of twenty or thirty men would relate to one another a conviction that death was soon coming to them; whereupon they moped and pined, obsessed with the notion, and nothing could cure them of it.

I endeavoured to argue a couple of them, who drank with me, out of this settled presentment. It was to no purpose: the Rider upon the White Horse was close upon them, they said, and they could not escape the stroke of his scythe. Already scores of them were dead from no visible ailment, but merely from superstition. A sergeant took me miserably by the hand and let me into a long, unheated room appropriated as a *morgue*, the place where dead bodies were kept until the thawing of the frozen ground permitted them to be decently buried. '*Alle meine guten Kameraden*,' he said wistfully, pointing about him.

It was a very strange and laughable sight that met my gaze, for the superintendent of the *morgue*, an apothecary, was evidently a very fanciful fellow. He had taken the bodies of these poor, pig-tailed, leather-breeched Germans, while still warm, and placed them fully clothed in various lifelike postures where death and the weather preserved them stiffly. Some were kneeling with hymn-books in their hands, their jaws open as if singing; others seated in chairs with cold pipes in their mouths; many leaning against the wall with hands in pockets or one leg carelessly crossed over the other; one man standing balanced on his head and hands.

At first I could not imagine them dead, despite their ghastly countenances, but dead they were. Two big tears trickled down my Grenadier's cheeks and wetted his great moustachios. '*Ach*,' he sighed, '*bald komm ich auch*,' 'Soon I too shall come hither.' And he raised a hand at various heights from the ground to indicate the respective sizes of unfortunate children who soon would be left fatherless, by his decease, at Wolfenbüttel in Germany.

He told me the characters and professions of the dead men, as if he were a guide in a museum of wax-works. Most of them were 'good comrades' from Wolfenbüttel; but there were many strangers too. This was a fringe-maker from Hanover, a surly fellow; that, a whimsical creature, a discharged secretary from the post office at Gotha; that, a renegade monk from Würzburg, but a good comrade; that, an upper steward from Meningen, a very pleasant man who could play the organ, but a thief; that, a cashiered Hessian major, very proud and evil; that, an unsuccessful playwright from Leipzig; that, a poor, bankrupt Bavarian pastry cook, the one in the corner a retired Prussian sergeant of Hussars, who spoke no more in life than now in death.

As I came away I pondered a metaphysical question:

whether in the same way as these Germans draw death upon themselves by the power of superstition, so a man might repel death by a contrary superstition of invulnerability—such as I myself had lately come to feel. 'Aye,' said I, 'but only so long as this presentiment of life is vouchsafed. It will vanish suddenly one day when that bullet is run into the mould which is destined for my skull alone.'

I communicated to Lieutenant Kemmis a plan I had for rousing the spirits of our company when we returned to Montreal, namely, of instructing them in the Indian ball-game, called by the French *la crosse*, which was a prime divertissement among the Mohicans. The ball was similar in materials and construction to that used by our Irish schoolboys in their ancient game of hurly, but was propelled with two sticks, or *crosses*, one in each hand, resembling large battledores. The field of play measured three hundred feet in length, with goal-posts at either end through which the contending parties sought to drive the ball with their sticks. The party that effected this twelve times in all was accounted victorious. The parties might trip, strike, grapple, wrestle, knock away each other's sticks, or employ any stratagem whatsoever, provided that the ball were propelled only with the stick and that no man lost his temper and shed blood. These matches among the Indians, of which I witnessed several while in the Buffalo settlement, were played with intense excitement. The greatest chiefs and most distinguished warriors took part in them, and important sums were staked upon the result by the spectators. The players, who were naked and slippery with bear's grease, played with a furious hilarity that was perfectly indescribable and grew most desperate as the game advanced until but one point remained to be notched by the winning side. The most remarkable circumstance was that no player was ever slain.

Lieutenant Kemmis readily agreed to my proposal for forthwith playing the game on the ice, with ten men a side, and himself for umpire. We improvised the *crosses* and the ball, and were soon sufficiently adept at the game to look forward with pleasure to imparting it to our men at the Isle of Jesus and playing matches in rivalry between the several companies. However, Lieutenant Kemmis, fearful of accidents, barred fistcuffs and kicking, and bade us play in our waistcoats rather than stark naked.

After our first game, which left us with limbs very stiff, but in the highest spirits, I wished that I were in General Riedesel's confidence and could recommend the sport to him as a medicine for his dispirited heroes.

We were aware that, with the end of winter, our period of inactivity would come to an end, and our campaign be resumed. To me, Canada had proved a very kind foster-mother. Indeed, it occurred to me that, were I ever obliged to remove from my native country and inhabit another, this would be my choice, though situate within winter's peculiar meridians. The climate of Montreal was especially salubrious and did I but take pains to master the French tongue—for the Canadian-French are very loath to learn the English—I might with industry and a small principal settle myself here very comfortably indeed. This feeling of gratefulness, still warm in my breast, will excuse that I have dwelt at such length upon the beauties and natural curiosities of the province.

I had the good fortune to visit Montreal on Holy Thursday, which they called *La Fête Dieu*, and which generally coincided with the departure of winter. On that day, at eleven o'clock in the forenoon, a great procession of the clergy in general, and the friars of all the monasteries, attended with a band of music, moved out from the great church and passed down the streets, occupying nearly a half mile of ground. They bore lighted candles in their hands.

The townspeople had prepared for this ceremonial by procuring large pines and firs from the woods, with which they lined the streets on both sides, making the boughs connect at the top, so that the religious spectacle proceeded under an umbrageous shelter, as if through a grove of living trees. The centre of the procession was occupied by the Host laid upon an open copy of the Scriptures in Latin, with a white cloth spread over, and above it a crimson canopy borne by six venerable priests. Boys in white vestments scattered flowers while others swung silver thuribles which they constantly wafted towards the Host, so that the smell of incense made the streets fragrant; and all the people sang joyful anthems. Protestant or no Protestant, I was pleased to pull off my cap, as had been ordered by General Phillips, the City Commandant, out of respect for the innocent emotions of these gay, good people—who fell with one accord upon their knees as the Host passed—and for the superb solemnities of the Romish Church.

On Holy Thursday the yellow wax candles that had been used in the ceremonial were cut into small pieces and distributed to the faithful, for a small pecuniary consideration, to be used as charms against tempests. If such a stump were lighted when the wind rose, its fury would —they thought—soon abate. A woman who kept a grog-shop near the barracks, with whom I was a favourite, presented me with one of these relics; informing me of its powers, and solemnly warning me against using it except for the purpose I have mentioned. I put it in my knapsack, after thanking her gravely, and thought no more about it.

Before the end of March the thaw had begun, Montreal having three weeks' advantage of Quebec in the matter of the spring's arrival, and it was no longer safe to play *la crosse* or perform our military exercises upon the frozen river. The river had been the parade-ground for some time past, for the snow lay deep upon the ground, but upon the ice it thawed daily in the sun and froze to small ice overnight—moreover, a steady footing was provided for the troops by the sweepings of the stables and byres which were thrown out upon the ice to be carried off when it should break up. One day, as we were at our platoon exercise, a sharp crack sounded under our feet like a discharge of grape and ice split across from bank to bank. We broke ranks in alarm and one man was injured by a bayonet in the general *sauve qui peut*, but the crack was of no immediate significance. However, the warm weather continued and soon the ice along the bank gaped with great chasms. Frequent roars of breaking ice were heard from the centre of the river, where the fantastic ice-mountains had formed. As the waters became swollen by the melting of the snow, these mountains fell into the stream and were hurried down towards Quebec with tremendous impetuosity until becoming wedged in narrow places between islands and heaping up there again in the form of new mountains. The greatest roar of all was heard at midnight of the last day of April when some obstruction, a half mile downstream from us, gave way. When we awoke in the morning, there was the river flowing clear and blue under the cloudless sky, and we were true islanders again; instead of carriages and sleighs driving across from the barracks to the mainland, canoes and *bateaux* came dancing down.

However, so long as there remained fragments of ice in the river, no navigation was possible to ships of burden, for these bergs, when frozen to the bottom, were no less dangerous than a rock—or than a charging spermaceti whale, when afloat.

We were distressed to learn that among the many victims of the thaw was Major Bolton, who was drowned in the Lakes on his way to Montreal, by the *bateau* he was in striking a submerged lump of ice with great force and sinking forthwith. Richard Harlowe brought us the melancholy intelligence; and in consequence of his employer's death he was obliged to quit The Eighth and be restored to the strength of The Ninth. When he was asked what had become of his wife, he replied that he feared her drowned in the Falls of Niagara, pursuant upon a threat that she had made him in a fit of rage. He affected to be disconsolate, and, whether or not he had banished from his mind all memory of his half-breed mistress, he at least refrained from boasting to us of that conquest. Towards me, he continued sullen and reserved.

During a fortnight the roads had been impassable, but now were quite dry and even dusty. Spring came with a rush, and we had hardly congratulated ourselves upon its delightful appearance when it passed on and gave place to summer. In a very few days the bare trees were in full leaf and the barren, frozen ground was green with grass and decorated with innumerable flowers.

Our annual supply of clothing, the new suit for every man for which stoppages were made from our pay, had not yet arrived, and we were told that we must commence the campaign in our old clothes, most of which were in a very ragged condition. But, to make them more presentable, all with long coats were told to reduce them to jackets, and their hats into caps; the cloth remaining over to be used as patches for rents and burns. The caps were now to be furnished with cockades of hair, but no hair being provided we were expected to go foraging for it—as the Israelites of old were expected by their task-masters to furnish themselves with straw for their bricks.

Terry Reeves, who had lately returned to us, his wound healed, and very sorrowful to be parted from his Indian squaw, led a foray of about twenty men of our company into a paddock where a herd of cows was grazing; intending to cut the hair from the ends of their tails. The plan miscarried. The farmer and a number of relatives who happened to be present in the farmhouse, because of a funeral feast in progress there, rushed out with sticks and began laying about them with great fury. Two soldiers had their heads broken and their bodies severely bruised before they could be rescued; they were foolish enough the next day to complain to Major Forbes, their officer, of this 'premeditated assault.' Major Forbes told them downrightly that they had got no more than their deserts. In the first place, it was an inhumane act to cut from the tails of cows those hirsute appendages provided by Nature for switching away the flies that so greatly plagued them in the hot season; in the second, they had evidently gone without their side-arms, which should always be worn, being the same to a soldier as a sword is to an officer; in the third, horsehair was far superior to cow's hair for the making of cockades. Terry therefore led a new expedition, under cover of darkness, to the artillery barrack at Montreal, where sufficient hair was secured for the whole company from the tails of the gun horses and officers' chargers found unguarded there in the stables.

❈ ❈ ❈ ❈ ❈ ❈ ❈ ❈ ❈ ❈ ❈ ❈

CHAPTER

19

OUR light infantry and grenadier companies were transported across the St. Lawrence River and marched to Boucherville, where we found the flank companies of the other regiments assembled, and took part with them in combined manœuvres under the approving eye of General Burgoyne.

General Burgoyne had spent the winter in England, together with several other officers of the army in Canada who were, like him, members of Parliament, and had there endeavoured to persuade the Ministry that he was far fitter to command the expedition against Ticonderoga than General Carleton. He alleged that General Carleton had been slow to press his advantage in the previous campaign, when he might have taken Ticonderoga almost without loss, and thus struck a resounding blow against the rebels; and that General Carleton was by no means beloved of the troops.

Now, the Secretary for War was Lord George Germaine. The greater part of the Army was unaware who this person might be, and gave no attention to the matter. But one day in this same summer I was greatly astonished to learn some particulars of his previous history. It happened in this manner. I had come upon old Sergeant Fitzpatrick and two sergeants of the Twentieth Regiment who, the day being July 31st, were drinking together in our bivouac. All wore roses in their caps to commemorate the glorious victory of Minden of which this was the anniversary, for before the battle the troops had lain in a rose garden and thus gaily decked themselves in contempt of the French. Now up rode stout old General Phillips. He stopped to shake the hands of his comrades-in-arms, but, says he, very sharply to Sergeant Fitzpatrick:

'How come you by this rose? I never heard that The Ninth fought at Minden.'

'No, General Phillips,' rejoined the sergeant, 'but The Twenty-third did so fight, with whom I then had the honour of serving, and in the leading line too. I remember your Honour on that occasion, how you split no less than fifteen canes on the rumps and sides of your sweating horses in bringing the guns up. And if I may make bold enough to say it, sir, I am right glad that to-day we have no Lord George Sackville in command of our cavalry.'

This Lord George Sackville had been in command of the British cavalry on that famous occasion and behaved very ill. An order had been given to the infantry to advance when they heard the beat of a signal drum. An aide-de-camp in a hurry conveyed the message that six British battalions and two of Germans were to advance at the beat of the drum; but this became mistakenly changed into an order to advance 'at beat of drum.' This they did forthwith, very courageously, despite a cruel cross-fire of artillery, before the French were marshalled in position; and by their unassisted efforts drove off the field a great mass of enemy infantry and—an unheard-of feat—a force of French cavalry of double their number. Lord George Sackville was hastily desired by Prince Ferdinand, the allied Commander, to pursue the routed French with his cavalry, but he stood fast, either from cowardice or because of personal pique against the Prince, pretending that he did not understand how the movement was to be carried out. Our noble Colonel, then plain Captain Ligonier, came galloping up to ask Lord George why he delayed. A Colonel Sloper, of the cavalry, cried out to Captain Ligonier, pointing in exasperation at his Lordship: 'For God's sake, repeat your orders to *that man*, that he may not pretend to misunderstand them, for it is near half an hour ago that he received orders to advance and yet we are still here. You see the condition he is in!' But the moment had passed, and Prince Ferdinand was robbed of the fruits of what was, even so, the most resounding victory of the whole century. Lord George Sackville, being in due course court-martialled, was found guilty and very rightly adjudged unfit ever again to command British soldiers in the field.

General Phillips now looked at Sergeant Fitzpatrick in a very peculiar manner. 'No,' said he shortly, 'Lord George Sackville does not command the cavalry of this Northern army, but Lord George Germaine sits in his chair at Downing Street; and there directs and co-ordinates the military operations of the Northern, the Southern, and the Eastern armies.'

One of the sergeants of The Twentieth then remarked: 'Aye, your Honour, I am sorry to hear that—for though I know little about this lord I have read that he is a sad Whig, having even been approached by that rascal Charles Fox to lead the Opposition. They say that he refused only because—as he frankly owned—to lead an Opposition was an ill paid and thankless task, and he had debts of honour which must be paid at all events. I cannot think that he will manage his task well. But better a thousand times to have such a Whig in the Secretary's chair than a traitor of the quality of Lord George Sackville.'

General Phillips very gravely: 'They are one and the same person. "*That man*," when he inherited the Germaine estates, changed his name accordingly.'

Well, this Lord George Sackville, or Germaine, nursed a long-standing hatred against a number of Generals and other officers: all such as had avoided his company since the notorious court martial fixed so sable a blot upon his name. Among these was General Carleton who had, besides, refused to job for him politically; and his Lordship therefore lent a ready ear to General Burgoyne's insinuations, and even recommended to the King that General Carleton should be recalled from the Government of Canada. King George scented rancour and prejudice. He consented that General Burgoyne, as an energetic officer, should be put in command of our expedition; yet he retained General Carleton in his government. General Carleton was much mortified and sent in his resignation: for General Burgoyne, as an independent commander, would now be taking orders directly from Lord George Germaine, General Carleton's professed enemy, and at the same time making requisitions upon the resources of Canada which must be supplied willy-nilly and with all dispatch. When this resignation was refused, however, General Carleton very loyally and generously did everything in his power to assist the arms of his supplanter.

It will be recalled that the British plan of attack was a simultaneous converging upon Albany, on Hudson's River, of three armies: General Howe's northward from New York, General Prescott's westward from Rhode Island, ours southward from Canada. To co-ordinate the movements of three separate armies requires a watchful and controlling central power, great nicety in calculating times and distances, and perfect secrecy. The task would be formidable enough in a country so enormous as America, and with so difficult communications by land and river, even when the three armies were directed along interior lines of defence, namely, lines drawn from the centre of the country outward to the frontiers; but was quite desperate when these armies must simultaneously attack inwards from positions on the frontier separated from one another by hundreds of miles of wilderness, and with no possibility of communication between them. For if then the central armies were well handled in opposition, they would mass in superior force against each of the three converging columns in turn, and destroy them piecemeal. It was plain madness to allow such a plan to be directed by any person at all, however gifted, from a distance of three thousand miles away—let alone one who had never set foot in America, or had any notion of conditions there, who relied for his information on prejudiced and inaccurate sources, who could not keep regular office hours or a secret, and who bore an inveterate grudge against the whole British Army. Yet such was the indulgence given by King George, long before he had shown any other signs of the lunacy that afterwards deprived him of his sovereignty, to Lord George Germaine!

I may here append that King George was as unfortunate in his choice of a minister to control his ships upon the sea, as in his choice of a minister to control his armies upon land: for the First Lord of the Admiralty was the ill-living, revengeful, and incompetent Earl of Sandwich, known to all as 'Jemmy Twitcher,' after the libertine of that name in Mr. Gay's comedy of *The Beggar's Opera*. It was he who, twenty years before, had been High Priest of that blasphemous and orgiastic fraternity, the Hellfire

Club, *alias* the Society of the Monks of Medmenham
Abbey; nor had he changed his nature since that day.
He was as cordially hated by his admirals as Lord George
Germaine by his generals, for he added hypocrisy to ill-
living, and wilful mismanagement of the Navy to hypocrisy. When the Court and Cabinet were set upon revenge against the notorious John Wilkes, the libertarian,
whose unseating and reseating as a member of Parliament
was the chief political topic of the years before the war,
his Lordship was called upon to discredit him in the House
of Lords. He did so by reading aloud to the scandalized
house a ribald poem composed by this Wilkes, and asked
the Lords to brand it as an impious and obscene document;
as if their Lordships were unaware that the same John
Wilkes, who had also been a Medmenham monk, had
printed this composition some years before, for private
circulation in the club. Shortly after this, at a performance
of *The Beggar's Opera*, that odious character, Mr.
Peachum, whose practice was virtuously to peach on his
scoundrelly associates when they were of no further
assistance to him, set the whole house in a roar by remarking how surprised he was that Jemmy Twitcher
should peach. As for this Jemmy Twitcher's mismanagement of his office: he starved the dockyards, sold contracts
through his mistress, Miss Ray, who presided at the
Admiralty as if a coroneted countess and was an un-
conscionable bargainer, allowed our strength in line-of-
battleships to fall far below the modicum needed for the
safety of our coasts, yet lyingly informed the Lords to
the contrary, pretending that three times as many frigates
were in commission as was actually the case. He also
oppressed and cheated those deserving old sea-dogs, the
Greenwich Pensioners, who were under his sole charge;
and conspired to ruin by calumny and subterfuge a
number of eminent and courageous captains and admirals
of the Navy—among them 'Black Dick,' General Howe's
brother, and 'Little Keppel.' But in spite of all these
wicked actions the noble Earl remained in power, as did
Lord George Germaine, until the war was irretrievably
lost: namely, five years after the period of which I am
now writing.

However, we could then know nothing of what lay in pickle for us, and had perfect confidence in General Burgoyne, in our own arms, and in the righteousness of our cause.

Our fleet had been strengthened by a new frigate, the *Royal George*; and a radeau, big as a castle, which was sunk at St. John's by the Americans in the previous year, had been raised from the river-bed. Our army consisted of some four thousand British troops and three thousand German. Two thousand Canadian levies had been expected to swell our numbers but the service proved unpopular. No more than one hundred and fifty appeared in arms with us; they hung back even from transport work. Besides these, there were the Indians, many hundreds of whom had promised to take up the hatchet.

At the beginning of June 1777 we marched out of Canada by way of St. John's and encamped on the western side of Lake Champlain; where we waited for *bateaux* to transport us, under convoy of the fleet, to the southern extremity of the lake, close to Crown Point.

In our passage down the lake we frequently encamped upon the islands, the brigades regularly following one another, and making about seventeen to twenty miles a day. The order of progress was so regulated that each brigade occupied at night the encampment vacated in the morning by the brigade preceding. It would have been a very pleasant time had it not been for the mosquitoes, which were more venomous here than anywhere else on the American continent, but only at Skenesborough, a little farther to the south, where (as General Washington himself averred) they would not scruple to bite through boot and stocking. At this time great clouds of turtle-doves were migrating from New York State past us into Canada; they were decorated with beautiful plumage of shifting hues and were much wearied by their long flight. It was with difficulty that they gained the trees near our bivouac to roost upon, and some even dropped into the water and drowned. Our people struck them down from the branches with sticks and wrung their necks as they fell. Turtle-doves furnished subsistence for six weeks of the year to the Canadian farmer, who erected ladders from the ground to the tops of the pines where the flocks were accustomed to resort. The turtle-doves perched upon the ladders, several to each rung. Coming softly to the trees by night with a musket full of small shot, the Canadian would fire upwards along each ladder and seldom fail to kill or wound forty or fifty birds, which he would subsequently eat in a delicious fricassee with garlic and sour cream.

An event remarkable, even if it can be dismissed as coincidence, occurred as we were approaching Crown Point. Picture to yourself the scene: a fine June day with the wide lake undisturbed by a breeze, and the whole army in array, forming a perfect regatta, a great number of Indians paddling ahead in their birchen canoes, twenty or thirty to a canoe, followed by the advanced corps, our Light Infantry and Grenadiers, the Canadians and a few American Loyalist volunteers, upon the gunboats; next, the two frigates, *Royal George* and *Inflexible*, towing large booms, the schooners, sloops, and other ships a little astern, including the newly raised radeau which transported the heavy artillery; after them the first brigade, with scarlet uniforms and flashing arms, in a regular line of *bateaux* and with the three generals in their smart pinnaces following; next, the second brigade, an equally brave sight, with the German brigades supporting; and far in the rear, the sutlers and camp-followers pushing along in a variety of craft.

The crystal surface of the lake became an indefinitely extended mirror reflecting the calm heavens, the tall trees of the islands past which we sailed, the great flock of laden boats and ships. It was like some stupendous fairy-scene of a dream, which the waking fancy can hardly conceive.

In our gunboat it happened that nobody was supplied with a tinder-box, though several of us felt the need of a pipe of tobacco. However, I rummaged in my knapsack and found there a dry piece of the fungus which I kept as a specific against the flux, together with a burning-glass and a candle-end of yellow wax. I concentrated the rays of the sun in a focus upon the fungus, which soon broke into flame when I blew upon it; whereupon I lighted the candle from this tinder and it was passed from hand to hand among the smokers on the benches.

All at once the sun was darkened by a cloud and a most violent and unexpected tempest blew up from the Green Mountains to the north-east, so that the whole vast sheet of water was agitated in a terrible manner. A small sloop carrying but little sail, not fifty yards from us, was laid flat on her side by the first gusts and the crew were obliged to chop away the masts in order to right her. I thought that the greater part of the army must of necessity be swallowed up, for the *bateaux* were most unmanageable vessels in rough weather and now heaved about frightfully. Suddenly a superstitious thought crossed my mind: I had inadvertently lighted the Holy Thursday candle in a flat calm and had therefore been instrumental in loosing the very danger that these two inches of bees-wax had been intended to allay! I noticed that one of my comrades still held the lighted relic under the shelter of his great-coat, where he was endeavouring to kindle his pipe from it. I snatched it from him, when it was instantly extinguished, and, lo, the storm began sensibly to abate. The whole brigade of *bateaux* weathered the storm safely except for two, carrying men of The Ninth, both of which swamped just as they got close in shore, but our comrades were within their depth and lost neither their lives nor their arms.

At the mouth of the River Bouquet, where we finally disembarked, a great body of Indians joined us, and General Burgoyne held a Congress with their chiefs and principal warriors. Not only had the Six Nations appeared in full strength, but their sworn enemies the Algonquins and Wyandots also. General Burgoyne addressed them through an interpreter in his oratund manner, as follows:

CHIEFS AND WARRIORS,

The Great King, our common Father, and the patron of all who seek and deserve his protection, has considered with satisfaction the general conduct of the Indian tribes, from the beginning of the troubles in America. Too sagacious and too faithful to be deluded or corrupted, they have observed the violated rights of the parental power they love, and burned to vindicate them. A few individuals alone, the refuse of a small tribe, at the first were led astray: and the misrepresentations, the specious allurements, the insidious promises, the diversified plots in which the rebels are exercised, and all of which they employed for that effect, have served only in the end to enhance the honour of the tribes in general, by demonstrating to the world how few and how contemptible are the apostates! It is a truth known to you all, these pitiful examples excepted (and they have probably, before this day, hid their faces in shame) that the collective voices and hands of the Indian tribes, over this vast continent, are on the side of justice, of law, and of the King.

The restraint you have put upon your resentment in waiting the King your Father's call to arms, the hardest proof, I am persuaded, to which your affection could have been put, is another manifest and affecting mark of your adherence to that principle of connexion to which you were always fond to allude, and which is the mutual joy and the duty of the parent to cherish.

The clemency of your Father has been abused, the offers of his mercy have been despised, and his farther patience would, in his eyes, become culpable, in as much as it would withhold redress from the most grievous oppressions in the provinces that ever disgraced the history of mankind. It therefore remains for me, the General of one of His Majesty's armies, and in this Council his representative, to release you from those bonds which your obedience imposed—Warriors, you are free—go forth in might and valour of your cause—strike at the common enemies of Great Britain and America—disturbers of public order, peace, and happiness, destroyers of commerce, parricides of state.

The General, then pointing to the officers, both German and British, who attended this meeting, proceeded:

The circle round you, the Chiefs of His Majesty's European forces, and of the Princes, his allies, esteem you as brothers in the war; emulous in glory and in friendship, we will endeavour reciprocally to give and to receive examples; we know how to value, and we will strive to imitate your perseverance in enterprise, and your constancy to resist hunger, weariness, and pain. Be it our task, from the dictates of our religion, the laws of our warfare, and the principles and interest of our policy, to regulate your passions when they overbear, to point out where it is nobler to spare than to revenge, to discriminate degrees of guilt, to suspend the uplifted stroke, to chastise and not destroy.

This war to you, my friends, is new: upon all former occasions, in taking the field, you held yourselves authorized to destroy wherever you came, because everywhere you found an enemy. The case is now very different.

The King has many faithful subjects dispersed in the provinces, consequently you have many brothers there, and these people are more to be pitied, that they are persecuted or imprisoned wherever they are discovered or suspected; and to dissemble, to a generous mind, is a yet more grievous punishment.

Persuaded that your magnanimity of character, joined to your principles of affection to the King, will give me fuller control over your minds than the military rank with which I am invested, I enjoin your most serious attention to the rules which I hereby proclaim for your invariable observation during the campaign.

I positively forbid bloodshed, when you are not opposed in arms. Aged men, women, children, and prisoners must be held sacred from the knife or hatchet, even in the time of actual conflict. You shall receive compensation for the prisoners you take, but you shall be called to account for scalps.

In conformity and indulgence of your customs, which have affixed an idea of honour to such badges of victory, you shall be allowed to take the scalps of the dead, when killed by your fire, and in fair opposition; but on no account, or pretence, or subtility or prevarication, are they to be taken from the wounded, or even dying; and still less pardonable, if possible, will it be held to kill men in that condition, on purpose, and upon a supposition that this protection to the wounded would be thereby evaded.

Base, lurking assassins, incendiaries, ravagers, and plunderers of the country, to whatever army they may belong, shall be treated with less reserve; but the latitude must be given you by order, and I must be the judge on the occasion.

Should the enemy, on their parts, dare to countenance acts of barbarity towards those who may fall into their hands, it shall be yours also to retaliate: but till this severity be thus compelled, bear immovable in your hearts this solid maxim (it cannot be too deeply impressed), that the great essential reward, the worthy service of your alliance, the sincerity of your zeal to the King, your Father and never-failing protector, will be examined and judged upon the test only of your steady and uniform adherence to the orders and counsels of those to whom His Majesty has entrusted the direction and honour of his arms.

After the General had finished his speech, they all of them cried out, '*Etow! Etow! Etow!*' and after remaining some little time in consultation, Little Abraham, as the most respectable and aged Chief among the Six Nations rose up, and made the following answer:

I stand up, in the name of all the nations present, to assure our Father that we have attentively listened to his discourse—we receive you as the Father, because when you speak we hear the voice of our Great Father beyond the Great Lake.

We rejoice in the approbation you have expressed of our behaviour.

We have been tried and tempted by the Bostonians; but we have loved our Father, and our hatchets have been sharpened upon our affections.

In proof of the sincerity of our professions, our whole villages able to go to war are come forth. The old and infirm, our infants and wives, alone remain at home.

With one common assent, we promise a constant obedience to all you have ordered, and all you shall order, and may the Father of Days give you many, and success.

They all cried, '*Etow, Etow,*' again, and the Congress then dispersed.

A war-dance followed that same evening.

I sought out Thayendanegea meanwhile in his wigwam, who greeted me with every mark of friendship. He was in full warpaint and grasped in his hand a war-banner, consisting of a spear dressed with coloured silks, feathers of the spruce-partridge and skins of polecats. I inquired privately of him the whereabouts and condition of Kate. He told me that she was under the protection of Miss Molly in his abode by the Genesee River, and already big with child; but counseled me to forget her. She had informed him of her decision never again to be my squaw, in any event, once I had quitted her for the sake of my Duty; she would return to Harlowe, soon as her child was born, for the sake of her duty as a wife. As my friend, Thayendanegea remarked, he deeply regretted her resolution, for (clenching his hands tightly together) he knew our hearts were and would always remain thus united in love, though in body separated. He added, however, that as a Christian he felt obliged to applaud Mrs. Harlowe's resolution, reminding me that whom God had joined, no man should put asunder, etc., etc.; a text which I heard with a certain feeling of remorse, being now again in British dress and company. My life in the woods during the previous winter seemed but a beautiful and idle dream.

I asked, what would become of the child? He replied: that was provided for already.

❀ ❀ ❀ ❀ ❀ ❀ ❀ ❀ ❀ ❀ ❀ ❀

CHAPTER

20

IF GENERAL BURGOYNE had in a manner made injudicious use of political power to supplant General Carleton in the command of our army, no scandal was caused by it; and General Carleton, as I have told, was very loyal in doing all within his power to ensure the success of our invasion of the United States. He even prevailed upon a few Canadian Habitants, during the very period when crops were sown, to hire him their teams for drawing our transport wagons and engage themselves as boatmen upon the lakes; others he set to improving the defences of St. John's, Chambly, and Sorel. This decent amity was not shown in a corresponding situation upon the American side, where the Commander of their Northern army, Major-General Philip Schuyler, was assailed in Congress by the intriguing New England representatives, headed by Samuel and John Adams: on the ground that he was a secret Loyalist. They pointed out, truly enough, that he valued the aristocratic spirit, which inspires officers to command and soldiers to obey, before the spirit of Liberty, which makes all men believe themselves the equal of, or superior to, those who are their betters by birth or education. They found an ally and instrument in Major-General Horatio Gates, who had been Adjutant-General of the Americans during the siege of Boston and was now second in command to General Schuyler.

This General Gates was no gentleman in behaviour and sensibilities, whatever his quality by birth, nor was he endowed with any officer-like gifts, though he had once held a commission in our Army, which was well rid of him. He was an urbane, sneaking, and ambitious person of good presence, with a talent for ingratiating himself into the confidence of mediocre men by traducing persons of character and merit: General Washington was later to feel and suffer from his spite. Although set by General Schuyler in command of the American advanced forces at Ticonderoga, General Gates murderously (as they themselves complained) left his people there to their fate. They were now suffering more pitiably than ever from bad food, disease, and lack of medical supplies. All were living in poor, thin tents and without greatcoats or sufficient blankets; and a third part of them were even obliged to go shoeless in a temperature that stood fixed below zero on Fahrenheit's thermometer. It is said that New Englanders had never sworn or taken God's name in vain until this experience of the camp at Ticonderoga forced them to it; where 'that most foolish and unaccountable of vices' took such root among them that every second word was now either the name of God or some base part of speech smacking of grogshop or nanny-house.

In November General Gates went down to Baltimore in Maryland, where Congress was assembled, and up again in February to Philadelphia, in which city their next session took place: insidiously pressing upon the Congress-men in lobbies, lodgings, and the street his superior fitness to command in General Schuyler's place.

Congress at last yielded to his persistent voice and passed a resolution giving him the independent command of the troops based upon Albany, just as General Burgoyne had been given an independent command of the troops based upon St. John's. However, General Schuyler did not assent so amiably to his supersession as had General Carleton. He suggested to his powerful friends in New York that this was an act of spite against him for the part that he had once taken in a land-dispute between New York and Massachusetts, over the possession of what is now known as the State of Vermont; and New York thereupon elected him as their representative to Congress, where he rose to demand an official inquiry into his conduct. This put the two Adamses into an awkward position; and in the end his merits were publicly acknowledged and he was sent north to resume his authority from General Gates. He arrived back at Albany early in June, the same time as we began our expedition down the lake; and immediately appointed Brigadier-General St. Clair to the defence of Ticonderoga, as a less offensive choice to the Massachusetts men than Brigadier-General Benedict Arnold, who was otherwise more fitted to undertake it. The next scene in this farce was that General Gates, who had not yet visited his army at Ticonderoga, grew reckless with rage and ran once more to Philadelphia to call Congress to account for their double-dealing!

General Burgoyne issued an Order of the Day to us on June 30th, to the effect that to-morrow we embarked for our assault upon Ticonderoga (which was fifteen miles distant from Crown Point, where we were assembled) and thence would drive forward into the interior of the enemy's country. The services required, he declared, were critical and conspicuous; but at all events 'this army must not retreat.' The British regiments of the Line, besides The Ninth, that embarked upon this hazardous campaign were very reliable ones, viz. The Twentieth, Twenty-first, Twenty-fourth, Twenty-ninth, Thirty-fourth, Forty-seventh, Fifty-third and Sixty-second.

No one can deny that we did very well at Ticonderoga, which was a double fortress consisting of the old French works, greatly improved, lying on the western side of the water, and a heavily fortified hill named Mount Independence, on the eastern. These two positions were linked by a bridge more than three hundred yards long, of colossal construction and protected by a massive boom. It should be explained that a short distance below Ticonderoga, to the west, occurred the crooked northern passage to Lake George; the broad continuation of Lake Champlain to the southward was called the South River.

My company had been formed with the light infantry companies of the other regiments into a battalion commanded by Colonel Lord Balcarres, an experienced and courageous nobleman. We expected very severe fighting, for the defences of Ticonderoga showed an even more formidable aspect than they had done when we stopped short before them in the previous October. Yet the exertions we were called upon to make were in the pioneering, rather than the military, way. The fact was that the Americans, reduced by the negligence of their generals to but three thousand men, were hardly sufficient in numbers to man the existing works. They had therefore neglected to fortify Sugar Hill, a rocky eminence, rather less than a mile in their rear, which rose six hundred feet from the water at the point where the South River and the Lake George inlet divide. They fondly imagined that, because they could not spare troops to construct and man a redoubt on Sugar Hill, it was not only inaccessible to British artillery, but out of range; though, as we later learned from prisoners, General St. Clair had a few months before satisfied himself by experiment that a twelve-pounder shell carried from the fortress to the summit, and could therefore carry in the contrary sense too.

General Phillips saw at a glance that Sugar Hill easily commanded the fortress; and remarked that 'where a man can go, a mule can go; and where a mule can go, a gun can go.' He called in the Lieutenant who was Engineer-in-Command of the Army, and asked whether he and his sappers could in a reasonably short time construct a road to the summit, up which gun-teams could haul howitzers of eight-inch calibre, light twenty-four pounders, and medium twelves. The Engineer visited this place—for we had by now environed the position for near three-fourths of its circuit, advancing through the woods with great caution on either side of the inlet, while the naval force kept in the centre—and was at first staggered by the broken rocks, the matted creepers, the huge fallen timber that encumbered its steep sides. Yet he undertook, if provided with sufficient fatigue-men, to make within twenty-four hours something that was worse than a turnpike road, but better than no road at all. So it was arranged, and my company was among those called upon to act as labourers upon this road. This was July 4th, the day which the Americans celebrated as Independence Day, and we could hear cheers for the United States of America coming down the wind to us. In the evening a dozen rockets were set off by them, and then one more, in honour of the thirteen States.

Under the Lieutenant's direction we heaved, pushed, fetched, carried, and sweated. A spur to our exertions lay in the consideration that if we could not thus force the enemy to evacuate their works by a threat of being shelled into Glory, General Burgoyne would call upon us to make a frontal attack upon them. We did not fancy a second Bunker's Hill victory; to advance across open country under fire of well-posted batteries, until we came to the tangle of forest-trees felled with their branches towards us, and finally, as we emerged in disorder from thence, to be picked off, one by one, by their excellent riflemen. A few lucky ones of us might make a lodgment and go at the enemy with the bayonet—who, as we knew, were ill-provided with his handy arm—but at a cost of perhaps half our force.

By dawn of July 5th a sort of road had been completed up Sugar Hill and the guns hauled up it on pulleys, by the combined powers of men, mules, horses, and oxen. As daylight grew, we were rewarded for our exertions by being permitted to peep through telescopes at the enemy works, where it was possible to count the defenders of each redoubt, and the guns in each battery, and to observe the enemies' vessels riding behind their gigantic bridge.

Said General Phillips to us: 'Thank you, my brave lads, for what you have done to-night. Let us rechristen this hill "Mount Defiance." ' Then the guns were laid, and shells and grape were sent plunging down into Mount Independence, and into the old French fort.

It was an unpleasant awakening for General St. Clair: he must choose either to hold his ground and lose his army, or quit his ground and lose his character. For the Americans had set great store by Ticonderoga ever since it had been captured from us, two years previously, by the fanatical Colonel Ethan Allen—'in the name,' as he said, 'of the Great Jehovah and the Continental Congress.' To yield the place without a struggle would strengthen the factious power of the New England Congress-men against General Schuyler and himself. He called a Council of War of his colonels, and there urged that to take the less glorious course of retiring, while they still could, would be ultimately of more benefit to their country. They assented, and he made the most of the short time that remained for getting away what he could of his men, stores, and artillery. Nothing could be done by them until nightfall, on account of our observers on Mount Defiance; but the sun no sooner set than two hundred *bateaux* were laden with baggage and sent off under escort of the five galleys that still survived from General Arnold's fleet; while the troops followed on foot. They did not take the usual route down the Lake George inlet, for the brigade in which we served commanded that water from a hill named Mount Hope, which we had seized without opposition and hastily fortified; we had two brigades of artillery there with us, besides. Instead, they took the only remaining route, which was down the South River, the troops in the old French fort marching over the great bridge and down the farther bank. A building was fired by one of their lesser generals, in spiteful disobedience to General St. Clair's orders, which lit up the scene and discovered great activity. However, it was doubtful whether they planned a sortie or a retirement, and we therefore stood to arms the greater part of the night. At daybreak an Indian scout, who had crept into the French fort under cover of darkness, reported that the enemy were gone. Immediately, we who were on piquet duty were ordered to enter the works; where General Fraser himself planted the British flag upon the rampart. After a short examination of the place, to make sure that the enemy nowhere lay in ambush for us, we hurried to the great bridge in order to search the works on Mount Independence.

This bridge was supported by twenty-two sunken piers of timber, the interstices being filled with separate floats, fifty feet long and thirty wide, strongly fastened together with iron chains. It was likewise defended, on the Lake Champlain side, by a boom composed of very large pieces of timber, fastened together by riveted bolts and double chains. Through this bridge the British seamen from our fleet were busily cutting a passage to allow the frigates to sail in pursuit of the enemy galleys and *bateaux*. Some were demolishing the boom; others had already removed a part of the bridge itself, between two of the piers; a third party were unshackling one of the great floats, to tow it away. They reckoned, by nine o'clock in the morning, to have cleared away an obstruction upon which the Americans had bestowed incredible labour over a period of ten months. We were obliged to halt a few minutes while we built a slight gangway for our passage over the breach.

Upon reaching the farther side we possessed ourselves of the heavy battery that defended the bridge. There we came upon four Americans lying dead drunk upon the ground beside a cask of Madeira. We counted ourselves very fortunate in this, for we observed that the matches were lighted and they had evidently been left behind to fire the guns off at our approach and blow us to pieces; but the wine had allured them to forget their instructions and drown their cares. The heads of some powder-casks were also knocked off and powder strewed in a train to them, with the object of injuring our men as they gained the works. A number of Wyandot Indians had attached themselves to our party, from a hope of scalps and plunder, and were curious in examining everything that lay in their path. One of them caught up a match that lay upon the ground with some fire still alive in it and began waving it about, the sparks flying in all directions. 'Down on your faces!' I shouted in alarm to my comrades, and not an instant too soon, for a spark dropped upon the priming of one of the guns. It discharged with a great roar, but in any case would have done no injury, for by some error the muzzle was elevated above the level of our heads.

Here, though I fear to impair the verisimilitude of my story with anything so preposterous, I cannot forbear to mention an incident which had occurred on the previous day. There were, as it happens, many reliable witnesses of it, and Lieutenant Anburey of The Fourteenth has recorded it in his well-known *Travels Through the Interior Parts of America*. A little after dawn, Smutchy Steel, being a sentinel of our piquet guard, observed a man in the woods reading a leather-bound book. He challenged him, with 'Who goes there?,' but the man was so closely intent upon his studies that he did not reply 'Friend' nor make any other response. Smutchy abstained from use of the bayonet, but ran up and seized him by the collar of his coat. Awaking from his reverie, the intruder said very calmly that he was Chaplain to the Forty-seventh Regiment, but could otherwise give no account of his presence there. Smutchy bade him stay where he was until the relief came; whereupon he was taken before Captain Montgomery, the nearest officer, who sent him under escort to General Fraser. General Fraser suspected him to be a spy, for The Forty-seventh were stationed two or three miles in the rear, and he thought himself acquainted with the face and name of every clergyman attached to the forces. He began to ask him several questions about the Americans, remarking that if he consented to answer them fairly he would escape hanging. The stranger pretended to be perplexed and persisted in his first story.

'Come, come,' said General Fraser, 'a person in your dishabille cannot pretend to be a man of God going about on his lawful occasions. Own to the cheat, pray, or it will go hard with you.'

'Sir,' said the prisoner, 'you have only to send to the Colonel of The Forty-seventh, and he will inform you who I am. I reported for duty at his headquarters yesterday evening with a letter of credit from the Governor-General of Canada.'

'And your name?'

He gave his name.

He was sent for examination to General Burgoyne, where his story was confirmed. I had no share in these proceedings, but Terry Reeves came running up to me at about seven o'clock with pale cheeks, and 'Oh,' he cried, stuttering, 'I have seen him.'

'Seen whom, Moon-Curser?' asked I. 'It was a ghost or banshee, by the look on your face.'

'Worse,' said he. 'It was the Devil. Him whom we last saw in the Newgate tap-room, the day that little Jimmy was tucked up.'

I shuddered involuntarily. 'You are dreaming, dear Terry,' says I. 'Or is it the apple-brandy?'

'Gerry Lamb,' he replied very solemnly. 'Would I ever mistake the sallow face, and the loose, wet lock, and the ugly chin to him, this side the grave? Or would you yourself, Gerry?'

I have already confessed to my superstitious weakness in the matter of the Holy Thursday candle. It will not therefore seem surprising to my readers to learn that this appearance, or apparition, of the Reverend John Martin worked strongly upon my imagination. It seemed a presage of the utmost calamity to our forces, though our great successes of the following week seemingly belied it. What is more curious still, this Popish priest, or Methodist minister, or Chaplain of the Established Church, this Reverend John Martin, once more disappeared so soon as he rejoined The Forty-seventh; but reappeared as suddenly, a fortnight later at Skenesborough, for a single day, and was thereafter lost to us. It has ever teased me to know whether or not the letter of credit from General Carleton was a forgery, or whether he had actually imposed himself upon that excellent personage.

We now explored Mount Independence; it was clear of Americans; and the rest of the brigade coming up, we set off again in pursuit of the enemy. The day was sultry, with the sun boiling behind a thin screen of clouds. We marched without a halt from dawn until one o'clock over a number of steep and woody hills, by a very rough track. A party of Indians went ahead, who being unencumbered by packs and heavy clothing could advance far more smartly than we; they brought back a score of stragglers to us, and we learned from these that the American rearguard was composed of chosen marksmen under the command of a Colonel Francis, one of their best officers. General Riedesel's Brunswickers were in our support, but they could not keep up with us on the march on account of heavy accoutrements and old age.

We were taking the Hibberton road, a roundabout route to Skenesborough, which was the American base near the extremity of the South River. We had halted about two hours and partaken of our dinners when General Riedesel rode up. He appeared in considerable excitement, and, 'Why, Red Hazel, my old friend,' General Fraser bantered, 'what means this flashing eye, this surly visage?'

He answered in tolerably good English that his God-damned old pigs were straggling and he could not prevail upon them to mend their pace.

Said General Fraser: 'Do not blame them, General. I remember no march so fatiguing as this in the whole course of the Seven Years' War in Germany. Here, accept a present of gingerbread. It was taken from the Americans at Ticonderoga out of a parcel left over from their celebrations of Independence.'

General Riedesel scrutinized the gingerbread, which was gilt and baked in the form of a mermaid. He gave her an amorous leer, then, with a sudden snap he bit her head clean off, and burst into an enormous peal of laughter—which so infected those who stood by that all immediately were convulsed with mirth. The mermaid's head then becoming lodged in the General's windpipe, he had like to be choked, but that Captain Montgomery, who rode up, smote him in the back with his fist. The gobbet shot out across the road, and he subsided, gasping and wheezing.

We marched on towards the enemy, who had gained Hibberton. When our scouts reported that they had halted three miles from us, about two thousand in number, we chose a defensible situation and lay that night on our arms. We slept until three o'clock in the morning, much tormented by the insects, and then renewed our march in the half-light. Two hours later we came up with the Americans and found them busily employed in cooking their provisions, though with piquets posted.

Then began a skirmish which, since the Americans were compelled to fight, became a pitched battle. When the piquets were driven in, our Grenadier battalion was sent round to cut them off from the Skenesborough Road which ran through Castleton; so they turned instead towards Pittsford which was thirty miles to the east, along a steep, rocky road. The Grenadiers, to intercept them, climbed a hill so sheer as to seem inaccessible; they could only gain the summit by laying hold of the branches of trees and hauling one another up the rocks by main force. Being thus headed off, the Americans showed fight and, while some attacked the Grenadiers, others turned about and fired at our light infantry companies as we hurried after them. Those Americans who had axes hurriedly felled trees, to serve as a breastwork behind which to receive us.

The brushwood was exceedingly thick and tangled, and their marksmen took careful aim at us as we stumbled up against the breastwork. I was proud to find how steadily our men behaved, though we could preserve no sort of order or dressing, nor use the manual exercise for platoon firing in which we had been perfected during our training. We made an improvement *ex tempore* upon it, however, by abstaining from any use of our ramrods: after loading and priming we merely struck the breech of the firelock to the ground, which sent the cartridge down, brought it to the present, and fired. We maintained a certain unity of action by singing in unison *Hot Stuff*, a rousing song that now enjoyed the same popularity among us as the famous *Liliburlero* (that chased King James out of three kingdoms) had enjoyed among our predecessors of The Ninth at the relief of Londonderry, the capture of Athlone, the victory of Boyne Water. With dry throats and swelling hearts we sang:

> *From rascals as these may we fear a rebuff?*
> *Advance, Grenadiers, and let fly your hot stuff!*

Each side in this engagement, which lasted near two hours, afterwards claimed to have been greatly inferior in numbers to the other. My belief is that the sides were about equal, though the denseness of the woods and the excitement of the occasion ruled out any counting of polls. It ended when General Riedesel, who had been impatiently waiting for his lagging troops to appear on the field and have their share in the glory, hauled forward fifty men of his vanguard and brought them into action. He bade them beat drum, blow fife and bugle, shout, sing battle-hymns and fire their muskets into the air to suggest to the enemy that they were the whole Brunswick Brigade; and this they did. The hullabaloo turned the scale: the Americans, who had lost their brave Colonel Francis, slackened their fire, and we charged with the bayonet. They did not receive us, but all ran off—except those who surrendered, and one or two lurking fanatics who remained behind, concealed in bushes, waiting for the chance to shoot at the 'tyrannical British officers.' One of these succeeded in killing a well-beloved captain of ours, as he was examining some official papers taken from Colonel Francis's pocket-book, and escaped unavenged. As I ran in the direction of the shot, I came upon Sergeant Fitzpatrick kneeling alone and bareheaded in a little hollow. He was giving thanks to God that his life had once more been spared, in the solemn words of the Psalmist: 'O God the Lord, the Strength of my Salvation: Thou hast covered my head in the day of battle.' His calm and tranquil aspect checked me in my bloody course; I returned to my comrades.

Smutchy was cleaning his rifle when he discovered, to his surprise, that in the excitement and confusion of battle he had put no fewer than four cartridges into his piece. His mouth being so busy with *Hot Stuff*, he had not thought to bite off the ends: he had snapped his piece in vain, because he had also omitted to prime the pan. If these cartridges had exploded together the overcharge would have burst the gun and perhaps injured him fatally. 'However,' Smutchy said, 'there was no confusion as to my baggonet'; and, glancing at it, I observed blood upon the blade. There was a sudden sick revulsion in my belly at the sight of a fellow-creature's blood smeared on steel, and I went apart into the bushes and vomited.

This having been a hand-to-hand engagement, unlike my first skirmish at Three Rivers, I must describe the course of my feelings during and after it. Before the fight opened, I was seized with apprehensions, in the knowledge that my life hung upon awful accident. This natural instinct, the anxiety for self-preservation, caused a quick pulsation and agitated my breast; so that during the hot climb up the hill-side my lungs came nigh to bursting. But, at the moment when the first bullet whizzed by me, all emotion vanished, my breast calmed, and my limbs drew upon an unsuspected source of energy. I was entirely lost in the ardour of the battle, wherein it was my duty not only to fight but to direct others in fighting. Reflection upon the brutal nature of war or the sanctity of human life suffered temporary suspense; I acted like one in a trance; and trees, bushes, my comrades, and the enemy, were as one sees pictures dancing in the flames of an open fire. It was not until we came to burying the dead that a thousand severe and painful feelings recalled the thoughtful mind and all the affections. The sight, especially, of dear comrades agonized with mortal wounds harrowed the recesses of my heart— some writhing and groaning in misery, some with brains oozing from shattered skulls, others sitting up or leaning on their elbows, pale with loss of blood, observing with a dull horror the extent of their injuries. I suffered sorrowful pangs, too, for the ragged enemy dead, whose cause their stubborn courage had in a manner ennobled. Worse than this, we found among the bushes two unfortunate Americans, wounded in the legs, who had lost their scalps to the Wyandots, but were pronounced recoverable by the surgeon. It was shocking to see a live man so ferociously disfigured; and I wondered that I had ever allowed myself to be enrolled in an Indian tribe.

I found occasion for reflection, too, upon the hairbreadth escapes with which many had been blessed in battle, while others were terribly taken off in the first onset. Lord Balcarres, our tall, gallant commander, whose glittering uniform made him the target of every rifleman in the American rear-guard, had his coat and trousers pierced with about thirty balls, yet escaped with a slight flesh wound in the hip; while Lieutenant Haggard of The Marines was shot dead between the eyes in the opening attack, and Major Grant of The Twenty-fourth through the heart, before ever the battle was joined—having been twice wounded in previous wars at this very place!

Not only solemn emotions possessed my unwrought mind. I recall with what an excess of laughter I greeted the story of Captain Harris's wound and his humorous sally. He was commanding the Grenadiers of The Thirty-fourth when he was struck, and scrambled on hands and knees to the shelter of a tree. Lieutenant Anburey of The Fourteenth, passing by, asked him: 'Are you badly hurt?' Though in great agony from a broken hip-bone, he clapped his hand to the part adjoining, which had also been pierced, and with an arch look, replied: 'You can ask my a—e, Anburey, you can ask my a—e!'

Now, a disagreeable happening to be related will show that the agreed rules of civilized warfare were either despised as tyrannical or not well understood by the New England soldiery. Stratagems and ruses are one thing, but to trade cunningly upon the mercy and humanity of the foe, quite another. General Schuyler, for example, made use of legitimate and witty ruse about this time. He arranged for a letter written by himself, as from a Tory partisan behind the American lines, and enclosed in the false bottom of a canteen, to fall into General Burgoyne's hands, which perplexed him for days.

But an altogether different case was presented at this battle of Hibberton (or Huberton or Hubbardtown as it was indifferently named). Two companies of Grenadiers stationed in the skirts of the woods, close to a clearing, observed a force of about sixty Americans coming across this clearing with their arms 'clubbed' or reversed, the recognized sign of soldiers who wish to surrender. The Grenadiers held their fire and stood in a relaxed posture, ready to disarm such voluntary prisoners; but when these had come within ten yards they turned their muskets round in a single concerted motion, and, firing a destructive volley upon the Grenadiers, ran as fast as they could into the contiguous forest.

This seeming treachery greatly exasperated the surviving Grenadiers, who gave no quarter for the remainder of the campaign; but I would name it ignorance rather than treachery—a mistaken application to warfare of a principle allowed as legitimate in trade throughout New England. The principle was that of *caveat emptor*, 'let the purchaser beware of being overreached,' and the good people of Massachusetts and Connecticut would tell you droll tales for your entertainment of how they had tricked and defrauded, not only strangers but friends and neighbours, in a manner that in Great Britain or Ireland would bar them from the society of respectable men. I was a long time accustoming myself, during my residence in America, to this moral obliquity, which I will say, however, very positively, did not belie their natural good fellowship and hospitality. Rather it was a sort of sport with them, as among the knavish, jovial horse-swappers of Yorkshire, or the tinkers of my own country. Yet it must have caused a householder a deal of inconvenience never to be sure that the sack of corn that he had accepted as 'country pay' —for where coin is scarce one must pay in kind—might not in reality be one-third corn and two-thirds chaff mixed with earth; or that in a consignment of hams that he had bought for his winter use from a travelling merchant, one-half might not be made of bass-wood, carved and painted to a lifelike similitude of the sample he had approved. If he were duped, he was expected to laugh heartily and to remark: 'I guess it was a regular pedlar's trick and serves me well right for being so green and sleepy-eyed.' Nor was scriptural authority wanting for this smartness. The son of Sirach in the *Book of Wisdom* had declared: 'A merchant shall hardly keep himself from doing wrong, and a huckster shall not be declared free from sin.'

The enemy had fled in great disorder, leaving two hundred dead on the field, and many more disabled by wounds: besides, the remains of a whole regiment, two hundred men, gave themselves up. But we did not press the pursuit for fear of out-running our supplies, of which we were so deficient that our breakfast that morning was bullock's flesh broiled in the wood-ashes and eaten without bread or salt; these animals were found running in the wood. We were not to know that General St. Clair's failure to reinforce his rear-guard had been due to the contumacious refusal of two militia regiments to march; and that, had we pressed the pursuit, we might have captured prisoners by the thousand, and supported ourselves upon the food and ammunition that they strewed behind them in their rout.

General Fraser had immediately dispatched a messenger to General Burgoyne, should he be at Ticonderoga, acquainting him with his success. He now desired to send the same message to him at Skenesborough should he have succeeded in destroying the enemy's forces at the bottom of the South River, and reached that place, whither he himself now intended to march. He therefore called for a volunteer to carry the message ahead of his advance; and when I informed his aide-de-camp that I had lived for three months among the Mohawk Indians, and was ready to go, the mission was confided to me. The General allowed me to choose a companion; Mad Johnny Maguire at once recommended himself. We set off together a few minutes later, being ordered to travel as expeditiously as possible. We took the road through Castleton, a wretched hamlet of twenty houses, which lay a few miles away. This place we avoided by a circuit, for fear of meeting the enemy, but stumbled on a great stone jar of cider in a field near by, covered with grasses against the sun, and refreshed ourselves from it.

It was not until the middle of the morning that we observed armed Americans: a large party of militia marching up the road towards us.

❀ ❀ ❀ ❀ ❀ ❀ ❀ ❀ ❀ ❀ ❀ ❀

CHAPTER

21

OUR fleet, having forced the bridge at Ticonderoga, had pursued the enemy vessels down the South River and overtaken them in the afternoon previous to our Hibberton battle. There was no escape for the Americans, who were at anchor in South Bay, a naval station close to Skenesborough. Two of the five galleys struck their flags, the remaining three were burned by their own crews: of more than two hundred *bateaux* the most were captured and the remainder sunk. The Americans, as they retreated, set fire to their stockaded fort, their storehouses, saw-mills, forges, repair-sheds, slips. The flame caught the hanging forest above the station, and up it all went in the greatest conflagration imaginable. Not one earthly thing was saved for the Americans, of whom about thirty were intercepted and captured by men of The Ninth, who had been disembarked before the attack began and ascended the hill from the flank. Others fled towards Castleton; and these were the men whom Maguire and I now observed coming towards us down the Castleton road.

Since we had no wish to engage in any fighting, we concealed ourselves in the bushes and let them go by; our vanguard would snap them up, we judged, in an hour or two. I had suggested the precaution of turning our jackets inside out, so that the fustian lining should show, instead of the scarlet, and render us less conspicuous—but Maguire said that this fashion reminded him too sadly of punishment drill at Waterford Barracks; he begged me not to make it an order. Since the scarlet of both our jackets was faded almost to a brick colour from long exposure to the torrid sun, I consented.

A party of about twenty Americans went by, arguing loudly among themselves on politics, their muskets slung. Behind them came two more men, a little dandiacal officer and a huge hairy-bosomed private soldier who limped. The private, as he passed our lodge, cried to the other: 'Hold hard, Andy, there's a tarnationed stone in my shoe. I must halt to shake it out.'

'I am thankful of a respite, Neighbour Benaiah,' replied the officer smoothly, sitting down plump a few paces from us. 'But, hark ye, I can't rightly agree with you that the Britainers intend to push on beyond Skenesborough. I calculate that 'tis but a feint to deceive us, and that's the reason of the plan of attack being openly published and advertised these months afore. No, my dear Benaiah, Johnny Burgine an't a-going to march down south on Albany with but eight thousand men agin the full thirty thousand we can oppose to him—for who's to guard his communications, eh? Be sure old nasty Carleton won't, seeing that he is Johnny's mortal foe and eaten with jealousy. No, no, dear Benaiah, and Billy Howe an't a-going to move up North to meet him, neither, and I'll tell you for why. I calculate old Billy Howe's a-going to transport his army by sea and land to the neighbourhood of Boston—for Boston, as we all know, is the centre and hearth of Independency; and Johnny Burgine, he'll return all his men, but a few, back up the Lakes and down the St. Lawrence River and join forces with him within the month. The Britainers an't such fools as they pretend, not by nation much, that they an't. I'm bound back home to Boston to repel the landing with God's help, and I'm a-taking the company with me.'

'No, neighbour Andy,' said Benaiah, 'that you are not. You shall stay here to captain us, you tarnal skunk, or we'll shoot you for sure. No hooking it off and giving us the slip, mind, you jockey! The bloody-backed rascals are here, and here we'll fight 'em, so soon as ever we have re-filled our pouches and sacks.'

The officer attempted to reply, but Benaiah with a growl told him to hold his rattle. Just then we heard shots, as of a brisk skirmish at some distance away in the direction whither we had been proceeding; whereupon the two Americans arose, the man Benaiah coolly and resolutely, his officer showing great apprehension, and passed on.

Maguire and I, who had both experienced a great desire to burst into laughter during this confabulation, now went cautiously in the direction of the shots. They ceased as we approached, and soon we came in sight of a detachment of our own regiment, under Captain Montgomery, who had secured a number of prisoners and were about to return to Skenesborough with them. We directed Captain Montgomery in the pursuit of Captain Andy's company; and in return he told us where to find General Burgoyne, to whom our message was addressed. We delivered it to him that evening, having come a matter of thirty miles, and arrived three hours in advance of the brigade. General Burgoyne was most affable to us and greatly encouraged by the news. Our reward was a bumper of Madeira wine apiece.

On his informing us that The Ninth had been detached that morning in pursuit of the enemy, who were retreating by Wood Creek towards Fort Anna, and that hard fighting was there expected, we begged leave to be allowed to join them; our excuse was that we bore a report to Lieutenant-Colonel John Hill, who now commanded The Ninth, of the losses we had suffered at Hibberton. These included the captain of our Grenadier Company, dead of his wounds, and a lieutenant seriously injured. The General consented to our petition, and we joined Captain Montgomery who was proceeding in the same direction. The next morning we were rowed up Wood Creek, which was shaded by enormous trees, in cedar-wood canoes: a gracious voyage. At the point where we were obliged to disembark because of obstructions in the stream made by the retreating enemy, we found ourselves in a camp of about five hundred Algonquin and Wyandot Indians, under the charge of the Deputy-Quartermaster-General of our army, Captain J. Money of The Ninth; they directed us to the Regiment. Several of these savages wore bloody scalps attached to their belts, and I observed with horror and disgust that one of these was that of a fair-haired woman. The warrior who wore it seemed fatigued after a long journey, and was rolling in the grass to refresh himself, as if he were a horse.

After marching along difficult roads and wading through rivulets, where the bridges had been destroyed by the enemy, we overtook our comrades about dusk. They had captured a number of American boats in Wood Creek laden with luggage, women and invalids, and were now encamped within a quarter of a mile of Fort Anna, which appeared to be strongly held. The fort consisted of a wide square formed by palisades with loopholes between; inside was a large block-house and a store-shed. The whole stood on a slight eminence above the creek, with a saw-mill adjacent, the mill-race of which gushed from a steep wooded hill.

I handed the message to Colonel Hill, who complimented me upon the speed with which I had delivered it. Knowing that I had some slight knowledge of surgery, he bade me report to Surgeon Shelly (who had exchanged with

Surgeon Lindsay from another regiment) as his mate; for
a hot engagement was expected. Maguire he ordered to
remain with Captain Montgomery's company. We lay
upon our arms all night, and I confess that I slept well,
undisturbed by fears of the morrow, for I now accounted
myself a veteran soldier. Lest the enemy should slip away
from us, we had posted piquets on the skirts of the wood
around the Fort, in front of which there was a cleared
field of about a hundred paces broad. The enemy did not
hold the saw-mill, which lay outside the palisade.

The weather was sultry and a storm approached, to
judge by the distant rumblings of thunder to the northward; but when dawn showed, the sky was still clear,
though sudden gusts of wind blew hither and thither.

A man then came running out from the Fort, pursued
with musketry-fire, which, however, did not injure him.
He declared breathlessly that he was a loyal subject of
King George and willing to serve in our ranks. Being questioned, he said that the thousand men in the Fort were in
great consternation, as expecting to be attacked and
stormed by us immediately. By the detachment of our
flank-companies to General Fraser's division, The Ninth
were reduced in strength to less than two hundred men,
including the officers. Colonel Hill therefore instantly sent
off a message to General Burgoyne, asking for support; for
the rest of our brigade lay eight or ten miles away. The
pretended deserter then slipped away, and it proved that
he had been sent to spy out our weaknesses: for within
half an hour the Americans came pouring out of the Fort
with great fury and shouting.

The sentinels of the piquets immediately discharged
their pieces, and their comrades hastened up from the
woods to support them. A number of Americans fell. The
remainder ran back to the palisade, re-formed, and came
on again with redoubled violence. From where I stood
with Surgeon Shelly, carrying his salve-box and bandages
in my hand, I could see nothing, for the woods were very
thick; but Captain Montgomery came marching by us with
his company and we fell in behind. The noise of musketry
in a close wood is very terrible, the discharges echoing
from tree to tree and the bullets smacking among the

leaves. Our whole line held firm and we shot down a number of men; but the rest ran across our right flank and we could hear their officers bawling to them to 'Follow-up, follow up.' Colonel Hill then put us to a severe test of drill by bidding us change front and retire up the hill to our left. At this moment a party of Americans in blue and buff came at us, firing as they advanced; Captain Montgomery fell, wounded in the thigh, from which the blood rose in a little fountain. Surgeon Shelly had just finished dressing the wound of another man with my assistance. He ran to the Captain's side and says he to me: "Sergeant Lamb, while I press upon the artery, wind the tourniquet tightly, close above.'

I complied with his order. We were glad of Mad Johnny Maguire's protection, for he ran forward with charged bayonet and sent the foremost Americans back; then returned to us, observing in a matter-of-fact voice, to the wounded Captain: 'They don't take the bayonet home, your Honour, so naturally as they should.'

I had nearly fixed the tourniquet ligature to Surgeon Shelly's satisfaction, when they came on again. 'Run, Sergeant; run, Maguire, my good man,' cried the Captain between his groans. 'Leave me, for I can't follow.' Off ran Maguire, but I remained for another few seconds until the bandage was secured and the Surgeon could remove his thumbs from the artery; then I, too, dodged among the trees, the bullets crashing about me and the enemy pouring up like a mighty torrent. I was thus the last man to ascend the hill; but heartily blamed myself as I ran that I had lacked the wit to snatch up the salve-box and the roll of bandages. These were now captured, together with Surgeon Shelly and the Captain. However, it was too late to return for them.

This manœuvre of Colonel Hill's was brilliantly executed: for indeed the Regiment, though rough in camp and on parade, was ready enough on the field, and we all made the summit of the hill except a few men. Here the ground was more open, and our companies drew up in Indian file, facing the enemy, each leading soldier discharging his piece in turn and then running to the rear of the file to reload; so that we maintained a well-directed

fire for nearly three hours. I took my turn in the line of
Lieutenant Westrop's company, who was shot through the
heart as he stood by my side. A few minutes after, a man
a short distance upon my left received a ball in his fore-
head, which carried off the roof of his skull. He reeled
round, turned up his eyes, muttered some nonsensical
words as if he dreamed, and fell dead at my feet.

Soon our fire slackened, for our ammunition was well-
nigh expended; and the enemy, perceiving this, boldly ran
across our front to cut off our retreat, nor could we prevent them.

Just at this critical moment, when all was still, came a
cry that made my heart leap with joy and threw the Americans into the utmost consternation: 'Whoo-oo-oo-oop' re-
sounded through the woods. Grounding my firelock, I
clapped my hand to my mouth and 'Whoo-oo-oo-oop,' I
replied, wildly modulating the note as I had learned, in
welcome to the approaching Wyandots and Algonquins.
The Americans scattered incontinently and, the fight being
over, The Ninth formed upon the hill. Colonel Hill then
led them down to the seizure of the Fort; but I remained
behind to care for the wounded.

It was a grievous sight to see the wounded men bleeding
on the ground. What made it more so, was that the rain,
of which only a few great drops had hitherto fallen, came
pouring down in a deluge upon us; and, still to add to the
misery of the sufferers, there was nothing to dress their
wounds, now that the salve-box was gone. I took off my
shirt, tore it up and with the help of a soldier's young
wife, Jane Crumer (the only woman who was with us, and
who kept close by her husband's side during the engagement), made some bandages from these strips and from
the hem of her petticoat, and bound up each man's wound
in turn. I had held Jane in affectionate regard for some
years. She was a slight-figured girl, not beautiful in a pic-
turesque sense, but with an excellent speaking voice and
fine eyes—a niece of Sergeant Fitzpatrick, with whom she
had lived before her marriage. Little Jane had attended
the arithmetic lessons at Waterford that I gave to his boys
and proved my aptest pupil.

Soon Maguire came in search of me, and, 'By the Holy,

Gerry, my jewel,' says he in great excitement, 'I can hardly see you for the rain that's in my eyes. Now here's a packet of news for ye. Those bloody savages who saved us were no Indians at all, but only Captain Money's codding. For he brought them up when he heard the battle noise, but they wouldn't come; so he sent them away and came running up alone, and it was he who uttered that whoop, not they, the heathen beggars—they were four miles hence. What's more, the rebels burned down the block-house and the saw-mill, but the rain has put the flames out and hardly a stick is charred, Glory be to Jesus, and amn't I lucky to be alive?'

I stopped the flow of his talk by making him help Mrs. Crumer and myself in conveying those of the wounded who could not walk to a woodman's hut some hundreds of yards away, the nearest place of shelter. This hut had been the scene of a skirmish towards the end of the battle, for one of our companies had seized it for use as a fort when the enemy tried to outflank us. The work was excessively fatiguing, since we must carry the poor fellows in blankets slung upon poles, and the rain made the ground very slippery.

We had come back from the hut for our third load, and there still remained nine men incapable of movement, when up rode General Burgoyne himself, with his jolly face and jutting chin, together with his 'family,' or staff, in order to view the battlefield. Recognizing me, 'So you arrived in good time to share the glory, my brave Sergeant,' he cried in a booming tone. 'Tell me, now, how did the battle go?'

I pointed out the positions, which he noted carefully—in order, I suppose, to remark upon them in his dispatches; and I then made bold to ask him for men to be sent to help me with carrying the wounded, which he obligingly consented to arrange.

Then he said: 'Should any of the Americans surprise you while you are performing this meritorious and humane duty, you must have a letter to give to their commanding officer, which should ensure the preservation of your life— if, indeed, the leaders of this rabble in arms have bowels of compassion like ordinary men.' He desired his aide-de-camp to lend him his back as an escritoire; and then and there, using a pen, a strip of paper and a pocket ink-horn, indited a very eloquent plea for my life and signed it with a tremendous flourish.

I thanked him and he galloped off. Jane Crumer looked after him, and then back at me, and laughed softly. 'There now,' she said, 'I confess I am quite disappointed. I expected him to pull out tinder, flint, taper, wafer, tape, and all, and seal the letter in headquarterly style. Why, he never even used a sand-castor!'

However, the General did not forget us. He sent up a dozen men of the Twentieth Regiment to act as a carrying party. I dispatched Maguire and Mrs. Crumer to Colonel Hill, to acquaint him with my situation; and the Colonel sent back Maguire, together with three other men and a quantity of provisions. The Colonel informed me that he was ordered to return to Skenesborough and that he left the wounded in my charge. Among these was Lieutenant Murray, with a flesh wound in his calf, who made merry with two fellow-Irishmen who were boasting of the blood they had shed in the service of their King and country, and the gravity of their wounds. In his blunt manner he exclaimed: 'By heavens, my good lads, you need not think so much of being wounded—for, by Jesus God, there's a bullet in the beam yonder by the door, and devil a compliment or pension will that poor timber earn!'

The losses of The Ninth on that day were thirteen killed and twenty-three wounded of all ranks; the gains were thirty prisoners, some stores and baggage and the Colours of the Second Hampshire Regiment of the Massachusetts army. We were commended in Orders.

As for myself, I remained for seven days as surgeon in charge of the hut, whither a supply of salves and bandages was sent up from Skenesborough, and a load of other necessaries. I encountered but one American, by name Gershom Hewit, of Weston, Massachusetts, a poor fellow whose right hand had been broken by a ball, and his leg injured. When I espied him, he was lurking in a thicket near our hut, in the hope of picking up scraps of food that we threw away. I had him covered with a musket when I told him to advance and be recognized. He expected me to shoot him out of hand, and was infinitely grateful when, seeing that he would never be able to soldier again, I dressed his wounds, provided him with victuals and drink, and sent him hobbling back to his own folk. He promised most faithfully not to reveal our whereabouts to his compatriots; which promise he kept.

We expected every moment to be attacked, and fortified the hut as best we could, cutting loopholes so that the wounded men also could fire on the enemy; but we were never molested, though every night during our stay we heard the noise of axes, as the enemy felled trees to hinder the advance of our army. We were proceeding against Fort Edward, on the upper reaches of Hudson's River, their new rallying-point. At the end of that time we returned to Skenesborough. All the wounded men, except three who died, were then nearly fit for duty; for, in preference to the drugs sent me, I had used a vulnerary recommended to me by the Indians, a sort of hartshorn which I found growing near the hut.

Now, Skenesborough was owned by a Scottish gentleman named Skene, a major on half-pay, who had served hereabouts in the previous war, and had been so taken by the beauty of the place that he obtained by Royal Patent a grant of 25,000 acres at the foot of the South River; and began to establish a great domain. It was he who owned the block-house and saw-mill at Fort Anna, and every other building for miles around. He was a Loyalist, and entertained General Burgoyne in a very magnificent way at his house in Skenesborough. Some say that all our subsequent misfortunes were due to this person. For though we were distant by land not more than twenty miles from Fort Edward, the effort of transporting our artillery and stores by this route would be gigantic because of the frightful nature of the country intervening: but all difficulties were denied or minimized by Major Skene, who calculated that a great military road cut from his quay to Fort Edward would render his estate more valuable by many thousand pounds. The alternative was to take us back by water to Ticonderoga, and thence to sail down Lake George, where the enemy could offer us no opposition. This would take four days with favourable weather;

and from Fort George, at the lake's end, a good wagon-road ran to Fort Edward—the defences of both places being in a ruinous condition. These stormed, another week should have brought us in triumph to Albany; had we left our heaviest guns behind.

However, General Burgoyne took the advice of his host. After two days but two miles of road had been built, notwithstanding the incredible exertions of men and teams; and General Burgoyne should then have acknowledged the error and called the task off—as did General Carleton when we sweated over-much to drag the two schooners entire from Chambly to St. John's. But Major Skene pretended that more favourable ground lay ahead, and reminded the General of his Order of the Day at Crown Point, 'This army must not retreat,' which piqued his honour. General Burgoyne had, moreover, sent his fleet of *bateaux*, his own and those captured, up the South River for supplies, and was ashamed to send a fast ship to recall them. He determined to continue the work at all events, the more so as many hundred of provincial Loyalists had arrived in the camp, some with arms, some without, and their expert services could be applied in the pioneering way.

General Philip Schuyler lay at Fort Edward with the beaten American army, amounting to little more than four thousand men; and had left in our hands above a hundred pieces of artillery and large supplies of flour and beef. Two regiments of New England militia he found so disorderly, and so addicted to plundering, that he dismissed them from his army; and what was left could not be depended upon as a fighting force. Yet he was resolved to spare nothing, not even his own good name, not even his life, to promote the cause of Independence which lay so near his heart. At Fort Edward there were cannon lying about on the grass, but no gun-carriages, and scarcely any entrenching tools; insufficient camp-kettles and not five rounds of powder and ball for his muskets. He could not hope to hold the place, but only to delay us until reinforcements were sent him. He had already angered Congress by a letter to them protesting against their dismissal of one of his surgeons without his leave; and now John

Adams was saying that the 'patriot armies will never successfully defend a post till they have shot a general'—meaning Generals Schuyler or St. Clair—'who has yielded a fortress, uncontested, to the enemy.' However, for the victualling of the army that remained to him after the desertions and his dismissals, and for the delaying of our advance, General Schuyler could draw upon his private fortune. He was the proprietor of an ancestral Dutch domain at Saratoga on Hudson's River, some miles downstream from Fort Edward, which was regarded as the best managed estate in all America, and where hundreds of skilled labourers were engaged in his service. Soon their axes, too, were added to those which we heard ringing in the forest, and marvellous obstruction they caused.

The woods here were composed chiefly of oaks of different variety, and the tough hickory, the hemlock, the beech, intermixed with great numbers of the smooth-barked Weymouth pines. They grew to a great height, though none appeared to be more than two feet in diameter; indeed, the girth of the woodland trees of North America was very small in proportion to their height and trifling in comparison of that of the forest trees at home—they sprang up so close together here, and in such rivalry of the sun, that their force was spent in gaining height rather than thickness. These trees, General Schuyler's soldiers and lumberers sent crashing to the ground, at intervals of a few paces, across every path and trail, creek and rivulet, between ourselves and Fort Edward; and ditchers with spades laboured, also, to dam and divert these waters to our hindrance. While he was thus adding hugely to our labours, General Schuyler was also subtracting from our subsistence by driving off all flocks and herds, and carting away or burning all standing crops which lay within the utmost range of our foragers.

It was while I was in the hut at Fort Anna that the Reverend John Martin reappeared at Skenesborough and preached a sermon to the troops on a Sunday morning. This was said to be a very dove-like, unwarlike address and more fitting for a parish church at a harvest festival than for the present occasion, which was a thanksgiving service for the success of our arms. The text was 'Be ye not like unto the ox and the ass, that have no understanding.' After the sermon a *feu de joie* was fired by the whole army, with artillery and small arms. We heard the noise in the distance and could make nothing of it, though we guessed it to be the explosion of a magazine.

I have spoken of the mosquitoes of Skenesborough, that bred there in the stagnant waters under the protecting shade of great trees, as the most malignant of all in America. The inhabitants were proof against their venom, but on us they raised great watering pustules precisely like those of the smallpox. The only sure relief was to be looked for in volatile alkali, of which we possessed scarcely any; but immediate bathing in cold water was better than nothing at all. To scratch was most dangerous, and many men were deprived of the use of their limbs for days from swellings due to this imprudence; two were obliged to undergo amputation. These insects added to the hardships of our men, whom on July 17th I rejoined, returning to my own company in the Light Infantry battalion. The road had then attained but one-third of the length projected, and the obstacles were growing more and more numerous. Exclusive of the labour of hauling away the fallen timber, we found it necessary, before we had done, to construct no less than forty bridges and a causeway, two miles in extent and consisting of large timber laid transversely, over a quaking morass. Nor were the bridges mean feats of engineering: many measured as much as forty feet in height and two or three times that in length, straddling over deep and muddy rivers. Occasionally small parties of the enemy attacked our piquets, but were easily repulsed.

The common soldier's labour now began to become severe in an extraordinary measure. Though working through a difficult country in the hot, sickly season, he was obliged to bear a burden which none except the old Roman veteran ever bore. He carried a knapsack, a blanket, a hatchet, a haversack containing four days' provisions, a canteen for water, and a proportion of his tent furniture. This, superadded to his accoutrements, arms and sixty rounds of ammunition made a great load and large luggage indeed. Yet the German grenadiers, with their enormous swords, long-skirted clothing, heavy brass-fronted caps and big canteens holding about a gallon, were even worse circumstanced. The carrying of the ra-

tions was the greatest grievance to our men, who all held
to the opinion that we should rather have been taken
round by water at our ease than forced to these cruel
labours. Many succumbed to the temptation to pitch the
whole contents of their haversacks into the mire, exclaiming: 'Damn the provisions, we shall get more at the next
encampment! The General won't let us starve.'

It was the last day but one of July before we reached
Fort Edward, having taken twenty days to cover as many
miles. This place consisted of a large redoubt with a simple
parapet and a wretched palisade, and barracks for two
hundred men; and stood in a little valley near Hudson's
River upon the only spot not covered with forest. The
Americans had withdrawn at their leisure thirty miles to
the southward; General Schuyler, very properly, as I have
indicated, risking to be court-martialled as a traitor and
coward for the sake of luring us deeper into American
territory. The farther we advanced, he was aware, the
greater the numbers of militia and frontiersmen who would
come out in defence of their homes, and the longer and
less defensible our lines of communication. General Schuyler was even single-minded enough so to yield ground as
to make a battlefield of his own domain and expose it to
ravage and destruction by both armies. This conduct had
its expected reward. The 'proud Bashaw of Saratoga' (as
his back-biters named General Schuyler) was once more
superseded in active command by General Gates; though,
much to the chagrin of the Adamses, the courts-martial
upon him and General St. Clair failed to commit either to
the firing-squad.

Unluckily for us, General Washington, who took the
part of both these excellent officers in their disgrace, now
insisted to Congress that, at least, General Benedict Arnold
should be employed by General Gates in a subordinate
command; and they consented. It was, however, with some
difficulty that he persuaded General Arnold to go to General Gates's assistance, for he was labouring under a resentment. When in the February of that year five American
Brigadiers had been raised in rank to Major-General, General Arnold was not among their number, though his
services enormously outweighed theirs, and all were junior
to him. Washington gave Congress his opinion of this un-

pardonable slight put upon the most capable officer in their army, and wrote to General Arnold himself, very delicately expressing his sympathy and begging him to take no hasty action, for he would 'do all in his power to correct an act of such flagrant injustice.' General Arnold was touched by General Washington's warmth and replied that 'every personal injury shall be buried in my zeal for the safety and happiness of my country, in whose cause I have repeatedly fought and bled and am ready at all times to risk my life.'

Had the matter not been thus arranged, and had General Washington, moreover, not reinforced this Northern army by stripping his own of some of its best troops—and sending up, besides, camp-kettles, shovels, pickaxes, field-guns and small-arms ammunition from his own arsenals, the campaign would have no doubt ended in a very different manner. Such disinterested conduct as his was by no means universal among the leaders of the American Revolution and deserving, in this instance, of his countrymen's highest praise; for General Washington was not certain but that our Southern army under General Howe might not suddenly attack and overwhelm him.

The jest of it was that General Gates, when he returned to his command, found himself far from welcome. Indeed, a strong brigade which had arrived from Vermont was for turning back in disgust, unwilling to serve under him, and other regiments expressed the same disinclination. But the magnanimous General Schuyler urged them not to make his supposed quarrel their own: for he had no quarrel.

� � � � � � � � � � � �

CHAPTER

22

THREE days before our arrival at Fort Edward, there had occurred a sad murder by a party of Wyandot Indians, led by a powerful chief named The Panther, of a Miss Jane M'Crea who lived with a relative of General Fraser's in the neighbourhood of Lake George. The occasion was the abandonment of Fort George, at the southern end of the lake, by the American garrison; and the flight, either to the American or the British camp, of almost all the settlers of the district, for fear of marauding parties. Since the news of Miss M'Crea's fate made a great noise in Great Britain and America at this time, I shall take the liberty of relating it in the words of that great American partisan, Dr. Ramsay:

This, though true, was no premeditated barbarity. The circumstances were as follows: Mr. Jones, Miss M'Crea's lover, from an anxiety for her safety, engaged some Indians to remove her from among the Americans, and promised to reward the person who should bring her safe to him with a barrel of rum. Two of the Indians who had conveyed her some distance on the way to her intended husband disputed which of them should present her to Mr. Jones. Both were anxious for the reward. One of them killed her with his tomahawk, to prevent the other from receiving it. General Burgoyne obliged the Indians to deliver up the murderer, and threatened to put him to death. His life was only spared, upon the Indians agreeing to terms, which the General thought would be more efficacious than an execution, to prevent similar mischiefs.

The above account has been challenged by some, who deny that Mr. Jones, an officer in a newly raised corps of Loyalist sharpshooters attached to our army, ever made any bargain with the Indians; and say that Miss M'Crea was found wandering in the woods. Others explain that the dispute arose between The Panther and a chief of the Ottawas who met the party as it was escorting Miss M'Crea to our camp in all civility and decency. Be this as it may, The Panther, also named 'The Wolf' by some authors, arrived in camp with Miss M'Crea's scalp in his belt, which had hair of a yard and a quarter long. Some of the many poets who later versified upon her fate described these tresses as being 'black as raven's wing'; others made them 'yellow as ripe Indian corn.' I cannot satisfy my female readers upon this question. The Panther was, it seems, unaware of the heinousness of his act, which was that expected of an Indian man of honour: it was held decent to avoid unnecessary bloodshed between fellow-warriors by sacrificing the subject of dispute, whether horse, dog, or woman, so that neither party should triumph. He consented at last, when he was acquainted with the sorrow and grief of Mr. Jones, to sell him the scalp for a trifling consideration, though Indians in general are most chary of parting with these relics even at a very high price. (Mr. Jones, by the way, never subsequently married but, surviving the war, retired to Canada, a morose and taciturn man.)

Had the threatened execution of The Panther taken place, his brothers-in-arms would have been bound by custom to revenge themselves upon our sentinels and advanced posts, for he was held in great esteem by them. General Burgoyne did very well not to press the matter, against the remonstrances of General Fraser. The chiefs of the confederacy of Wyandots, Algonquins, and Ottawas, then called a council under the presidency of a Frenchman, Monsieur St. Luc le Corne, who had once led them in their wars against the English. At this meeting they informed General Burgoyne that their warriors were most discontented by the restraint in which they were kept, as never before when they had served as allies of the French. M. St. Luc remarked: 'General, we must brutalize affairs, you know.' General Burgoyne replied warmly: 'I would rather lose every Indian in my army, Monsieur St. Luc, than connive at such enormities as you would condone.' The next day, therefore, these tribes deserted by the hundred, loaded with such plunder as they had collected; only Indians of the Six Nations being left with us, and not many of these.

It cannot be a matter of much surprise that the murder of Miss M'Crea and General Burgoyne's pardon of The Panther were painted in the darkest and most disagreeable colours by the Americans, and that reports of similar outrages were fabricated by them and printed at large in their newspapers to discredit us. Dr. Benjamin Franklin, who should have known better, circulated a document of his own composition, purporting to be an extract from a letter written by a certain Captain Gerrish of the New England Militia. This piece, which appeared in the *Boston Inde-*

pendent Chronicle, described in minute circumstance the taking of booty from the Seneca nation, among which were eight packages of scalps lifted from American soldiers, farmers, women, boys, girls, and infants. A forged invoice and explanation from one James Cranford, trader, to Sir Guy Carleton in Canada was appended, and his supposed request 'that this peltry be sent to the King of England.'

But it astonished me later to learn that such cheap lies obtained circulation and credit even at home. *Saunders' News-Letter* of August 14th 1777 gravely asserted: 'Seven hundred men, women, and children were scalped on the sides of Lake Champlain. The Light Infantry and Indians scoured each bank, women, children, etc., flying in turn before them.' Now the fact is that between St. John's and Crown Point there were not more than ten human dwellings, the whole country being upwards of eighty miles of woods and wilderness. Could inhabitants who never existed be either scalped or made to fly before their enemies? Yet, necessary as it would seem for such public scandal-mongers to acquaint themselves with the topography of the places in which they fix their scenes of horrid action, their readers are usually as ignorant and willing to believe evil as themselves were to concoct it, so that the lie travels far. As a former Light Infantry man I hold this libel against my corps in particular detestation.

At Fort Edward our expedition was faced with a further stubborn task, namely, to clear our communications with Fort George, twenty miles from us, which was to be our base of supplies. General Schuyler, who was not superseded until a fortnight later, had sent a thousand axe-men up each of the roads and tracks connecting these places. Moreover, the road, once cleared, must be solidly laid to bear heavy transport. For between us and Albany, our destination, lay two broad and swift rivers over which our artillery must somehow be conveyed: thus, in addition to the artillery itself and our supply wagons we must also bring along large numbers of *bateaux* and a quantity of planking to form two solid pontoon bridges. One-third of the team-horses expected from Canada had not arrived

to haul for us, nor could our foragers, scour the neighbourhood as they might, discover more than a mere
fifty ox-teams. Thus a deal of the hauling was by man-
power.

Great ill feeling was caused among us that the Brunswick foraging-parties failed to add to the common stock
the cattle and sheep they took, yet drew from this stock
their share of what we put in. We seldom now tasted
fresh meat, but were reduced to our British salt beef, salt
pork, and biscuit once more; and while our officers were
content each to take all his worldly goods upon his
shoulders in a knapsack, the German officers positively
refused to be separated from their superfluities, but maintained a great train of vehicles to carry them. Our officers
felt that this was unjust, and regretted having left at
Ticonderoga, in the Light Infantry storehouse, many
comforts which had become necessaries in a climate of
this sort, and which could be conveyed upon a single
tumbril. Colonel Lord Balcarres wrote asking General
Burgoyne's permission to send a small party back to 'fetch
a little baggage.' This permission was refused, on the
ground that no party of men, however small, could be
spared; and it was desired that no officer, either, should
be given leave of absence for this purpose.

Lord Balcarres thereupon went in person to General
Burgoyne and said frankly that he stood greatly in need
of certain articles, such as shirts and stockings, left at
Ticonderoga, and must fetch them at all events. Though
he had been forbidden to send out any party of men,
however small, nor any officer, he warned the General
that he would obey this order only in the letter—he would
send out a single sergeant, as being neither an officer nor
a party of men. General Burgoyne took this in good part,
but enlarged upon the danger to such a lonely emissary,
for the woods were filled with prowling rebels. Lord
Balcarres thereupon declared that he had a man in mind
for the task who could be counted upon successfully to
accomplish it; and was then good enough to name Corporal, acting as Sergeant, Roger Lamb of The Ninth.

General Burgoyne recollected me as both the messenger sent on from Hibbertown and the surgeon with whom

he had spoken at Fort Anna. He not only consented but ordered that, if I accepted the mission, I should hasten the delivery to him of a quantity of other stores newly arrived at Ticonderoga, taking command of the recruits and convalescents there and bringing them back with me as escort. The cause of General Burgoyne's anxiety for the stores was that his advance was held up for lack of them. His foolish counsellor, Major Skene, had advised him to supply himself at the expense of the enemy, who had a richly stocked magazine and supply-base at Bennington, thirty miles to the south-eastward. Major Skene declared that the supplies at Bennington were but weakly guarded, that the district was populated with none but Loyalists, and that the Brunswick Dragoons, who still lacked horses, might have their choice of several hundred that were collected there. General Burgoyne thereupon sent off a force of Germans, with an advance guard of Indians, who, coming up against a strong force of New Hampshire militia and farmers from Vermont—under General Stark, a former British officer who had been overslaughed for promotion and now took handsome revenge —were utterly routed, losing five hundred men and all their artillery, ammunition and wagons. Thus his need of fresh supplies was worse than before.

Lord Balcarres now sent for me and explained what he wished done, without disguising the dangers of the journey. 'But,' said he graciously, 'my opinion of you is already so high that I feel perfectly sure that you will successfully undertake for us this very necessary service. See, here is General Burgoyne's pass, made out in your name.'

I undertook the commission with alacrity, not a little proud to be chosen as the depository of his Lordship's confidence and that of our Commander-in-Chief.

We were stationed at Fort Miller at this time, which lay fifteen miles beyond Fort Edward. The month was early September, although I cannot now recall the day, since my journal remained unposted for two months from July 8th, the day of the fight at Fort Anna. I set out from Fort Miller at noon, taking with me no blanket, but only some provisions, a rifle and twenty rounds of ball-cartridge. That it was a hazardous journey I knew well, for several of our men had been attacked when bringing up supplies or running messages. However, I kept off the beaten track, like an Indian, and by four o'clock came safe to Fort Edward—where a sergeant of the regiment stationed there gave me a drink of rum—then off again towards Lake George, after ten minutes' halt.

In this lonely journey through almost continuous pine forest, broken with tangled clearings, I met with no single soul, and stopped but once or twice by the way to refresh myself with the wild raspberries of excellent flavour that there abounded. I recalled, with little satisfaction, that this was the very way that had been taken by the wretched survivors of the Massacre of Lake George two years before my birth. The victims of this massacre were some scores of British soldiers—the number is not exactly known—together with their women and children. They were the garrison of Fort William Henry at the lake head, who had capitulated from hunger to the French general, Monsieur de Montcalm. He had allowed them all the honours of war and a safe convoy under guard to Fort Edward, but his callous and inhuman subordinates permitted these unfortunate people, whose ammunition had been taken from them, to be plundered and murdered by the Indians in the French service, led by M. St. Luc le Corne.

One of the survivors, Captain Carver, wrote very pathetically of his escape. Being first robbed of his coat, waistcoat, hat, buckles, and the money from his breeches pocket, he ran to the nearest French sentinel and claimed his protection, who only called him an English dog and thrust him back with violence among the Indians. He was next struck at with clubs and spears, most of which he dexterously dodged, though a spear grazed his side, and some other weapon caught his ankle. When he took refuge among a party of his countrymen, the collar and waistband were all that remained of his shirt. The war whoop then sounded and a general murder began, with the scalping of these defenceless men, women and children; yet French officers were observed walking about unconcernedly at some distance, shrugging and smiling. The circle of the British becoming greatly thinned, Captain Carver burst out from it, but was caught at by two stout chiefs, who hurried him to a retired spot where they could dispatch him at their leisure. He had almost resigned himself to his fate, when an English gentleman of some distinction, as Captain Carver could discover by the fine scarlet velvet breeches he wore, his only remaining covering, happened to rush by; and one of the Indians relinquished his hold, intent on this new prize. The velvet breeches showed fight, and Captain Carver broke away in the bustle; glancing around, he saw the unfortunate gentleman dispatched with a tomahawk—which added both to his speed and desperation. To be brief, after many similar hazards, the Captain escaped to the briary forest and, after three days in the cold dews and burning sun without sustenance, and with the loss of a shoe, reached Fort Edward at last more dead than alive.

Heaven evidently avenged the massacre by striking down Monsieur de Montcalm at Quebec and finally driving the French from Canada. As for the Indians, they perished of smallpox, which they took from the French, almost to a man; for while their blood was in a state of fermentation and Nature was striving to throw out the peccant matter, they checked her operations by plunging into cold water, which proved fatal to them. The reason that the French were held in such esteem by the Indians was that they interfered little with tribal customs, not even acknowledging the unwritten law of Christendom that all innocent and defenceless persons of whatever nationality, and especially women and children, must never in any circumstances be deliberately resigned to the barbarity of savages. They even winked at the practice of cannibalism, for about this same time Monsieur de Carbière's Ottawan Indians drank British blood from skull-goblets, and ate British flesh broiled, as Father Roubaud, a Jesuit priest, has testified in his history.

In avoiding the road, I made a circuit through the woods which brought me past a broad sixty-foot waterfall to the very pond near which the massacre took place. It was now called Bloody Pond. Dark had fallen and the dews were chill. The shallow waters of the pond were covered with beautiful white lilies. I was greatly fatigued by this time, and withdrawing from the pond to a deep part of the wood, lay down to sleep under a tree. The night dews awakened me shivering with cold about two hours later, and I resumed my march. I was no Indian, and had from drowsiness lost my sense of direction. By three o'clock in the morning I had no notion where I might be. Happening to see a light on my left, I cautiously approached it and perceived that it came from the open door of a log-house, against which was outlined the figure of a man wearing a large round flopped hat.

As I stood there, wondering what he might be, whether rebel or loyal, I heard a sudden shivering cry and a few unintelligible words, as if some woman or child were being put to the torture. Confused thoughts of Bloody Pond still crowding my head, I strode forward with my piece primed and cocked, resolving to take instant vengeance on the villains, come what might.

I called to the man: 'Hold up your hands, I have you covered'—with which summons he complied. Coming close, I found him to be a man of sturdy frame with unpowdered dark hair cut short and hanging around a white hat; his face was of a wild, melancholy cast. He smiled at me and asked in a smooth, wheedling, yet not unpleasant voice: 'What dost thou here with that weapon of murder, Friend?'

I pushed him aside and burst into the room—and there saw at once that I had absurdly mistaken the cry: the agony was not that of death, but of birth. A woman lay on a wooden bed in the corner of a plain, neat room, her face covered with her hands, her knees drawn up; and another woman, wearing a little black bonnet, was ministering to her in the capacity of midwife. I checked my impetuous career, and turned back in shame to the man in the doorway. 'Forgive my foolishness, sir,' I said. 'I was confused. I had thought it was the Indians at work.'

'Have no fear of the Indians. They are an honest and well-conducted folk, unless they are abused, or partake of ardent spirits and so become tired.' ('Tired' I found to be his term for 'intoxicated.') 'They have shown me and my family much kindness, for the sake of William Penn, who was their friend.'

I then observed that he was a member of the Society of

Friends, or Quakers, and not a wet Quaker, neither—the sort who affect silver buckles on their shoes, lace ruffles at neck and wrist, and powder on their hair—but of the dry sort who wear drab, threadbare cloth coat and breeches, cotton stockings, and plain, square-toed shoes.

'I was going out to the patch to commune with the Lord, praying Him to mitigate the suffering of this poor soldier's wife,' he said simply. 'Wilt thou accompany me, friend, and join thy prayers to mine? For it is written that "When two or three are gathered together in Thy name"—here he lifted his eyes reverently to Heaven— "Thou wilt grant their request." My inner voice assures me that thy steps were directed to my door for this very purpose.'

I answered nothing, but went with him; and presently we kneeled down together in the dews at the edge of a field of tall hemp which he had planted. There he began to pray with exceeding slowness, trembling in all his body as he wrestled with the words. They came out one by one, often in repetition, as if wrung from a strict compression of his heart: 'Grant—O Lord—to this—my—poor —poor—sister—my—sister—now—O Lord—labouring— labouring—labouring—with child—cheerful—courage— now—oh—humble—courage—to   endure—endure—O— Lord—to endure—the punishment—of her mother—her mother—who sinned—her mother—our mother—Eve— who—sinned—in Eden.'

'Amen,' said I greatly affected; and as we rose from our knees, the woman's pangs lessened, for we heard the other comforting her and calling her 'poor soul' and 'dear honey.' But the child was not yet born.

'Who is the woman?' I asked, in a low tone outside the door.

'Friend, I do not know her name. She was brought to my house by a Mohican Indian, a follower of the Christian Thayendanegea, or Captain Brant, a chief of that nation. She affirms herself to be the wife of a soldier in the Ninth Regiment and relates that she was braving the perils of these woods alone and on foot, from Montreal, in order to come up with him. She was seized, she says, with the sickness of labour in the forest, where she must have perished had the Indian not found her and brought her to me. Yet I wonder that she is dressed in Mohican fashion, not in English dress.'

The Quaker woman then emerging, I asked her trembling: 'Will she live? Does all go well?'

She replied shortly, 'With God's help. There is nothing amiss.'

The pangs began again at that moment, and the woman returned to the house. I was so torn with emotion that I caught at the Quaker's sleeve and, cried I, 'Come back, sir, to the hemp patch, and let us wrestle this out together.'

He was nothing loath, and turned back with me.

I do not know what I prayed in my agony of heart, but the honest man knelt by me and cried, 'Amen, Amen!' to my wild outpourings, until the cries from the cabin ceased; and presently the woman in the bonnet came out with a little creature wrapped in a cloth and, says she, 'Josiah, O Josiah, kiss 'un, the sweet little girl.'

Josiah took and kissed the child fervently, and so did I, with indescribable emotions. 'The mother is sleeping now,' the woman said.

I told the good Quaker, who begged me to enter his house and partake of a dish of tea: 'No, I thank you, Friend Josiah—for a true friend you have been to me—I cannot accept. I must go forward to Fort George, according to my orders. Direct me, I beg, for I am lost.'

He said piously, 'No man is lost who loves God and his neighbour.'

Now that dawn was at hand, he showed me the path plainly, and I thanked him.

I said, 'Friend Josiah, tell the woman, whoever she may be, that Sergeant Roger Lamb of The Ninth will be passing this way again in about four days' time, with a party of men, and will be happy to convey her to the army in one of the wagons. And tell her this, that I wish her and the child well, from the bottom of my heart.'

I made him repeat these words exactly after me, shook hands with him in affectionate farewell, and directed my steps towards Fort George.

I reached this place as the sun rose; and upon my presenting to the officer in charge of the garrison my letter from General Burgoyne, he provided me with a captured American *bateau* to take me up Lake George to Ticonderoga. The Canadians called this lake by the elder name of Lake Sacrament, from the purity of its water, which they were in former times at the pains to procure for sacramental use in their churches. The bed was of fine white sand, giving a pellucid clearness to the lake, which was four-and-thirty miles long and nowhere more than four miles wide. Lake George embosomed above two hundred islands, which were for the most part but barren heath-covered rocks garnished with a few cedar and spruce trees. There was abundance of fish here, such as the black bass and a beautiful large speckled trout, remarkable for the carnation of its flesh. I drowsed rather than slept in my passage through this romantic waterway, which was performed in the finest weather.

We went ashore at Diamond Island with a message for the Captain in charge of the stores-depot there. The island was so called from the transparent crystals that abounded in the rocks upon it. A soldier of The Forty-Seventh presented me with one which he had found lying loose in the sand, consisting of a six-sided prism, terminated at both ends by six-sided pyramids. When placed on a window-sill in the sun it threw little rainbows on the walls and ceilings, he said. Diamond Island was once overrun with rattlesnakes, whose sloughed skins lay about on all sides, and was in consequence avoided by every one. However, one evening a *bateau* conveying a herd of hogs was caught in a storm while sailing near by and overset. The Canadians and the hogs swam together to the shore, where the former spent the night in the trees and the latter ran off earnestly grunting. The next day the Canadians hailed a passing vessel and were taken off: but some time later, returning to the island, they found the hogs immensely fat, and hardly a single rattlesnake remaining. When they slaughtered one of these hogs they found by what means the island had been rid of its noxious tenantry; for its stomach was full of the undigested remains of rattlesnakes.

Near Halfway Island I witnessed a curious sight, namely a migration of grey squirrels and black: of whom hundreds were attempting to swim across the lake, which was then as smooth as glass, from the western to the eastern shore. We passed a number of their drowned corpses; and others which we overtook, nearly exhausted, ran up into the *bateau*, upon our putting down an oar before them. The boatman secured a dozen of them and said that he would put little chains around them and tame them for pets. Their bushy tails had acted as a sort of float to support them in the water; but the legend that they will raise their tails to act as mast and sail in a breeze I judge ridiculous.

A great curiosity hereabouts was the double echo, which our boatman showed us by calling out in a shrill voice the name of his wife, Louise Marie, which was repeated in melancholy fashion by the curved sides of a mountain, from two distinct quarters at once. I confess that my heart cried, 'Kate, Kate' no less loud and longingly, though my tongue was silent.

For the rest of the journey I slept. A brisk southerly breeze, springing up, carried the boat swiftly forward under sail. Disembarking above the Falls, I made the rest of my journey on foot to Ticonderoga, by way of Mount Hope, passing by a camp of American prisoners of war and several storehouses, and arrived late that same night. I was a day completing my business at the Fort, and two days more in retracing my way down the lake. I now conducted a brigade of *bateaux* containing a great deal of baggage and stores, recruits and convalescents to the number of sixty. In addition, a crowd of Canadian French came with me, supplied by General Carleton at General Burgoyne's request, to work the *bateaux* on Hudson's River. I urged upon my command the necessity of speed, and kept every man who could work an oar busy in urging the craft forward.

While I was at Ticonderoga I noticed the remains of a bonfire that some of our young officers had made, of an enormous stack of paper-money issued by order of the American Congress. Several tightly bound quires of bills, of high denomination, had remained unburned and hardly scorched. It occurred to me that it was as foolish an act to destroy these printed promises to pay in specie, as it would be to tear up a private note of hand. I therefore placed the bulk of them to store and took a commission for myself of five thousand dollars. The bills that I chose for myself were of twenty-dollar denomination, as being less bulky for my haversack, and had upon them a rude cut of a zephyr in a cloud disturbing the ocean waves, and the motto *Vi Concitate*, or 'Disturb with force!' I thought the device appropriate, though to *raise the wind* by the issue of such paper unbacked by specie was a doubtful procedure, and when the fraud was discovered by the common people was likely to cause great dissension. The four-dollar notes, which I rejected, showed a wild-boar running on a lance, with the printed sentiment, 'Either death or a decent life'; it was not clear whether the Revolutionary cause was represented by the resolute lance or by the courageous boar.

Returning without adventure to Fort George, I hastened to call upon the Quaker Josiah, during the time that the wagons were being loaded from my brigade of *bateaux*.

I knocked at the door, my heart beating loudly against my ribs, and waited with the utmost impatience to be admitted. Receiving no reply to my summons, I pushed open the door. There was nobody at home, but a weak cry from an adjoining room sent me hurrying to where the child was lying in a cradle of maple-wood, its tiny body covered with gauze against the mosquitoes, and naked because of the great heat of the day. Around its neck was tied my Charles groat on a slight blue ribbon.

I could not wait, for my military business was urgent; but I had the good fortune to meet with Josiah a half mile from the hut. He informed me that the Negress who attended his wife, an emancipated slave, had two days previously lost her infant, of a cough. Kate Harlowe had thereupon resigned the child to the care of this woman, and the guardianship of the good Quaker and his wife, saying that she herself had no milk to give it, nor was the battlefield any place for a mother and her new-born child. But her place as a wife was beside her husband. The very day after I left her there, Josiah said, she had bidden the family farewell and set out to meet her husband, though against their wishes and continued entreaties.

The Quaker turned and walked a little of the way with

me back to the Fort. He spoke very honestly of the short-
comings of numbers of his co-religionists. Not only were
there Wet Quakers, who loved the world too well, but
(it seemed) there were even Free Quakers who bore
arms in the war. Yet, he said, such plain murder—if I
would forgive the term, being a soldier—was perhaps less
heinous in the eyes of God than the hypocritical action of
some of his former companions at Philadelphia. In refusing
to serve in the wars, or to pay the tax imposed upon
them for their refusal, they acted in conformity with their
faith; but he detested that they had voted the sum of
twenty thousand pounds for 'wheat, barley, and other
grains,' letting it be known that among 'other grains'
might be counted those of gunpowder—and thus becoming
accessories of murder. In disgust of which unrighteous
folly he had left them, and come to live in the wilderness.

I asked him: 'Friend Josiah, if you think me a murderer,
why do you walk at my side in so social a fashion, and talk
with me so pleasantly?'

He replied: 'Our Lord, Jesus Christ Himself, did not
hold himself apart from the Roman soldiers, nor even from
a Centurion, their officer. And John the Baptist bade
soldiers be content with their pay.'

'If Saint John said that indeed, surely he was condoning
murder? For the payment was for their being soldiers,
namely, for the practice of killing.'

He made no reply, but paced on with compressed lips.

I asked him again, thinking that perhaps he had not
heard me: 'Expound, Friend Josiah: why did he who was
counted worthy to baptize the Saviour of Mankind thus
address soldiers, bidding them be content with their pay?'

He answered, 'Had even the Saviour Himself told them,
"Thou shalt not kill," they would have mocked at Him
(though such was the command of the Father), for they
had taken the soldiers' oath to Caesar and could not unsay
it. They were already murderers, as thou sayest. To them
could be given no higher notion of virtue than they were
capable to follow. And to thee, friend Roger, as my inner
voice assures me, the Lord would not say, "Thou shalt not
commit adultery," for thou knowest this commandment
well, yet hast disobeyed it in a manner that cannot be

undone. Instead, He would say, "Keep thy evil imaginings away from this woman, since she is the wife of another, and pray God that thou fallest not again into the same snare."'

With that he grasped my hand, the tears wetting his cheeks, and left me. His last words were: 'The child will be taught to worship God in this Wilderness.'

I returned very pensively to Fort George, where I made inquiries after Kate Harlowe, whose path would have led her past the outer sentinels; but she had not passed that way. I concluded that the sound of my name had refreshed her affections, and that she had returned to the company of the Mohican Indians rather than link herself again with her husband Harlowe, and thus bring equal pain upon herself and me.

The next evening I had the gratification of conveying the stores and baggage in safety to the army, and of being thanked by my officers for the manner in which I had executed the orders confided to me.

❋ ❋ ❋ ❋ ❋ ❋ ❋ ❋ ❋ ❋ ❋ ❋

CHAPTER

23

BY MY conveyance of these stores, the army was the richer by a month's supply; the bridge of boats being thrown across the Hudson's River two miles above the village of Saratoga, on the 13th and 14th of September 1777 we crossed and encamped on Saratoga plain. Here the country was exceedingly beautiful but utterly deserted by its inhabitants. We of the Light Infantry formed the vanguard and, following down the opposing bank, soon came upon a delightful stream, the Fishkill Creek, peopled with exotic wildfowl, broken into artificial cascades, and trained around several tiny islands planted with unusual flowering shrubs. Beyond, a broad green lawn sloped

easily down to the water's edge, and at its head stood
General Philip Schuyler's spacious mansion, with a row of
noble pillars extending its entire length from ground to
roof. The mansion at Skenesborough had been very well,
for so remote a place, but it was by comparison with this
but a large and well-appointed block-house. This had both
elegance and maturity and we saw clearly that the spirit
of subordination, rather than that of 'Liberty, Liberty,
Liberty' animated the General's artisans and tenantry,
whose cottages could be seen in the distance clustered
around a good-looking church.

The transition from the hideous and unkempt country
about Fort Edward to this European paradise was striking.
We found ourselves treading with humility and soberness,
as we flanked the lawn in order to search the house,
avoiding to violate the well-tended flower-beds and the
neat borders of the gravelled paths, and stepping delicately
between the rows of cabbages. It might almost have been
Castle Belan, near Timolin, which I had visited as a recruit
on my march to Waterford; but that here painted wood
was generally employed instead of bricks and stucco. The
house was embellished within, as we had expected, with
solid and beautiful furniture, rich hangings and carpets,
china and silver in glass-fronted cupboards, of which but
little appeared to have been moved. In the dining-room we
observed two or three lifelike portraits of General
Schuyler's ancestors who were notable Dutchmen, and a
fine equestrian portrait of His Majesty King George. Out
of respect for the decency of these surroundings we abstained from plundering the least thing, but searched the
attics, cellars, and outhouses, discovered nothing and
passed on; but left a guard against the depredations of
our Indian allies. The solid grist-mill, saw-mill, barns, and
other buildings were also found clear of the enemy.

There was but one road in the neighbourhood, following
the course of Hudson's River down to Albany, thirty
miles away: it was flanked by forests, commanded in many
places by rocky heights and often separated from the
broad flood of the river only by a precipice. This was the
road we must take, and many tributary creeks and thick
forests lay between us and our destination; and, as a half-

way obstacle, the deep and rapid Mohawk River. The enemy was encamped ten miles from us, at Stillwater, in a strongly entrenched position known as Bemis Heights. Our communications with Canada were long and exposed; we had with us but a month's provisions; most of our Indian allies had left us; and what with the losses at Bennington and elsewhere, we were reduced to less than six thousand troops, including Germans and American Loyalists, against perhaps fourteen thousand of the enemy. The odds against us were increased by the greater discount that must be made in our case for men necessarily employed on other services than that of fighting: such as baggage and ammunition guards, and attendants upon the sick and wounded. Not three thousand of our men, of whom something better than two thousand were British, could be put into action at any given time; whereas the American fighting strength fell short of their total forces by far less. We did not, however, allow ourselves to consider the possibility of a check. Being ordered to attain Albany, there to join hands with our Southern army under General Howe which was to advance up Hudson's River, we were resolved at all hazards to reach this rendezvous before our supplies failed: where we would be once more provided with all necessaries.

A very disagreeable circumstance was that a diversion of ours, to the westward, had signally failed. This was made by Colonel St. Leger, who had gone by way of Lake Ontario and taken with him a battalion of American Loyalists, a few regulars and a thousand Indians of the Six Nations, led by Thayendanegea, under the guidance of Colonel Guy Johnson's brother, Sir John Johnson, Bt. Colonel St. Leger routed and killed General Herkimer, in a stubborn battle—though Thayendanegea was disappointed of his neighbour's scalp—and besieged an American force at Fort Stanwix, which seemed upon the point of surrender; he hoped soon to possess himself of the whole valley of the Mohawk River, a place well known for the number of settlers who remained loyal to King George. But General Benedict Arnold upset all his plans by a cunning stratagem. He prevailed upon a half-witted Dutchman, Hon Yost Schuyler, whom the Indians, because of his peculiar ways, held in a sort of religious awe, to go among the Indians and announce with excitement the approach of an enormous army of Americans under General Arnold. This he did. The Indians were alarmed and inclined to believe this tale, for Hon Yost—who performed this cheat in order to save from the gallows his Tory brother, whom General Arnold held—displayed a coat riddled with what he said were British bullet-holes. Sir John and Thayendanegea pooh-poohed the tale, but it was confirmed by an Indian in Arnold's pay who came up shortly afterwards; he, when asked, 'Are the Americans few or numerous?' pointed above his head at the leaves of the forest. After him came another Indian, whose lie was that General Burgoyne's army was cut in pieces and General Arnold was hurrying to Fort Stanwix by forced marches. Indians, though not cowards, have always sedulously avoided pitched battles, preferring to harry the flank and rear of an advancing foe. These tribesmen now, persuaded by the Cornplanter of the Senecas, immediately decamped, in spite of all the persuasive eloquence and rum that Sir John offered them; the Loyalists followed, and Colonel St. Leger, left with only his few regulars, had no alternative but to break off the siege and retire too. Most of the Loyalists had flung away their arms in terror; so that the Indians, balked of other scalps, took a few of theirs in disgust of such cowardice. Among Indians, to lose even an arrow was considered unwarriorlike, and for the like misdoing or mischance a man was flogged on the bare back by his women folk. Sir John and the Colonel each blamed the other for the common misfortune and drew their swords upon each other. Murder would have been done had Thayendanegea not interposed and recalled them to their duty as Christians.

From the Schuyler mansion we followed the road for three miles between forest land and continuous fields of fine wheat and Indian corn, half a mile broad. Of these, some had been harvested; some burned by Vrouw Schuyler, the General's wife, as she quitted her home at our approach; but a great deal left standing. The harvest was very welcome to our Commissaries, and men were instantly set to work to garner, thresh, and grind the wheat, at the mill, into flour. The maize was cut as forage for our beasts. Still we encountered no enemy, and the whole army moved forward on the following day, September 15th, encamping that night at a place called Devaco —or Dovegat, or Dovacote, or as you please—which lay on a crooked inlet of the river, where the cornfields ended. Beyond this place innumerable obstacles were encountered, such as felled trees, broken bridges over the numerous streams and rivulets which fed the river, and the road itself was cut away wherever it ran at the edge of a height. The army halted for two days while engineers and pioneers repaired this damage, and our Indians went forward as scouts to note the enemy's disposition. We then advanced to within three miles of the enemy's position, halted, and sent forward the repair-parties once more. On September 18th our engineers were obstructed by the enemy in their task of rebuilding a bridge, and we guessed that on the next day we would come to grips.

All this time it had rained heavily, which made our advance the slower, but our people's greatest wish was that the bad weather would continue, for rain spoilt musket-fire, by wetting the priming-pan, as effectively as it had hindered archers in the ancient days by slackening their bowstrings. If it came to push of bayonet, we believed ourselves the victors. We had, moreover, confidence in our own steadiness under fire, in the experience of our officers, and in the comradely unity that bound us all together, barring only some regiments of the Germans.

The American fortifications on Bemis Heights, a hill contiguous to the river, had been laid out by the same engineer, the Polish patriot, Kosciusko, who had planned those at Ticonderoga; and were executed in the same swift and solid way by American labourers. But, as at Ticonderoga, the Americans had omitted to hold or fortify a hill, lying a short distance away, which overlooked their stronghold. General Burgoyne was aware that General Gates, in the lobbies of Congress, had presented the yielding of Ticonderoga as a very heinous offence. He therefore hoped that this other fortress would be held by General Gates with the stubbornness wanting in General St. Clair; and that, even when it was raked by our guns from the commanding hill on the left, the whole American force would be kept cooped up in it. If this happened, great slaughter would be done. We could encircle the Heights by working round through the woods, and cut the road behind, whereupon any man who attempted to escape must either face our volleys from the woods that surrounded the fortress, or swim the river.

On the next day, September 19th, battle was joined. General Phillips, with the Germans and the heavy artillery, pushed up the road which ran close along the river. General Burgoyne with four battalions of which The Ninth formed the reserve, and four light guns, took the centre; while General Fraser with the Grenadiers and our-selves (the Light Infantry battalion), a battalion of American Loyalists, one regular battalion, the rest of the artillery and a few score Indians, was sent to make a wide circuit through the woods on the right. Our task was to seize the hill afore-mentioned which was the key to victory, while the other columns provided a diversion. A combined assault through broken and thickly wooded country is always difficult to achieve in unison, unless signals be given by bonfire, mirror-flash, or signal-gun. It was therefore well that a signal had been arranged, for the centre and left could not have foreseen how long a time would be spent by us in arriving at our agreed position, which was abreast of them at two miles' distance from Bemis Heights. The ground we had to traverse was a frightful tangle of rocks, thickets, ravines, bog-holes, briar-patches, standing trees, and trees overset by a hurricane of some years be-fore. An occasional relief to this wilderness was found in what the country people termed 'clever meadows,' namely, unexpected grass-grown clearings; the flocks and cattle that came by devious paths to graze on them belonged to the farmstead of one Freeman, built on a hill near by, which formed our centre.

It was late in the morning before we were able to fire our signal-gun, in default of a mirror-flash, the sun being obscured, to which General Burgoyne and General Phillips replied with other guns; and then forward we went. It appears that General Gates had no notion but to do just as General Burgoyne had hoped—to stay snug in his trenches and tamely permit himself to be surprised and raked from the hill. But, unfortunately for ourselves, General Arnold was in a position to challenge and dispute this inept method of waging war. He had recently, after all, been raised by Congress to major-general's rank; as a reward for opposing a British landing on the Connecticut coast, where he happened to be on a short visit to his sister, and, though our people succeeded in destroying the important magazine of Danbury, taking tithes of their forces as they retired. His conduct on this occasion, where again he was foremost in attack and hindmost in retreat and but narrowly escaped death, had commended him so highly to the army that General Gates came to hate him very deeply.

Now General Arnold demanded, with eyes that seemed to shoot out fire, permission to lead out at least a part of his own Division in the direction from which the first signal-gun had been heard, in order to prevent our out-flanking the Heights. General Gates refused this request, with a demand to General Arnold to mind his own business; but to one angry man was joined another, the same Colonel Dan Morgan of the Virginian Riflemen who had come so near to storming Quebec two years previously. Colonel Morgan, having been exchanged against a British colonel captured by the Americans, had re-formed and trained his regiment until it was the most formidable in their whole army. The marksmen it contained were now for the most part not Virginian backwoodsmen but Presbyterian Ulstermen settled in Pennsylvania, and some Pennsylvanian Germans. They could march forty miles in a day, subsist on jerked beef and maize-porridge, and for mere sport would often shoot apples off one another's heads, taking turns, at sixty paces. Both Arnold and Morgan had been drinking hard liquor all that morning, in a manner to make them reckless of what they said or did, yet not so as to destroy their judgment of what needed saying or doing. They railed at their Commander in so contumacious a manner that he was terrified for his own safety: for General Arnold kept clapping a hand to his pistol and swearing terribly. Finally General Arnold declared that if he could not go with permission he would go without, and at the head of his entire command; where-upon General Gates yielded sulkily, saying that he might take Colonel Morgan's riflemen and half a brigade of New England militia, but no more.

These forces came out against us about noon, on a front of two miles, and drove in our screen of Indians. The Loyalists and Canadians could not hold their ground either, but ran through our ranks. There ensued a very confusing skirmish, in which the Americans advanced with too great impetuosity, running in twos and threes against our leading platoons. We caught them with well-directed volleys, killed a number and took twenty prisoners. But they were far swifter of foot than we, and avoided the bayonet. The one failing of the rifle-gun, as against the musket, which it enormously outranged, was the difficulty of reloading. Towards the end of the war, little use was made of these weapons of precision, since it was found that delay between shots more than counterbalanced the advantages of their exactness.

It happened that our company under Captain Sweeten-ham was heavily engaged in this onset; he and I, with ten others, found ourselves separated and surrounded by a large number of riflemen who were dressed in Indian fashion, with no covering at all but leggins and breech-clout. The Captain was soon wounded in the shoulder and the foot, four other men fell and the remainder of us had no choice but to retire, plunging into a ravine choked with tall reeds and escaping through a cedar thicket. It fell to me to cover the retreat, for the others went off in a hurry, forgetting that the Captain was able to proceed but slowly. A bullet carried off my cap, another grazed my side, a third broke the lock of my fusil, which I was forced to abandon. A company of The Fourteenth coming up in support, the fire grew very hot, but the Americans broke off the fight when the cry of a wild turkey, many times repeated, sounded through the woods: it was Colonel Morgan's rallying-cry, which they instantly obeyed.

After attending to Captain Sweetenham's wound, I sent him off under Mad Johnny Maguire's escort to the general hospital in the rear; and felt content that I had in a manner made amends for the trick that I had once played on him in forging his signature. Then I returned to the scene of the combat, intending to re-arm myself with a musket of one of our dead or an American rifle-gun and the necessary ammunition. I was proceeding cautiously back through the cedar thicket when I heard the voices of two men passing my front, and crouched behind a bush. It was a large, heavy rifleman driving a disarmed British non-commissioned officer before him with the muzzle and butt of his piece; the prisoner pleading for mercy.

'Now, my wee lad,' cried the rifleman in a thick Ulster brogue, which I will not attempt to reproduce in writing, 'sit you down, for we must have a clack together.'

Richard Harlowe—he it was—had lately been raised to corporal's rank and detached to our company to take the place of another who had fallen sick. He sat down, as bidden, on a tree-stump within view of my lurking-place, and the rifleman stood over him in a threatening posture.

'Don't think I do not know your bonny face, Ralph Pearce, or exult in having you here in my power at last; though be sure I should be glad enough to have Colonel Pearce, your father, sitting next to you, who drove me from my house and trade in Lurgan town, and forced me to sail here across the black ocean. Come now, Ralph Pearce, you who married my little sister Molly against your father's wish and mine; and who threw her off when he threatened to disinherit you; and who afterwards cheated at the cards and was dismissed from your regiment; and trafficked with the Pretender; and went back to poor Molly, to rob her of the jewels you had given her, and broke her heart: tell me now, Ralph Pearce, for I am curious to know—will you die with an easy heart?'

Richard Harlowe, or Ralph Pearce, made a sobbing noise in his throat, begging for his life to be spared. 'No, Alexander Bridie,' he said, 'no, I am not fit to die. Spare me, in Christ's name, for I am not fit to die.'

'I have lived a rough life,' continued Alexander Bridie, 'I have taken life in revenge for one-twentieth less of injury than I have suffered at the hand of the Pearces; and when we have taken life, we folk at the head of the Susquehannah River, we take the scalp too. With you, my charming Ralph, I shall reverse the procedure: first your

scalp, and afterwards your life.' He drew out a long
Albany knife and whetted it across his palm.

I was struck with confusion by this recital. Should I
hazard my own life for the sake of this scoundrel Harlowe,
rushing unarmed to his rescue, when by his death I should
so greatly profit? Yet if I left him to his fate, would not my
conscience ever afterwards reproach me for having not
only seduced the wife of a comrade-at-arms, but stood
idly by while he was mutilated and murdered?

My better feelings prevailed. I ran forward, hallooing,
with a rotten stick grasped in my hand as my only weapon;
which seeing, Harlowe somersetted backwards over the
stump, dodged among the bushes and was free.

Alexander Bridie brought his piece to his shoulder, aiming at me, and I gave myself up for dead. But suddenly he
himself staggered and fell down dead, as a flying tomahawk fetched the back of his head and cleft his skull
almost in two.

As I stood staring, a lithe figure came mincing from
behind the cedars and with giggles and squeaks, squatting
upon his hams, took up the rifleman's fallen knife and
with it excoriated the accustomed trophy. It was the
Mohican *bardash*, Sweet Yellow Head, and after him appeared the majestic form of my friend Thayendanegea,
with three new scalps swinging at his girdle.

Thayendanegea clasped me to him, embracing me
fondly and calling me 'my son Otetiani.'

He took me apart into the thicket and said: 'I have news
for you, dear Otetiani. This expedition has failed, as did
the other expedition we made two months ago against Fort
Stanwix, when Arnold, the Dark Eagle, tricked us. I am
now about to fetch the Red Men home. I have explained
to General Burgoyne my decision and urged him to retire
while there is yet hope. But he will not listen. He is in-
fatuated.'

I asked, 'Thayendanegea, what has occurred?'

He replied, 'Nothing has occurred. That is the devil
of it.'

'How do you mean?'

'The Southern army was a hundred miles distant from
Albany when the campaign began. Now it is not half this

distance away—no, it is twice that distance. For General Howe has transported twelve thousand troops to the mouth of the Delaware River and is advancing against Philadelphia, as though he had no interest in us and were waging a private war of his own. General Washington opposes him. The few thousand men that remain in New York, under General Clinton, are insufficient to come to our help up Hudson's River.'

'But the Eastern Army that was also to converge upon Albany from Rhode Island?'

'It has not started. It will not start. General Burgoyne has been sent out on a fool's errand. Now also, my allies report that a strong division of Americans under General Lincoln is advancing against Ticonderoga to cut off your communications with Canada; already, I think, they will have done so. I told General Burgoyne: "I must now take my nation home. If we stay, your people and mine, yours will be captured as being white men, but ours will be massacred as being red. Why do you stay?" He replied, "I cannot believe that General Howe, or Lord George Germaine, would so deceive me. It is a fiction, is it not, confess, brave Thayendanegea, to excuse your departure?"'

'And did he credit you in the end, my Father?'

'He did, and, to his honour, bade me depart in peace and take all my nation with me. You are enrolled in my nation, dear Otetiani. Come with me, since I have permission for you to come. Come, and reside with us again. We love you dearly, my son. According to the Christian law, Mistress Kate is the wife of another; nevertheless, you will be accounted as married to her according to Mohican Law, if you acknowledge her child as yours. She is now at our town of Genesee, her heart consumed with love for you.'

'She has positively assured me, Father, that she will never again speak to me.'

'She tells me this: she gives you now another chance to rejoin her. We will take off the little one from the Quaker's hut and find a wet-nurse for her from among our own nation. It is ill that a white child should drink the milk of a black woman. You will be happy with your wife and daughter. You will fight in our battles, and be revenged upon the American rebels, and assist in winning back America for King George.'

Almost he tempted me, but since I had clung to my way of duty before, I resolved not to swerve from it now, our cause being in such straits. I showed him my deep gratitude for his concern in my behalf, but declared that I could not so stretch my good conscience as to decamp from my post in the hour of danger. I would rather perish nobly in good company than live with Kate and bear the disgraceful name of deserter.

He told me, after a long silence: 'Dear son, you have chosen right.' He embraced me, and departed.

Meanwhile, the aspect of the battle had changed. General Arnold with three thousand men had countermarched from the flank to the centre, where he attacked General Burgoyne, who was holding the house and the paddock of Freeman's Farm with eight hundred regular British troops. Here the action was very heavy, with shot for shot and bayonet against clubbed rifle, for nearly four hours. The American marksmen climbed into the tops of high trees and there took popping shots at our officers, for twenty of whom they accounted. General Burgoyne himself was nearly taken off, a rifleman wounding his aide-de-camp (who rode in fine furniture) in mistake for him. Three subalterns of The Twentieth, none of whom had exceeded the age of seventeen, fell, and were buried that night in a common grave. Our battery of four brass guns was several times taken and retaken, but the Americans could make no use of them, for so often as they were lost, our gunners, of whom but a quarter remained unwounded, carried away the linstocks—to fetch them back once more when the guns were recovered. Had General Gates reinforced Arnold, as he was constantly urged to do, the line would have given way, for The Twentieth were near breaking. But he did nothing, and we were saved by General Phillips who, towards evening, brought up some field-guns at a trot and treated the enemy to a great shower of grape. Behind him came General Riedesel's Brunswickers to take the enemy in flank. General Phillips himself rallied The Twentieth, who had lost half their number in killed and wounded, the Minden veterans acclaiming him with a hoarse shout. The Americans fell back. Though General Arnold, on foot now and pistol in hand, urged them to a crowning effort, they were exhausted and could do no more. In the gathering darkness he led them round in safety behind the impenetrable thicket which covered the American centre. So the battle ended, but for slight encounters as a few Americans, lost in the forest, tried to regain their lines through our posts. By midnight all was silent.

We lay upon our arms that night and at daybreak moved forward to within cannon shot of the enemy, where we strengthened our camp by cutting down large trees, which served for breastworks. We threw our dead together into wide, shallow pits, and scarcely covered them with clay; the only tribute of respect allowed to fallen officers was to bury them apart from their men. Among the Massachusetts dead were found one or two young women, who from the fact of one of them having a cartridge clasped in her hand, had no doubt accompanied their husbands or brothers on service in order to load spare firelocks for them in the line of battle. General Fraser shook his head when this circumstance was brought to his notice. 'When women are brought into this damned business,' he said, 'it argues a resolution that will take some beating down.'

Taking all the results of this battle, our advantages from it were few indeed. We kept the field, but the possession of it was all that we could boast, for we were so much weakened that we could not at present press the attack. The Loyalists had nearly all gone off with the Indians. Their disappearance left us at a loss, from their having evinced a wide knowledge of this district and served us in the capacity of guides. Such levies are always precarious assistants to regular troops; they shrink from blows and scanty subsistence and their untrained condition gives them a temper easily dispirited by reverse. It needs the training of years and the tradition of former battles before a regiment can gain that cool presence of mind which will carry it forward unguardedly, to destroy itself if necessary in the cause to which it is devoted.

Two days later a letter reached General Burgoyne from

Sir Henry Clinton at New York, confirming Thayendane-gea's ill news. This was the first messenger from the South that had arrived since the campaign began in earnest, nor had a single one of General Burgoyne's own ten messengers succeeded in passing safe through hostile territory. The letter, written in cipher, ran merely: 'You know my poverty; but if with 2,000 men, which is all that I can spare from this important post, I can do anything to facilitate your operations, I will make an attack upon Fort Montgomery: if you will let me know your wishes.' Fort Montgomery, on Hudson's River, lay eighty miles to the south of Albany.

This placed General Burgoyne in a predicament. Now, if he decided to extricate our army from the difficult position in which it was caught and, disobeying orders, retired to Canada, he would be behaving very shabbily towards General Clinton, who counted on him to advance. Yet the longer he waited, the more insecure his position. He had that very day been informed that the American general, Lincoln, had successfully attacked our posts and depots about Ticonderoga and the northern end of Lake George; and that he had captured nearly three hundred of our men, several gunboats and the whole of our remaining *bateaux*, with their crews, rescued a thousand prisoners and possessed himself of Mount Defiance, Mount Hope, and other outworks of the fortress. We were thus cut off from Canada.

General Burgoyne sent the same messenger instantly back to General Clinton, with a reply written small on thin paper, and screwed inside a silver bullet. The messenger reached Fort Montgomery, which, by General Burgoyne's account, he expected to find in British hands, and there inquired of two soldiers, whom he took to be Loyalists, for General Clinton. Such incredibly ill luck attended this expedition that the person before whom he was taken was not Sir Henry Clinton, but a distant relative of Sir Henry's in the American service, who was then Governor of the State of New York. No sooner had the messenger discovered his error than he turned aside and swallowed the silver bullet: which was, however, recovered by means of an emetic. Upon its being unscrewed, the message was found and General Burgoyne's intentions discovered:

which were to hold General Gates in play while Sir Henry made a diversion below Albany to draw away his troops. But General Burgoyne revealed that our supplies would not last beyond October 12th.

The messenger was immediately hanged as a spy. 'Out of thine own mouth shalt thou be condemned,' was the jest that hurried him into eternity.

We kept within our fortifications for the next few days, not having sufficient strength to attack the Americans, but being most averse to retreat. We hoped also that our continued presence at Saratoga would serve the obscure and perplexing strategy that had fixed us in our present situation, at least by preventing General Gates from marching with his fourteen thousand men to the aid of General Washington. General Burgoyne could not have guessed that he was the victim of a monstrous blunder; but it was so. The story is as follows: Lord George Germaine had in May drafted a dispatch to General Howe, ordering him to march up Hudson's River. This dispatch was in reply to one from General Howe, who did not agree to the plan for co-operating with General Burgoyne in this manner, but favoured instead an attack upon Philadelphia, as the enemy's capital city. However, upon calling at the War Office one morning, on his way to Sussex for a holiday, and finding the draft not yet copied fairly out, Lord George Germaine could not wait to sign it, but continued on his journey. The dispatch was therefore not signed, and therefore not sent, and his Lordship either clean forgot about it or assumed that it would take care of itself. Unfortunately, in another dispatch Lord George had, it seems, approved of the attack upon Philadelphia as a subsidiary enterprise; and General Howe was therefore unaware that he was still expected to assist in the attack upon Albany, or that our army had already set forth single-handed upon this project.

The American General, Charles Lee, who often hit the right nail upon the head, remarked of General Howe, not altogether unkindly: 'He shut his eyes, fought his battles, drank his bottle, had his little whore, received his orders from North and Germaine (one more absurd than the other), shut his eyes, and fought again.'

Though we did not yet know it, the battle had brought out much bad blood in the American camp. General Gates, 'that man-midwife,' as General Burgoyne privately named him for his sneaking and unctuous ways, made no mention whatever, in his report to Congress, of General Arnold's presence upon the field of battle; and the chief colonel of his staff spread the absurd story that General Arnold had avoided the fight and spent the whole day in camp, drinking. By this means the single person who prevented us from storming the Heights and breaking through to Albany, and who had therefore saved General Gates's reputation, if not his life, was teased and provoked into mutinous rage. He resigned his command. Every Northern general but one, General Lincoln, then signed a memorial entreating General Arnold to remain with them for one more fight at least; but General Gates withdrew his command from him, and allowed him to remain in the camp only in the capacity of a private person.

The war-like feeling of New England was intense at this time, largely because of the indignation and alarm that had been inculcated in the various provinces by reports of Indian savagery. The militia mustered in enormous numbers and for once paid attention to their officers; deserters were whipped and returned to duty by the Selectmen of their townships—one father even sent back his two recreant sons in chains to the General commanding a Provincial division with the Roman request, 'Deal with them as they deserve.'

❋ ❋ ❋ ❋ ❋ ❋ ❋ ❋ ❋ ❋ ❋ ❋

CHAPTER

24

ON OCTOBER 6th our rations were diminished by one-third, because of a great shortage of provisions, but without exciting any murmur or complaint in the camp. We were already reduced to salt pork and flour, with a little spirits; not even the officers being able to procure tea, coffee, or fresh meat. Our regimental clothes were in a sad state, not having been renewed that year: they had become rotten from the great variety of weather in which we had worn them and ragged from the briars and rough country through which we had fought our way. Our horses also went hungry; for the river-side pastures were soon exhausted, and covering-parties to protect our foragers could not be spared. Most of all we felt the want of sleep, for the forests around us were alive with the enemy, who kept us continually upon the alert and compelled us to lie upon our arms for a great part of each night. The Americans even had the assurance to bring down a small field-piece to fire as their morning-gun, and so close to our quarter-guard that the wadding from its discharge flew against our works.

We had heard a great concerted howling two nights before from the right of our position, which disturbed our sleep; and the same noise arose again on the night following. General Fraser believed that it proceeded from dogs belonging to our officers, who had gone off by night to hunt; he ordered them to be confined, under pain of any stray dog being hanged by the Provost of the Division. However, upon the noise continuing and scouts going out to investigate, it was found that great packs of wolves had assembled and were howling as they scratched at the shallow graves of our poor comrades; nor would they be balked of their banquets, but continued their horrid cries until they had dug up the flesh and consumed it.

On this same night General Burgoyne called his chief officers to a Council of War. He told them, that our army had evidently been intended from the first to be *hazarded* and that it might now require to be *devoted*. He asked their advice. Generals Fraser and Riedesel were for retiring at once to Canada, General Phillips gave no opinion, General Burgoyne himself was for making one last attempt to force a passage to Albany. There being no objection raised to his view, about noon of the next day, October 7th, he took out fifteen hundred of us with ten guns, against the enemy's left, in an attempt to turn them off Bemis Heights. The Generals above named commanded the three divisions. What was left of our army stayed in the camp, except the bâtmen who went out for forage under cover of this advance. Before we set out we were given our last issue of rum, to hearten us.

We advanced in good order to within a short distance of the enemy's works, where we halted in a large field of uncut wheat and shook out along a zigzag fence, posting our cannon in rear. We were inviting an enemy attack, hoping to cause them heavy losses and then to press victoriously upon a rout with the bayonet. We of the Light Infantry held the right of the line, and my company, being the eldest there, held the extreme point. At four o'clock the battle began with an attack upon our left by many thousands of the enemy. There our Grenadiers sustained the attack with great firmness; but the Americans broke the Brunswick regiment to the Grenadiers' right, and General Riedesel and his staff used their swords among the fugitives to rally them behind the guns. We were then quickly recalled from our position, where we were already hotly attacked by Colonel Morgan's force, to save the Grenadiers from destruction. They were fighting hand to hand now against odds of ten to one, and some of our fieldpieces had been taken and retaken five times.

To break off an action against superior numbers without loss is a matter of great difficulty; General Fraser accomplished it for us by ordering a charge-bayonet which sent the riflemen running. But, alas, to twelve marksmen had been consigned the task of aiming at the person of General Fraser and none other. Dressed in the full uniform of a general, with laced furniture upon his iron-grey charger, he presented a most conspicuous target. One bullet grazed the horse's crupper, another passed through the mane, but a third pierced the General's body, passing in close under the breastbone and out near the spine. He was carried away, mortally wounded, and the command of the right wing devolved upon Lord Balcarres.

This was the first occasion that I saw General Benedict Arnold in action. He had been forbidden by General Gates to leave camp, but had struck with his sword at an officer sent to restrain him, wounding him; and then galloped into the fray with oaths of fury. He was in an ecstasy of enthusiasm, to which resentment of General Gates, natural courage, and a great deal of hard liquor contributed perhaps in equal measure. He rode in undress, and bareheaded, directly across our front, waved a sword about his head, shouted in a cracked voice and grimaced in high excitement. The New England militia troops were inspired by him to unusual valour wherever he led. He carried three whole regiments of Massachusetts infantry with him in a dense body against the centre, where the remainder of the Germans broke before him at the second charge. A comic aspect of this heroism was provided by an aide-de-camp of Gates, who had orders to arrest General Arnold and bring him back to camp. The unfortunate man was made to play follow-my-leader throughout the day and led into some mighty hot spots, but never came near enough to lay his hand upon the angry man's collar.

General Gates himself was not seen by his troops during this action: he spent the greater part of the day in discourse with a wounded prisoner, Sir Francis Clark, whom he was trying to persuade, by political argument, of the righteousness of the American cause. Sir Francis, who was dying, did not budge from his convictions, and, says General Gates to one of his aides, 'Did you ever hear such an impudent son of a bitch?'

It was a stiff rear-guard action that we fought, some companies retiring while the others faced about and fired volleys with precision and effect. We were now covering the retreat of the centre and the left, but were sufficient to the task and came safe back at last into the camp, where we hurriedly refilled pouches and cartouche-cases. All the guns had been lost, by the shooting down of the teams: without these it was impossible to haul them back. Twenty-five officers had been killed and wounded in the space of less than an hour, and several experienced sergeants, including my friend and benefactor Sergeant Fitzpatrick, who died very easily, shot in the lungs. 'Well, Gerry,' he said panting, as I bent over him, 'I believe I have got my furlough—to the Promised Land. The Rev. Charles Wesley always bade us build our hopes of what God might do for us hereafter on what He has done for us here. I trust to that. My loving duty to poor Mrs. Fitzpatrick, my affectionate wishes to my niece Jane, my compliments to the Captain, and God bless you!' Soon after, he expired.

General Burgoyne had escaped unwounded, though shots had pierced his hat and his waistcoat. The bâtmen had been surprised in the act of cutting fodder and came back empty-handed.

This was not the end of the day. General Arnold next rode against our camp with a brigade of Continental troops. He unwisely chose the position held by the Light Infantry and supported by heavy pieces of artillery. We gave his Americans musket-fire and grape as they tried to rush the open space in front of Freeman's Farm; and repulsed them with great loss. Even this did not daunt General Arnold: in the fading daylight he effected a combined assault on the horseshoe redoubt which covered the right of our position. Here the German reserve was stationed, and his attack this time did not miscarry, for he broke through the weak Canadian companies that lay between the Germans and ourselves and took the position in rear. The Brunswick colonel was killed; his men fired a last volley and then surrendered. General Arnold was entering the sally-port, sword in hand, when his horse rolled over, stone dead. As he was pitched from the saddle, a wounded German fired at him point-blank and shattered the thigh-bone of the same leg that had been broken below the knee at Quebec. General Arnold prevented an American soldier from bayoneting his adversary, swearing that the German was a fine fellow and in the way of his duty. The pursuing aide-de-camp here finally caught up with General Arnold. 'General Gates's compliments,' he gasped. 'You are to do nothing rash, but return at once to the camp.'

General Arnold called a surgeon, who shook his head on examining the wound and recommended amputation. 'Goddam it, sir,' cried this remarkable man, 'if that is all that you can do with me, I shall see the battle out on another horse.'

As for our people, they were greatly fatigued and even the sentinels found it hard to keep their eyes open. I was busied with the wounded, until late that night, when an order came to us to abandon our post and take up a new position half a mile in the rear, on the height above our general hospital. This natural fortress lay close to the road and the river and was protected by a deep ravine. The order was obeyed with the greatest regularity and silence. We could hear the Americans bringing up their artillery for an attack at dawn, and thus the wisdom of the withdrawal became apparent, for our camp was not cannon-proof and the enemy had outflanked us by the capture of the horseshoe redoubt from the Germans.

Early in the morning General Fraser, who had dictated and signed a last Will, breathed his last: his request was to be buried by us without any parade within the great redoubt. All that day we offered battle, and several brigades of the enemy formed against us in the plain with the evident intention of assault. However, a howitzer shell from our batteries, bursting in the middle of a column, caused such carnage that they all ran off into the woods and showed no further inclination to attack. An assault across a level meadow against so strongly entrenched a force as ours was too much to expect of irregular troops; and it was a mistake on our part to discourage them by howitzer fire before the attack was well launched. To have met them in the open would have been a most agreeable change from the continual wood-fighting and skirmishing in which the advantages of our discipline had been lost. In a dense thicket every man is his own general, and subordination to orders where combined movements are impossible of execution becomes a vice rather than a virtue, for the most obedient soldier is at the greatest loss.

At sunset, since the enemy did not attack, we buried General Fraser, carrying the corpse in procession up the hill in full sight of both armies. Generals Burgoyne, Phillips, and Riedesel joined the cortège. The Americans, regarding the prosecution of the war and the killing of our officers as of more importance than scruples of reverence to the dead, cannonaded the procession; and their shots threw up the earth around us as we stood bare-headed at his grave, attentive to the service. I have since heard it said that on perceiving their error the Americans fired a minute-gun only, as a mark of respect; but if so, they used shot in mistake for wadding. The chaplain of the Artillery, Mr. Brudenell, continued his steady reading of the office without alarm or hesitation throughout the cannonade.

At nine o'clock we were obliged to move back again, for the Americans were marching in great force to turn our right flank; we abandoned our general hospital, with five hundred sick and wounded, to the enemy. Terry Reeves was among the wounded, and I said farewell to him with a heavy heart, for he had fought very gallantly and proved a true comrade to me. Our company was with the rear-guard, General Phillips commanding us. It was two hours before the order came to march, and we had for some time expected a night-assault by the enemy, who re-formed in the same place as they had left that morning. We could see the twinkling lanterns which the officers carried, and their movements up and down the lines. Yet, we came off safely, and the enemy did not pursue us until late on the following day, which was October 9th. For lightness of travel we had left behind our tents and other furniture.

This was a miserable journey, the rain pouring down without ceasing, and the road exceedingly bad and muddy. The Americans had again broken down the bridges over the creeks, which must be repaired to allow our wagons and guns to pass and then broken down once more to hinder the enemy's advance. Our *bateaux* in the river which had kept abreast of our advance now returned with us, the crews poling them with difficulty up the shallows. The train of wagons, as the rain grew worse, became bogged and not to be extricated by any means, the horses being weak for lack of fodder and our own strength quite worn out. These wagons had been hastily constructed in Canada of green wood and the warping of the timber made them very stiff to drive, even in the best of weathers. We held no conversation among ourselves on this march, so heavy our hearts were, nor cracked a joke, nor sang a song. We halted for some hours, at Dovegat, where we formed in expectation of an assault. None came, and on we went.

I found myself in ill company, that day, trudging beside Richard Harlowe. The knowledge that he was indebted to me for his life seemed to embitter him yet further against me; but on the contrary (by a strange infirmity of human nature) warmed my heart towards him. This infirmity the great Shakespeare noted in his tragedy of *Julius Caesar* where the memory of how he had once saved Caesar's life from drowning weighed more with Cassius—when invited to join in murdering him—than any memory of kind treatment at Caesar's hands. I even offered to carry Harlowe's musket for him, since he limped from an inflamed heel and seemed unable to support the weight; but he sullenly refused and I did not repeat my offer.

So we continued in a silence disturbed only by the horrid imprecations of Corporal Buchanan, who had been sent to take Sergeant Fitzpatrick's place in our company. At nightfall our vanguard reached the village of Saratoga, and found that a large body of the enemy had seized the rising ground on the near side of the Creek, where the Schuyler mansion stood, and were fortifying it. However, the rain prevented the enemy from using their rifle-guns and they were pushed across the ford by threat of bayonet; where they joined another large body that was fortifying the opposing bank in order to cut off our retreat. So fatigued were most of our people on arrival at Saratoga— we had spent near twenty-four hours in accomplishing a march of eight miles—that they were indisposed to cut wood for fires, to dry their drenched clothes, but lay down as they were upon the sodden ground. I remembered, however, the situation of a hen-house near General Schuyler's range of barns and store-houses, and, with the permission of an officer, led my company to it out of the rain.

About the middle of the night I was overcome by a terrible nightmare. In this dream I fancied that I was caught in a raiding party of Wyandot Indians, my arms were pinioned and I was led away to be burned. I struggled against my captors with all my strength, but unavailingly, and was lashed with strips of elm-bark to a stake. There a fire was kindled about my feet. The Indians mocked and jeered me, seizing brands of hickory wood from the fire and scorching my flesh with it in every part of my body, without pity. Foremost among my persecutors was Richard Harlowe, who at last seized a bucket of red-hot embers and emptied it on my head, crying: 'Coals of fire! Coals of fire! There's nothing burns the head like coals of fire!' Then the Reverend John Martin appeared in the guise of a Wyandot sachem. He grinned at me and, said he, 'Here I am again. Ye'll never be rid of me. I am here, there, and everywhere, like the Royal Artillery.'

The heat was unbearable, the flames roared high, I was choking with the smoke; and then some-one seized me by the middle and threw me across his back. He staggered with me out through the flames, and laid me upon the grass. I awoke then, to know that the fire at least had not been a dream, and that Smutchy Steel had rescued me from the blazing hen-house, when I was near smoth-ered. The fire had been providentially noticed by Lieu-tenant Kemmis as he went to his lodging at the mansion; he ran up and shouted a warning. My comrades awoke, but could not escape, for the door proved to have been secured from the outside with a stout snib. Had the Lieutenant not been at hand to enlarge us, by turning this snib, we should infallibly have burned to death.

Some flaming straw from the hen-house, being carried upwards by the heat, now lodged in the roof of a barn near by and the whole range of buildings caught fire. We were hard put to it to rescue from the flames the sick and wounded who had been housed there. My two hours of sleep before the conflagration were the first that I had enjoyed since the third night before; and I slept no more that night, neither. Our company discussed together who could have been the incendiary, but came to no conclusion. It was remarked that, of those who had taken shelter in the hut, only Richard Harlowe was absent when the alarm was given. But, there being no other circumstances to incriminate him, he was not charged with arson, and the matter subsided.

On the next day, October 10th, the *bateaux*, with what little provisions remained in them, were constantly fired upon from the other bank of the river, which was distant but thirty yards. Many fell into the hands of the enemy and several of the boatmen were killed or wounded. We now recrossed Fishkill Creek, and General Burgoyne sent a force of artificers up the river, under a sufficient escort, to occupy and repair the pontoon-bridge built for us four weeks previously. They found it still afloat and the task would have been completed by the following daybreak had not their escort been urgently recalled by General Burgoyne who wished every available soldier to be present with him for a battle which he hoped might be decisive for our arms. A company of Loyalists, left behind as a guard, fled upon the approach of a small body of the enemy, and the artificers were forced to do likewise. But General Burgoyne at least succeeded in sending his military chest safe back into Canada, under slight escort, assisted by the Indians.

We were entrenched on the low ridge of hills overlooking Fishkill Creek and its artificial islands, and a broad space was now cleared of everything that could afford cover to the enemy. By an unkind necessity of war, the Schuyler mansion on the opposite side of the creek was, at General Burgoyne's order, burned to the ground, for it afforded an admirable shelter behind which General Gates's army might mass for the assault. My heart was sore to see this noble house and the mills beside it go up in flames: and my high estimation of General Schuyler's character was confirmed when later I learned that he bore us no ill will for this destruction, declaring that, had he been in General Burgoyne's shoes, he would have done the same. He had, indeed, in the first year of this war, ruined the beautiful estate of his neighbour Sir William Johnson, Bt. (father of Colonel Guy and Sir John Johnson) which was situated in the Mohawk valley: carrying off his Scottish tenantry as prisoners and killing his famous herd of peacocks, the feathers of which his militiamen stuck in their caps as trophies.

It was raining still, and indeed rain fell continuously for a whole week from the time of our retreat. 'So much the better for us,' we thought, fingering our bayonets with expectant ardour. In the middle of the morning the American attack was launched under cover of a thick fog. Their vanguard, consisting of above a thousand of their regular troops, covertly passed over the Creek and advanced towards us up the slope. At that moment the fog lifted and their whole line was disclosed. We gave them grape-shot and platoon-fire and waited for their nearer approach in order to charge with the bayonet; but they broke and ran in remarkable disorder. We expected them to re-form and return to the assault, but in vain. Instead, their centre halted and took post, facing us, on the other side of the Creek, while Colonel Morgan led his large command two miles upstream and there crossed; wheeling round, he then halted on the fringe of the forest which bordered our right flank. Three thousand more Americans pushed along the farther bank of Hudson's River, now denuded of our forces, capturing a number of our *bateaux* with their crews. Opposite us they posted batteries of guns which could rake our position from end to end. They also placed guards on all the fords and ferries as far upstream as Fort Edward, and built a redoubt commanding our pontoon-bridge.

General Riedesel now proposed to General Burgoyne to abandon our baggage and guns and retreat during the night, forcing a passage over a ford four miles below Fort Edward, and striking across the forest to Fort George before the enemy beyond the river could be reinforced. General Burgoyne refused, still hoping that the Americans would dash their army against us in a wild onslaught.

On the following morning, October 11th, some of us were given the dangerous and difficult duty of transporting the sacks of provisions from the *bateaux* upon our shoulders into the camp, and rolling up the barrels. Musketry and shell-fire from across the river killed many of our number.

Very great indeed were the distresses which we were called upon to suffer, yet they were borne with fortitude; and we were still ready to face any danger when led on by officers whom we loved and respected. Numerous parties of the militia now joined the American forces, so that General Gates was soon at the head of twenty thousand men. They swarmed around us like birds of prey. By our losses we had been reduced from the seven thousand men with whom we set out from Canada to half that number, not two thousand of whom were British.

Our camp was a mile and a half long, and a half mile broad. We were exposed to continual round-shot from the enemy batteries, which made it inadvisable to light fires: for the smoke or flame provided a target at which aim was immediately taken. Thus we were obliged to subsist upon raw victuals—salt pork and a paste made with flour and water. Moreover, the whole army was provided with but one spring of water, which was muddy, and we were feign to drink puddle-water or rain caught in our caps. To fetch water from the Creek by day was to be shot dead; and three armed parties who went down under cover of darkness did not return. We were greatly galled by popping shots from the riflemen in the tree-tops; and, in the small redoubt where we were huddled, would amuse ourselves by hoisting a cap upon a stick above the parapet. Instantly shots would be fired at it, and it would be perforated by two or three balls. We were forbidden to reply, in order to save our ammunition for the general assault that was still expected, and took this very hard. Soon we were beyond caring for the cannonades. We lighted fires, regardless of the danger, baking our flour paste into the usual cakes upon stones laid in the embers. Our store of spruce-beer was expended and any one who possessed a reserve of rum could find a ready market for it at one guinea the pint.

At another Council of War on the next day, October 12th, General Riedesel prevailed upon General Burgoyne to attempt the retirement that he had refused to make two days before. Five days' rations—all that remained—were therefore issued to us by the Commissaries, and we awaited orders to issue from the works when dark came. However, our scouts reported that the enemy had sent out so many detached parties that it would now be impossible to execute this retreat without setting the whole American army in motion against us. General Burgoyne therefore changed his mind once more, for though he trusted General Riedesel, he did not trust the Germans under his command. It was notorious that they were suffering too greatly to be dependable marching companions; and had concerted to fire one volley only, if attacked, and then to club their arms in token of surrender.

I was now assisting the surgeons in a building which was a principal target of the American artillery—a log-house of two storeys well advertised to them as constituting our general hospital. It was suspected by these over-ingenious people that our generals would be smart enough to make the hospital serve a double purpose, by sheltering themselves and their families under a roof that invited a humane respect. Some slight colour for their belief was provided by Madame Riedesel's ornamental calash which stood near the door; this pretty blue-eyed lady and her three young children having taken refuge in the cellar of the building. Therefore the round shot came bounding in and out of the upper chambers where we were at work. A surgeon, Mr. Jones, had his leg so crushed by flying masonry that we were obliged to amputate it. In the middle of this operation, which he endured with great fortitude, another ball came roaring from across the river, and when the dust had cleared we found that Surgeon Jones had been dashed from the table on which he was laid and was lying groaning in a corner: his other leg had been taken clean off! This was only one of many horrible happenings, of which a full Detail would turn the stomach.

The wounded were crying out for water, and we had none to give them. A bâtman volunteered to run down to the Creek and bring up water in a pail, but he was struck down before he had gone many steps. Then the same Jane Crumer, who had assisted me at Fort Anna, and whose husband was among the gravely wounded, cried out that the Americans were not such beasts that they would fire at a woman. She went leisurely out from the hospital, paused by the dead man to unclasp his fingers from the pail that they still clutched; then, waving amiably to the enemy across the river, she continued to the water-side, drew water, curtsied her gratitude and returned. Not a shot was fired at her. She went to and fro with her pail until she had fetched sufficient for all.

On October 13th, General Burgoyne summoned yet another Council, to which all officers from the rank of Captain upwards were invited. It is said, that to Major Skene, who was present, General Burgoyne remarked with a pardonable show of irritation: 'Sir, you have been the occasion of getting me into this quagmire. Now be good enough to show me the way out.' To which Major Skene made the absurd reply: 'Scatter your baggage and stores in every part of the camp, and while the rebel militia are scrambling for the plunder, you will have time to get away in safety.' This remark, however, was not recorded in the minutes of this proceeding, which may best speak for themselves.

Minutes and proceedings of a Council of War, consisting of all the general officers, field officers, and captains commanding corps, on the Heights of Saratoga, October 13th, 1777:

The Lieutenant-General having explained the situation of affairs as in the preceding Council, with the additional intelligence that the enemy was intrenched at the fords of Fort Edward, and likewise occupied the strong position on the pine plains between Fort George and Fort Edward, expressed his readiness to undertake, at their head, any enterprise of difficulty or hazard that should appear to them within the compass of their strength and spirit. He added that he had reason to believe a capitulation had been in the contemplation of some, perhaps of all, who knew the real situation of things; that, upon a circumstance of such consequence to national and personal honour, he thought it a duty to his country, and to himself, to extend his council beyond the usual limits; that the assembly present might justly be esteemed a full representation of the army; and that he should think himself unjustifiable in taking any step in so serious a matter, without such a concurrence of sentiments as should make a treaty the act of the Army as well as that of the General. The first question he desired them to decide was:

Whether an army of three thousand, five hundred, fighting men, and well provided with artillery, were justifiable, upon the principles of national dignity and military honour, in capitulating in any possible situation?

Resolved, *nem con.* in the affirmative.

Question 2: Is the present situation of that nature?

Resolved, *nem. con.* that the present situation justifies a capitulation upon honourable terms.

General Burgoyne then drew up the following letter directed to General Gates, relative to the negotiation, and laid it before the Council. It was unanimously approved, and upon that foundation the treaty opened:

After having fought you twice, Lieutenant-General Burgoyne has waited some days in his present position, determined to try a third conflict against any force you could bring to attack him.

He is apprized of the superiority of your numbers, and the disposition of your troops to impede his supplies and render his retreat a scene of carnage on both sides. In this situation he is compelled by humanity, and thinks himself justified by established principles, and precedents of State and of War, to spare the lives of brave men upon honourable terms.

Should Major-General Gates be inclined to treat upon that idea, General Burgoyne would propose a cessation of arms, during the time necessary to communicate the preliminary terms by which in any extremity he, and his army, mean to abide.

General Gates then transmitted the following proposals to General Burgoyne; whose answers are appended:

(1) General Burgoyne's army being exceedingly reduced by repeated defeats, by desertion, sickness, etc., their provisions exhausted, their military horses, tents, and baggage taken or destroyed, their retreat cut off, and their camp invested, they can only be allowed to surrender prisoners of war.

Answer: Lieutenant-General Burgoyne's army, however reduced, will never admit that their retreat is cut off while they have arms in their hands.

(2) The troops under His Excellency General Burgoyne's command, may be drawn up in their encampments, where they will be ordered to ground their arms, and may thereupon be marched to the river side to be passed over in their way towards Bennington.

Answer: This article inadmissible in any extremity; sooner than this army will consent to ground their arms in their encampment, they will rush on the enemy determined to take no quarter. If General Gates does not mean to recede from this article the treaty ends at once. The army will to a man proceed to any act of desperation rather than submit to this article.

General Gates did recede from this article, and the following was substituted in its stead:

The troops to march out of their camp with the honours of war, and the artillery of the entrenchments, to the verge of the river, where their arms and artillery must be left. The arms to be piled by word of command from their own officers. A free passage to be granted to the army under Lieutenant-General Burgoyne to Great Britain, upon condition of not serving again in North America during the present contest; and the port of Boston to be assigned for the entry of transports to receive the troops whenever General Howe shall so order.

It becoming generally known to both armies that the articles of capitulation were being discussed, the enemy's fire slackened; and, though the rain continued, our condition was sensibly bettered. Our remaining oxen and other cattle were slaughtered and some fresh meat distributed to us. Our people began to greet and discourse with the Americans on the opposite bank of Hudson's River; and a few riflemen even emerged from the forest on our right and exchanged rations and keepsakes with the Light Infantry and Grenadiers. On the morning of October 18th Mad Johnny Maguire came down to the river with me and several others. My comrades began shouting across the water friendly challenges to wrestling and boxing matches, and a big fellow with a gun seven foot long cried out, evidently to me: 'You now, the tall sergeant with the moon face, will you kindly oblige me with a sweet turn at the blackthorn stick?'

These were the accents of the city of Dublin, and I burst into loud laughter. 'No, my Kevin Street bully,' I replied. 'The small sword is my weapon.'

The American grew very wrath and 'Don't you dare to laugh at Cornelius Maguire, you rascal lobster,' he said, 'or I'll swim over this stream and scuttle you with one blow, so I will.'

At this, something appeared to strike Mad Johnny Maguire's mind very forcibly. He darted from our midst and plunged into the river. 'Och, Corny, Corny,' he cried, 'I hardly knew ye.'

Cornelius Maguire, seized by a similar impulse, plunged in to meet him. They found their feet on a shallow place near the middle, where they hung on each other's necks and wept. Their 'Och, Johnny, my darling brother,' and 'Och, Corny, my jewel,' soon cleared up the mystery for us. Cornelius Maguire had emigrated to America twenty years previously, at about the same time that Mad Johnny Maguire had entered the British Army. Each had been totally ignorant that he was engaged in hostile combat against the other's life.

Our minds were set at rest on October 18th, when we learned that General Gates had yielded to General Burgoyne's threat of a desperate assault, should his demand for honourable terms be rejected, and that the articles were now signed. It was consoling that we had preserved the dignity of the British character and extorted from a successful foe, vastly outnumbering us and straining every nerve to tarnish our honour, so plain an admission of the awe in which they held our enfeebled arms. We were aware, however, that General Gates was prompted to rapid compliance not only by our resolute front but by news of Sir Henry Clinton's capture of Forts Montgomery and Clinton with a charge-bayonet five days before. The Seventh, Twenty-sixth, Sixty-third, Fifty-second, and Fifty-seventh were the regiments employed on this honourable service. The great iron chain-boom, weighing fifty tons, there stretched by the enemy at prodigious expense across the river, had been speedily removed, and our ships freed to sail up the river as far as Albany. General Gates feared for his arsenal in that town and resolved to finish off one business before becoming involved in another. It consoled us for the surrender of our thirty-five pieces of brass ordnance and our five thousand muskets, to learn that General Clinton had captured more than that amount of cannon, together with great stores of powder and provisions, in Fort Montgomery.

Our minds were filled with delightful thoughts of a safe and prompt return to our own land, where we might hold up our heads as men who had fought stoutly, and where we would also find great arrears of pay awaiting us to console us for our present indigence and hardships.

Mad Johnny Maguire and his brother fell into a severe dispute, since they were resolved never again to part, as to whether Johnny should now discharge himself from the British Army and settle down with Corny on his farm at Norwalk in Connecticut, or Corny should quit the American army and the two together go west into the new territory of Kentucke. The moral issue was debated with great warmth and, their fraternal love being as strong as their respective loyalties, it was with difficulty that we could restrain them from reciprocal injury.

❋ ❋ ❋ ❋ ❋ ❋ ❋ ❋ ❋ ❋ ❋ ❋

CHAPTER

25

OBEYING our officers' orders, we piled up our arms in a meadow, near the confluence of Fishkill Creek and Hudson's River, and emptied out our cartouche-cases. It was found that not fifteen rounds a man remained to us. A great stench arose in this meadow from the decaying bodies of horses that lay about it. They had been allured there, from the deep ravine where we kept them within the camp, by the scent of rich grass—the enemy shot the poor beasts down as soon as they began grazing. There were soldiers who now wept at being parted from the muskets that they had carried so long and cared for so well, and that seemed almost a part of themselves; and I own that for days I missed the familiar weight of my piece upon my shoulder, and felt in a manner naked without it. No American troops were present at this melancholy scene, General Gates having confined all to camp except a few companies of riflemen who lined the fringes of the forest as a precaution against any treachery on our part. Lieutenant-Colonel Hill preserved the colours of The Ninth by taking them off the staves and sewing them in the lining of a mattress. He eventually was able to present them to His Majesty at St. James's Palace, who rewarded his faithful services with the appointment of aide-de-camp to himself and the full rank of colonel.

That same day, October 17th, we were marched off in the direction of Boston. We passed through the long ranks of our enemies, who had spent the whole morning scrubbing and cleaning their persons and firelocks in order to make the best appearance possible. There were fourteen thousand of them in the parade and some thousands more posted in reserve. The men were in general taller, thinner, and more sinewy than ours. Our veterans remarked that they would have liked these rebels better had they shown that command of mind which should dignify an army when victorious in the field; for it seemed to them that the features and tones even of the American regular troops betrayed an improper exultation. Lieutenant Anburey of The Fourteenth, in his published account of these transactions, has written: 'As we passed the American enemy, throughout the whole of them I did not observe the least disrespect, or even a taunting look, but all was mute astonishment and pity.' Neither I, nor such of my surviving comrades as I have consulted, can account for the discrepancy between what we saw and what the Lieutenant saw, unless by the suggestion that we were of a more jaundiced and irritable temper than he: for pity there was none, but either sour looks or good-humoured sallies at our expense, to which we did not care to reply. The truth is, we had been so scribbled against, by their newspaper writers and pamphleteers, as base mercenaries and British scum, and so preached against by their ministers, who represented us in Biblical imagery as mere monsters—with swords for tongues, claws for hands, hoofs for feet, and our mouths dripping with the blood of children and virgins—that few Americans could cast out this strong prejudice from their minds. Add to this, that we could hardly expect from peasants, fighting in defence of their homes, the same courtesies as passed, for instance, between our armies and the French, when professionally opposed in battle upon the neutral soil of Germany or the Low Countries.

The American regular or 'Continental' troops wore buff and blue uniforms with stout knapsacks, and carried muskets, twenty thousand of which had been secretly bought from our enemies the French by an American emissary in Paris; the riflemen were conformedly dressed in linen hunting shirts and leggins; the militia were clad, according to their own parochial fancy, in coats of military cut but of many different stuffs, colours, and facings—their firelocks also showing much diversity of quality and pattern. Besides these troops there also were numerous companies of well-whiskered rustics in workaday dress, many of whom carried immensely long guns of the sort used for duck-shooting, but some only pitchforks or knives bound to poles to serve as pikes. It was the monstrous many-coloured, fleecy wigs affected by the elder men that caused us most amazement and recalled the times of good Queen Anne, when men wore haystacks upon their heads.

The Americans certainly had proved very smart in repairing their deficiencies of warlike material. We had at first thought that they would have to yield for want of gunpowder: for the quantities that they won by capture, or by sale from the Spanish, French, and Dutch were wholly insufficient to their needs. But a simple countryman had approached the Massachusetts Assembly with a specimen of his own manufacture of gunpowder, from the saltpetre contained in rotten stable-refuse, and undertook to show them how more could be made in eight months than the province had money to pay for. His process was adopted. Flour-mills, which were very numerous in New England, were thereupon converted into mills for gunpowder, and of this product there was soon a superfluity. The Americans also were very short of lead for bullets and ran into their molds clock-weights, waterspouts, cisterns, leaden ornaments from house-fronts, statuary, and printers' founts of type, and were reduced at times to pewter spoons and dishes. Paper for cartridges, neither too thin nor too thick, was hard to come by, and the Continentals were supplied on one occasion with a whole edition of a German Bible printed in Philadelphia. The leaves of vestry-books were also much used in New England for this purpose. In one respect, we learned, the smartness of the Yankees recoiled upon them. For the French muskets supplied being insufficient to the needs of the whole American army, the militia were sometimes served out with trade-muskets, showy and defective, that had been manufactured for sale to the simple fur-getting Indian, or to the African chiefs of the Guinea Coast who took them in exchange for slaves. They frequently burst at the first discharge and proved fatal to the soldiers who bore them. Most of the muskets used against us were manufactured by country blacksmiths in imitation of the Tower musket, but not to a single standard, so that if a part were damaged the piece would be useless until a new part could be forged to match.

When the head of our column arrived opposite the enemy's general headquarters, General Burgoyne in plumed hat and a rich new uniform delivered up his sword with a flourish to General Gates, wearing a plain blue frock, cocked hat, and spectacles, who received it courteously and returned it to him. The other officers were likewise permitted to retain their swords and fusils. Major Skene, by the bye, wrote himself down humbly as 'a poor follower of the British Army.' During these proceedings their musicians played the tune of 'Yankee Doodle,' which had now become their national paean, a favourite of favourites, and used alike among them as the lover's spell, the nurse's lullaby, and the soldier's marching song. The word 'Yankee' signifies 'coward' in the Cherokee Indian tongue, but from being used as a term of reproach it had become a word of glory to all New Englanders. The verses of the tune were exceedingly frivolous.

During the delay of some minutes caused by the compliments exchanged between the Generals, I found myself halted opposite some Massachusetts troops: I believe they were a Captain Morean's company. Among these I recognized James Melville, or Mellon, who had been prisoner at Quebec. I asked him: 'Fighting again? Did you not give your parole?'

He grinned and replied: 'They gave me a paper to sign. But I owe King George nothing. A forced promise, I'll swear, is no promise.' He then asked his officer for permission to break ranks and give me a drink from his flask: which was refused, as the orders were very strict against this. Yet he tossed the flask to me, I drank rum from it and was about to toss it back when he cried to me that I might keep it in return for my former benefits to himself; which I did, gladly.

We now retraced our steps once more along the road to

Stillwater, which was a gloomy enough stage on our two-hundred-mile journey; encamping on the hill over the ravine where we had abandoned our tents and our wounded. The tents were gone, but the hospital was still crowded with our sick, who were receiving considerate treatment. To my joy I found Terry Reeves sitting at the door on an upturned keg, nearly recovered from a bullet wound in the foot; he did not wish to be parted from us again and hobbled forward with the company the next day. We were shocked to discover on a visit to General Fraser's grave that some rough Americans had added to their former disrespect of his obsequies by exhuming the corpse. Their excuse was that they thought that we had concealed guns in the grave, and muskets in the coffin. It was certainly their custom to credit us with a 'smartness' altogether foreign to our British nature; but more likely the hope of these frontiersmen was to find, in the pockets of the General's uniform, a watch, or money, or some article of value that had been overlooked by the mourners in the anxiety and solemnity of that evening's work.

We crossed Hudson's River by General Gates's bridge of boats at Stillwater; the township was very well named from the sudden calming of the turbulent stream opposite it. The American army passed us, marching down to Albany against General Clinton's small army—which, however, soon retired upon hearing news of our disaster.

That morning a thanksgiving sermon had been preached before the American army. The Chaplain fully set forth to his hearers that the Almighty had done more for them than they had done for themselves. He preached from Joel ii. 26: 'But I will remove far off from you the Northern army, and will drive him into a land barren and desolate, with his face towards the East Sea, and his hinder part towards the Utmost Sea; and his stink shall come up, and his ill-savour shall come up, because he has done great things.' Great things our Northern army had indeed accomplished in the way of battle, and none could deny it; that General Howe had not come to our assistance with his twenty thousand men, or that General Clinton's force had marched too late, was no fault of ours. Now we were, in the words of the text, being driven into a land barren and desolate, with our face towards the East Sea; and as for our stink and ill-savour, the inhabitants of the country soon made it plain to us how grossly their nostrils were offended.

Saratoga was distant from Boston some two hundred miles. From the outset of our march we experienced much hardship, sleeping in barns and being given but scanty provisions. The way before and about us presented an uncheering appearance, mountainous and uncultivated, with no pleasing scenery to amuse the eye. I was now able to congratulate myself on my prescience in burdening myself with the Congress bills, which passed current in these parts. I still retained one thousand dollars of them. The remaining four thousand I had given to the surgeon of the hospital to purchase comforts for the poor fellows under his charge; which gift, I believe, saved many of their lives. Of what was left I kept one hundred dollars for my own use and divided up the remainder among the men of my company: I regarded it as plunder and to be put into the common stock. We therefore fared better than most of the army so long as this money lasted. New England rum, which we purchased at Bennington, the first place of pleasant appearance that we arrived at, kept us alive through the very cold nights of our passage over the Green Mountains. Many soldiers paid for their drams by selling their cartouche-cases, which seemed unnecessary luggage now that our muskets were taken from us. The mountain roads were almost impassable to our wagons, and when we were half over, a heavy fall of snow occurred, which caused several men to die of cold. A soldier's wife bore a child under the lee of a baggage cart that cruel night, and both survived.

The Americans were very glad to sell our people Continental paper in exchange for 'hard money,' as they termed gold and silver. At Bennington, in Vermont State, they offered nine paper dollars for each golden guinea, thus halving the professed value of the paper, and when we had crossed the Green Mountains and arrived at Hatfield and Hadley in Massachusetts, on the Connecticut River, we could get eighteen. The price of guineas grew still better, the nearer we came to Boston, and by the time we had passed through the back country of Massachusetts and approached the sea-board, we came to realize how low was the confidence of the more sagacious Americans in the ability of Congress to redeem these paper promises. For at Worcester, two or three days' march from our destination, we could get as much as thirty-five dollars for a guinea. As the war continued, the value of a paper dollar declined to less than one penny and at last the entire issue, having served its purpose of raising the wind was silently repudiated. But what appeared strange to us was that though the Americans depreciated Congress money in this way, by offering to sell it to us at so great a discount, yet always, whenever they sold any article at a price in paper dollars and we paid in hard money, they made no allowance for the difference in exchange; but for the honour of their country reckoned a paper dollar the equal of a silver one. We were the Egyptians, as it were, whom these Children of Israel—who, by the bye, bore Biblical names almost to a man—spoiled of our silver and gold.

In this march we were able to make many comparisons between the appearance and manner of life of the inhabitants and what we recalled of the Canadians and our own people at home. First, let me say, that though the wants of the country owing to the war were already very great, from its reliance upon England for stuffs and manufactured goods of quality, the inhabitants appeared well-fed and cheerful, and immeasurably better provided with the conveniences of life than the country people of Ireland. The women were dressed in bright and well-fitting clothing and had a remarkably independent air. Every place through which we passed was now raising two or three companies of troops to join General Washington's army, so that on the industry of these women depended the life of the countryside, and well they knew it.

I must observe here that no town that we came to had a settled or finished look, nor can it have been solely a fault of the war that life was here universally lived as if it were a doubtful campaign against the forces of Nature; with no opportunity to enjoy the fruits of victory, but a constant impulse to engage in new battles. Accidents that in our own country would serve to drive a man half-mad seemed here to produce little alarm or agitation. Nothing was either splendid or beggarly, and when a man was knocked down, he speedily picked himself up again in a manner impossible on our Continent. The labourer was everywhere content with a house of rough logs, unwhitewashed, unpainted, and not always boarded even on the inside. All around this habitation was, in general, as barren as the sea-beach, without flower-beds, paths, or lawns, but only heaps of cast rubbish and refuse; and if there was a cultivated plot called a garden, they used the plough to it, not the spade. Especially there were never any forest trees left standing for shade or adornment in the neighbourhood of a dwelling: Americans detested trees as much as our farmers detest weeds or stones. From the face of the country being everywhere overspread with forest the eyes of the people became weary of it: so that I have read of Americans landing on barren parts of the north-west coast of Ireland and expressing the greatest surprise at the 'improved state' of the country, so clear of trees! I never but once during all my seven years in America saw a well-laid out and completed estate, and that was General Schuyler's at Saratoga that we had been obliged to devastate. What contributed to the untidy and hasty effect of North American negligence was the stumps of trees left standing where virgin forest had given way to the plough. They were not grubbed up but allowed to rot slowly, while the plough avoided them with crooked furrows. They stood up two or three feet at the natural height of an axe-stroke; since a man could cut many more trees in a day in this style than if he levelled the stumps with the ground. Hedges were lacking, being held to rob the soil; and instead everywhere ran rough fences of various construction, which were more convenient than charming.

This want of attention to the amenities of life had been hereditary from the first settlers. Land and timber were cheap, labour dear, and a man would be held a fool who spent his time beautifying his home and its environs, when he might be planting an orchard of fruit-trees or clearing a few acres of forest to make into a maize-field. It may be recorded here that the only American who was ever known to grub up the stumps of his trees at once was their General Stirling, who called himself Lord Stirling. He had come to England, before the war, to pray for the revival in his favour of the extinct Stirling peerage, but the House of Lords disallowed his claim and forbade him under pain of public disgrace to assume the title. When the Americans popularly conceded it to him, he showed his gratitude by a sincere and steady devotion to their cause. He was most adhesive to the dignity of his rank, and the removal of the tree stumps was in keeping with these punctilious traits of his character.

The cattle hereabouts were numerous and extraordinarily large; and so were the hogs, which they fattened upon maize. Maize, or Indian corn, was the only grain to which the climate was favourable; for wheat was inclined to the blight, barley grew dry in the ear before maturity—so that ale was a rare delicacy in America—and oats yielded more straw than grain. But maize throve exceedingly and was the staple for both man and beast.

These Americans were so little gregarious that a rural township never consisted, as in Canada or anywhere in Europe, of a social collection of houses, inns, and places of religion surrounded by the fields and orchards of the inhabitants; we seldom saw more than a dozen houses together and the rest were here, there, and everywhere. It was as if each family wished to assert its independence of neighbours and form a village consisting of its own house and barns. When a son married, he would seldom be content, I was told, if he could not remove with his wife to a distance of two hundred miles away or more, and clear new land with his own axe.

I must say that America was certainly no Lubberland, or Land of Cockaigne, where the streets are paved with half-peck loaves, the houses roofed with pancakes, and where the fowls fly about ready roasted, with knife and fork plunged in their backs, crying, 'Sweet, sweet, come eat me!' It was the land of hard work and steady habits.

The women were brisk and handsome and kept their youthful looks some years longer than ours at home, though their hair turned grey sooner. For some reason, the climate did not appear to encourage wrinkles, and old men and women had a ruddy, smooth look which would contrast very cheerfully with the crumpled parchment faces of our own parents and grandparents. Their teeth, however, were very bad and their breaths sour, which some attributed to their hasty manner of eating and to immoderate fondness for molasses—which they consumed at

every meal, even with greasy pork. Another cause may
have been the great severity of the winter which kept
them short, for months together, of green vegetables and
salads and also encouraged them to profuse tippling of
spirits. New England speech seemed to proceed rather
through the nose than the mouth, yet was not unpleasing
in effect, if the person discoursing was one of sensibility;
and was so clearly articulated that, where a number of
people were talking together in a crowd, an American
voice, though not raised, could be distinctly heard cutting
through the confused babble of the rest, with hardly a
syllable lost.

New Englanders were, then as now, generally esteemed
the most inquisitive people in the world. They greatly
lacked for entertainment in the country and made up for
this with gossip and with minding the business of other
people. No stranger who arrived, however greatly fatigued,
at an inn but was pestered by the company and by each
newcomer who dropped in, to reveal his name, destination,
origin, family condition, trade, intentions, and political
colour. This provided good sport, for the stranger was
always suspected of misleading his interrogators, who
would try to trick him into contradictions. If he proved
sulky, hospitability would dry up, and if he asked questions in return he would get more grins than answers. It
can be conceived, then, what interest the passage of our
army excited, especially when it was learned that among
our officers were no fewer than six members of Parliament and a number of peers. Lieutenant M'Neil of our
regiment was annoyed at the giggles and ironical curtsies
of a row of very handsome young women who came out to
see us at Worcester; and when a small queer great-grand-
mother in a tall hat, standing a little beyond them, raised
her hands to Heaven and stared at us with astonishment,
he turned to her tartly: 'So, Mother Goose,' he said, 'must
you too come wandering out to see the lions?' She replied
archly: 'Lions, lions! I declare now I had mistook you for
lambs.'

We were sorry for young Lieutenant Lord Napier. He
was much troubled by the curiosity of the women at the
house where he was lodged, who imagined that a Lord
must be something more than man and kept peeping in at

doors and windows, in the hope of seeing a creature with angels' wings or a devil's hoof and tail, or I know not what else. At last four of them, pushing boldly into the room inquired: 'We hear you have got a Lord among you. Pray now, which may he be?' Then they looked sternly at Lieutenant Kemmis, as if to say: 'Dare to deceive us and it will be the worse for you.'

Unfortunately for Lord Napier, he was fresh from a tumble in the mud, and had not yet got his clothes sufficiently dried to allow the dirt to be brushed off; one side of his face was bemired, too. But Lieutenant Kemmis, knowing that there would be no peace until these women were satisfied, pointed to his Lordship and cried out in the resonant tones of a herald-at-arms: 'Ladies, there you behold the form and person of the Right Honourable Francis Napier, of His Majesty's Thirty-first Regiment of Foot, Baron of Merchiston in the Kingdom of Scotland, Baronet of Novia Scotia, Hereditary Lord Almoner to the Akhoond of Swat, Grand Squire of Gotham, Lord of a hundred inferior lordships in the Land of Cockaigne, Knight Grand Cross of the Order of Liliburlero, and much besides which I have forgot. Gaze on him, ladies, for you will never look upon his like again.' They gazed very attentively at his Lordship, who blushed beneath his mud. At length one of them exclaimed: 'Well, if *that* be a Lord, I never desire to see any other Lord than the Lord Jehovah.' Nevertheless, a number of other women came in to see the show, for which privilege they had paid entrance-money to the landlord.

The last stage of our march was from Weston to Prospect Hill, near Cambridge, which lies six miles from Boston. Exceedingly heavy rain fell, but our people bore up very well and sang choruses as we approached the end of our travels, to proclaim that our spirit was undaunted. The most sanguine among us did not imagine that we would have less than two or three weeks of waiting before the transports appeared which would take us home to Britain; but it was argued that the cost of keeping so many men in fuel and provisions would prompt the people of Massachusetts, whose Court had passed resolutions for procuring suitable accommodation for our army, to be rid of us as speedily as possible—or so soon at least as we were no longer able to pay for our subsistence in coin.

Meanwhile we determined to make the best of our lot, which was, to be short, deplorable. We were put that evening, drenched to the skin, into the temporary barracks that had been erected for the shelter of the revolutionary troops during the siege of Boston. These had since been dismantled and allowed to fall into utter decay. In a number of cases thirty or forty persons, men, women, and children, were indiscriminately crowded together in one small, miserable open hut. Our provisions and fuel were on short allowance, our bedding was a scanty amount of straw, and we had no furniture of any sort but our own camp-kettles, and these General Burgoyne had with difficulty saved for us from the enemy, who wished to seize them as legitimate plunder.

How mercifully is the future hidden from the eyes of man! Had it been revealed to us by an Angel that our army, by Congress's profligate repudiation of the Convention, was to remain in captivity for five miserable years, I believe the great mass of us would have run mad, falling upon our guards with our bare hands in a desperate attempt to wrest back our freedom.

In what manner I myself, after having been closely confined for a twelvemonth, succeeded in escaping to the British Army in New York, and there took up arms once more against the Americans; and travelled, before the war was over, through another eight states of the American Union, Northern, Southern, and Middle, is a separate story from this. For I then changed my title from 'Sergeant Lamb of The Ninth' to 'Sergeant Lamb of The Twenty-third, or Royal Welch Fusiliers.' Yet into that account Kate Harlowe must again enter (whom now I thought altogether lost to me) and several comrades of The Ninth, who also escaped, and Mrs. Jane Crumer, and even that unaccountable personage, the mock-priest John Martin. But, for the present, I have told enough. I have, it will be observed, endeavoured to demark the right line of duty and behaviour which the soldier in the ranks ought invariably to pursue. I may have lost my aim, but even in its failure I trust that my motive will be thought laudable.